# FORBIDDEN SHADOWS

E.J. DALES

*For my mom and dad who always encouraged me to use my imagination.*

*For both of my grandfathers for passing down their creativeness and the ability to tell stories.*

*For both of my grandmothers who gave me their stubbornness and feistiness that helped me to achieve my goals.*

*For my sons who I get to pass down my encouragement, creativeness, stubbornness and feistiness so that they can fulfill their dreams.*

*Love you all! ~EJD*

# CONTENTS

# Character Legend

The symbols represents which character's point of view
will be seen in any particular chapter or scene.

Detrick County, New York's unusual temperatures made it hotter than normal for the beginning of June. A gray, hooded figure stood in the shadows of a canopy of trees. He watched with intensity as a towheaded boy sat in the shade underneath a Bloodgood Japanese maple. The crimson leaves created an umbrella, casting a shadow on him. It seemed like only yesterday he himself hid in shadows at the hospital during the birth of the lad, Asher, on October 13, 2169. The hooded figure found it hard to believe it'd been exactly sixteen years, seven months, twenty-three days, five hours, and sixteen minutes ago.

Over sixty years ago, he'd sat underneath same Japanese maple tree at the same age as Asher. The day he found out the identity of his father.

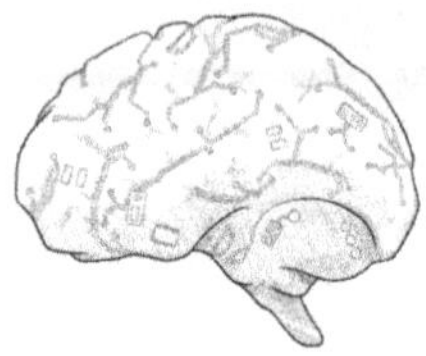

A wetness splattered upon Asher's pale cheek. His lanky fingers wiped a sticky reddish substance off his face. He brought his chewed fingertip to his nose and sniffed a sour smell consisting of chocolate, strawberry...and molasses? He looked up in the tree to see if maybe a bird had dropped him an unwanted gift. He felt another spray, followed by the sound of a young boy's giggles.

Asher looked over his shoulder. Timothy's rusty copper hair was plagued with cowlicks. Perched under a pair of wings made of freckles, a devious smile revealed his two upper central incisors with a gap in between. His bluish-gray eyes beckoned toward Asher as if saying, "Come and get me, I dare you," as the ten-year-old squeezed the trigger of his squirt gun. A stream of cinnabar-colored liquid showered Asher's face.

"Right between the eyes," said Timothy. He laughed mischievously.

"What the hell," said Asher. He turned off his hBook, and the holographic image hanging over his watch disappeared. He scrambled to his feet to wipe the substance from his eyes. "What is this?"

"Drinkable blood. It has chocolate milk, strawberry syrup and molasses in it. It looks blood when I shoot you," said Timothy.

"Molasses?" Asher scraped his tongue on his teeth after he tasted the odd mixture.

"Yeah, I couldn't find the corn syrup." Timothy gave another squeeze of the trigger. This time, a blotch of dark red formed in the center of Asher's white T-shirt. "Bam! You're dead."

"I'll show you who's dead, you little booger." Asher jolted toward Timothy, a playful grin on his lips.

Timothy's eyes grew wide along with his smile. "You know you can't catch me." Timothy's hybrid legs took charge—he ran as if he had the power of The Flash, his favorite superhero.

Asher sprinted across the green lawn, which was speckled with dandelions and buttercups. He snickered under his breath as Timothy tumbled and rolled. Winded, Asher pounced on Timothy like a frog hopping onto a lily pad.

"I know you fell on purpose," Asher said through his twisted smile. He straddled Timothy as his fingers plunged into Timothy's ribs, moving frantically as if typing on an antique keyboard, forty words per minute. Timothy squirmed. "That tells me you want the tickle treatment!"

"Stop," said Timothy with a laugh, his face turning red.

Asher knew from experience "stop" meant "keep going." If Timothy really wanted Asher to stop, he would've pushed him off with his hybrid arms as easily as flicking a booger off his finger.

"Say it and I'll stop." Asher continued to tickle him.

"No, I won't."

"Say it!" An ear-to-ear grin, showing Asher's awkward smile, plastered on his face.

"Okay, okay, stop first," Timothy pleaded, swatting Asher playfully with his hybrid arms.

"Not until you say it!"

As if defeated, Timothy forced the words out between giggles. "Asher is the bestest brother ever!"

"And?"

"I want to be like you when I grow up."

This caught Asher off guard. These weren't the normal words Timothy would mutter to end the tickle treatment. He was supposed to promise his dessert to him tonight. Asher rolled off, and Timothy sat up, out of breath.

"You want to be like me?" asked Asher.

"Yeah, I want to be a big brother too and treat my baby brother like we were blood, like you do with me."

"There are other kids here you can become a brother to, you know."

"They're more like friends than siblings. You're the only one who treats me like a brother."

"Mr. Whitaker likes you," said Asher. Mr. Whitaker had been at Willow Wood for six months, 2 days, and 11 hours. Mr. Whitaker would have nothing to do with Asher, but he always seemed to smile and brighten up when Timothy was near him.

Timothy's shoulders dropped along with his expression. "He's only two."

"That doesn't mean he doesn't need a big brother. You would be a perfect big brother for him."

"If I become Mr. Whitaker's big brother, does it mean you won't be my big brother?" asked Timothy.

"I will always be your big brother," Asher reassured him.

"And you think I would be a good big brother to him?"

"I can't think of anyone else who would be better," Asher said. "The best part is you can give Mr. Whitaker the tickle treatment." Asher pounced onto Timothy. This time Timothy used his hybrid arms and legs to push Asher onto his back. Timothy straddled him, giggling while his fingers explored Asher's armpits. Both boys were laughing.

Asher had never realized how much he meant to Timothy.

"Timothy Remington Smizik! Asher Levi Smizik!" A powerful female voice echoed off the grounds of Willow Wood.

Timothy's fingers stopped in mid-tickle, his eyes widened, his lips pressed together. "Mom called us by our full name. That's bad. Real bad," he said. Timothy referred to Vicki Smizik as Mom.

"Timothy Remington Smizik, you go clean the mess you created in the kitchen. There is molasses everywhere."

"I'm outta here." Timothy jumped up and ran toward his tree fort as The Flash.

Asher let out a deep sigh. Every time his mother called him by his full name, that meant a grounding, he instantly knew why. Dr. Emily must have told her she caught him breaking Willow Wood's number one rule: talking to an outsider on his computer. Dr. Emily had caught him after his mother left to do errands earlier in the day.

"There you are," said Vicki Smizik. Her strawberry-blond hair bounced as she crossed the yard.

The Victorian hotel rose up behind her. The forest-green paint had chipped off in places, causing the hotel to look like it had a bad case of chicken pox. The white shutters and trim were now eggshell, almost a beige from the harsh weather they had borne throughout the years. Moss and algae grew on the shutters on the shadowy side of the house, a shield protecting them from the invasion of rain, snow, sleet and other ammunition Mother Nature could throw at them. The weather-abused roof had missing shingles and many needed to be replaced. A few windows had cracks in them, looking like a trail a rabbit would leave behind in the snow. The back porch had patches of missing lattice underneath, letting children and critters alike sneak under the porch, or, for others, sneak out. Repairing and preserving the hotel and grounds had become difficult due to lack of income. Willow Wood had a strict policy of no outsiders allowed on the property, everything had to be taken care of by the thirty-plus hybrid children or the two adults who lived there.

Asher tried to avoid eye contact. The black of Vicki's pupils were surrounded by a ring of craggy, silvery flame swallowed by beryl blue. If he dared to look closer, he would see the sadness of heartbreak, the pain of sorrow, and the fire of a spirit that would never burn out.

"I know," Asher mumbled. He wanted to run away like Timothy did instead of facing conflict, however, if he did, his grounding would be ten times worse.

Vicki sat next to her son. Her "I don't care who sees me today" clothes showcased her pear-shaped body. "Would you care to tell me why?"

The hot sun blanketed Asher's face. A breeze whisked through, causing the dandelions and buttercups to dance. He shrugged.

"The one rule we have here at Willow Wood that must be obeyed is no talking to outsiders."

"I know." Asher still refused to look at his mom.

"Look at me when I'm talking to you," she ordered. Asher reluctantly turned his head to see his mother's face firm with anger and disappointment, yet under complete control.

"Why did you do it?"

Asher shrugged.

"Asher, if the hybrid police or, worse yet, the hybrid hunters find out about Willow Wood—"

Asher finished his mother's sentence. "I know. They would cleanse the garrison chips from all of the kids." Asher knew how serious cleansing was; only five percent of hybrids survived the procedure.

"If hybrid hunters caught you and the others...well, I don't even want to think about it." She let out a bodily shake of fear.

"I'm sorry, Mom." Asher looked down to the ground, defeated.

"Who were you talking to?"

"A girl. She's a hybrid too."

"Hybrid or not, you cannot chat with outsiders. It's too dangerous. It could be a trap, a way to lure hybrids into the sights of the hybrid hunters."

Asher remained silent.

"Dr. Emily analyzed the computer, and she doesn't think you got pinged. To be on the safe side though, she disconnected the computer and fried it."

Asher looked up. "I had books I haven't read yet on the computer."

"They're gone now."

"Am I going to get a new computer?"

"We don't have enough money to get the roof fixed, let alone to get you a new computer. For the time being, no."

Asher's shoulders fell limp like a plant without enough sun. "Can I use your computer?"

"You're grounded from using any computers."

"Grounded? How long?" His head shot sharply toward her.

"Will a week be long enough to teach you the importance of not chatting with an outsider, or do you need it to be longer?"

Knowing better than to argue with his mother, Asher said, "A week will do."

She lifted her son's chin. "I love you, Asher."

"I know."

She shook her head as if in disbelief. "The older you get, the more and more you look like your father."

Asher sent her a peculiar look. His mother hardly ever mentioned anything about his father. The last time she did was two years, three months, and twenty-seven minutes ago. Asher went to save Timothy, who'd climbed onto the roof of Willow Wood. Timothy ended up saving Asher instead. "If your father was here," were the words she snapped.

"Why don't you ever talk about my father? I mean, is he like Darth Vader or something?" He referred to the villain in a recent remake of the twentieth-century film *Star Wars*.

This time Vicki turned her head to look down to the ground.

Asher recognized the cue that she didn't want to talk about it. He longed to know more. It was hard enough already trying to figure out who he was. The enhanced brain power implants made it worse. Many times, especially as he grew older, his mind wouldn't turn off from analyzing the facts he already had. He wanted to know more about the man who gave him XY chromosomes. He didn't know anything about him, including his name, except they exhibited similar traits. His father's DNA played a role in his appearance, mannerisms, quirks and personality. He wanted to know how much of a role.

He didn't know if he would ever learn anything more. He couldn't talk to anyone outside the compound...ever. Now he was grounded for a week. Asher's cheeks flushed.

"Being a hybrid sucks!" Asher bolted up and stormed toward the Japanese maple tree. He wanted time alone. His mother followed.

"Liam," she said.

Asher stopped in mid-stride and turned around. "What?" he asked, confused.

"Liam is your father's name. Liam Mrkonic."

Asher kept silent, processing this new information.

"I'm sorry for keeping your father such a secret from you. I'm trying to protect the two of you."

"From the hybrid police and hybrid hunters?" asked Asher.

"There is that, but your father works for Earth Force Alliance (EFA). I'm sure you can understand why that might be a problem."

Asher let his mother's words settle in as he shot her an incredulous stare. His body quivered as a sudden coldness hit his core. Maybe his father was Darth Vader after all. At least if he were in prison he would be paying for his crimes. EFA? They'd played a big part in the hybrid civil war twenty years ago. Since they were a government agency, they had to fight for the government's views, and in this case, hybrids were to be banned. Asher remembered reading in a history book if the hybrids had taken control of EFA assets, they would've won the war. Now he learned his father worked for an agency who only protected the rights of normals, something he was not. His thoughts were interrupted as his mother spoke again.

"You do remind me of him," Vicki continued after Asher's silence. "Your height, for one thing. A lot of your expressions remind me of him. And of course, you have the Mrkonic ears."

Asher touched his ear, which stuck out like a radar antenna. "What is he like?"

"He was an athlete in high school."

"I don't have that part of him, do I?" Asher smiled, Vicki laughed.

"I'm afraid you inherited your mother's athleticism, or lack thereof."

"What else?" Asher wanted to learn more. He wanted to know more about himself, his genes, his DNA.

"Well, he loves all sports teams in Pittsburgh. He played the drums with a passion."

"Pittsburgh? Is that where he lives?"

"Cranbury Township, a small town outside of Pittsburgh."

"Would he like me?" The question came out of nowhere.

"If he would meet you today, I'm sure he would like you."

"Could we take a trip to Cranbury? I would like to meet him," said Asher.

Vicki let out another sigh. "It's too dangerous for you to be out there."

Asher exhaled in a huff. Her answer had never changed over the years. "Mom, I'm sixteen now. I'll be seventeen in October. I can handle it out there. Pandora says hybrids hide among normals all the time."

"Is Pandora the girl you've been chatting with online?"

"Yeah."

"She is right. Hybrids do manage to live in the shadows among normals and not get caught, however the risk is far greater. You're safer here."

The old man, still observing from the shadows, let out a silent sigh. He could watch no more. In two minutes and forty-three seconds, Neon, a girl with hybrid eyes, would be climbing out from her quiet place underneath the back porch of Willow Wood, and joining them. He couldn't take the risk of being spotted by her.

He took one last look at the boy and his mother. "I love you," he whispered. He knew he would never see her again.

Vicki Smizik came out of Timothy's bathroom holding a bunch of dirty clothes. "Did you brush your teeth?"

"Yes, Mom," Timothy said as he opened his mouth, exposing his teeth.

She gave him the mother stare. "Do I need to smell your breath?"

Beaten, he schlepped into the bathroom and brushed his teeth. When he came out, he found Mom shaking her head in disgust as she pulled old pieces of pizza and a piece of food no longer recognizable out from underneath his bed.

"Tomorrow before you do anything, you will clean your room," said Vicki.

Wearing only The Flash pajama shorts, Timothy crawled into his bed. He bent forward and pulled out a two-foot-tall, black, hairy stuffed ape named Berman from beneath the covers. Berman had been a gift to Timothy from Asher the first day Timothy arrived at Willow Wood.

"I never thought I would see the day Asher would part with Berman," Vicki said, tossing the pizza into the trash.

"Tell me the story?" Timothy had heard it a million times. It always made him feel wanted.

Vicki sat beside him on the bed. "Well, the day you arrived, you were crying. Dr. Emily and I could not get you to quiet down. The older kids even tried. We had traveled far, and all I wanted was for you to rest. Then Asher came in with Berman. He carefully picked you up and sat down, with you on one leg and Berman on the other. He started making sounds like a gorilla, and your cries turned to laughter."

Timothy listened hard.

"Asher asked if you could sleep in his room, and from that day on, you were roommates."

"Until he kicked me out," said Timothy.

"That's because he became a smelly teenager. He wants his privacy now. He still loves you more than ever."

"I know," Timothy admitted.

"Asher will be in soon to tuck you in. I love you."

"I love you too, Mom."

Vicki kissed Timothy on the forehead and sealed it with a motherly smile. "I'll see you tomorrow," she said as she left the room.

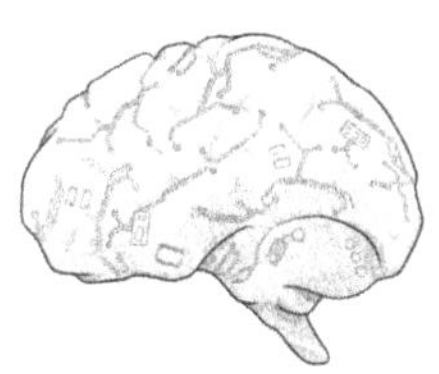

Asher switched off the radio on his nightstand. He enjoyed listening to podcasts before he went to sleep. Tonight's topic wasn't anything new. Alita Blackwood, a hybrid activist, and her followers recently blew up two cargo shuttles that had anti-hybrid detection equipment. The pilots and crew of both shuttles were killed.

He began reading the history book he'd memorized that spoke of the hybrid civil war while massaging his sore hand. Each night Asher would tell Timothy a bedtime story. Before Asher would leave Timothy's room, they would fist bump. Tonight, Timothy got careless and bumped Asher's fist a little too hard.

Unlike Neon, whose garrison chip enhanced her vision, or Timothy, whose chip enhanced his arm strength and leg speed, Asher's enhanced the satellite chip in the limbic system in his brain-controlled memories. He could remember conversations word for word he'd heard at the age of two, when his body fully accepted his hybrid implants.

The satellite chips in his posterior parietal cortex, ventral temporal occipital cortex, and prefrontal cortex caused the garrison chip to enhance his mathematical skills too. He did not need a calculator to solve difficult math equations—he was a calculator.

Asher's brain was in overdrive after today's events. He lay there thinking about a time when normals and hybrids could coexist, a time before normals felt threatened by hybrids' enhancements. Hybrids got the better jobs, tainted sports records, and started to show superiority. Normals took action to ban hybrids from certain professions like politics, sports, CEOs of companies, and others. Alita Blackwood and the Phantom Prophet fought for hybrid civil rights. Alita Blackwood took the aggressive route, while the Phantom Prophet took the more passive route. Both failed, for the normals won the civil war and banned hybrids altogether.

Then his brain would jump to his father. After all these years, he finally knew his father's name. This caused him to wonder even more about his father and how much he may or may not be like him in looks, personality, likes and dislikes.

His thoughts jumped track again and went to the conversation when Timothy said he wanted to be like him. He wasn't quite sure what to think about that. He knew it was a powerful compliment, but was he as great as Timothy made him out to be?

Asher left out a sigh. He hated when he couldn't turn his brain off.

He knew he had to distract himself so that he could fall sleep. He closed his eyes and his hand went exploring under the bed sheets. The section of his sheets where his hand was started to move back and forth in a rhematic motion.

Asher's closet door swayed open with a force. He sat up in panic, pulling his hand out from under the sheet.

Out of the closet stepped Neon. Her bi-colored hair, neon-blue on top and neon-green on the bottom, dripped tiny droplets down her face and neck. She didn't appear fazed by Asher's reactions.

"Neon!" hissed Asher. He grabbed the comforter that was halfway off the bed and pulled it up around his long, gangly body. "I know you think you have your own private entrance. Can't you at least knock first?" Neon always entered and exited his room through the closet door. Both Neon and Asher were the only ones who knew about the secret in the closet.

"Why?"

She had a good point. Neon could see through walls and doors, sheets, even clothing. She had also made a promise.

"You promised you wouldn't use your vision on me." Asher grabbed his pillow and placed it in front of him. Even though Neon could see through the pillow, it put his mind at ease having the extra barrier in front of him.

"Why are you here?" Asher asked. "It's after midnight."

"I had the best swim ever." Neon's green-and-blue hair glistened.

"Swimming?" replied Asher. "The pool is closed by nine."

"I didn't swim in the pool. I went to the river."

This didn't surprise Asher. "That's outside the walls. You're not allowed to leave Willow Wood."

"I hate those walls. This place is a prison."

"No, it's not. It's...home," he said, though his actions betrayed him. Talking to Pandora on the computer was his passive way to escape Willow Wood and remain in the safety of the stone walls surrounding it. Neon took the more aggressive path by physically leaving the confines of Willow Wood whenever she wanted.

"Easy for you to say," said Neon. "You've never been outside those walls. I have, and I know what adventures are out there."

Asher was one year old when he'd moved to Willow Wood. Neon, who was Asher's age, had only been at Willow Wood for five years.

Asher didn't reply. She had a point.

"Tomorrow night you and I will go to the river."

"Why would I want to go? I can't swim."

"You don't have to go in the water; we can go canoeing."

"Canoeing?"

"Yeah, there's a canoe down there."

Asher had to admit, a part of him wanted to go. He'd never been canoeing before. The new moon hid in the shadows of Earth, he wouldn't be able to see anything. He didn't have night vision capabilities like Neon did. Still, it wasn't the new moon that held him back.

"I can't sneak off the property. I'm in enough trouble already. And you're going to get caught one day."

"What are they going to do? Ground me?" Neon sat on the edge of the bed.

"It's not safe out there for us. You know that." Asher scooted back into the corner and pulled his sheets up farther.

"You can't hide here forever. You need to go out and have fun. Get adventure in your life. Don't you ever wonder what life would be like if we weren't hybrids?"

Asher shrugged. "Not really," he lied.

"What do you mean, 'not really?' Either you have or you haven't. With your brain implants, you could tell me how many times you've thought about it."

"Okay, fine. I have."

"Do you think hybrids will ever become legal again?" asked Neon.

Asher shrugged and pulled his foot out from underneath Neon's butt.

"It seems like the only person fighting for us is Alita Blackwood."

Asher's eyes widened. "Mom says she's a terrorist."

"I don't think she's a terrorist. Her group only targets normals who support laws making hybrids illegal. She's a rebel. She is fighting for the rights of hybrids. If we ever become free, it will be because of Alita Blackwood and her followers fighting for us."

"You can fight for a cause without being violent." Asher thought of activists who fought for a cause that didn't result in fighting and killing, like Mohandas Gandhi, Martin Luther King, Jr., and Nelson Mandela in the twentieth century, or Ksenia Kozlova, Gabino Carioca and Liling Ming from the twenty-first century, or the Phantom Prophet in the twenty-second century.

"Not when you're a hybrid." Neon gazed into a world Asher couldn't see. "I'd join Alita Blackwood now if I could."

"What's stopping you?"

"You'll miss me too much."

Asher looked at the closest thing he had to a sister. Unlike his relationship with Timothy, he considered Neon his best friend, nothing more, nothing less. "You wish."

"You say that now, but the day we go our separate ways, you will miss me."

Asher couldn't deny it.

"You're telling me you would take an innocent life to save your own? That's not right, Neon. I couldn't do it."

"I got news for you, Asher." Neon crossed her arms. "There are no innocent people out there. And if I had to, I would kill one who suppresses us—kills hybrids—to ensure the safety of myself and other hybrids."

Asher shook his head. "You're crazy. That's as bad as them—what makes you different?"

"I'm right. That's what's different," she argued.

"I couldn't do it," Asher said. "Besides, what about the Phantom Prophet? He fought for hybrid civil rights. He did it peacefully and didn't kill anyone."

"And look where it got him. Dead. You would kill if your life depended on it."

Asher had nothing to say. He didn't know what he would do if he had to decide if a person lived or not.

"Changing subjects," Neon said. "I have to tell you, I saw a man across the river tonight. He was watching me."

Red flags went off in Asher's mind as his eyes snapped to Neon's face. "What do you mean, watching you? How could he see you? It's a new moon tonight."

"He had on night vision glasses. Besides, he got to see a full moon." Neon cast a devilish grin.

Asher started to get out of bed. "We need to tell my mom. He could be a hybrid hunter."

Neon pushed Asher back down. "Relax. Keep you naked ass in bed. He was no hybrid hunter. I've seen them before. This guy is probably a weirdo hoping to see more than the full moon."

"I still think we should tell my Mom."

"Trust me. He was no hunter." As always, Neon came across confident and sure of herself.

Asher was torn. He knew if he told, Neon would get in trouble. Plus, everyone would have to evacuate. Maybe he was a perv, like Neon said. Yet, why was he out so late at night? Did he know Neon would be there or was it a coincidence?

Neon let out a yawn. The contagious action spread to Asher.

Neon stood up. "I'm going bed. Tomorrow night, it'll be fun. You'll see."

"I'm not going."

Neon headed back to the closet. "That's what you think." She stepped in and closed the door.

Asher sighed with relief, relaxing his guard, although he still had the sheets covering everything below his abdomen. He jumped as the door swung back open.

"By the way, don't think of me as you finish up your nocturnal activity." She shot him the smile of a trickster and disappeared behind the closet door once more.

"Neon!" yelled Asher.

"Kidding," came from behind the closet door. Asher knew better.

The yawns became more frequent. He lay in his bed, trying to come up with a plan to get out of going to the river tomorrow night. He didn't know why Neon had this invisible power over him, making him do things he didn't always want to do, like the time they'd tried to leave Willow Wood to check out the nearby village. Neon made it to the other side of the front gate. Asher had only made it halfway over when his mom caught them. Who would've thought she would be coming back from an overnight trip a day early?

He couldn't go beyond the wall then, and he knew he couldn't do it now. There were too many dangers out there. His eyelids drifted shut, and yawns were replaced by the gentle breathing of sleep. Pleasant dreams filled his head. They would soon be interrupted by the nightmare of reality.

The Cuban stared up at the starry blanket. He finished his last swallow of goat's milk and wiped the remnants off his raven-colored mustache. Stubble covered his bronze-umber skin. Long sideburns and a short ponytail sat under his black Cuban military cap.

His eyes echoed the way he felt toward hybrids: dark and cold. The whites of his eyes contrasted sharply with the pitch-black irises filled with intensity and despair.

He took a deep inhale of his Cuban-made panatela from his native land. He closed his eyes and exhaled as he went over the plans for tonight's raid on Willow Wood, a small estate in upstate New York where hybrid orphans lived. A thirty-minute drive was all that stood between him and those hybrids. Normally, they would use scorpion drones on a raid like this. The machines would shoot out tranquilizer darts from their tails, which was where they got their name. That wouldn't work this time. After scoping out the layout, he discovered a network shield around the property causing the scorpion drones to crash and burn.

Cortez didn't mind though. Actually, he was quite pleased they couldn't use drones tonight. Not only did he like it, he relished the chance to get his hands dirty in a raid. It made him feel alive and in charge.

He looked at his watch and took one last drag of his panatela before rubbing it out in the palm of his gloved hand. He marched over to the operations mobile and climbed in through the back.

Marissa Navarro sat on a stool. Her muscular, cracked fingers strummed her guitar. Being born and raised in Antarctica had caused her skin of honey and amber to weather hard. Her old, leathery face gave her the appearance of being twenty years older than she actually was. Shiny black hair with strands of crimson hung over her muscular shoulders. Her eyes held a greater darkness, resembling cold winter nights and starless skies where all dreams, desires and optimism seemed galaxies away.

Despite her hard looks, a sweet, soothing lullaby flowed from her cracked, florid lips, almost hypnotizing. JD, her pet pig, lay at her feet, resting peacefully by the sweet lullaby. Without taking her attention away from her guitar, she spoke. "I trust the crew is in place."

"Yes and they're waiting for the go-ahead." He stared deep into her eyes, trying to find that one weakness of hers he could use in his favor.

She placed her guitar against the wall, bent over and petted JD. "Come on, JD, it's time to get us some hybrids."

The pig snorted and stood with Navarro. She grabbed a miniature crossbow and pulled her hood over her head.

"Press on." She abruptly walked past the Cuban and left the ops truck.

Cortez scowled as JD jumped off the truck. A small smirk, almost unnoticeable, hinted on his face. When the day came he cut the talons Navarro had latched deeply into him, he would be eating himself fresh bacon.

"Asher, get up! We have to go now!" Asher's panic-stricken mother stormed into his room momentarily to wake him, then left the door open on her way out.

Despite the sound of an unsynchronized herd of gazelles and cries of scared monkeys outside his bedroom door, the tentacles of sleep nudged Asher back into the sea of covers. He had to be dreaming. His internal clock told him it'd been two hours, six minutes, and forty-seven seconds since he fell asleep.

"Asher! Hybrid hunters are coming," said Timothy, rushing into Asher's bedroom. He ripped the sheets off Asher with his bionic arms quicker than any normal human. "Get up!"

"What?" Asher did not comprehend the words. Coming out of a dead sleep had that effect on him. His biological brain cells grasped at the chance to catch up to the same level of alertness as his technological hybrid brain implants.

"Hunters are here!"

Sleep began to drift away as the situation made itself clear.

Asher's mom flew back into his room. "Why aren't you up yet?" She grabbed Asher's narrow wrist and yanked him out of bed. "Let's go."

"I'm not dressed." Asher wore only a pair of white briefs to bed.

"There's no time. The hunters are here," she said.

"Mom, are we going to die?" asked Timothy.

She didn't reply.

Hearing Timothy's question made the situation real—the sugar rush Asher needed to wake up. The confusion cleared instantly. His life and the other kids' lives at Willow Wood Estates were in jeopardy. If hybrid hunters caught them, they would be killed and sold as spare parts on the black market.

Asher's gawkiness showed as his spindly body fell to the floor with a thud. His legs were entangled in his blankets. Timothy helped unwrap him, and, with ease, he pulled Asher up to his size thirteens.

"Come on, Asher. We have to go," said Timothy.

Timothy, Asher, and Vicki entered the hallway. The house emitted an eerie silence.

"Why is it quiet?" asked Timothy.

"Everyone else must've already evacuated the house," Asher replied.

Vicki looked both ways down the hall. "Come on, this way," she said urgently.

They ran to the staircase at the end of the hall. Asher peered out the big glass window and saw from a distance what looked like a group of lightning bugs headed their way. He knew the green glow wasn't from a lightning bug, they didn't blink. The glow of night vision goggles cast a look of a demon. He swore his heart stopped beating. Were one of those hunters the man Neon had seen at the river? Why didn't he tell his mom? This could've been prevented.

"Asher, take Timothy to the egress tunnel."

Asher's peripheral vision caught Vicki's movement at the bottom of the stairs. "Mom, where's Neon?"

"I saw her take Mr. Whitaker to the egress tunnel," answered Timothy. "I didn't want to leave without you."

"Get yourself and Timothy to safety," Asher's mom instructed.

"Aren't you coming?" He looked out the window again and could make out a swarm of four-wheelers zooming up the multiple acres of the front lawn. A bright flash lit up the surrounding area, and the front door exploded. Shards of glass, wood, and other debris flew through the air. "Mom?!"

The hallway filled with smoke. The lower half lay in ruins. His ears rang from the blast, drowning out the last six words echoing in his head. "Get yourself and Timothy to safety." A rusty, metallic salt-like taste flooded his mouth. He spit out a mixture of dirt, saliva, and blood.

Asher looked at Timothy. Violent coughs rumbled out of his mouth, and he had a laceration by his right ear. Fear took control. A tsunami of photon bursts surged through the hole in the wall where the door and his mother were moments earlier.

The hybrid hunters were here.

Asher scanned below and found a pile of debris with his mom underneath. Blood streamed from her forehead. A piece of wood protruded from her chest. He could hear her gasping for air.

Asher's brain implants told him to run, to get Timothy to the egress tunnel. His emotions told him otherwise, to climb down to the first floor and save his mom.

Silhouettes appeared on the front porch.

"Timothy, as fast and quiet as you can, shut every door on this floor, except my room. I'll meet you there."

"We'll be trapped in your room."

"No, we won't. Go!"

Timothy sped down the hall, shutting the doors as he passed them. His hybrid legs and arms made the task look easy.

Asher peered around the corner, spying on the action below. He spotted a woman wearing what looked to be a combination of wine-colored leather entangled with black canvas fabric. Dark hair with deep red strands hung out of her hood, onto her shoulders. She seemed to have a fearless, sick confidence about her. A pig followed her as she strolled over to Asher's mom.

She spoke with an accent Asher had never heard before. At least not in person. "I'll make this easy for you. Tell me where the hybrid brats went, and I will end your pain instantly."

"No," gasped Vicki.

The woman kicked Vicki hard in the side. A fountain of blood spewed out of her mouth as she coughed. She gazed toward Asher, then closed her eyes and stopped breathing.

"She's dead," said one of the men.

"Just to make sure." The woman held up a miniature, handheld crossbow, took aim, and fired a dart into his mom's ear. After a muffled pop, Vicki's head cracked open and oozed gray and reddish matter.

Asher screamed, though he couldn't hear his own voice. Rather, he found himself glaring at the Antarctician, who turned and slid her hood off, revealing her harsh and evil face. She smiled, showing the most perfect white teeth Asher had ever seen. She whipped up her crossbow and fired a shot.

Asher fell back as the dart pierced the wall next to him and exploded.

"Get yourself and Timothy to safety." His mother's voice echoed in his head. Asher wiped his eyes and scurried back.

"You know what to do," the woman ordered in a calm, authoritarian tone. She motioned her glove-covered hand toward the spot where Asher had stood only seconds before. Asher raced to his bedroom.

Timothy poked his head out from underneath the bed.

"Did you shut all the doors?"

"Yeah, but why?"

"No time to explain. Get into my closet."

"Your closet? They'll find us there for sure."

Asher opened his closet door and pushed Timothy into the cramped space. He wedged himself in and closed the door, his neatly hung clothes falling off the hangers. Asher hoped the hunters would check the rooms with the doors closed first. After all, why would anyone hide in a room and leave the door open?

In the dark, Asher's lanky fingers fumbled on the wall. "Where is it?" he whispered to himself.

"Ouch, you're hurting me," whined Timothy.

"Shhh." He had to calm himself down and focus to retrieve the information on the whereabouts of the latch from his implants. His finger fell upon a knot. He pressed it, and a small door, about the size of an entrance to a doghouse, popped open by his feet. Hours before, Neon had used this secret passageway to visit him after her midnight swim.

Asher found Timothy and pushed him into the passageway.

"What are you doing? What is this?"

"Quiet. Get in." He cramped himself down and slid through the doorway, shutting it behind him.

Asher tried to hold back sneezes and coughs as they crawled through the web- and dust-infested passage. He tried to ignore the pain as his boney knees scraped across the hard, musty wood. He couldn't see, he didn't have to.

"Ewww, what's that smell?" said Timothy.

"Quiet."

"It smells like a dead animal." Timothy sounded nasally. He must've been pinching his nose.

"Keep going. We have to move faster."

"It's hard to crawl with one hand."

"Use both hands," whispered Asher.

"It really stinks."

"Hold your breath then." In the dark, Asher could hear Timothy take a deep breath and hold it.

They scurried along in the dark, cramped corridor. A thud echoed in the passageway, followed by a breach of air escaping Timothy's lungs. "Ouch! I hit a dead end."

"There's a ladder. We have to climb up it."

"Up? We need to go down," said Timothy.

"We have to go up before we can go down. Let me get in front of you." Asher and Timothy wormed past each other, giving Asher the lead. "Follow me."

The two began to climb the wooden ladder.

"Twenty-one, twenty-two, twenty-three..." Asher stopped. He twisted around and scuffled into another small passageway. Timothy followed right behind him. Asher crawled, counting the strides. "Sixteen, seventeen, eighteen..." He pushed open a small door. The familiar aroma of cinnamon, Neon's favorite smell, flooded his nostrils. Her room consisted of bright neon colors that glowed when her black lights were on. Digital posters of her favorite music group, Pig Snout, covered her walls. All five band members, who were in their mid-twenties, were wearing only speedos. They were muscular and had the physique of a person who took to the gym every day and earned their shower. A poster of a teenage boy with a guitar hung above Neon's bed. Although Neon would deny it, she fantasized about being with Mitch Kalon, the hottest teenage singer on today's circuit.

"The hunters must've been in here already. Look how messy it is."

"You've never been here before, have you? It's always this way."

"She won't let me in. She says it's 'invading her privacy,'" mocked Timothy.

"A wrongdoer recognizes a wrongdoer," mumbled Asher.

"What did you say?"

"Nothing important, let's keep moving." Asher went to the bedroom door and peered out. The hall appeared to be empty. He closed the door and locked it.

"Why are we in Neon's room?" asked Timothy.

"We have to hurry." Asher didn't have time for questions. He needed to focus on getting them to safety.

Asher led Timothy to the connecting bathroom. It smelled of hairspray and cinnamon. Makeup containers littered the sink, and a few had found their way to the floor.

Asher opened up the linen closet and shook his head in disgust at the pile of dirty towels blocking his escape route. He tossed the damp towels in random directions, fighting off the panic and the fear that their pursuers were going to capture them...kill them.

Towels cleared, he pressed on the hardwood floor, and it popped open. He lifted the door.

"Timothy, get in."

"Why am I always the one to go first?"

"Because I said so. Now go."

Timothy rolled his eyes as he crawled into the passage. "It's dark in here. At least it doesn't smell like dead farts."

"Crawl until you come to a ladder, then climb down. It empties out in the old wine cellar. Make sure no one is in there before opening the door."

Timothy acknowledged the instructions and disappeared into the darkness.

Asher could hear the hybrid hunters outside the bedroom. He crawled partly inside the passage. His muscles froze refused to move when he heard pounding against the bedroom door. The hunters were breaking down the locked door. Asher grabbed the dirty towels and lowered the trap door, ensuring the dirty towels covered the top of it, hoping to hide their escape route. Footsteps thumped above. Asher didn't move.

He covered his mouth as he let out a gasp. Part of a towel caused the trapdoor to be open up a crack, casting a small beam of light upon Asher. The floor board creaked above him. He could see a pair of worn and dirty black combat boots. A callused, dirt stained hand reached down. Asher's heart stopped or at least it felt like it did. The hunter picked up one of Neon's makeup containers.

Asher let out a sigh of relief as the boots disappeared from his sight and the thumping dissipated until he heard nothing. His internal clock told him that the hunter was in the bathroom for 58 seconds, but to him, it felt like 58 years.

Asher lifted the trap door and poked his head out. He could feel his eyes widen when he saw the hunter in Neon's room rummaging through her personal belongings. He froze. The hunter had his back towards Asher, but how long would it be until the hunter turned and saw him?

"Hey Krankshaft!" A women's voice sounded from the hallway. He didn't recognize the voice, so it couldn't have been the woman who killed his mother.

"You should see all this cool shit in this room," replied the hunter.

"They found a tunnel in the house that appears to be an escape route. Navarro wants us to guard it, just in case that kid tries to use it."

Asher still couldn't move. With his head still sticking out of the trapdoor, he held his breath as he watched the hunter leave Neon's room. Another sigh of relief came from Asher, this time bigger, heavier and slightly louder. The hunter left the room without looking back into the bathroom.

He pulled his head back into the secret passageway. This when he closed the door, he ensured that nothing was in the way keeping it from being closed completely. Because the adrenaline flowed through his veins like a river during the spring rains, he made it to the ladder and climbed down rapidly, ignoring the fact that he wasn't all that quiet in doing so.

He breathed another sigh of relief as he entered the wine cellar.

"I hear the hunters upstairs," said Timothy. "Is Mom going to be okay? Are we going to rescue her?"

Asher ignored the question, the answer hurt him deep within. "This way." Asher led them to the opposite end of the wine cellar. He listened before opening the door that led into the basement. The damp, musky air caused Asher's nose to twitch in the darkness. They ran to a basement window.

Asher's height allowed him to open the window that led underneath the back porch. "Stay under the porch and be quiet. Wait for me," he instructed Timothy.

Once he hoisted Timothy through the window, Asher tried to lift himself up. He couldn't do it, he had no upper body strength. He found a chair. It had to be what Neon had used when she snuck out. Using it, and with the help of Timothy's bionic arms, he managed to climb out.

"We should stay and help Mom!" said Timothy.

Asher closed his eyes, trying to get the vision of his mom's dead gaze out of his head. Having a perfect memory wasn't always a blessing. For Asher, it was moments like this one when his hybrid implants became a curse, unable to remove the vivid and horrid memories.

"She's dead, isn't she?"

"Yeah." A lump in Asher's throat wouldn't let any other words out. Timothy's arms wrapped around him as he planted his head into Asher's bare chest. Asher could feel Timothy's tears run down his ribs.

Timothy pulled back a little and looked up at Asher through bloodshot, swollen eyes. "Are we going to die too?"

"No, I'm going to get you out of here safe."

"What if they capture and kill us?"

"They won't." Asher hoped Timothy believed him, because he didn't believe it himself. He peeked through the lattice toward an old outhouse, a secret entrance to one of the egress tunnels. Several wearers of night vision goggles blocked their escape route. The egress tunnel entrance in the house had to be blocked with hybrid hunters. Asher didn't want to take the risk of going back into the house. He crawled on the soft earth to the other side. There were no lights. He didn't know if the hunters had looked under the porch yet or not. He didn't want to take that risk either.

He had to get them off the estate. Asher had never been off the estate before. Fortunately, he had seen satellite images of the acreage and heard stories from Neon when she disobeyed the rules and went exploring.

They would have to make their way to the stone wall first, through the thick woods next and finally to the river, hopefully their new escape route using Neon's canoe. His brain implants told him they were 1.627 miles away. Asher feared the idea of canoeing in the dark. He had no other choice. At least, no choice that didn't involve facing their pursuers head-on. How hard could it be to maneuver a canoe with hybrid brain implants?

He removed the lattice, trying not to make any noise, and poked his head out. He pulled himself through and helped Timothy out.

Asher felt a deep chill as the night air breezed over his body. As they set foot on the ground, Asher wished he had taken the time to throw on a pair of shoes. His feet didn't take kindly to the terrain. If Neon were with him, her feet wouldn't care about the texture of the ground. Her feet were calloused and used to it. Neon did not like wearing shoes and didn't unless she absolutely had to.

"This way. Follow me," Asher whispered.

They scurried into the backwoods. *Okay, we went 500.7 feet. We should be coming to the stone wall*, Asher mentally calculated. Sure enough, they exited the woods. Across a small field stood the stone wall, eight feet and two inches high. Asher calculated they would have to run 296.4 feet across the field to get to the wall, and another 7,793.46 feet beyond the wall to the river. His calculations, as usual, were spot on. He whispered a prayer to a God he did not know personally that the canoe was still there.

"Let's get to the wall."

Timothy's hybrid legs gave him speed Asher did not have. He darted across the field like a cheetah chasing its prey and up the stone wall like a spider, his mechanical legs and arms making the difficult task a breeze.

Out of breath, Asher reached the wall. Timothy sat on top with his legs dangling off the side.

Asher saw night vision goggles. It wouldn't be long before the hunters emerged from the woods. Panic-stricken yet motivated by fear, his mother's last words, and his promise to Timothy he wouldn't die, he jumped and barely grabbed onto the edge. He struggled trying to pull himself up. As he started slipping to the ground, Timothy jumped down.

"What are you doing?" Asher asked.

"Let me boost you!" Timothy clasped his hands together to form a stirrup. "I can hold you."

Asher put his foot into Timothy's hand. With a small grunt Asher found himself airborne. His nail bitten fingers scraped across the top of the brick wall as he flew over and landed hard on the ground, knocking the air out of him. Timothy had given him too strong of a boost.

Timothy appeared on top of the wall. "You okay, Asher? I didn't mean to throw you—"

The world went into slow motion. A blast struck Timothy in the back. Asher scrambled to catch him. He let out a grunt as Timothy landed on him. The pain coursing through Asher's body made the pain from the initial toss feel like a butterfly kiss.

"Timothy!"

He didn't answer.

"Don't you be dead on me." Asher placed his hand on Timothy's chest. He felt a slight movement up and down. "Yes, you're still alive."

Asher groaned as he tried to pick up Timothy. His hybrid arms and legs made him three times heavier than the average ten-year-old boy. Asher gripped Timothy under his armpits, and with energy from an unknown source, he dragged Timothy to the river. He hoped the canoe was still there.

# CHAPTER 4

"There's the canoe! I'm going to get you help," Asher said between breaths.

With little to no grace, Asher flopped Timothy into the canoe with a thud. The boy let out a muffled groan.

Asher pushed the canoe into the current of the unknown with a large grunt. Timothy let out another stifled moan as Asher climbed in, almost tipping the canoe.

"Oars? Where did Neon put the oars?" Asher muttered, feeling around the bottom of the canoe frantically. They weren't in the boat. Asher looked toward the shore. He couldn't go back and get them. He used his hands to get as far away from the shore as possible until the current took over.

Laser bursts from the hybrid hunters' weapons flew around them until the current took the canoe around a bend. Asher heard a weird sound, like bubbles popping and wind howling. The sound grew louder and louder. He looked behind him and saw a scorpion headed their way.

"Shit!" said Asher.

"You said a curse," said Timothy in a weak voice.

There was no way for them to outrun or hide from the drone. A whisking sound came from the far shore, and a sparkling light ball whizzed past the drone. A second one missed the drone as well. Finally, the third ball of light crashed into the scorpion, right before it fired upon Asher and Timothy. The explosion lit up the night sky. Asher knocked the breath out of himself as he lunged forward to cover Timothy from the flying debris. He didn't know who had shot the drone. Who else was in the dark?

Asher and Timothy were safe from the hunters for now. They still had to face the unknown dangers of the foggy river. The water picked up speed.

"Frick!" said Asher as the canoe hit a rock, causing them to spin. "How do I control this damn thing without oars?"

Timothy groaned each time the canoe rammed against a rock or made a turn. "Make it stop."

Asher could barely hear him above the rapids.

"I don't know how, booger." He gripped both sides trying to steady the canoe. With each bump, tip and turn, the canoe took on water. Asher could barely see Timothy had shifted in the canoe, his head rolling to the side. The water in the canoe threatened Timothy's lungs.

"Stay with me, Timothy." Asher stretched and turned Timothy's head away from the puddle of water beneath him. Timothy let out another groan. Asher couldn't make out all of his words.

"Can't...my...arms...legs."

"It's okay, we're going to get you—"

The canoe turned and dipped down, and Asher lost his balance. A cage of wetness strapped onto his body, pulling him underwater. Fighting against the cold, rushing water and complete fear, he managed to get his head above surface. He gasped for air before he submerged again. The little breath he had, he lost as the current slammed him into a rock. Asher's head surfaced again, and he clung to a rock coated with river scum. The water frothed over him, causing his scrapes and wounds to burn.

"Timothy!" Asher called. The rapids raged with the roaring of death.

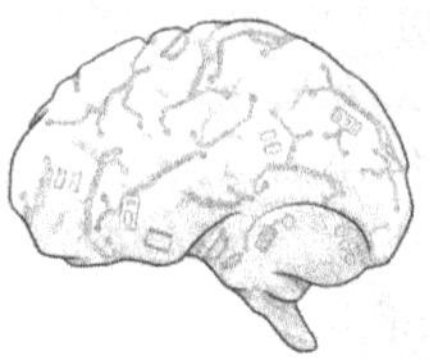

Asher heard voices. He couldn't control his shivering. He opened his eyes, still clinging to a rock. A water-soaked log wedged against him, keeping him pressed against the rock and his head above water. The morning sun peeped through the fog. He must've passed out still hanging onto the rock.

"Hello! You okay?"

Asher looked at the shore. His head throbbed, his recent memories hazy like the fog that followed the river downstream.

"You on the rock! Hello!"

Asher saw a man with a dog. He didn't know or even care if the man with umber skin was a hybrid hunter or not. If he was, he seemed far too old for a hunter. He had to be in his seventies at least. The top of the man's head was dark skin surrounded by pillows of white clouds that ran down the side of his face and under his mouth and nose. His earlobes glistened as the sun woke up from its night's sleep. He wore a pair of red shorts, the color a lifeguard would wear, and a plain white T-shirt. Having only the lady who killed his mother to compare him to, Asher couldn't envision this elderly man as a hybrid hunter. Asher couldn't flee even if he wanted to. His body had no energy left to get him ashore.

"Are you okay?" The man's distinctive voice had a sound of its own. A voice perfect for animation and narration of hFilms and hVision.

Asher mustered all the energy he had left to speak. "Where's Timothy?"

"Who's Timothy?" said the man. His eyes scanned the river.

"My brother." The haze in Asher's mind started to clear.

"I haven't seen any others. Only you. Are you hurt?"

The dog walked into the water up to his underbelly, and he stopped and let out a bark.

Asher felt his forehead. He winced as his fingers came across a small gash above his eye. "I have a cut on my head. I think I'm okay."

"Can you swim?"

"No, I don't know how."

"First thing, you cannot panic. You have to stay calm. Can you do that for me?"

Asher hesitated. Fear and panic wrapped tightly around him. "Timothy! I have to find Timothy. He's hurt."

"Let's get you to shore first, and then we'll look for your brother. Can you stay calm and do what I say?"

"I think so?" It was a question, not a statement.

"That's not reassuring. Relax. I'll get you to land." The man sounded confident. "What's your name?"

"Asher."

"Okay, Asher, people call me Gully Jumper, or Gully for short. You're going to have to trust me. Okay?"

"I have to find Timothy!" Asher couldn't stop the panic rising in his voice.

"We will. Now listen to me."

"Okay." Asher scanned the area, hoping to see Timothy on the opposite shore waving to him with a look of "Come and get me!"

"You have to let go of the rock, get your feet pointed downstream, and try to float on your back."

"I can't let go. I can't swim."

"You don't have to swim. Only float. Do this." Gully cocked his head back, waved his arms at his sides, and moved his legs up and down, demonstrating how to tread water and float at the same time.

"I'll drown if I let go. I have no body fat to float."

"No, you won't. All you have to do is let the river take you to calm waters."

Asher closed his eyes. He could hear the man encouraging him. The dog barked. He took a deep breath and pushed off the rock.

"There you go, you're doing it!" Gully followed on land with his old canine friend leading the way.

Asher slammed against a rock. Wedged between two rocks was Timothy's corpse, his bluish-amber eyes nothing more than lifeless, colored marbles. Glazed over with an icy appearance, they were stuck in their position, staring pointlessly at Asher and reminding him he didn't get Timothy to safety, like his mom told him to do. Asher had broken his promise.

"Don't panic, Asher. Listen to my voice. You can do this."

Asher lost all control and tumbled through the rapids like a piece of driftwood. His head bobbed and his arms flailed through the white-caps. He could see Gully racing after him.

"Damn it!" said Gully.

Asher gasped for air, coughing up water in his windpipe. He pounded against the rocks like a pinball.

Asher had no more energy. He was physically, mentally, and emotionally depleted. He had nothing left to give. He went under, knowing there would be no coming back up. A part of him didn't want to. Not with his mom and Timothy both dead.

Pain ripped into his head as a hand grabbed onto his hair. Asher felt himself moving upward. He wheezed, trying to get air to replace the water that went into his lungs. He coughed and gagged; his lungs, which were once losing, were now winning, forcing the intrusive liquid out of their domain.

"I got you, bud," said Gully as he treaded water for both of them. "Relax. You're going to be okay."

Asher was too exhausted to fight or even speak. Gully swam ashore to safety with Asher in tow. The dog greeted his owner with his tongue hanging out as if smiling, his golden tail wagging, and a small bark as if saying hello.

Asher lay on the stony shoreline. His head throbbed, and not one place on his body didn't hurt or ache in one way or another. He could taste blood seeping into his mouth around his lips. Nothing hurt more than his heart.

"I like morning swims, but I wasn't expecting this one." The old man laughed.

"He's stuck." Asher's voice shook as he kept envisioning Timothy wedged between the rocks. "Have to save Timothy, he's stuck. I saw him."

Gully looked up the river. "I'll go look. You stay here."

Asher didn't move. In total exhaustion, he passed out.

Asher screamed. He sat up, sweat dripping down his face. He found himself wrapped up in warm blankets on a soft feather bed. He found himself in a pair of dry, baggy sweatpants and a gray hoodie.

"Are you okay in here?" asked Gully as he entered the dimly lit room.

Seeing Gully, Asher remembered what had happened. This man saved him from the river's rage and then went on to find Timothy.

"Did you save Timothy?"

Gully's body slumped.

Asher knew the answer anyway. He had seen Timothy's lifeless body with his own eyes. His bottom lip quivered, and his shoulders dropped in resignation. "It's my fault. He can't be dead." Asher kept hearing the final six words his mother had spoken to him, echoing in his throbbing head. "Get yourself and Timothy to safety." He'd failed his mom, he'd failed Timothy. He wished Neon had been with them. Neon would've gotten them all to safety. She'd lived on the streets before. She knew how to escape from serious danger.

"I'm sorry, Asher."

Asher didn't say a thing. He shut his eyes only to opened them again. When he'd closed them, a vision of Timothy's dead face had appeared.

"Here, sip this."

"What is it?"

"Vegetable broth."

Asher reluctantly reached for the cup. His muscles ached with each move. He smelled the broth, and his mouth watered. He took a sip. The broth felt good as its warmth spread across his chest.

"Is he still stuck on the rocks?" Asher winced at the thought of his surrogate brother's final resting place between rocks with fish, birds, and other animals feasting on him.

"It took me a bit to find him, when I did, I realized I needed special equipment. I carried you here, and by the time I got back to the river, his body had disappeared. The current must've taken him. I'm sorry. Is there someone I can call for you?"

Asher looked down at his broth and shook his head. "Where am I?" he muttered.

"You're at my cabin. You're safe here."

Asher took another sip of the warm broth. Although his internal clock told him it was 5:33 p.m., he felt as if the man expected him to tell him things. Things Asher didn't want to discuss. "What time is it?" He wanted to derail any thoughts the man had about what had happened to him.

"It's around five-thirty. Dinnertime. You slept all day. Are you hungry, or is the broth enough? I have stew on the stove."

Asher grimaced. "No, thank you. This broth is fine. Not really hungry." Asher didn't eat meat. If he did, he might have accepted the offer. Besides, he didn't have much of an appetite.

"Asher, was it only you and Timothy who made it out of Willow Wood in the canoe?" Asher's eyes widened. His eyes flicked to the doorway. Could he make it? *How did he know?* he wondered.

Gully held his hands up in a gesture of peace. "Relax. I'm not here to hurt you. You're safe."

Licking his lips Asher tensed. He didn't want to reveal anything, but he wanted to find out what Gully knew. "Willow Wood? What's that?"

"It's all over the news. Willow Wood was a secret estate that housed hybrids. It was raided last night." Gully's eyes tried to pierce Asher's

"Hybrids?"

"I see, you're trying to play it safe. I understand. If you're going to try to act ignorant, make sure your facial expressions act the part as well."

Asher didn't say a thing.

"Like I said, you're safe here. I'm not a hybrid hunter. I'm actually one of the good guys."

Asher looked at his broth, not wanting to look at the man. "Did the news say if they captured anybody?"

"No, one fatality. A woman, they didn't reveal her name yet."

Tears filled Asher's bloodshot eyes. "It's my fault."

"I'm sure it wasn't."

"It's all my fault," he repeated. Asher wanted to say more. Guilt and regret gripped tightly around his aching heart, choking it. If only he'd told his mom about the man Neon had seen, she could be alive now. And if he would have gotten up when his mom first tried, Timothy could still be alive. Asher put the cup of broth on the nightstand and slouched under the covers, pulling the blankets over his head. Asher rolled and turned his back towards Gully, trying to hide from the events of last night.

"You are alive, Asher. Let's focus on that."

Asher tried sniffing the tears away under the blankets.

"I understand you want to hide under those sheets. Trust me when

I say you will not be able to hide from past failures, fears, or who you truly are. You must face all of them head to head. Take a stand. I know you're not alone. Your friends will stand with you."

The man sounded like Asher had many friends. He only had one, and Neon was more like an annoying sister than a friend. The thought he had no friends raced through his mind like a missile. With Timothy and his mom dead, and Neon MIA, he had no one to help him face those things.

"Are you going to turn me in?" The blankets muffled Asher's voice.

"Why? Because you're a hybrid?"

Asher didn't answer.

"Like I said before, you're safe here."

Asher lowered the sheets from his head. "The hybrid hunters didn't kill or capture anyone else?"

"The news didn't report any more deaths or captures, then again, the news crew wouldn't know if the hybrid hunters took their victims to another location."

At the start of Gully's sentence, a tiny glimpse of hope sparked in Asher's heart. Maybe Neon, Dr. Emily, and the rest made it out alive. It wasn't his mom or Timothy, it was at least something to hope for. That glimmer died as Gully finished the sentence.

"Why are you being nice to me?"

"Let's just say I have a very close friend who is a hybrid. He's saved my hide more than once. I think differently about hybrids than the government and most normals do."

"Thank you, sir, for helping me. How did you find me?"

"I was in the right place at the right time during my morning walk with Kane."

"Who's Kane?"

The man smiled. "Kane. Sit up."

The golden-coated dog poked his head over the footboard.

"He's been lying here in front of the bed all day. Normally he doesn't lie in that spot."

"What kind is he?"

Kane's large body jumped on the bed, and he rested his head upon Asher's lap. His tail wagged as if he'd known Asher for a long time.

"Half St. Bernard and half golden retriever."

"We had a few dogs at Willow Wood. I don't know what happened to them."

"What's your plan now?"

Asher wanted to tell him about the safe house in Jamestown. Could he really trust Gully? Was Gully trying to be his friend to get key information from him? Asher remembered his mom telling him several times he couldn't trust anyone on the outside. "Nothing in particular."

"You're welcome to stay here as long as you like."

Asher shouldn't trust the man. At the same time, he couldn't face the outside world alone yet. Gully seemed nice enough. The way Asher figured, if the man wanted him dead, he would have killed him already. No, Asher would stay and formulate a plan. "Thank you, sir. I think I'm going to rest a little bit more."

Gully smiled and took the cup from him. "If you need me, yell. Come on, Kane."

With a tired bark, the old dog slid off the bed and followed his master into the living room.

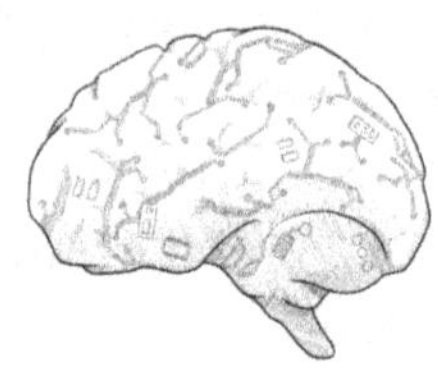

Asher's bladder woke him up in the middle of the night. The images from his nightmare about his mom and Timothy were still vivid in his head. A strange, arithmetic growl came from the living room. It sounded like an antique chainsaw.

"Owww," groaned Asher as he forced his aching body out of bed. He found the bathroom and looked in the mirror. He touched the cut over his eye, examining it. Guilt. Regret. Sadness. All of them showed their ugly faces in the mirror. "I'm sorry, Mom. I'm sorry, Timothy."

Asher finished his business and went back to bed. The growly tune continued with its annoying music. He sat on the edge of the bed. Thinking. Contemplating. Calculating. He changed his mind. He couldn't stay here.

His stomach joined the choir. It gurgled, reminding Asher he hadn't eaten a real meal in the last twenty-four hours. Following the wishes of his hunger, he sneaked into the kitchen, careful not to wake Gully, who was sleeping on the sofa. He found a loaf of bread on the counter. He swiped it and headed to the front door.

Kane popped his head up and looked at him.

Asher opened the door and stepped into the darkness, not looking back. He had to go to Jamestown, first he had to find a computer.

The man in the gray hood stood in the dark shadows of the night. The porch light flickered as a shadow came out and passed by it. When the shadow vanished in the darkness of night, the gray-hooded man went to the cabin.

Kane jumped up and wagged his tail as the man entered.

"Hey ya, boy." He petted the dog on the head.

"What's going on?" Gully sat up abruptly. "Oh, it's you," said Gully as he tried to get his eyes to focus.

"Asher's gone. He left about ten minutes ago."

"And Timothy?"

The gray-hooded man's body drooped. "As we suspected. His body was recovered by Dr. Monroe."

"I'm sorry."

"I am too." He paused. "I am too."

"Piss off, bitch!" Brett Lundy yelled as he slammed the front door of his well-to-do house in Meat Cove, Nova Scotia. He ran his muscular hands through his feathered brown hair, giving him a pop-star look.

"Cara on your case again?" asked Jinx, Brett's on-again, off-again girlfriend. Her dyed ebony hair was cut high and tight. She wore dark makeup around her eyes, which she had tinted solid black, looking like they plucked out. Jinx had several piercings on both ears, on her nose, lips, and brow, and more under her black denim pants and black T-shirt with the words, "I'm a bitch. Deal with it!" Gothic tatts were scattered across her pale skin.

"She thinks she's my mother. She is fricken six years older than me. I have half-siblings older than her." Brett's fists clenched. "The senator only married her because she's a fricken trophy wife." Brett refused to call the senator Father, Dad, Pa, or any other fatherly names. Anger erupted from his brown eyes as if they were solar flares.

Jinx wrapped her arms around him and gave him a deep kiss. Brett pushed her away.

Bitter and disgusted, Brett said, "You were eating corn nuts again, weren't you?"

"It's no worse than the smell from your constant burping after you eat your breakfast consisting of a whole dill pickle, beef jerky and Mountain Dew."

"Don't you start on me too," said Brett.

"I'm sorry, baby."

"Stop calling me that." Brett hated being called nicknames of affection. He didn't really care for Jinx. He kept her around because she put out and her brother owned a 2169 Gemini they used to sneak off without permission whenever they wanted.

"Man, she really irked you this time. I think you need good giggles."

He stopped and looked at her. "You got any?"

"No, but I know Jenny does."

Brett didn't mind Jenny. However, her friend Keisha got on his nerves, especially when she laughed.

"One more year and we don't have to buy it off the black market," said Brett.

"I'll be glad when I turn eighteen," Jinx said. "I can legally move out on my own. We could get an apartment together."

Brett didn't reply. If it wasn't for her connections, getting weed and alcohol, and giving him sex practically whenever he wanted it, he would probably dump her for good. No more on-again, off-again. They got into a fight practically every day, it always ended in sex.

Brett, now thoroughly stoned, laughed as he ate his favorite snacks—Froot Loops and French fries. He looked at Jinx, Jenny, Keisha, and a new girl. All of them were stoned as well. He couldn't remember the new girl's name. Her blouse partly revealed large breasts that excited him. He wanted to get a piece of that.

The sun had gone down, and the fivesome ended up at Jinx's house. Her parents had a business meeting in Boston, leaving Jinx's older brother, Carl, in charge. Carl had gone on a date with his boyfriend.

"You guys want to play hide-n-go-seek?" asked the new girl. She had long bleached-blond hair and tits Brett couldn't keep his eyes off.

"That's a fricken child's game," said Jinx.

"Not the way I play it," the new girl replied. "Although there should be the same amount of boys as girls."

"How do you play it?" asked Brett.

"We turn out all the lights in the house to make it pitch dark. We girls hide in the house, and the boys have to find us. If the boys find us, we have to take off a piece of clothing."

"I'm in," said Brett, not letting her finish.

"Let me get this straight. We take off our clothes and Brett doesn't?" asked Keisha. "That's not fair."

"Once Brett finds all of us, then he gets to hide, and we look for him."

"I'm in, cunnermans!" Brett said again.

"House, turn off all interior and exterior lights," said Jinx. The house went dark.

"Remember, you can't leave the house," said the new girl.

Brett counted, and the girls quickly found spots to hide. He enjoyed the game. Especially the part where he got to fondle, grope, kiss, and tease each girl, except for Keisha. Brett couldn't be bothered with her.

He ran to the garage wearing nothing other than his boxers, thinking it would be a good spot to hide, among other things. When he entered, he could see the dim shape of the 2169 Gemini. He ran his hand across the sleek hood. He opened the door, climbed behind the wheel, and took a swig of his whiskey. He wanted to go for a ride.

"Found you," said the new girl. She caressed his body. "Take them off."

Brett climbed out and pulled off his boxers. She embraced him, and they kissed deeply. Brett placed his hands on her breasts.

"Lights on," said Jinx.

The garage light turned on. Brett pushed the new girl away. Jinx and the other girls joined them. All five were completely naked.

"Now what?" asked Keisha.

"Let's go for a ride," Brett said, looking at the Gemini.

Jinx laughed. "We are in no condition to go for a ride."

"Carl is moving to Erie, Pennsylvania next month. There aren't many opportunities left." Brett climbed back into the car.

"I need to get my clothes," said Jenny.

"Who needs clothes?" Brett pushed in the override code Carl didn't know he had. The car let out a vroom that sounded sweet to anyone's ear.

"I'm in," said the new girl. She climbed into the backseat. Jenny and Keisha followed. Jinx sat up front in the passenger's seat.

The garage door opened, revealing Carl walking up the driveway. "What the hell? Get out of my fricken car!" He ran into the garage and opened the driver's door before Brett had a chance to lock it.

Carl's dark eyes pierced through Brett as an angry pucker stood out of his acne-plagued face, which he tried to hide by growing his tar-colored bangs to cover his pale gray eyes.

"Frick off, cunnerman," said Brett.

"Get out of my car!" Carl yelled. His arm, more flab than muscle, grabbed Brett by the neck and tried pulling him out.

"You frick face!" Brett climbed out and without hesitation gave Carl a right hook, followed by a left uppercut. The cracking of teeth was followed by a thud as Carl's head hit the cement floor. He lay stunned.

"Brett, what did you do?" Jinx yelled. The girls were getting out of the car.

"Get back in. We're going for a ride." Brett climbed in and slammed the door shut. Jinx let out a huff and did the same. If Brett had looked at the other girls, he would've seen fear motivated them to get back in the car. The tires squealed, leaving Carl behind.

The drama of Carl subsided once a bottle and a joint were passed around.

"What's a cunnerman?" asked the new girl, snuggled into the back with her arms crossed over her bare bosom.

"It's Brett's new favorite insult," Jinx said. "He used to call everyone idget until he went to Pennsylvania for a week."

"What does it mean?" asked the new girl.

"Hell if I know. I thought it had a cool ring to it."

"Where are we going?" Jenny asked after taking a swig from the bottle.

"Besecker's for breakfast." Brett's eyes felt weird as well as his head. His vision became blurry, and he slurred a little. "Jinx, program Besecker's into auto-drive."

Jinx's fingers danced on the computer screen on the dashboard. "Besecker's in Clark's Harbour?"

"That's the one. They make the best breakfast."

"Wait! Clark's Harbour?" asked Jenny. "That's on the opposite end of Nova Scotia. We'll be driving all night."

"That is why we're going there for breakfast and not a midnight snack," Brett said with a short laugh.

"Excuse me," Keisha said. "Are you all missing the fact that we're naked?" She giggled. "Our clothes are back at the house." She giggled more.

"We'll worry about it later. Light up another joint." Brett took the joint from Jinx. He took a deep inhale and let it out slowly. "Let's party, girls!"

Brett groaned as he tried to open his eyes. It felt like a galactic warship had fired heavy rounds into his head. The light made it worse. He smacked his lips and tongue around, feeling his cottonmouth. If there were galactic warships in his head, then there had to be an air wing of star runners in the middle of a dogfight in his stomach.

He found himself wearing an orange jumpsuit with the initials CHPD over the left breast. Part of the letters and the front of his jumpsuit were covered with what Brett thought the star runners discharged in his stomach.

Brett looked around the small, dingy gray room. It had a cot, a toilet, a sink, and a garbage can. Brett looked down at the garbage can and saw evidence he had missed the target. Looking at the vomit made Brett's stomach turn. "Where the frick am I?"

He looked toward his crotch. "Frick! I pissed myself." Movement outside the door caught his attention.

"Voice recognition, Sgt. Johnson Knapp, badge number 235, Clark's Harbour Police Department," came a voice outside the door.

"Voice recognition authenticated," replied a metallic, hollow, male voice.

"Open Cell Five."

Brett's door clicked. The handle turned, and in walked a policeman.

"You're awake," Sgt. Knapp said as more of a statement than a question.

"Really? You sure state the obvious." Brett's head pounded.

"Listen here, son, the better you cooperate, the easier it will be."

"I'm not your son. Where am I?"

"You're at Clark's Harbour Police Headquarters. You don't remember anything from last night, do you?"

Brett tried to think. It hurt his head too much.

"Just as I thought. Let's get you cleaned up and get food in your stomach."

"Can't you give me a hangover shot?"

"Nope. Not allowed to administer medicine. Even if I was, I wouldn't. If you can't handle your recreational activities' aftereffects, then you shouldn't be doing them to begin with."

"Spare me the lecture, cunnerman." Brett couldn't put last night's puzzle together. He could remember only a few pieces. "Where are the girls I was with?"

"They have already been released to their parents. We're still waiting for yours to show up. I have other things I need to take care of, let's go. You need to clean up before the senator arrives."

Brett stood up too fast. The air wing dogfight going on in his stomach attacked again. Liquid chunks erupted out of Brett's mouth, spewing onto the floor. Brett fell back down to the cot.

"Still upset I see." The sergeant guided him to the garbage can. Brett dry heaved a few times. "It sounds like you got everything out of your stomach."

Brett wiped the vomit from his lips and chin with his hand, then proceeded to wipe his hand off on Sgt. Knapp's pants. He lay back down on the cot and placed his arm over his eyes. What he wouldn't give to get a dose of the hangover medicine he keeps in his bedroom. He didn't know which felt worse, his head or his stomach.

"Your charges are serious. Drunk in public, indecent exposure, resisting arrest, disorderly conduct, and grand theft auto. I'm sure if we think hard enough, we can add to the list."

"Gee, thanks." His stomach gurgled.

"Excuse me, Sgt. Knapp?"

Brett knew the voice without looking up.

"Yes?"

"I'm Oscar Drake. I work for the senator." Oscar's eyes bore down on Brett. "How is he?"

"I have a fricken hangover from hell and I'm in jail. How the frick do you think I am?"

Oscar worked for Brett's father. Without looking up, Brett could picture Oscar standing there at the door. No doubt the florescent light reflected off his clean-shaven head, which didn't make sense. He'd always thought black absorbed light, not reflected it. His dark brown eyes were surrounded with what looked to Brett like snow a dog pissed on. His goatee sat neatly trimmed around his trout lips. His arm muscles bulged under his black suit and white shirt, causing the threads to strain, trying not to snap.

"Thank you, Sergeant. I can take it from here," Oscar said.

"Be my guest. I'll be down the hall if you need me. Once he's cleaned up, we can discuss his release."

"Thank you again, Sergeant."

Sergeant Knapp left the cell.

"What were you thinking?" Oscar asked Brett, who still hadn't moved since he last lay down.

"Let me guess, the senator sent you instead of bringing his fat ass down here himself."

"You know your father has a very busy schedule. Especially since he announced his candidacy for North American President last week. Once the media finds out, they are going to have a field day with your little stunt."

"Who gives a shit?" Brett forced himself to sit up and look at Oscar. "The senator is more worried I'll blemish his political career than he is for me."

"Brett."

"Tell me it's not true," said Brett.

Oscar didn't reply.

"That's what I thought. He doesn't give a shit about me. Why should I give a shit about him and his fricken candidacy for president?"

"I'm not going to stand here and argue with you about your father. We need to get you cleaned up and back home."

"I can't wait till I become a legal adult. Then I won't have to listen to you."

"True. That means stunts like this will follow you around for the rest of your life. It means I won't have to come all the way down here to get your sorry white ass out of jail."

"If that's the way you feel, then leave me here," Brett said.

"I would if I could. I did tell your father I would come and get you."

"Stop calling him my father. We might have the same blood, but he's not my father. The only reason he doesn't send me away is to save his popularity amongst the voters." Brett knew Oscar wouldn't argue. If the senator sent Brett to a private boarding school, his prospective voters would see he didn't care one way or the other about public education. It wouldn't look good if he tried to convince them he was for public schools while his own son went to a private one.

"Do you want to go to a private school?" asked Oscar.

"If it means getting away from him and his trophy bitch, yes."

"I can make it happen."

"How would you convince the senator to let me go?" Brett asked.

"Like the senator, I know people. With their help, I think we can get the senator to sign off on this."

"Really?" Brett doubted it.

"I went to a private academy when I was your age," Oscar said. "My physics teacher, Hai ying Wu, took me under her wing. She tends to favor kids like you."

"What are you saying? You were a badass too when you were my age?"

"What I am saying is you are in the fast lane to self-destruction. I'm afraid if you don't correct your course now, there will be no turning back."

"I'm fine with the direction I'm going. You won't find my ass in prison, the senator will make sure of that," said Brett.

"It is my job to make sure we don't find your ass decaying in a gutter or a back alley. Brett, you're out of control, and if I don't help you now..."

"I would say talk to the hand, but I'm afraid if I move again, I'll give you more than my hand. Besides, I thought you were on my side."

"I am on your side. That's why I feel you need to go to this academy. With the help of Hai ying Wu, who is now Dean of Academics, we'll convince the senator it's in his best interest you attend. If anyone can convince your father to let you go, it will be her."

"Where is this academy?"

"Earth Force Alliance Junior Academy NAS *Pocono*," replied Oscar.

"EFA?" Brett removed his arm from his eyes and looked at Oscar. He laughed. "How could I ever doubt you, Oscar? The senator is going to blow steam out of every orifice of his body. He's been trying to shut down the program for years. Let's do this."

"I am not going to talk to Dean Wu on your behalf for you can piss your father off again. This is a chance for you to tap into the potential hidden deep within you. I see it escape once every other blue moon, nevertheless it's there, and if anyone can get it out, it's Dean Wu."

"Untapped potential. Now you're starting to sound like Mrs. B," said Brett.

"Mrs. B? Is she the old lady you've been sneaking off to see every Sunday?" Oscar asked.

Brett sat up, surprised. He thought for sure no one knew about his visits to Mrs. B.

Oscar looked at Brett. "You didn't think I knew, did you?"

"You better not fricken tell anyone," Brett threatened.

"Oh yes we don't want anyone to know you actually care about something other than pissing your father off."

"It's not what you think." Brett didn't like when people found a vulnerable spot in him. Mrs. B was an old lady he'd been visiting for a couple of years now as she slowly lost her mind. Sadly, she didn't recognize him anymore. She kept calling him Thane, her husband, who he'd never met. Nevertheless, he continued to visit her every Sunday. He didn't know why, and he couldn't explain it, for some strange reason, the old lady touched his heart in such a way he had to attempt to touch hers as well. Brett's mother was the only other person who touched his heart that way. "The academy is coed, right?" He tried changing the subject.

"Yes," replied Oscar.

"This gets even better. Call your hookup. I want to do this."

"This isn't going to be a walk along the beach, you know," Oscar said.

"I don't care how tough it is, as long as it's far away from Trophy Bitch and the senator."

"Okay then. Let's get you cleaned up and out of here, and I'll make some calls."

Brett smiled as he took the change of clothes from Oscar. This would be the biggest thing he ever did to really piss the senator off. He hoped this Wu lady could convince the senator to let him go, the biggest pit he had to jump over to make this happen. He couldn't wait to see the look on the senator's face. What started off as a miserable day had turned into one of the best days of his life.

Asher's internal clock told him he'd been hiking for two hours and thirty-six minutes. He didn't dare go back to Willow Wood, and Jamestown seemed too far to walk. His journey took him through a dense and damp forest. The trees reached up into the sky as if they were painting twinkling lights upon a black canvas. The dead leaves and branches crunched under his feet as he limped along after having twisted his ankle earlier in his trek. Asher knew the woods at Willow Wood. He could walk around blindfolded all day and not bump into anything, unless Timothy had put an obstacle in front of him on purpose to trip him. He had memorized where every tree, bush, and other fixtures of the yard were, like the garden, pool, well, and play-ground. He could calculate with his implant how far it was to each obstacle. A mental map in his memory chip would guide him through the woods. These woods were different...and for the first time in a very long time, he had no idea where he was going.

Crickets, a bubbling stream nearby, owls, and frogs joined together in an eerie chorus. Wildflowers, rotting wood, and animal scat caught the attention of Asher's nose.

His muscles hurt, he couldn't stop yawning, and he had no idea where he was going even though his implants kept him from walking in circles. He didn't know what dangers lurked in the chill of the night. After walking for an additional thirteen minutes, he came to the forest's exit.

"Finally," he said with relief as the woods broke out into a minute town. He stood behind a tree and watched, examining, ensuring there were no hybrid hunters lurking or milling about. Once satisfied, he headed into the open.

He looked at the simple street. He had never been to a town before. Part of him wanted to explore and take it all in. He knew he couldn't get caught. Even though he had read thousands of books, he didn't know how to act normal in the presence of normals. He stood nestled behind a tree, debating his options.

"What do I do?" Asher mumbled under his breath. "Maybe this wasn't a good idea after all." With Neon, he wouldn't hesitate a nanosecond to continue on.

Asher bit a piece of his fingernail off and spit it out. He could tell by the short burst of concentrated pain near the cuticle his right index finger began to bleed. Asher's internal clock read 2:13 a.m. There wouldn't be too many people up, if any. "You can do this, Asher." He let out a deep breath and marched forward.

He played masquerade with the shadows from the streetlights as his mask. He held his breath each time a person passed by, hoping they wouldn't notice him. The only way they could tell he was a hybrid would be to do a scan on him, revealing his brain implants. He couldn't help fearing maybe normals had a sixth sense for detecting hybrids. He wondered if normals acted differently than hybrids. His mom and Dr. Emily were both normals, and didn't act any differently, they protected hybrids. With his limited experience, he had no way to know.

He passed another group and wondered why so many people were walking on the streets this late at night. Was this normal in the outside world? He crossed an intersection lit up by neon signs from several taverns, bars, and dives and saw where the crowds were coming from. People filtered out of the mouths of the buildings.

One of the signs caught his attention: *Cyber Mania, café, internet, virtual reality games and more. Open 24 hours.* "Internet?" This could be what Asher wanted. The answer to get him to the safe house in Jamestown. He didn't know how to reach Dr. Emily or anyone else from Willow Wood. The only person he knew how to reach was Pandora. He'd promised his mom he wouldn't contact her again. He didn't have a choice, did he?

One of the last times he'd chatted with her, Pandora said the two of them should meet. She and her dad were both hybrids, and they lived in a safe hybrid village. Asher liked the thought of going to a village and not being trapped on a large piece of property with a stone wall around it. Plus, as much as he wanted to reconnect with Neon and find Dr. Emily, there would be much to face...too much pain. Would they blame him for the deaths of his mom and Timothy?

Asher cautiously opened the door to Cyber Mania and entered the small lobby. The door squeaked, and a solid tone shot out of the ceiling in three quick bursts. He walked in, and his nose instantly did a double take at the disturbing aromas that filled the air.

The lobby had a few stained chairs and a service counter where a boy with shaggy hair slouched in the corner. His eyes were droopy and bloodshot. He had a peaceful and mellow look about him. The boy noticed Asher and stood. He brought a joint up to his lips and inhaled, closing his eyes, and slowly breathed smoke back out.

"You want a hit, brah?" asked the boy.

"Uh, hit?" He'd never had marijuana before, even though it was legal in North America for those who were at least eighteen. He refused politely. "No, thank you. I would like to get on the internet, please."

"Card."

"Huh?"

"I need your payment card then I can turn on the internet for you, brah."

Asher gave the clerk an awkward smile. "I don't have a payment card." He turned to leave, feeling defeated.

The clerk took another hit. "Wait," he said. "If you can keep it a secret, I'll let you use the equipment for free. You need to do me a little favor, brah."

"Favor? What kind of favor?" Asher was skeptical. Thanks to Neon, he'd learned to be skeptical when it came to people wanting favors.

"Clean the bathroom for me. This way my boss doesn't get mad at me."

Asher thought for a second. He cleaned bathrooms at Willow Wood for the younger kids. It wasn't bad of a job, except for the time when the toilet backed up and overflowed after Timothy used too much toilet paper.

"Can I use the computer first?" asked Asher.

"Brah, I'm not an easy mark for you to use the computer and slip out the back entrance without doing your part."

Asher had only heard the term once. "Okay, I'll do it first."

"The supplies are in the closet. Ignore Old Mary. When she has too much to drink, she comes in here and sits on the pot and sleeps it off. There are times when she sits in there and sings. You stay out of her stall, you'll be fine. Supply closet is in the hallway."

Asher gathered cleaning solution and towels and made his way to the facilities. The distinct aroma of urine and fecal matter hit him as he entered the ladies' bathroom. On his right were two stalls. The first one had its door hanging crooked, due to a missing hinge. The second stall was missing the door completely. With no one in the stall with the broken door, Old Mary must've been sitting in the stall with no door. Asher did not want to see an old lady sitting on the pot. The thought disturbed him.

On the left were two chipped and cracked porcelain sinks. Inside were rust-colored stains from the dripping faucets. It looked like at one time there were mirrors above the sink. The floor had small tiles with cracks, scum, and water intertwining. The ceiling revealed pipes housed dust, cobwebs, bug corpses, and a fecal trail from rodents.

Walking into the empty stall, he crinkled his nose and tried to keep the bread he'd eaten earlier in his stomach. The toilet's seat sat half off the toilet. Urine, shit, toilet paper, what appeared to be bloody tampons, and possibly a used condom filled the toilet to the top of its edges.

"I'd stay away from that toilet if I were you," said an elderly voice from the second stall, followed by a sweet singing tune. Asher had never heard the song before, and the melody contrasted with the surroundings.

Asher didn't say anything. He put on the black rubber gloves that were too large for his hands and flushed the toilet. He backed up in case it overflowed, and he knocked the wobbly door completely off its remaining hinge. The toilet overflowed, spewing its contents onto the cracked, discolored floor.

"I warned you to stay away from that toilet," said the voice. It went back to the song.

Asher couldn't avoid the second stall anymore. He looked in and saw Old Mary. She had shoulder-length white hair, her thin face filled with crow's feet and wrinkles. Her clothes weren't what Asher expected. He'd thought she would be wearing clothes that made her look like a homeless person, instead she had on a blue blouse with khaki slacks. Asher sighed with relief seeing her slacks were pulled all the way up.

"Do you like the song?" asked Old Mary.

Asher shrugged. "I guess." He actually did like it, unfortunately his current surroundings were overpowering his other senses.

"I wrote this song with a former boyfriend when we were teenagers. Many years ago."

Asher didn't respond. The toilet stopped flooding. He could hear the trickling water running into the drain on the floor.

Asher spent the next forty-seven minutes cleaning the ladies' room while Old Mary sang her song. He liked the singing, it helped take his mind off reality while he cleaned. When Asher finished, he gathered up his cleaning supplies and moved on to the men's room. He prayed, to a God he didn't know, hoping the men's room was in better condition.

Before Asher exited, Old Mary spoke once more. There comes a time in everyone's life where they have to step out of their forbidden shadow and face what's before them."

Asher had no idea what a forbidden shadow was, but for some reason he felt like Old Mary was trying to warn him of something. But, what?

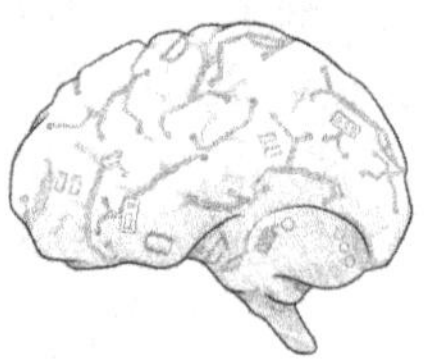

Asher ran his fingers across the small table—they smelled of bleach despite the oversized gloves he'd worn. At least he'd finished cleaning and was now online. Computer images appeared. He found the site to contact Pandora. After a slip of the fingers, a holoimage appeared above the desk of a girl. She had brown eyes and two jet-black braided ponytails, one on each side resting on her usual black T-shirt with a skull on the front. Asher swore she had no other clothes. He never saw her wearing anything else. Pandora appeared to be wide awake, considering the time of night.

"Asher?"

"Pandora, I need your help."

"What's wrong? Where are you? It doesn't look like you are in your bedroom."

"Hybrid hunters raided my home last night. I managed to escape."

"You okay?"

He touched the cut on his forehead. "I guess." Asher didn't know how to answer the question. "I need your help. I'm in a small town. If I send you a location gram, could your dad come and get me?"

"Yes, you can come here, and we'll figure out what to do," she said.

This is what Asher had hoped for. He wasn't quite ready to face the others yet. He ran his fingers on the table again. He paused, doubting his decision. Did he have any other options? He hit the send button before giving in to the doubt that encompassed his brain. "There, I sent you a location gram."

"I got it. Oh good, you're not too far from where I am. I was afraid you might be in another state, or country, even. Are you alone?"

"Yeah, I am at a cyber place. I'm in my own booth. There is a clerk though. I think there are a few people in other booths, not sure. Then there's Old Mary hanging out and singing in the women's bathroom."

"Old Mary?"

"Don't ask."

"Are you safe?"

"I think so." At least he hoped he was.

"Stay where you are. My dad and I will be there shortly."

"Okay. Thanks."

The holoimage disappeared. Asher searched the internet and found articles about Willow Wood. There were no pictures of the pig lady who'd killed his mother. Instead, there was a man Asher hadn't seen at the raid. After seeing the hybrid police badge on his breast pocket, he knew why. The man appeared to be Caucasian with the skin of one who'd spent a lot of time out in the sun. The peculiar thing was the pigment around his eyes was much paler. He looked like a racoon in reverse. He had the same skin pigmentation disorder around his knuckles too.

Asher bit his lip. An idea—an insane idea, in Asher's opinion—popped into his head. He typed a name into the holotable's search bar:

*Liam Mrkonic*

A slew of pictures appeared with contact info below them, all with the name Liam Mrkonic. *I need to narrow the search*, Asher thought. Since his mother had grounded him from his computer, he couldn't do any searches on his father after he'd learned his name. He typed in Pittsburgh, PA. Only three pictures remained. Asher deleted the one of the short, chubby black man. He looked at the second one and knew he didn't have to look at the third. A strange chill coursed through his body. The hairs on the back of his neck stood up. He had a strange feeling in his stomach.

*Is that him? My father?* The man had a slender face, like Asher. Blond hair and broad shoulders. Asher felt like he was looking at a picture of himself in the future. He glanced at the address: *7659 Foul Rift Road, Cranberry, PA.*

Asher jerked around as the door to his booth opened. He flicked the holotable off, as if afraid of his mom catching him breaking the rules again. There in the doorway, holding a large firearm, was an old lady with short, white hair with patches of purple. Asher guessed she was in her mid-seventies.

The women stopped and stared at Asher. She had a strange look on her face, almost as if it'd been a long time since she'd seen him.

"Asher, come with me. Hurry." Her raspy voice sounded like she'd smoked for a lifetime.

"Who are you? How do you know my name?"

"No time. You're in danger."

"No one knows I'm here." There was something about her, he couldn't figure it out. It was like a memory had escaped his mind. *I don't forget*, he thought.

"There's no time to explain." The old lady grabbed Asher's wrist.

Asher couldn't believe how much strength she had, considering her age. He struggled, though trying not to make a scene, as she yanked him out of the booth.

Two men stormed through the front entrance. Without looking, one lifted his handgun and fired toward the area where the clerk hung out. The old lady fired a few shots.

"This way!" She led Asher to the back door. When she opened it, there stood two more armed hybrid hunters. She shot both before either could fire a round.

"Who are they?"

"Hybrid hunters. Cortez is the worst. He works for Navarro, the bitch who killed your mom." Asher and the woman ran down a dark alley. "I have a vehicle around the corner."

"How do you know that? How did they know I was here?" Asher's brain was on overload with all the questions.

"After the bastards raid a hybrid dwelling, they monitor all communication devices within a circumference of the site, hoping any hybrids who escaped will try to contact help."

*That's what I did*, Asher thought. Since she'd saved his life from the hunters, he followed her. They rounded the corner and came to a dead stop. Old Mary leaned up against a car, like she knew they were coming.

"You," said the lady with Asher.

"Alita Blackwood. It's been a long time," Old Mary said.

"Old Mary?" said Asher.

"Not Old Mary," Alita Blackwood said.

"That's what the clerk calls me. I didn't bother telling him differently," Old Mary replied.

"Autumn Fletcher," Alita Blackwood said with disgust. "I really thought this time he would come himself instead of sending you."

Confused, Asher tried to make sense of Old Mary, or Autumn Fletcher, whoever she was, and how she knew Alita Blackwood. How did Alita Blackwood know where to find him? Did his call to Pandora reveal his location to her? How did she know his name? He had an eerie feeling in his stomach he knew her. He couldn't figure out how, he didn't forget anything, which meant there could be trouble in his near future.

"He had other matters to attend to." Autumn Fletcher opened the car door.

"Other matters or not, you can't have the boy. I got to him first." Alita Blackwell placed a tight grip around Asher's bony arm. He couldn't believe her strength. Not nearly as strong as Timothy's grip, still strong though, especially for an elderly person.

"You know you can't keep him, and anything you try will right itself," said Autumn. "Asher, get in the car."

Asher looked up to the sky. He heard a buzzing. The same buzzing he'd heard on the river, only louder.

"Drones!" he yelled.

Alita Blackwood released her grip and fired at the drones, lighting up the sky with a fiery orange flare. Autumn Fletcher reached into the vehicle, pulled out a large rifle, and started firing too.

"Get in the car!" yelled Autumn.

He dove into the front seat, hitting it in such a way causing his breath to escape from within. Autumn kicked the door closed with her foot. The car jerked as it skidded off down the street, leaving the two ladies behind to defend themselves against the drones.

Asher watched the scene as he sped away. He wished he had Neon's vision. As the car turned, a couple of other vehicles pulled up, firing off blasts. Each lady got into a different car and sped off in opposite directions.

"Where am I going?" Asher asked himself. He fumbled on the dashboard.

*2 West 3<sup>rd</sup> Street*
*Jamestown, New York*

Autumn Fletcher must've programmed it to take him to Jamestown. "How did she know?" Asher had a strange feeling inside him. He swore he heard voices speaking to him within his mind, telling him to his destination.

With shaky hands, he programmed in a new address. *7659 Foul Rift Road, Cranberry, PA.* He paused. "I'm sorry, Mom. I have to meet him." He pressed the execute button, and the car adjusted for the new destination. Asher slumped in the seat as he headed to Pittsburgh.

"I didn't think you were coming," Autumn said, out of breath.

A plump old man with a trimmed, white beard and a full head of white hair sat behind the steering wheel.

"Have I ever let you down before?" The old man had a faded, eastern Canadian accent.

"I know you didn't ask me that question, Thane Blass," said Autumn.

"I prefer to be called Game Master." Thane Blass smirked.

"Yeah, you're a master all right, and we both know of what." She sent him a smirk back. Her head turned as they passed the road they were supposed to turn down. "You missed your turn."

"Nah, I'm hungry. I thought we would stop and get breakfast before we head to Gully's."

"Breakfast? I almost died back there, and you want to go eat breakfast now?"

"Yeah, it's too early to eat lunch."

Autumn let out a sigh. "Honestly, I have no idea how all of us put up with you over the years."

"That makes two of us. I have no idea how I've been able to put up with all of you all these years." He gave her a wink.

Tabitha Dorney's fingers danced over the piano keys flawlessly. She'd started lessons at the age of three and had been playing the piano for thirteen years now. Music was in her soul; music was her soul. Everyone, including her pesky sister, Penelope, and deaf brother, Ryan, knew better than to interrupt Tabitha when she was playing the piano. She stopped abruptly and made changes to the notes on the holographic sheet music in front of her.

"Don't stop. That was beautiful," said her father, Mr. Dorney.

"I can't find the right notes to fit this spot." She brushed her strawberry-blond hair off her pale, freckled face. "Maybe if I change the lyrics."

"You'll come up with it. I have faith in you. It'll probably happen when you least expect it." Mr. Dorney had much love for his family.

Short in stature, he had small love handles seeping over his belt, and his straight gray hair with blue streaks were spiked up haphazardly. He'd seen the style in one of his Japanese manga and decided to go with it in an effort to look young.

"Let me guess, Dad. Stop over thinking." She kept her attention on her music notes, trying to figure out what to change, how to make the melody work. Though she had written songs before, this one was different and she couldn't figure out why.

"Exactly." Her father smiled at Tabitha. "I'm sure going to miss hearing you play."

"What do you mean, Dad? I'm not going anywhere."

"You applied for EFA Junior Academy, didn't you?"

"Dean Wu said at my interview it's normally the first ten kids on the waiting list who are accepted. I'm number thirty-three. Figure the odds on that one." Her fingers fumbled along the ivory keys. She wanted to go. She could apply again next year and only attend her senior year, however, she wanted the full two-year experience.

"I received a call from Dean Wu today. She took you off the waiting list."

Tabitha jerked her head toward her dad. "You mean I won't have a chance next year, either?"

"No, she took you off the waiting list. You are accepted as a full-time cadet starting in September."

Tabitha squealed with delight. She got up and hugged her father. "Does Mom know?"

"Not yet."

"I can't wait to tell her," said Tabitha.

"Tabitha," her dad called after her.

She stopped in the middle of the doorway. "Yeah, Dad?"

"Are you sure this is what you want? Pensacola Music Academy already said they would accept you."

"Dad, I love music beyond words. I've never left Florida, except the time we went to Texas for Uncle Murry's wedding. I want to get out there and let my music be inspired amongst the stars."

"I will support your decision, even though I am going to miss you terribly."

"I wish Pop Pop was still alive. He would be excited." She missed her grandfather dearly. He had been gone for a few years. Her heart still felt like he'd died yesterday.

"Are you kidding? He would move the earth to keep you from leaving him."

"I miss him," she said.

"It's been four years since they tried removing the garrison chip without success. I suspect we may never get over his death. We'll learn to live with it, never get over it. Now, let's go tell your mom your good news."

Chief Hospital Corpsman Liam Mrkonic sat in his recliner and turned the holovision on. He had finished rocking out on his drums to Cross Bones, F.A.W., Logan Steele, and his personal favorite, The River Rat Gang. He wore a distressed, faded black Silver Tongue T-shirt, drenched in sweat in the pits and down the neck and back. His Pittsburgh Pirates ballcap rested on his sandy hair, which had started to show signs of gray. He'd been wearing the ballcap for twenty years, minus the times he wore his EFA uniform.

He popped open a bottle of Iron City beer, took a swig, and burped. He wiped two days of growth on his face and let out another belch, then turned on the Pirates game. They were playing away against the Cuban Reef Sharks.

Chief's coffee-bean and forest-moss eyes rolled as he let out a miserable sigh when the doorbell rang.

"Who can it possibly be?" he mumbled to himself. "Mick, if that's you...!" He got up and answered the door.

A man with a golden suntan and a pigment malfunction around his eyes stood before him. "Liam Mrkonic?"

"I'm him. How can I help?"

"I'm a detective with the hybrid police." He pulled out an official badge. "May I come in and ask you a few questions?"

"Come on in. I'm sorry, I didn't catch your name," said Chief.

The detective walked into the living room. "Mac, everyone calls me Mac." He turned his attention to the holovision. "Pirates fan, huh?" he said in disgust.

"What team do you like?" asked Chief.

"Philadelphia Phillies, of course."

"Should've known. How can I help you, Detective?" Chief motioned the detective to take a seat. He muted the holovision.

"How do you know Victoria Smizik?"

Chief fell back into his recliner, shocked. Other than his brother, Mick, he hadn't heard a single person speak her name in years. "We were high school sweethearts. We were engaged at one point. Is she in trouble?"

"She's dead."

All the blood flowed out of Chief's face. He managed to push a word out of his dry throat. "How?" He took off his ballcap and held it close to him. Vicki had bought him the ballcap on their first date, to a Pirates game.

"Two days ago. Hybrid hunters raided an estate in New York where a group of hybrids lived. She was killed during the raid."

"Why was she there?"

"I was hoping you could tell me," said the detective.

Chief stood and walked over to the fireplace mantel. He stared through the bricks, focusing on nothing in particular. "I haven't seen Vicki in over seventeen years. We broke off the engagement when I joined EFA."

"It appears no one else has seen her in the last fifteen or sixteen years. Matter of fact, the last document I could find pertained to her was the application for marriage to you. She fell off the grid. Do you know why?"

"I'm sorry, Detective, I don't."

The detective stood and looked around. "You live here alone? Any family to speak of?"

"I have a brother who lives here in Pittsburgh. This place belonged to my parents before they died. I'm actually on leave, in between commands. I report to my new post next week."

"Where are you coming from?" asked the detective.

"I spent the last two years at Denver EFA Hospital. I'm now headed to the NAS *Meservey*. She's an old battle cruiser, still it'll be good to get underway again." His speech was hollow, almost automatic. He couldn't believe Vicki had died. A wound he thought was healed many years ago had resurfaced like a wet burp after a holiday meal.

"I'll let you be. I took up enough of your time. If you find out anything, can you contact me?"

"Absolutely." The two men held their wristwatches together as the detective's contact information transferred to Chief's watch. "I'm sorry for your loss. Thank you for your time." The detective saw his own way out as the chief collapsed into his recliner. He stayed until sleep took over.

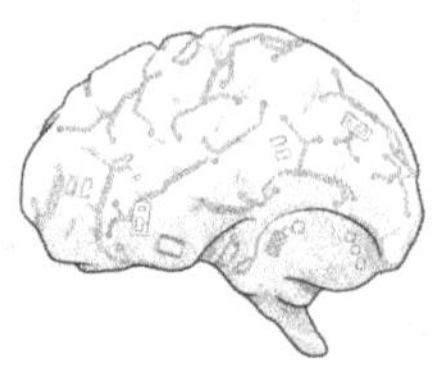

Asher's palms were sweaty, his stomach in turmoil. "Here goes nothing."

He crept up the brick sidewalk towards the front stoop. His feet became heavier with each step. An old weatherworn doormat on the stoop read, "The Mrkonics." He let out another breath and rang the doorbell. Time appeared to stop. He rang it again, and no answer. *Guess he's not home*, Asher thought. He wasn't sure if he was relieved or disappointed his father didn't open the door—maybe a little bit of both.

Giving in to doubt, he said, "Maybe this was a bad idea anyway." He turned and stepped off the stoop, then he heard the door open.

"May I help you?" asked the man who'd opened it.

Asher turned and saw his dad in person for the first time. He didn't know what to expect. He couldn't find his words.

"May I help you?" the man repeated.

"Are you Liam Mrkonic?"

"Yes." The man appeared leery.

"Do you know Vicki Smizik?"

Liam paused at the question, looking a little bewildered. "Yes, I knew her."

"She's my mother." Asher paused, the wound of her death still deep and bleeding. He tried to be careful with his next sentence. He couldn't help himself. He blurted it all out. "My name is Asher Levi Smizik. I'm your son."

"Why are we here?" asked Xiao-Niao Li. The house had to be four times larger than her own. Her dad worked as a cremator for a cemetery near Baltimore, which put her family on a tight budget. The music blared and caused the house to vibrate. Xiao thought for sure people in the next town over could hear.

A boy on an airlift motorcycle glided down the street, hovering over the road. As he came closer, his tires lowered, and he sped up onto the front lawn, yelling and laughing. He hopped off and ran inside the house. The back of his jacket read: *Clearview Bears 2183 Forensic National Champs.* A pair of bear claws held up the word *Bears*. The boy's hair stood on end as if filled with static electricity, and waves of different light-up colors moved through the strands.

"It's a Clearview Prep School tradition. The rising seniors throw a party for the rising juniors," said Olivia. "Next year we'll get to throw the party."

Xiao pushed her silky black hair over her ear away from her eyes, a nervous habit. "I don't know why I let you talk me into doing this," said Xiao. "You do know there are alcohol and drugs in there?"

"And sex too." Olivia's magenta hair blew in the summer wind.

"I am not having sex with a boy I don't know," Xiao insisted.

"Then have it with a girl." Olivia winked with a green eye. Olivia and Xiao had been friends since first grade and appreciated each other's humor.

"Really? You know I'm not going to have sex with you either." Xiao smiled. Or at least what she considered a smile. Most others would consider it an ever-so-slight arc of the lip line.

"Damn," Olivia said. "Come on, let's go inside."

"Maybe we better not. I should go home and study."

"Now it's my turn to say really. It's girls like you who give Chinese women a bad rap."

"And it's girls like you who give Latinas a bad rep," Xiao replied.

"You bet your sweet ass I do." Olivia had a shit-eating grin on her face. She let out a long sigh. "It's summer break. School doesn't start for another two months. Put the studying away and let's go in and enjoy ourselves. It's not like you accepted the invite to EFA Academy."

Xiao felt an invisible spirit telling her to go home. Against her better judgment, she followed her best friend into the abyss of partying teenagers.

Fifteen minutes later, Xiao sat in a dark corner by herself, studying relativity and quantum relativistic theories via her holowatch. The more she had memorized, the better equipped she would be for her AP classes at Clearview Prep.

"Is that homological algebra?" a boy asked.

Xiao didn't bother to look up. "Yes."

"I'm no mathematician, but I'm pretty good with numbers. Tell you what, give me yours and watch what I can do with it."

"Not interested," Xiao said, annoyed. She wanted him to go away, only she had promised Olivia she'd stay for an hour.

"For some reason, I was feeling a little off today. When you came along, you definitely turned me on."

"Will you stop and go away, please?" Xiao looked up. Too focused on her schooling, she didn't want any boy to come along and distract her from her goals. This boy was different. He caught her off guard. Her heart sped up. His hair, a medium brown, shared the same color with Pu'erh tea, dark but gentle in any light. His eyes, though. She'd never seen a person with one blue eye and one brown. People got their eyes tinted different colors all the time. These didn't have an unnatural look like most tinted eyes had.

"I tell you what. If you have one slow dance with me, I will go away and you can get back to your theories. If you refuse, I can stand here throwing pick-up lines at you all night long."

"Go away." Xiao turned her attention back to the hologram.

"I'm Knute Tuckerson. My friends call me Tuck. You can call me anytime."

*Cliché*. Xiao ignored him.

"If nothing lasts forever, will you be my nothing?"

Xiao continued to read.

"You remind me of a magnet, because your pull is strong." Tuck didn't give up. "My buddies bet me I wouldn't be able to start a conversation with the hottest person at the party. You want to go get ice cream or something with their money?"

"Okay, fine." Xiao turned her holowatch off.

"Really, you want to go get ice cream?" Tuck's dimples showed when he smiled.

"No, I will give you one dance, and then you have to leave me alone." Xiao combed her hair away from her ear and let out an exaggerated sigh. If one dance got him away from her, then she would do it. Although she wouldn't admit it to herself, she liked his smile.

Tuck held out his hand. Ignoring it, Xiao stood and went closer to the dance area. There were many couples embracing each other to a slow song by Mitch Kalon. She placed her hands on Tuck's broad shoulders, and he put his on her hips. They swayed with the music.

"Do you have a name, Quantum Girl?"

"Xiao-Niao. My friends call me Xiao. After this dance, you can call me never."

Tuck let out a small chuckle. "I believe you cracked a joke."

"Who says I'm joking?" She brushed her hair away from her ear again.

Tuck smiled. "Are you a rising junior too?"

"I said I would dance with you. I didn't say I would answer your questions too."

"Such hostility. I'll make one more deal with you. Let me ask you three questions, and then we can end this dance early." He gave her a devilish smile.

She sighed and rolled her eyes. "Fine. What?"

"Question one: Why Clearview Prep?"

"It's the best prep school in Maryland."

Tuck stayed quiet.

She felt like she had to add to her answer. "I did get accepted to EFA Junior Academy, my second choice if I didn't get into Clearview Prep. I already gave EFA my rejection letter."

"I thought about applying to EFA. The thought of me being up there and you being at Clearview Prep was something I couldn't live with."

"Will you stop already? It sounds like you've been stalking me."

"Sorry, I tend to say cheesy things when I'm nervous."

"Why are you nervous?" asked Xiao.

"I find you attractive, and the fact you're trying to push me away makes me want to try that much harder."

"What's your third question?" Xiao didn't notice a different song was now playing.

"My *second* question is: if you would rather study quantum theories, then why come to the party to begin with?"

"My best friend dragged me here. Trust me, coming here wasn't first choice on my agenda tonight."

"I don't believe that. I mean, if you really didn't want to come tonight, I don't think you would be here. You don't come across as one who goes against her will."

"I'm dancing with you, aren't I?" asked Xiao.

"Thank you for proving my point." Knute smiled, showing his teeth.

Xiao rolled her eyes and let out a small sound of aggravation. "What's your last question?"

"Hmm, I have to make this a good one. Kiss me if I'm wrong, but dinosaurs still exist, right?"

She dropped her arms and tilted her head sideways. "You don't give up easily, do you?"

"Nope."

One kiss wouldn't hurt. It wasn't like they would become an item or anything that would cause her to lose focus on school. He was cute.

"Okay," she said. She put her hands back on his shoulders and brought her face close to his. They both closed their eyes. The only time she kissed a boy was when Olivia dared her to kiss Dick Nutter during a game of truth and dare Olivia dragged her in to.

Out of nowhere, her arm was grabbed and jerked her away. She opened her eyes and saw Olivia.

"Livi, what are you are doing?"

"The hybrid police are here. They're raiding the party."

"So? We have nothing to worry about."

Olivia kept silent as they pushed their way through the crowd. "Olivia?"

"I'll explain later. Let's get out of here first."

Xiao had her back pressed up tight to a house a couple of blocks away from the party. She breathed rapidly, and strands of her dark hair were plastered on her face from sweat. Olivia went ahead to see if they were being followed.

Xiao ran the options through her mind. *Why is Olivia afraid of a hybrid raid? She's not a hybrid. She can't be.* Xiao had known Olivia pretty much her entire life. *What if she is? No, dismiss that thought right now, Xiao-Niao Li.*

"Run!" yelled Olivia. She came around the corner with fear plastered on her face, her eyes wide, lips pressed together and trembling. "Scorpions are coming!"

Xiao didn't move. "Olivia, tell me what this is all about."

"There's no time. The scorpions will be here soon."

"There is no reason why we should be running from the hybrid police and their drones." She stood with her arms crossed. Her lips firm, her eyes fixed on Olivia, not blinking.

"I promise you, I will explain everything as soon as we're safe."

The sound of an airlift motorcycle drew their attention. Xiao noticed the boy she'd seen go into the party earlier. Two drones with red-and-blue lights flashing and a siren blaring chased him down the dimly lit street. A drone hissed as tranquilizer pellet shot from its tail coiled above the main body of the drone. The boy swerved and skidded on his side, then landed motionless on the street.

The loud souped-up engine of a muscle car roared as it zoomed around the corner, wheels screeching. The front was painted purple, and a gradient effect moved into black at the back. The rims glowed with blue light, and the windows were tinted. The engine looked like it had tried to break itself free from the hood, which held a silver pterodactyl hood ornament with glowing green eyes, the grill shaped into wings. It doubled as a horn, and its bone-tingling cry let drivers know to make a hole.

"Get in!" Tuck yelled from the driver's seat as the passenger door lifted upward.

"Oh, he's cute," said Olivia as she dashed across the yard and hopped into the backseat. Xiao ran to the car, stopped, and looked at the boy lying in the middle of the road. Two scorpions hovered over him, keeping watch. The buzzing of more drones bore into Xiao's ears.

"Xiao, we have to go now!" yelled Tuck.

Xiao climbed in, and the car jerked and sped down the road, her door still slung open. "I'm not in yet," she yelled. She yanked the door shut.

"We're being followed. Three scorpions," said Olivia, looking out the back window. "Can you outrun them?"

Xiao could see the drones through the glass roof. Their tails looked ready to fire upon them.

"No, sorry. Don't worry. Ursula here has a few tricks under her hood."

"Who's Ursula?" Xiao held onto the dashboard, her knuckles growing white.

"My car," Tuck replied as he patted the dashboard like one might pet their dog.

Xiao looked at Tuck. "You named your car Ursula?"

She turned her head toward the road and screamed.

Tuck slipped the gearshift and floored it, leaving a trail of white smoke. He shifted the stick again as he rounded a corner.

"You're going to get us killed!" yelled Xiao.

"It's better than the alternative," he replied, shifting yet again.

"Why do you have a stick shift? They're a thing of the past."

"We have fricking scorpions on our ass, and she wants to know why I have a stick." He swerved again.

Xiao's face plastered to her window. "Let me out!" Her muscles tensed every time the car swerved or made a turn. Xiao swore part of her stomach stayed behind at the last corner.

"Is she always like this?" Tuck asked Olivia.

"Yes," she replied.

"I am not." Xiao turned around to look at Olivia. "Why are we running from the drones?"

"Wait! You don't know why?" Tuck asked. "Aren't you a hybrid?" He swerved around a corner, hitting an object on the sidewalk. "I hope it wasn't a person."

"It wasn't," Olivia assured him, looking out the back window.

"No, I am not a hybrid. Neither is Olivia, which is why I don't understand why we're running from the police."

"I thought she wanted to get you out of the party fast because you were a hybrid," said Tuck.

Xiao huffed. "I am not a hybrid."

"And her?" Tuck nodded toward Olivia.

"I can assure you she is not a hybrid either."

"Umm, Xiao," mumbled Olivia. "You know how we promised each other when we first became friends we would never keep secrets from each other?"

"Yes, holding a secret only you know can be easier to carry with your best friend." A horrible thought popped into Xiao's mind. "Is one of your family members a hybrid?"

"No," replied Olivia.

"Thank God," said Xiao. "That's one secret I wouldn't want to carry."

Olivia fell silent.

"You're the hybrid?" Tuck asked Olivia.

"I told you, she's no hybrid. We've known each other since we were five years old. If she was a hybrid, I would have known." Xiao wondered why she tried to deny the fact staring her in her face. If Olivia had hybrid implants, then their friendship would be a hoax. Olivia wouldn't lie. Would she?

"Yes, I'm a hybrid," Olivia said.

"I can't shake them," said Tuck. "Xiao, open the panel in front of you."

Xiao didn't respond.

"Open the panel!" Tuck yelled.

Xiao sat numb.

"Olivia, can you reach the panel?"

"Out of the way, Xiao." Olivia leaned over the seat. She stretched and opened the small panel revealing a red button with a lightning bolt on it.

"When I tell you to, push the button, and hold it in until I say stop." Tuck slammed on the brakes and drifted the car into a 180-degree turn. The drone lights were about two blocks away and closing in.

"This one is for you, Maddy." Tuck shifted the car into gear and pushed the accelerator pedal. The car shot off like an escape pod from an exploding ship. He flipped a panel down on the left side of his steering wheel. The button had flames.

"Hang on, girls, we're going for a ride." He pushed the button, and Olivia flew backward. Flames shot out of the back, and the car took air.

"You're going to hit the drones!" yelled Xiao.

"Push it NOW!" Tuck shouted.

Out of sheer panic, Xiao listened. She used her whole petite hand to push the button. The pterodactyl hood ornament screeched as lightning bolts shot out of its green, glowing eyes. The drones sputtered and crashed as the lightning bolts shot at them like a lion tamer's whip.

The car struck the pavement hard. Olivia flew back as Tuck slammed on the brakes. Xiao still held the button down.

"Let up, Xiao, before you use up all my power."

She let up slowly and looked at her hands as if she'd committed mass murder. "I am going to get expelled from Clearview for sure," she muttered.

"Did we get them all?" asked Tuck.

"I think so," Olivia replied.

"We better get out of here before backup comes." Tuck slipped his car into gear and sped off.

Tuck pulled up in front of Xiao's house. He had already dropped off Olivia.

"Are you okay?" he asked.

"How could she lie to me?"

"She was scared, and your reaction didn't help. Looks like she was right not to say anything."

"I've known her for a long time."

"Maybe she wasn't allowed to tell you when she was a kid. Then as she got older, it was too much to share, to risk losing you. That was one of my parents' concerns when they were debating whether to have my sister become a hybrid. If close friends and relatives found out, would they lose their relationship, or worse, would they turn them in? My sister felt the same way."

"Is Maddy your sister?" asked Xiao.

"Yes."

"What happened to her?"

"When she was seven, she was diagnosed with speckled brain disease. My parents took her to a doctor for hybrid implants to keep the disease from spreading. During the procedure, the doctor's office was raided by the hybrid police. She never received her implants. She was dead within a few months."

"How old were you?"

"She died on my ninth birthday."

Xiao felt her heart going out to him, which was rare for her. "What happened to your parents?"

"Lawyers found a loophole and got them off with probation only. She technically didn't have the implants yet."

Xiao took in the weight of what Tuck had told her. Olivia had luck on her side to still be alive. She could have been killed moments earlier.

Tuck turned and looked at Xiao. "You all right?"

"I don't know. I better get going." She needed to get away. She opened the car door.

"Dinosaurs still exist, right?" He gave her a sly smile.

She closed the door without a word and headed inside. As she walked in, Tuck sped away. She didn't look back.

Her own words haunted her mind: "Don't worry, Livi, I won't tell." How could she lie to her best friend? She'd never lied to her before. Olivia started it. She lied first.

Xiao walked upstairs and knocked on her parents' door.

"Come in," said Xiao's father.

She walked in. Her father lay on the bed reading, while her mother sat at a holoeasel practicing Chinese calligraphy.

"Did you get good studying in with Olivia?" her father asked.

Xiao's mother smiled. "My guess is she did not. It's hard to study at a party."

"You knew I went to a party?"

"I know it may be hard to believe, I was your age once."

"You knew I was going to a party and you still let me?" Xiao didn't understand.

"You have never given us a reason not to trust you," said her mother. "We know regardless of what you do, you will always end up doing the right thing."

Xiao took a deep breath. If the authorities found out she had been involved in Olivia's escape, her life would be over. Tuck told her not to be concerned. He had taken measures to ensure his car wasn't traceable. Xiao still had her doubts.

"Is there something you want to tell us?" asked her mother.

Tears leaked from her eyes. She nodded.

"Where's my nephew?" Mick Mrkonic bellowed as he barged into the house unannounced.

Liam came from the kitchen. "Keep it down. He's in the game room on the computer."

"I want to meet my nephew. I've had this hanging around the shop for nearly seventeen years now. I thought it was time to give it to find it a new home." He held up a faded, dusty stuffed Pittsburg Pirates parrot.

"This is not the time. Besides, he's sixteen years old. I'm sure he outgrew stuffed animals long ago."

"What's the matter with you, Liam?" Mick asked.

"Like I said on the holocomm, this kid shows up at my door

claiming to be my son," said Chief. "At the same time I found out Vicki..." He trailed off. "It's not a coincidence. The kid ulterior motives, I'm sure."

"He probably wants money. Get a genetic test done before signing anything and call it a day." Mick, a practical man, owned a pawnshop and other various shady businesses Chief chose to know nothing about. Chief had a clean criminal record. Mick, not so much.

"I don't need a DNA test." Liam looked over to the door. "When I opened the door and saw him standing there, it was like looking at myself in a mirror twenty years ago. His hair is a little lighter than mine, and he has his mother's eyes. Plus, he has the Mrkonics'—"

Mick finished the sentence for him. "—family ears. The poor kid." Mick turned serious. "And how are you holding up? You know about Vicki?"

Chief could barely get the words out. Although his brain had written her off long ago, his heart had not. "Not sure," he confessed. "She was involved in a hybrid raid. A detective was here earlier, before Asher..."

"She named him Asher, your middle name. She kept the Mrkonic family tradition of naming their first-born son with his father's middle name. Good thing I don't have any kids...at least I know of. Could you imagine any son of mine would be son going around with the name of Gad? I still don't know how mom and dad come up with that."

"Stay focused here, please. This detective was asking me about Vicki. They found her body at a place in New York that hybrid hunters raided.

"She was with hybrids?" asked Mick.

"Yes, she was."

"What was she doing living with...wait, is he a..." Mick's eyes grew big as a revelation went off in his head.

"Yes, and not too loud," warned Liam.

"Wow, doesn't this make your life complicated. What are you going to do?"

"I don't know. He can't stay with me."

"Why not? Because he's a hybrid?" Mick shook his head. "This kid, your son, lost his mother. Now you're going to throw him out to fend for himself?"

"I sure can't take him to the *Meservey* with me next week."

"Isn't there any high-ranking brass you can talk to?" asked Mick.

"What am I supposed to do, tell them my unknown hybrid son came to live with me and can I please take him along?" Sarcasm flooded out of his mouth.

"You can't send him anywhere else. He has to stay with you."

"Really, Mick? Haven't you been listening?"

"The kid lost his mother and probably all of his friends. We both know Vicki would have set up a backup plan in case a tragedy like this happened. She would not thrust Asher on you like this."

"Who knows what she would've done." Chief could feel anger rising. Too much, too sudden. How could she do this to him? As much as he wanted to be angry with her, he still loved her. The love had resurfaced again the moment he answered the door to Asher.

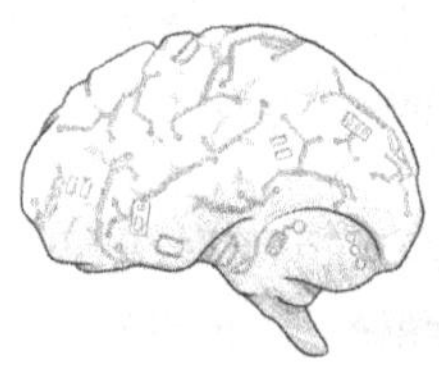

"You went to your father's?" Pandora's image shimmered above the holotable.

"I know it was a stupid idea," said Asher.

"What's he like?" she asked.

Asher shrugged. "He doesn't want me. I could tell."

"He's a normal, what did you expect?"

"Am I too far for you and your dad to come get me?" Asher couldn't stay here. Maybe Pandora would let him crash for a while, until he figured out what to do.

"And go where?" Asher had told her all about the raid at Willow Wood.

"One of the safe houses in Jamestown or Buffalo?"

"No. I don't want to see them...the other survivors, if there are any." Asher couldn't look at anyone from Willow Wood in the face. He didn't want to tell anyone Timothy and his mom had died because of him. This is why he went to see his father.

"Then where would you go? I know it's hard right now. Losing your mom, but—"

"I thought I could still live with you and your dad," said Asher, interrupting, not ready to talk about his mom with Pandora. His heart argued with his brain, causing him to change his mind. Should he go live with Pandora? Should he see if there were any survivors at the Buffalo and Jamestown safe houses? And then there was the option of staying with Chief.

"Why would you do that?" asked Pandora.

"You said last night you and your dad would pick me up at the Cyber Mania place and take me to your village."

"I didn't talk to you last night, Asher. Last time we talked was the day before the raid."

"Then who did I talk to last night?" Asher's mind started spinning. "Maybe it was a trap. Maybe that's how the hybrid hunters found me. How would they know to disguise themselves as you?"

"I don't know, Asher. It's not safe for you. Send me your location, and I'll see if we can come and get you."

A warning went off in his head. What if last night's Pandora was an imposter? Or this one. Was this a trap to get him? Maybe him talking to Pandora got Willow Wood raided.

"I better go." Asher disconnected the feed.

He leaned back in his chair and closed his eyes. He jerked them open when the image of Timothy's dead face and his mom's maimed body appeared. He couldn't trust Pandora—Mom had been right. The truth stung him deeper than the deaths themselves. Had he been the ultimate cause of the raid from the beginning? He had jumped to conclusions, blamed Neon for sneaking out. His contact with Pandora could have been behind it all. He had to figure out what to do. What information did she have now? He was at his father's. Would she be able to put it all together to find him in Pittsburgh? He hoped not.

Asher wandered down to the basement garage where he had left the car he used the night before. He wondered if it had any tracking devices on it. If a hybrid hunter tracked him, they would have shown up by now. He scanned the basement. It had ancient classics like foosball and an air hockey table, a pool table, a holotheater and a bar. The walls were decked out in anything related to the Pittsburgh Pirates, Pittsburgh Steelers, Pittsburgh Penguins and the basketball team, the Pittsburgh Anvils.

He climbed onto a barstool, resting his head in his arms on top of the bar. He wanted to cry. Confused, he didn't know where to go. Maybe he should turn himself in and get cleansed. With any luck, he wouldn't survive the process.

He watched a monitor before him, wedged between the rows of liquor, showing a slideshow rotation of personal pictures Chief must've programmed. Each picture stayed up for ten seconds before switching to a new one. Asher's eyes widened as an image came up of Chief and his mom. They had Pittsburgh Pirates gear on. Chief stood behind his mom, bending over with his arms around her. Both of them were smiling. Asher wondered if Chief's hat in the picture was the same one he wore now. It looked pretty old.

He never knew his mom to look so young. She looked happy.

"Our first date. It was the first game we saw together," said Chief.

Asher jumped and turned around.

"Have you been to a game?"

Asher shook his head. He didn't want to be here anymore.

"You want to go?"

"Why?" Asher surprised himself with the question.

Chief walked behind the bar. He bent over and pulled out an Iron City beer. "You want anything to drink?"

"I'm fine." He crossed his arms over his stomach to hide the fact it was growling.

Chief opened his beer. "We have a situation here."

"Don't worry, I'll leave. I'll try to erase any memories of you. If I'm captured, they can't link us. That's what Mom would've wanted." Asher's eyes didn't leave the top of the bar.

"That's not the situation I'm talking about. The issue is no son of mine will leave Pittsburgh before seeing a Pirates game."

"No, I want to go. This was a mistake." Asher stood and headed toward the stairs.

"No, the mistake would be me letting you leave thinking your visit here was a mistake."

Asher stopped and turned. "It is a mistake."

Chief laughed to himself. "Fifteen minutes ago, I would've agreed with you."

"What changed your mind?" Asher asked.

"Let's say your Uncle Mick—the pain in the ass he can be—has a way of opening my eyes." Chief motioned Asher with his head to sit back down.

Asher complied.

"Asher, I don't know what I'm supposed to do here. What I do know is I can't let you walk out the door. If something were to happen to you...well, I won't let it happen."

"You want me to stay?" Asher became confused. He had already made up his mind to leave.

"Next week I have to report to my new EFA command. How about staying with me until then? In the meantime, you and I can figure out together what the plan will be for you once I leave. Plus, the Pirates are in town, and Pittsburgh has great food. I bet your uncle can score us tickets to Mitch Kalon's concert this weekend."

Asher winkled his nose.

"Yeah, I don't care for him either. We'll skip the concert." Chief chuckled. "What do you say we go to Rudy's for an early lunch?"

"What if I'm caught?"

"We will make sure it doesn't happen."

Earlier that day, Mick disposed of the vehicle. Now he had no idea on how he would get to Jamestown if he decided to go there instead of staying with Chief. In addition, exhaustion had started to set in. How far could he run before getting himself caught anyway? Maybe here he could at least get food to eat. Maybe sleep in a bed. Maybe avoid seeing the survivors a little bit longer. He wondered if Neon had survived.

Asher's stomach left out a loud and long growl.

"Sounds like your stomach needs to be fed. You like pierogis?"

Asher nodded his head. "My mom used to make them all the time."

"Oh, I wonder if they were her mother's family recipe. Man, they were good. Come on, you have an anxious uncle upstairs waiting to meet his nephew."

Brett and Jinx stood waist-deep in the pool behind Brett's home. Their lips and tongues were doing a fierce dance inside the other's mouth. Jinx pushed Brett away with a smile. "Easy there. You're going to get me all horny again."

"Is that a bad thing?" Brett sloshed through the cold pool water toward her. Both of them were naked. "You know who's ready for round two?"

Jinx laughed. "We finished round one."

"Your point?" Brett cocked his head.

"You must be horny if you can pop a boner in cold water. I figured your balls had shrunken to the size of Tic Tacs."

Brett gave her a smile. "I could be naked in an Antarctic dome city and still be horny when you're standing by me naked." His right forearm, tattoo ink still fresh, wrapped around her. The tattoo looked like nose art on an ancient World War II plane. Her bleached-blond hair blew in the wind. His left arm slipped around her side to meet his right arm, which held a new 3D tattoo logo for the band F.A.W.

He pulled her close and kissed her deep and hard again. She returned the gesture. He backed her up against the pool wall, and a soft moan escaped Jinx's occupied lips as her legs floated up, one on each side of Brett.

"Brett, get out of the pool." Senator Lundy stormed across the deck connected the pool to the house. His clean shaven face had a hard and firm look.

"In a minute. I'm rather busy right now." Brett continued to kiss Jinx.

"You get out of the pool, now!" demanded the senator.

"I'm about ready to come in the pool if you leave me alone long enough."

"You get your damn ass out of that pool now. And tell your whore to get her slutty ass off my property."

Jinx looked up at the senator. "I'm right here."

Brett pushed Jinx off of him with a disgruntled sigh and climbed out. He didn't care if the senator saw him naked. He grabbed Jinx's clothes and threw them to her in the pool.

"Brett, now they're wet, you idiot."

"Screw you!"

Jinx threw on her wet top and climbed out. She stormed toward the back gate, her wet clothes in tow.

"I better not see you on my property again!" yelled the senator. He turned his attention to Brett. His trophy wife came out onto the deck. He grabbed Brett's right arm with force, turning it to see the tattoo. His pudgy thumb covered part of it. The part where the leather skirt covered the lady's genitals.

"Ow, you asshole."

The senator slapped Brett across the face. "You don't speak to me like that. What is the meaning of this?" He glanced down at the tattoo.

Brett didn't answer. He wanted to punch his father in the face. Like everything else, the senator would pay to cover it up, and Brett would be the one to be sorry.

The senator looked at the tattoo and then at his wife. "I thought you said this was a naked picture of you?"

"It is," the trophy wife assured him. She marched over with her large, fabricated breasts bouncing. "I tell you, Brad, she was naked. That is me."

"In your dreams," said Brett. "A girl like this," he said, motioning to his tattoo, "I would want to bone. A girl like you...hell, you couldn't give the horniest person alive a boner, let alone get them to screw you." Brett winced as another slap hit his face.

"You will go inside, get dressed, and Oscar will take you to get those tattoos removed."

"No."

"Do I need to assist you?" the senator said, cold and harsh.

Brett didn't look away from the senator's glare. "Go ahead, do it!"

The senator let go of Brett's wrist. He quickly grabbed it again. The portion of the skirt the senator's thumb had covered was now gone, revealing the woman's pussy.

"I told you!" said the trophy wife.

"Is this a heat sensitive tattoo?" asked the senator.

"It sure is. When I'm cold, she's dressed. When it's hot, she's hot."

"Why would you do this shit? Don't you know I'm running for president? If the media found out about this—go get dressed. I'll have Oscar waiting for you."

Brett had heard enough. He headed to the house with no intention of going with Oscar to have the tattoo removed.

"All of them removed!" yelled the senator from behind. "Including the skull and snake on your back."

"Frick you!" Brett mumbled as he entered the house.

"Why would you do that?" Oscar asked from behind the wheel.

Brett nestled up against the door, his head resting on the window. His eyes were closed. He didn't reply.

Oscar's muscular hand shook Brett.

He opened his eyes and removed his earplugs. "What?"

"Why would you get a tattoo of Cara naked? You knew the senator would get pissed off."

"It's your fault, you know" said Brett.

"How is it my fault?"

"You told me this Dean Pu of yours."

"Dean Wu," interjected Oscar.

"Whatever, you said she could talk the senator into letting me go to the Academy. Dean Chu or whatever her name is failed, and now I'm still stuck with the senator and the bitch."

"Brett, getting a tattoo with heat sensitive ink revealing your step-mother's triangle isn't going to get you to the academy." He smiled and let out a small laugh. "Although it was pretty funny. I wish I was there to see her face when she first saw it."

"It *was* good," Brett said with a smile. He liked Oscar. He trusted him, unlike any others.

"I know why you got the lady tattoo, and I can guess you got F.A.W.'s tattoo with its offensive design. Why the skull and snake on the back?"

"I thought it was cool," replied Brett.

"You realize you will have to have it removed too."

Brett sat up ignoring Oscar's last comment. "Oscar, I have to get out of that house. If I don't, you won't be picking me up in jail for grand theft auto. You'll see me in jail for murder."

"I know it's rough. Your father is a powerful man."

"I got a bruise already where he squeezed my arm. Look!" Brett revealed the bruising around the tattoo. "I tried to turn the bastard in a couple of times. He has social services in his back pocket."

Oscar didn't say a thing.

"If only I could get to the Academy. Things would be better. The asshole won't let me go." Brett imitated the senator's voice. "One of my campaign promises is to cut the EFA Junior Academy program. It would not help my candidacy if you attended there."

"Not a bad impression. I think I might know a way to get the senator to change his mind. You have to promise me if you go, you work your ass off and stay out of trouble."

"I told you when you picked me up in jail I'm all in." Brett shifted himself, giving Oscar his full attention. "Your first idea didn't work. We're running out of time here."

"I know we are. That's why we need to get the media involved."

"Media? I like it already. Continue." Brett smiled as Oscar unveiled the new plan.

$S$ *nap. Kerplunk*. The eight ball fell into the side pocket of the pool table. "Game." Asher smiled. He and Chief were at a local pub, shooting pool.

"This is the last time I'm going to challenge you to a game of pool." They'd played three games, and Chief hadn't even come close to winning any of them. "You play a lot?"

Asher laid his cue stick on the table. "No, this was the first time."

"First time?"

"Yeah. This is easy. Pool balls collide with nearly perfect elasticity. This means the kinetic energy in their motion is almost completely preserved, and very little of it dissipates into heat or other energy sinks. If you have perfect control over how you strike the cue ball and where to aim it, you can always predict what will happen. It's all math, simple really."

"Simple my ass," said Chief.

"Yeah," Asher said.

The weirdness of the last three days had started to dissipate as Asher and Chief adjusted. Asher felt a different kind of connection with Chief—for one, Chief hadn't scolded or grounded him for anything.

"When are we are going to eat?" asked Asher.

"Eat? How can you possibly be hungry?" Asher saw Chief's eyes glance towards the table of empty plates that once contained Kelly fries, pierogis, sweet potato and black bean quesadilla and mozzarella sticks.

Asher shrugged.

"If only I could eat like you do and not gain any weight, I would be one happy person. How does pizza sound?" asked Chief.

Asher shrugged again. "Sure."

The dark pub lit up as the door opened. Mick came in, paused, and scanned the room. When his eyes locked onto Chief and Asher, he headed straight toward them as if on a mission. "I got an answer to Asher's situation."

"Not here," said Chief. "Let's go to the head. I have to tap a kidney."

"Don't expect me to hold it for you," said Mick with a smirk.

Chief ignored the comment. "Asher, you stay here, we will be right back."

Chief and Mick walked into the musky smelling bathroom. It was clean, but everything in it looked old. He checked the stalls to ensure they were alone. He went to a urinal and unzipped his pants. Mick was already standing at one, relieving his bladder. "I know you mean well, having Asher live with you is a huge liability for Asher," said Chief.

"I'm past that idea now. I have a new one," said Mick.

"This ought to be good."

"I have a source."

"You always have a source," Chief interrupted.

"You want to hear this or not?" asked Mick.

"Forgive me, dear brother. Go ahead."

"What do you know about the NAS *Pocono*?" Mick asked.

"The *Pocono*? She's a Junior Academy ship, if I'm not mistaken. It's a damn shame too. Dad used to be stationed on her during her prime. She's known for the Currituck Dive where Ensign Harrison Currituck dove into a planet killer asteroid to keep it from hitting Earth. Why you ask?"

"My source says the Dean of Academics is conducting interviews here in Pittsburgh for this coming school year."

The door to the bathroom swung open and in walked a man. He went into a stall and closed the door. Mick and Chief steered their eyes to the wall in front of them. They both zippered up and went to the sinks to wash their hands.

"I don't know, Mick. If he gets in, he still has to pass the medical screenings on the ship. You know he has nerve damage from his accident." Chief tried to speak in code so that the patron in the stall wouldn't understand what they're talking about.

After washing their hands, they stepped out of the bathroom and found an empty corner. Chief could see Asher from a distance, playing a solo game of pool.

"It's too risky, Mick."

"This's the best part, brother. You get transferred to the *Pocono*. This way you get to stay in EFA and Asher can be with you. Since you would be the leading chief petty officer of medical, you can ensure Asher's scans come out normal."

"For one thing, doing a tour on an Academy ship is a career killer."

"Do I need to knock some sense into you dear brother,"

"Mick—"

"Liam, I love you. You lost your soulmate and almost lost your son because the career came first. It's too late to start over with Vicki. It's not too late to be a dad. Don't make the same mistake twice."

Chief sighed. He looked over at Asher and noticed that he was looking his way. Chief signaled with his arm for Asher to join them.

Asher walked over. "Yes, Chief?"

"If we can get you accepted to EFA's Junior Academy program this fall and I'm stationed on the same ship as you, would you be willing to do it?"

Asher shrugged. It didn't sound like something he would really want to do. He knew Timothy would have wanted to go. But, thinking it over, he still didn't want to go to Jamestown, and he didn't know how to survive on the streets like Neon. "Okay. If it means I can stay with you."

"Good, I'll let my source know," said Mick. "Now, brother, you better get him prepared for the interview."

"Hey, Asher," said Chief. "Give me an example of how math is used in the game of pool."

"If the cue ball is X times as far from the rail as the object ball, imagine two perpendicular lines extending from the rail to the two balls. Aim for a point on the rail X over X plus one{\displaystyle {\frac {X}{X+1}}} of the distance to the object ball's line."

"I think he's prepared," said Mick.

Navarro sat back in her chair in the mobile ops van. JD lay on the floor next to her feet. Navarro's lips were tight as she watched the video of Alita Blackwood and another, older woman battle the drones and then escape in different cars. She played it again and freeze-framed it. A picture of a tall, lanky, blond teenager flickered on the screen.

"Who are you?" she asked herself. "Why does Alita Blackwood want you?"

Cortez entered the van and placed his empty flask of goat milk down. He looked up and saw the picture of the boy on the screen. "I tell you; the kid is a nobody. He's another hybrid she's tried to save."

"I think you're wrong. She would've sent coadjutants if that were the case. No, she chose to go herself. Why?" She shifted her attention to Cortez. "Any luck finding out who the other woman was in the video?"

"Facial scans came up negative. She is as much a mystery as the kid."

"Did you track down any of the three vehicles they escaped in?"

"No, it appears they went stealth."

"Damn it, Cortez. I want answers. I'm tired of her constantly evading me." Navarro stood abruptly, causing JD to pick his head up off the floor and look at his master. She stormed up to Cortez and looked into his eyes the best she could with the height difference. "You find me answers, or you will find yourself volunteering for the next organ shipment. Do I make myself clear?"

Cortez replied with a nod of the head.

"Good. Crew ready?"

"Yes, everyone is in position."

"Let's move out."

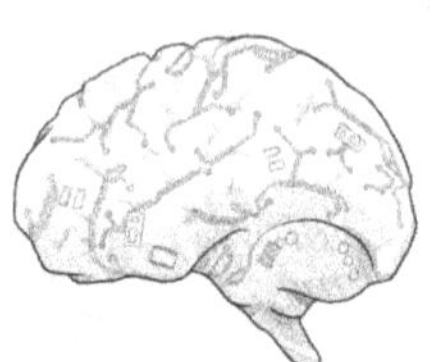

Asher sat in the mancave at the holotable. Using his hybrid memories, he created four human figures identical to who they were modeled after. He arranged them into a group, like they were getting their picture taken.

"Your mom hadn't changed," said Chief. "What are you doing?"

Asher shrugged. "In the room I'm sleeping in, there's a family portrait of you, Uncle Mick, and your parents. I don't have a family portrait. I figured I could make one myself. Dumb, huh?" Asher looked away from Chief.

"Not at all. I take it the girl with the crazy hair standing next to your mom is Neon?"

"Yeah."

"Who's the boy?"

Asher looked at the ground. He'd told Chief everything about the night of the raid, except for Timothy. He believed he killed Timothy. He didn't want Chief to know.

"That's Timothy," he replied softly.

"I take it he's with Neon and the others. MIA."

"He didn't get away." Asher flicked the holotable off.

"I'm sorry, Asher. You want to talk about it?"

"No." Asher stood and went back upstairs. It was hard enough creating an identical image of Timothy let alone telling chief what really happened. He held back the tears that were forming in his eyes.

The doorbell sounded. Chief came scrambling up from the mancave. "Go back down while I see who it is." Asher complied.

He heard yelling upstairs. Even with the yell muffled, he recognized the voice.

"Asher! I see you down there!" came Neon's voice through the closed door.

"Neon?" Asher ran up the stairs, tripping along the way.

Asher opened the door like the gates at a horse race, with each horse representing an emotion. Seeing her face caused mixed emotions —guilt and shame, joy and excitement. The emotional racetrack kicked up dirt and debris as he stood there staring at Neon.

"Why didn't you come to the safe house?"

Asher shrugged as he stepped into the hallway.

"Wow!" Neon said, looking at Chief. "That's you in twenty years."

Asher managed to put his diverse emotions to the side long enough to speak. "Neon, this is my father. Chief, this is Neon.'"

"Is this where you're staying now?" Neon looked around the room. Knowing how Neon thought, Asher knew she scanned the house with her X-ray vision.

"For now." Asher hid his trembling hands inside his pants pockets.

Chief poked his head outside and looked around, then shut the door and locked it.

"Relax, Asher's father. I wasn't followed. I've been on the streets before. I know what to do." She turned her attention back to Asher. "I heard your mom didn't make it."

Asher sat down in the living room. He looked at the floor and shook his head. He couldn't bear to look into Neon's eyes while confirming his mom's death.

"I'm sorry. Is Timothy with you? I didn't see him in the house. He's the only other one missing."

Asher shook his head. "He didn't make it." Asher spoke the words softly that he could barely hear them himself.

"Timothy? Damn. That sucks." Neon showed no emotion at the news of Timothy's death. She always said showing your emotions to other people was telling them you're weak. He gulped, knowing his emotions surfaced many times.

"Neon, can I get you something to drink?" asked Chief.

"I need food. You wouldn't believe what it took to get me here. The leftover lasagna in the fridge looks pretty yummy."

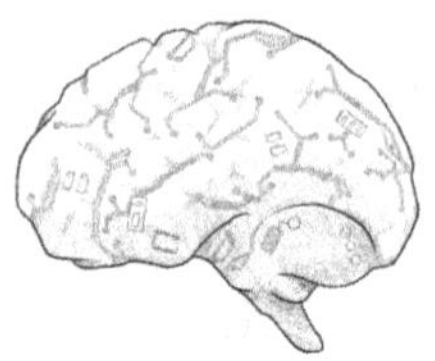

The two teenagers spent a few hours talking. Mostly, Neon talked while Asher tried to hide his emotions of regret, guilt, shame, and sadness. Although she tried pressuring him to reveal the details of the night of the raid, he managed to skirt around it. He couldn't reveal how weak he truly was. He shuddered at the thought of what Neon would think of him if she learned he killed Timothy. Not to mention if she found out Alita Blackwood tried to save him. She'd be all over him trying to get information to try to find her and join the cause. He did his best to let Neon talk and answer as few questions as possible. The fewer things he said to her, the fewer times he had to face those dark emotions.

Chief flicked his holowatch on, and a bust of Mick appeared. "Hey, brother," said the holoimage.

"What's up, Mick?"

"Is Asher around?"

"He's up in his room with a girl—from his old neighborhood," Chief said.

"Are you making him keep the door open like Mom did?" asked Mick.

Chief smiled. "I am, actually."

"Pathetic," said Mick shaking his head. "Tell him my source came through and he has an interview."

"When?"

"In one hour," Mick replied.

"Seriously. With no warning?"

"Sorry, she's on a tight schedule. She's doing this as a favor to my source."

"Who is your source...wait, do I even want to know?"

"No."

Chief rolled his eyes. "Where is the interview?"

"At the house."

As if on cue, the doorbell rang. Chief peeked out the window. "Uh, Mick. Would the dean happen to be a short, old Asian woman?"

"That's what I was told. How did you know?"

"She's here, standing outside my door."

"Makes sense. My source told me she'd be there in an hour about an hour ago."

"One day..." Chief flicked off his watch and opened the door. "Hi, you must be here for Asher."

Asher headed down the stairs. An old woman with gray hair tied in a bun sat in one of the chairs. Her face looked firm and hard. Asher's heart pumped faster, his blood flowing like a locomotive. He stopped and glanced behind him. Chief gave him a reassuring smile. Neon had her arms crossed and shook her head and pressed her lips tight together. Neon didn't approve of this opportunity that Asher had before him. She thought the Academy would be another prison, a prison that would brainwash him into becoming a normals sympathizer, a norsym.

"I don't have all night, Mr. Smizik. That is, if you are Asher Smizik," said Dean Wu.

Asher took a deep breath and headed down, trying not to look at her. Numerous thoughts swarmed inside him. *What if she has a sixth sense that will detect that I'm a hybrid? What if I say something during the interview that leads her to suspect me of being a hybrid? What if I fail the interview? What if I pass the interview?*

Asher felt a scratchy feeling under his chin. His lanky fingers reached up and felt the tag to his shirt. *Oh no*, he thought. *Not only do I have my shirt on backwards, it's inside out too.* He had changed in seconds when Chief called up to say his interviewer had arrived.

After what felt like a trek across the nation, he arrived in the living room. He sat across from her, looking at the floor.

"Mr. Smizik."

"Yes, ma'am," Asher said, refusing to look up.

"Do you know why I am here?" asked Dean Wu with a firm tone.

"Yes, ma'am. To see if I warrant acceptance to EFA's Junior Academy."

"No, that is not why I am here."

Asher looked up. *Oh God, she knows I'm a hybrid. She's trying to bait and hook me. I knew this was a bad idea. Should have listened to Neon.*

Dean Wu continued. "I'm here because a very close and personal friend of mine owed your uncle a favor. I am here to pay that favor off."

"Does that mean I'm not going to the Academy?" Asher asked softly.

"First, when you speak to me, I expect you to look directly at me. Secondly, you have to speak louder with confidence, otherwise you won't make it at the Academy." Her hands were folded on top of each other, resting on her cane. Asher noticed what appeared to be a burn scar on her right hand. It was unusual to see a person with a scar. Most people use an anti-scarring medicine that causes the scar to completely disappear.

"Yes, ma'am." Asher found it hard to look at the dean. Through many accounts of literature, from William Shakespeare to the Bible, it was said that "the eyes are the windows to the soul." He didn't want anyone to see the inside of his soul. He knew they wouldn't like what they saw, he didn't like himself. He glanced toward the stairs where Chief and Neon were peeping around the corner. Chief nodded at him, giving him encouragement. Neon pressed her lips together and shook her head. Doubt rose up again.

"Tell me, Mr. Smizik, what do you do for fun?"

"Fun?" Asher didn't know what questions to expect. He definitely didn't expect this one.

"What are your hobbies?"

"Uh." Asher stumbled over his words. "I like to read."

"Reading is good. What was the last book you read?"

"*Fahrenheit 451*," he said.

"That is quite an old book. Written in 1942 by Arthur C. Clarke."

Asher looked up. "No, ma'am."

"Are you saying the Dean of Academics is wrong?" Her voice was coarse.

"No, ma'am." Asher looked back down to the floor.

"You don't truly believe that, now, do you?"

"No, ma'am."

"Who do you think wrote *Fahrenheit 451* then?" Dean Wu's hands had yet to move from her cane.

"It was written by Ray Bradbury in 1953."

"I see. What is the significance of the title?" asked Dean Wu.

Asher noticed she didn't blink. Her eyes were locked on him.

"Mr. Smizik?"

"Sorry, ma'am, what was the question?"

"What is the significance of the title *Fahrenheit 451*?"

"The significance of the title, 451 degrees Fahrenheit, the temperature at which book paper catches fire and burns. Also note the epigram by Juan Ramon Jimenez: 'If they give you ruled paper, write the other way.' Jimenez, 1881–1958, was a Spanish poet who won the Nobel Prize for Literature in 1956 and was largely responsible for introducing Modernism into Spanish poetry. The implications of both concepts—one, a simple fact, and the other, a challenge to authority—gained immense significance by the conclusion of the book," Asher said with complete confidence, as from his perfect memory he recited word for word the information from the CliffsNotes he'd read earlier.

"Although this book was written over two hundred years ago and we don't burn books—or, in this era, delete books—does anything in today's society reflect the same theme as Mr. Bradbury's book?" the dean asked.

Asher shrugged.

"Mr. Smizik, you have to do better than that."

Asher knew exactly what reflected the same theme in today's world. Could this be a trap to reveal his true self?

"Hybrids?"

"Are you asking or telling me?" said Dean Wu.

It didn't seem like a trap. Asher continued. "Hybrids."

"Tell me how."

"The fire chief tells Montag, the protagonist, that because each person is angered by at least some kind of literature, the simplest solution is to get rid of all literature. In our society, people get mad at hybrids because their abilities can be enhanced. Ridding the world of controversy puts an end to the dispute. The only problem is that the books couldn't fight back. Hybrids can."

Dean Wu didn't say a word. Asher offered her his crooked smile.

The awkward silence broke when Dean Wu spoke. "Why do you want to join the Academy?"

The change of topic threw Asher off. He had himself ready to answer more *Fahrenheit 451* questions.

Being truthful, Asher answered, "I don't know if I want to go or not." He looked down at the floor, ashamed of his answer.

"Why would you not want to join the Academy?" The dean's eyes pierced into Asher.

"I haven't done anything like this before, and I don't know if it's for me. I would have to leave my best friend." He glanced over his shoulder to see Neon.

"Why do you want to go to the Academy?"

"I lost my mom and my...brother a few days ago. I know Timothy dreamed about the Academy. I want to go to fulfill his dream. Plus..." He paused. "Plus, I met my father for the first time. He didn't even know I existed until now. I want to get to know him. If I go to the Academy, he could ask for a transfer there."

Dean Wu nodded. "If he doesn't get transferred?"

Asher shrugged.

Dean Wu stood. "I have seen and heard enough. I will leave now."

Asher stood. Chief and Neon came down the stairs.

"Did he make it?" asked Neon. Asher gave her a glare for asking that question.

"You will have to ask Asher," Dean Wu replied.

Asher was confused. She didn't tell him either way. "I don't know."

"I think you do know, Mr. Smizik. Dig deep and you will find that answer."

Asher closed his eyes. He replayed the entire interview, word for word, in his mind. There, something he hadn't noticed before. After he said why he wanted to go, she nodded. She had a little grin, barely noticeable, upon her face. Very subtle, but there.

"I made it?"

"Again, Mr. Smizik, are you asking me or telling me?"

Asher smiled. "I made it. I am going to the Academy."

Chief patted Asher on the back. "Good job, I'm proud of you."

"Big mistake," said Neon, not keeping her feelings to herself.

"That friend of your uncle that I owed the favor to," Dean Wu started to say.

"Yeah?" replied Asher.

"You remind me a lot of him. I think you will do well. I will see you in September. Good evening, Mr. Smizik, Chief." She ignored Neon.

"Thank you, Dean," said Asher.

Dean Wu stepped outside and turned around. "Mr. Smizik, your comparing *Fahrenheit 451* to our society was excellent. Do you think there are Montags out there?" She pointed toward the road with her cane.

Asher shrugged. "Maybe?"

Dean Wu didn't say a word. She turned and headed to the sidewalk, where she got into a car. Asher watched her drive off.

"Now I need to get that transfer," said Chief. "I'm proud of you, Asher."

"Asher, you can't go," Neon said. "You'll be trapped up there."

"I appreciate your concern for Asher. This is his decision, not ours. I have faith he will make the choice that is right for him."

Asher didn't pay attention to Chief or Neon. He concentrated on the last question Dean Wu had asked. *Are there Montags out there?* Why would she ask that question?

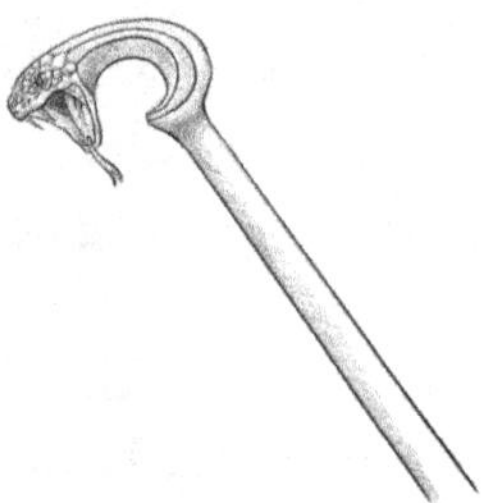

Dean Wu climbed into the passenger seat. A tall figure with a gray hood sat behind the wheel. "How did it go?" he asked.

"As suspected," replied Dean Wu.

"You had him scared to death, didn't you?"

Dean Wu smiled. "I think you already know the answer to that question." She looked out the window. As they drove away, she could see Asher's eyes following them until they were out of view.

Asher stepped out of the shower and dried himself off. No sooner had he wrapped the towel around his waist the bathroom door burst open. Asher jumped.

Neon laughed. "I haven't seen anything jump that high since Timothy threw a frog on the hot grill." She stood in the doorway. A ponytail dangled from the left side of her head. She wore a tight neon-yellow shirt and a pair of black shorts clenched around her lower figure.

Agitated, Asher asked, "Don't you ever knock?"

Chomping on gum, Neon said, "Turn off your engine. You're starting to get overheated."

"I'm not overheated. I'm sick and tired of you coming into my space without any respect for my privacy." Asher turned his back on her and occupied himself at the sink with his normal morning bathroom routine.

"If that's the way you feel, maybe I won't go to the baseball game with you today."

Asher put his deodorant down and turned to face Neon. "I'm sorry. It's just…"

"I get it. Check this out. We get to go on a real adventure today. Even if it's a boring baseball game." Neon let out a yawn.

"You ever think maybe I don't want to have a real adventure? I'm not like you, Neon." Asher brushed passed her and went into his room across the hall. Neon followed.

"You should've thought about that before coming here. You might not want one, but you need one. Everyone has to have one good adventure in their life." Neon sat down on the unmade bed.

"Says who?"

"Says me," she replied.

"You say that as if you've acquired enough travel points on the air shuttle of life for a free trip to the Tekulve-Lockley Wormhole. I got news for you. You have no more travel points than I do. They won't even get you to the corner of this room."

Neon's eyes made contact with Asher's groin.

"Knock that shit off." Asher grabbed his clothes and went back the bathroom, slamming the bathroom door. He could hear Neon outside the door.

"I had to see for myself. It looks like you are actually growing a pair now."

Asher opened the door and avoided looking at Neon as she leaned against the hallway wall, gazing up at the ceiling. Asher went back into his room and once again she followed him and fell onto his bed. He had only a pair of shorts on. He picked out a shirt from a pile of clothes next to his dresser. He brought it up to his face and took a big whiff of it. His nose twitched at the acrid smell. He tossed it to the side and grabbed another one. Asher had a small selection of clothes to wear. Chief had started a new wardrobe for him, since all of his clothes were at Willow Wood. Not everything they ordered had come in yet. Most of his clothes were hand-me-downs or purchased at a thrift shop, not new ones like these. He actually enjoyed surfing the internet looking for new clothes, looking at the hologram of himself showing what he would look like in a particular outfit. If he found a design he liked, he could change it to whatever color he wanted.

Neon rolled over onto her side and propped her head up on her hand. "You act like you're going on a first date."

Asher grabbed yet another shirt and smelled it. He pushed the shirt deeper into his face and inhaled deeply. He shook his head, satisfied, and put the shirt on. "I'm not like you, Neon. You were out there the first eleven years of your life." He pointed to his window. "I've only been to the pub a few times, and that was during the day when there weren't many people there. Going to a stadium filled with people at night—" He stopped, not wanting to share his fear with Neon.

Neon got off the bed. "I think you're being selfish."

"Selfish, because I am scared to death about going tonight? I wish my mom was here telling me that everything will be all right. But she can't be here. She's dead. Remember?" Asher's eyes flashed with anger.

Shaking her head, Neon answered. "Always negative. You realize, Asher, of all of us Willow Wood kids, you're the only one who's going to be in a consanguine environment. The rest of us are going to live in foster safe houses, which will probably be more of a prison than Willow Wood was."

"Consanguine?" Asher asked in a half-sarcastic tone.

"What, you think you're the only one who knows big words?"

"You only know that word because I used it last night."

"True, that doesn't change the fact that I'm right." Neon crossed her arms and gave Asher a challenging expression.

Asher pulled out a fair of socks and slammed the drawer shut. He sat on the edge of the bed, pulled his large foot up, and put a sock on it. "I know. I always thought I would live out my days at Willow Wood with my mom, Timothy, you and the others. Now I'm stuck living with my biological father for the first time and going to an academy in space. My world is not mine anymore."

"It's still yours," said Neon. Her tone softened. "You're having an adventure and exploring a different part of it now. That's all."

"I wish you could come to the NAS *Pocono* with me," said Asher.

"Not me. I wouldn't want to go."

"Where's the sense of adventure you were lecturing me about?"

"I love adventure, not people who are barking orders and having to wear shoes the entire day."

"Point."

"Asher! Neon! We leave in five minutes!" Chief yelled from outside Asher's room.

"If you don't want to go to the Academy, tell Chief. You don't have to, you know. You and I can explore the world together. Maybe even join Alita Blackwood's cause to get us to become legal citizens."

Asher didn't miss the gleam in Neon's eyes. "What is it with you and Alita Blackwood?"

"Look into that memory chip of yours. I told you. She's the only one fighting for our freedom."

"I think she could do it in more of a peaceful stance, like the Phantom Prophet tried to do," said Asher.

"Peaceful stance? He was killed for his peaceful stance."

Chief tapped on the door and poked his head in. "You two ready? Mick's here." Chief was wearing his Pirates hat and a black Pirates jersey with gold lettering. Number 44 was on the back with the name Cooper.

"I have to finish putting my shoes on."

Chief opened the door wider and looked at Neon. "I see Neon is at least wearing the proper colors."

"My wardrobe is limited." Asher felt bad. He looked down at the floor. Why did he ever come to see his dad?

"This is my bust," said Chief. "I should've gotten Pirates gear for you. If you want, I can give you one of my jerseys, and I'm sure I have a spare ball cap lying around."

Asher shrugged.

"Neon, why don't you head down. Asher and I will be there in a minute."

"I can wait for you guys," Neon said, chomping on her gum.

"Neon, I would like to have a moment alone with Asher," said Chief.

"Oh, I get it. Okay. Ash, I'll 'see' you down there."

Asher grimaced at Neon calling him Ash. He preferred Asher.

Once Neon left, Chief came over to the bed and sat down next to Asher. "Care to talk?"

Asher shrugged. He wished Chief would leave him alone. "I'm okay." Asher got up and headed to the door.

"I tell you what. Once we get to the stadium, I'll take you to the souvenir shop. I can buy you a whole new wardrobe there."

"If you want." Asher opened the door to find Neon. "I knew I'd find you here spying. Come on, let's go." Asher brushed past her and went downstairs. If only he could go back in time to change things. A life without adventure, home at Willow Wood with his mom and Timothy—that was what Asher longed for.

utumn Fletcher, Gully Jumper, and Game Master Blass pulled up to the curb not far from a black iron gate that blocked the driveway to a large mansion in Meat Cove, Nova Scotia. A gaggle of reporters swarmed the gate, trying to peek inside.

"Are reporters always here?" asked Autumn.

"No, it's because the senator is running for president," Game Master Blass replied.

"I really don't want to be here to see this," said Gully.

"I agree," Autumn chimed in.

"I went to see that swim meet with you last week, Gully." Then he turned his attention to Autumn. "Last month, I went to that boring piano recital with you. I want to be here for the press conference, and I want you two to enjoy it with me."

"Thank you, Thane, for inviting us. I am really excited," said Gully sarcastically.

Game Master Blass smiled. He watched as more reporters gathered around.

"I'm sorry, Master Brett, your father is in a meeting. He cannot be disturbed." A butler stood guard in front of the door that led to Senator Lundy's home office.

"I want to show him that I got the bitch removed from my arm." Brett twisted his limb to show his bare forearm.

"I'm sorry, sir, you will have to wait."

"Let me guess, he's talking to that Dr. Monroe guy from Akron Industries, isn't he?" Brett looked into the butler's eyes. "You're hard to read, I'm right. I can tell."

Brett stood there for a second. He looked at his watch. "Who else is in there?"

"I'm sorry, Master Brett, I am not at liberty to say." The butler showed no emotion.

"I'm out of time anyway. I have the media waiting for me. When the senator gets done with his meeting with Dr. Monroe, that mafia guy Gianni Finelli, that real estate bitch Amanda...what's her last name? Pike. Amanda Pike. I'm sure there are others I'm forgetting. Let them know I'm at the front gate giving a press conference."

The butler's brows lifted.

"I am going to announce my acceptance to EFA's junior academy and I will be leaving when the new school year begins." Brett gave the butler the biggest shit-eating grin he could muster and left.

"Who is coming out of the gate?" asked Autumn.

"It's him," Game Master Blass said.

The three elderly people watched as Brett came out and stood in front of the reporters.

"Hello, and thank you for coming," said Brett. "I thought you would like to know that I was offered and accepted a seat onboard the NAS *Pocono* starting this fall. "If you wonder how I was able to be selected to attend Earth Force Alliance Junior Academy with my school records, my father, Senator Brad Lundy, managed to pull powerful strings. To prove that I am not lying, I thought I would bring Pinocchio." Brett pulled down his pants and boxers to reveal a tattoo of Pinocchio's face. "Now, if his nose starts growing, either I'm lying or just plain horny."

The gate opened and out rushed Senator Lundy and Oscar.

"Get him out of here," the senator said to Oscar.

"I'm not done with the press conference," Brett argued.

"Come on, Brett, let's go." Oscar herded Brett with his arm. Brett pulled up his pants and disappeared through the gate with Oscar.

Game Master Blass smiled. "I've seen enough. Let's go."

"Couldn't we have gone before that display?" asked Gully.

"And miss all the fun? Not a chance," Game Master said. The three climbed into the car and drove off. "I love that kid."

The senator stormed into Brett's bedroom. Brett lay on his bed. Oscar and the senator's wife stood there too.

"I don't know what the hell you were thinking," yelled the senator. He could feel a vein bulging from his pudgy neck. He looked directly at Oscar. "I'll deal with you later."

Oscar nodded and left.

"Relax, he had nothing to do with this," Brett assured him.

"What about the press?" asked the trophy wife.

"I dealt with them. I managed to sidestep it for now." The senator clenched his fists and released them repeatedly. "Now for you. Is this your way of forcing my hand to send you to that spaceship?"

"Part of it," said Brett. "The other part is I want away from you and that bitch."

"You watch your fricking language, young man."

Brett rolled his eyes.

"You want to go away that bad? Fine. I'll send you to that military school in Newfoundland."

"I want to go to the EFA Junior Academy. I already committed there."

"You probably used your allowance to bribe your way in."

"What can I say? You taught me well."

The senator growled. "I am not sending you there. I don't care what you do, there is no way I am sending you there. We will say that you were offered a seat at the military school in Newfoundland and decided to attend there instead."

"Okay," said Brett.

The senator stepped back. "This isn't like you, giving in."

"Bribery isn't the only thing you taught me. Let's see…" Brett started to count on his fingers. "Fraud, embezzlement, tax evasion, conspiracy, extortion, racketeering, money laundering, tampering with evidence, perjury and obstruction of justice."

"That's enough," yelled the senator.

"I didn't say my favorite one of all. Blackmail." Brett looked at his fingers. "I'm out of fingers. I guess I have to use Pinocchio's nose." He stood to pull down his pants.

In a rage, the senator cuffed Brett with the back of his hand.

"You asshole!" Brett no longer seemed calm and in control.

"Brad, can I talk to you privately for a minute?" asked the trophy wife.

"Now?" The senator could see blood seeping out of Brett's mouth.

"Yes."

The senator grabbed her arm and pulled her away. "What is it?"

"Maybe it's not such a bad idea if we send Brett to the EFA."

"What are you saying?" the senator asked in disbelief.

"Think about it. He won't be around reporters. He will be isolated. We can even ensure that no messages from him get off the ship without us looking at them first. We won't have that same control if he goes to Newfoundland or stays here."

"I told you, if I enroll him there, what kind of message does that send? I'm publicly opposed to the Junior Academy program."

"That's right, you are. When you send your son there, tell everyone you're sending Brett there to prove you're willing to give the EFA one last shot, to try the program firsthand. Then when Brett fails…" She looked over to him. He sneered at her. She turned her attention back to the senator. "Or more likely gets kicked out, you can use that to your advantage. Until he does, we are free of him."

"You might have something." The senator thought through different scenarios—how the plan could benefit him and his campaign, and how it could backfire. "We will have to spin this to make sure that Brett doesn't think he won."

"Let the little prick think he won. We'll see what he thinks once he gets up there in space." She smirked.

The senator thought long and hard. He made his decision and

called Brett over. "You will not leave this house or make contact with anyone outside of it until it's time for you to report to the damn space school."

Brett gave him a smirk. He was glowing, thinking that he'd won.

"One last thing. I warned you about tattoos. Kiss Pinocchio goodbye, I am bringing a tattoo remover in here to take care of your tattoos the old-fashioned way."

Brett put his hands in front of his crotch.

"I'll make sure it gets done even if I have to chain you down myself." He stormed out of Brett's room with the trophy wife right behind.

Brett opened his bedroom window. He lit a cigarette and inhaled the smoke, releasing it slowly through his nose. He turned when he heard a knock on the door.

"Yeah?" Brett usually tried to hide the fact that he smoked around certain people, but he didn't care anymore. His cheek swelled, and he could still taste blood from where he'd bit his lip.

The door swung open, and Oscar walked in. "I see you're at one of your healthy habits again."

"No lectures." He took another drag.

"I heard your father is bringing in tattoo remover to take care of Pinocchio."

"I don't care. I got rid of the F.A.W. logo. I used tattoo concealing lotion on the bitch and skull tats. When I leave this place, I'll apply the reappearing lotion. This way I can show them off to everyone at the academy. I'm cool with having Pinocchio permanently removed."

"Pinocchio wasn't part of the plan."

Brett took a long drag from his cigarette. He blew smoke out of his nose like a raging bull snorting before charging the matador.

"I improvised." Brett flicked his cigarette out the window.

"You have to keep your nose clean the next few weeks. You can't do anything that might cause your father to change his mind."

"He can't stop me."

"You're not as invincible as you think you are."

"I know the senator. I know how he operates. I know that bitch too. I knew she was going to sweet-talk him into sending me. 'To protect his presidential campaign' was probably her excuse. I'm sure by now the senator learned that my acceptance letter has been distributed to the media. Now he has to do damage control. I got this." He lit up another cigarette. "I got this." He smiled.

# CHAPTER 17

Chief, Mick, Neon, and Asher entered Park 84, Home of the Lumber Company, the stadium where the Pittsburgh Pirates had played their home games for the last seventeen years. They walked through the entrance for ticket holders who had seats in the City of Steel section, right behind home plate.

"One of my sources managed to get us seats in the best section for tonight's game. With our tickets, we get a free dinner buffet, cushioned seats behind home plate, and free concessions throughout the game. Plus, no charge for the POV glasses," said Mick, excited.

"Who's your source?" asked Asher.

"Some questions are best left unanswered," said Chief.

"What're POV glasses?" Neon asked.

"They're glasses you can wear while watching the game," Asher replied. "You can choose to watch it through the eyes of any player on the field or the umpire."

Asher looked around the lobby at a wall covered with numerous portraits. He didn't recognize any of the men in them. One picture caught his eye, though. It showed a former Pittsburgh Pirates player, the Baseball Hall of Famer Gehrig West, autographing a ball for a young boy in the front row of the stadium. A tall man stood next to the boy. Asher placed his finger on the man. His arm broke out with goosebumps, and the hairs stood at attention. An indescribable feeling coursed through his body.

"If your dad looks like you in twenty years, that guy looks like you in sixty," said Neon. "Maybe that's a distant relative."

"Asher," Chief called.

"Yes, sir?"

"It's going to be about a twenty-minute wait for our table. How about we get you the Pirates gear I promised? You look like you should be at a funeral instead of a baseball game." Chief winced after he spoke the words.

"I'm okay," replied Asher.

"Asher, come on, let's go get new clothes," Neon said.

Chief looked at Mick.

"Hey, Neon, how about you stay here with me?" Mick said. "You can help me save the table when it's our turn."

"Save the table yourself," replied Neon. "I'm going shopping with the boys."

"I thought maybe the two of us could discuss what you'll do once my brother and Asher go to the *Pocono*," said Mick.

"Nothing to discuss. I already have my plans laid out. Let's go, guys, we're wasting time."

Chief looked at Asher, then at Neon, and back at Asher. Asher let out a small sigh. "Neon, I'm okay. You can stay here with Uncle Mick."

Neon shot a glare at Chief. "Fine." She brushed past Chief and walked to the wall with all the pictures on it. Asher couldn't see well through the crowd of people, but it looked like Neon wiped her eyes.

"Come on, Asher. We won't be long," Chief promised. Reluctantly, Asher followed his father into the crowd.

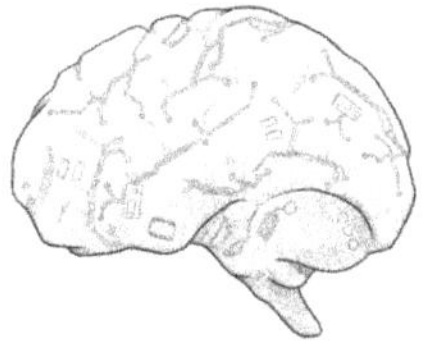

Asher stepped into the stadium store. There were jerseys, hats, bats, baseballs, beach towels, and all sorts of souvenirs. Asher couldn't believe how many people were jammed in the store, bumping into each other as they browsed the merchandise.

"The store is filled with a lot people." Asher crossed his arms, hoping to form a barrier between himself and all the shoppers. His chest tightened, and he found it hard to breathe. He felt hot all of sudden, and he swore his insides were quivering. What if there were hybrid police here? Or worse, hybrid hunters. Could he find himself on the way to a cleansing station before the end of the first inning? His feet wouldn't move. It felt like Gorilla Glue was on the bottom of his soles. He looked up at Chief, hoping for assurance that everything would be okay.

Chief must've read Asher's mind. He gave Asher a reassuring smile and placed his arm across his shoulders. His arm magically took part of his worries away. Did Chief really have his back? He seemed calm and not threatened at the scene before them. Asher began to breathe easier. With a nudge of the arm, they entered the sea of shoppers.

Chief looked at what Asher had picked out thus far from the stadium store. He could tell his son had no fashion sense. In Asher's defense, his choices were limited and they weren't allowed to leave the stadium. Asher picked out one yellow and one black Converse sneaker with the Pirates emblem on the side. To go with the sneakers, he chose a pair of Pirates socks, each in opposing colors. Moving up, Asher liked a pair of black-and-gold Pittsburgh Pirates boarder shorts. The top of the shorts were black, and as the color traveled downward, it faded to Pittsburgh's gold.

"Okay, we have shorts, socks, tennis shoes. Now we need to get you a jersey and hat. While I am at it, I'll get a jersey too. Never can have too many Pirates jerseys. Do you see one you like?"

Asher didn't respond; his eyes focused on a girl in line at the register. She wore a Phillies shirt and hat. Her long brown hair with blond highlights swayed in the breeze that went through the store. Her bright smile had caught his attention. When she turned and looked in Asher's direction, she smiled even more. Asher had the oddest yet warmest feeling explode in his heart.

"She is a cute one," Chief said, looking in the same direction as Asher.

Asher snapped out of his daze. "What?"

Chief smiled. "Do you see a hat you want?"

Asher turned his attention back to Chief. "I have to look." Asher kept glancing in the girl's direction. He noticed her peeking at him as well. "You going to get a new hat too?"

"I'm not quite ready to retire this hat yet," he said.

"Why?" asked Asher.

A solemn expression appeared on the Chief's face. "Almost twenty years ago, your mom and I went on our first date. It was at a Pirates game when they played at StarKist Stadium. I haven't worn any other hat since." He paused. "Yeah, I'm not ready to give it up yet."

Was this the only thing he had left of his mom, and if he got rid of it, it'd be like saying goodbye to her forever? Asher wished he had a memento of sorts for both his mom and Timothy. Maybe when he got back to Chief's he could make his own.

By the time Chief escorted Asher to the racks of jerseys, the girl had left the store. If only he knew where she watched the game from. He wouldn't know how to approach her, let alone talk to her. Besides, Neon would do everything in her power to keep him away from a normal.

"Which one you want? How about number thirty-two, Mercury Ripper? He's the best in the league," said Chief.

Asher looked at the variety of jerseys. "Is it okay if I have this one?"

Asher held a gold jersey, a 2133 replica, the word *Pirates* spread across the chest with the number fifteen snuggled under it. On the back, it had a large number fifteen with the name West above it.

"West, huh? Your grandfather would've been proud. That was his favorite player. Now all you need is a ballcap, and I know the one." Chief picked up a black hat with three gold stripes and a gold letter P in front center. "Perfecto!"

"You don't have to get me all this," Asher said shyly.

"I don't mind. I actually enjoy it. Now, you said you like to read, right?"

"Yes."

"I know the perfect book to get you. This way you can catch up on Pirates' history." Chief went to the book section and scanned the covers displayed on the wall, each with a specific number. He spoke his name and the numbers corresponding to the books he wanted.

"I ordered six books here for you. It should last you a while. We can get them downloaded at the cashier's desk."

"Thank you, Chief!" Asher looked forward to reading the books Chief picked out for him.

"Now, there are two more things we have to get you, and I think we'll be set."

"No, this is enough," Asher said. His dad had bought too much already.

"A Pirates baseball in case you see a player you want to autograph it, and a Pirates pennant to hang in your bedroom."

Asher didn't know what to think. He knew Chief considered his home Asher's home now, it felt...different. It felt like anything but home. He still considered Willow Wood to be his one and only home.

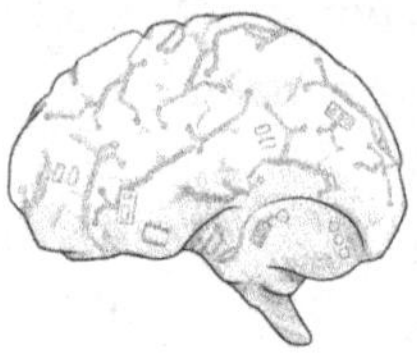

Asher walked through the tunnel that lead to the stadium seating. He let out a burp. He can't remember the last time he ate as much as he did at lunch time. He stopped at exit the tunnel to take in what lay before him. He'd never thought he would be in a public place with thousands of people like this. As scared as he was to be around people—afraid of being found out—for the first time in his life, he felt truly free. The smells of popcorn, hot dogs, and beer fluttered past his nose. The mugginess weighed heavily on his skin. Chatter and cheering echoed throughout the park. He could see the players warming up on the field. Asher jumped a little as Chief placed a hand on his shoulder.

"Welcome to Park 84," Chief said with a childlike grin. He closed his eyes and took a big inhale through his nose. "Nothing beats coming to a Pirates game."

The usher escorted them to their seats. They were in the fifth row behind home plate. As Asher consumed his surroundings with delight, the fear of the crowd dissipated temporarily.

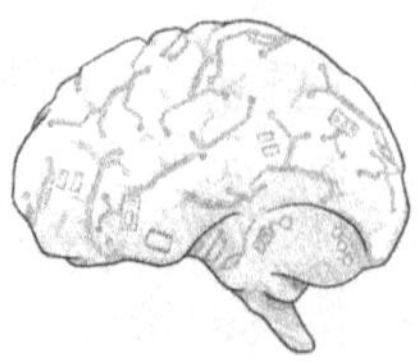

Asher, and especially Chief and Mick, were disappointed at the start of the game. In the first two innings, the Pirates gave up nine runs to their divisional and state rivals, the Philadelphia Phillies. The teams were in a tight race for first place in their division. All games counted against a longtime divisional rival.

At the bottom of the ninth inning, and even with the blowout innings at the start, the Pirates didn't give up. "I can't believe it," said Asher. "We scored a run in every inning. If we score another one, we'll tie them."

"I'm hoping for two runs," said Chief.

"Zero runs, two runs, Whatever. At least the game will be over with," said Neon who didn't cover the fact she was bored.

"If the Pirates tie, that's when we get free baseball," answered Mick.

"Free baseball?" she asked.

"A regulation game is nine innings," Chief replied. "If the score is tied after nine innings, then we go into extra innings. They call that free baseball."

The Pirates scored only one run in the ninth, which called for free baseball.

At the beginning of the bottom of the tenth, the score remained 9–9, and the Pirates had two outs.

"Maybe we can get a two-out rally going," said Chief.

Asher watched as the batter worked the count full. Then came the pitch. The batter swung. The bat cracked. Everyone stood, and the stadium erupted into cheers as the batter jogged around the bases.

"That is what you call a walk-off home run!" Mick shouted.

"Take a look at the scoreboard, Asher. You see how the Pirates scored one run in every inning?" asked Chief.

"Yes."

"That's called a full picket fence, and it has never been done before. You witnessed history. Other teams scored in every inning, never one run in each. Some innings had multiple runs. This is a great day for baseball."

Chief gave Asher a one-armed side hug. A strange and unfamiliar excitement flowed through his body. Asher looked at the smiling man and hesitantly gave him a side hug back. Despite being paranoid in large crowds, he actually enjoyed himself. He hoped he could do it again in the future.

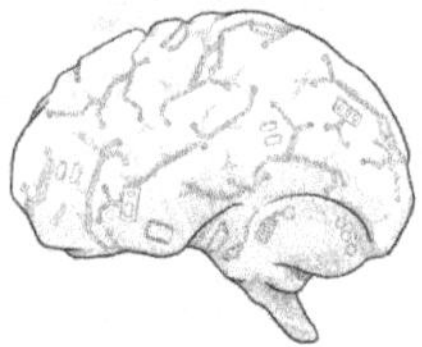

On the way out of the stadium, they stopped at the restrooms. Mick and Chief stood in the concourse waiting while the two teenagers went to empty out all the soda and lemonade they drank.

"I'm ready," said Asher as he exited the bathroom.

"We're still waiting on Neon," said Mick.

"Hey, Mick, you see that guy over there with the Phillies attire on?" Chief said.

"Yeah," Mick replied.

"That's the detective I told you about."

"What do we do?" asked Asher. "Is he following us? Does he know?" His chest got tight. Anxiety crept into him.

"Let's not get paranoid. Once we let that beast in, it will be hard to tame it," said Mick. "I know that from experience with..." Mick noticed a glare coming from his brother. "Never mind where I got it from, just don't let it in."

The three watched the detective as he milled around, talking to other Phillies fans. A woman came out of the bathroom and joined him.

"I'm ready. Where are the kids?"

"They already headed to the shuttle," he replied. He spotted Chief and walked over to him. "Chief Mrkonic, right?"

"Yes. You're the detective that came to my house a few weeks ago."

"Small universe. I don't know how the Pirates pulled it off."

"The better team won," said Chief.

"We'll talk about the better team when the Phillies go to the World Series this year." He diverted his attention to Mick and Asher. "Pardon me. I'm Mac."

"I'm Mick, and this is Asher."

The detective shook hands with Mick and Asher. Asher tried to control his breathing as the detective gripped his sweaty palm. He couldn't help wonder if the detective had a sixth sense when it came to finding hybrids.

Mac looked at Asher, then Chief. "Are you two...?"

"He's my son, Detective."

"You said you didn't have any family except for your brother."

"It's funny. After you left, I found out about Asher. I had no idea he existed."

"That's true, Detective," Mick chimed in.

"Those bathrooms are disgusting," interrupted Neon at the perfect moment. "Who's that?" Her attention turned to Mac.

"He's hybrid police detective," whispered Asher, not taking his eyes off them. He had stepped back, afraid of the detective's possible sixth sense when it came to finding hybrids. "I saw him on the news. He was at Willow Wood after the raid, and he came to Chief's house too."

Chief and Mick shook the detective's hand in farewell. Asher and Neon watched him with intensity as he joined a woman and disappeared down the concourse.

"How did he find us?" asked Neon.

"I think it's coincidence," Mick replied.

"What did you say to him?" asked Asher.

Chief looked at Asher. "I told him the truth."

"The truth?" Asher said.

"I told him you were born out of wedlock. That your mother never told me about you. That she recently died, and it was her wish for you to live with me."

"Did you tell him that I..."

"I left that part out. Come on, let's get out of here."

"For your information," Neon said, "if we come back here, I am not using those bathrooms. They're disgusting."

"You could've waited until we got back to Chief's," said Asher.

The two of them started to bicker.

"If you didn't know any better, you would think they're siblings," said Mick.

"Or husband and wife," Chief said with a chuckle.

Asher scrunched up his face.

"Not in this lifetime," Neon responded.

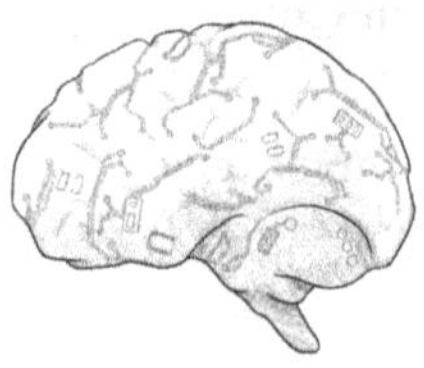

Walking through the crowd to exit the stadium, Asher had the feeling of being followed. Every time he looked around; he saw nothing peculiar. Then he spotted a person ducked behind a truck in the parking lot.

"Neon."

"Yeah?"

"Is there anyone on the other side of that Coca-Cola truck?"

Neon shifted her eyes to the truck. "Yeah. It's a woman. I want to say an old woman."

"What is she doing?"

Neon snapped her head away from the truck.

"What's wrong?"

"It's a hybrid. She has hybrid eyes too."

"You guys coming?" asked Chief.

The two teenagers continued to walk. Asher had no doubt that Alita Blackwood followed them. He hoped Neon wouldn't realize who hid behind the truck. That was a direction he didn't want to travel.

At dusk, the sun adumbrated the man in the gray hood and made him appear like a ghostly version of himself. A summer breeze whisked past him as he watched Asher and the others enter Chief's house.

"I know what you're thinking," the man said to himself. "Don't worry. You're safe here. Alita Blackwood won't get you. I will make sure of that."

An annoying chime echoed in Chief's ears as he entered North Side Pawnshop. The uninviting place had bars on the windows. Dust-covered junk cluttered the main lobby. Security cameras were aimed in all directions.

On the backside of the lobby stood a glass counter with jewelry that people had pawned for money. Rufus, a large ugly mutt, lay in front of the counter.

"Hello, Rufus," said Liam.

The dog immediately got up and went over to him, wagging his tail. Long strands of slobber drooled from his mouth. Rufus always greeted Liam with excitement. For others, he stayed in his spot, guarding his domain.

"Where's your poor excuse for a master at?" Liam rubbed the

canine's head with one hand and slipped him a treat with the other. The dog swallowed the treat in one bite. Liam didn't visit the pawn-shop very often, when he did, he always brought Rufus a treat.

"I was wondering when you were stopping by," Mick said, coming from the back room.

"Did you get it?" Liam asked.

"Have I ever let you down?"

"There was that baseball game I seem to remember."

"I got you tickets."

"Sure you did. In the section where all I had to do was stand up on my tiptoes to touch the moon."

"I was barely out of middle school. I didn't have the sources back then like I do today."

"That game was important to me." Liam placed his hand on his Pirates hat and used it to rub his head.

"Was that the game?" asked Mick.

"Yeah, my first date with Vicki."

"You left in such a huff you even forgot your hat and glove."

"That was the only time I did, too." Liam's thoughts went to that game and the days, months, and years that followed.

"Liam, do you need a brotherly hug right now?" Mick gave him a look of pity.

Liam laughed and pulled out an untraceable burner pay card. "How much is the identity package?"

"You think I'd charge my big brother, the person who bailed my ass out of jail more times than I care to remember?"

"Yes, I do." He smiled. "Now how much?"

"Consider it a gift to my nephew."

"Thanks, Mick."

Mick handed over the package.

Liam placed the chip next to his watch, which beeped and projected a hologram of documents. "You didn't change his name or birthday or anything?"

"No, I didn't. There was no Asher Smizik registered. We decided to go with his true identity. The closest we can keep things the same, the easier it is to remember."

"Asher has a perfect memory. He won't forget the details," said Chief.

"It's not Asher's memory I'm worried about." Mick gave him a brotherly glare.

"Oh," Chief replied. "No one will be able to trace this identity as a fraud?"

"Relax. My business associate is the best there is for items this sensitive. The only thing closer to a real birth certificate, school records, and other credentials are the real thing, and no one will be able to tell the difference." Mick reached under the counter and pulled out a wooden cigar box. "I believe you ordered this too?"

Liam took the box and opened it, revealing a row of cigars. He took one out and held it under his nose. He closed his eyes and took a deep whiff. "Thanks, Mick."

"The rest is under the cigars," Mick said. "I'd leave them in there until you need them. They are the most advanced ones in existence."

"Untraceable?"

"Untraceable? They're one of a kind. Authorities won't even know what to look for."

Satisfied, Liam closed the box and grabbed the identity package off the counter.

"You and Asher off to *Pocono*?" Mick said. "What does Asher think of all this? Every time I see the kid, he is wearing forced happy smile to cover the hurt and pain he is going through. I know you noticed that too."

Liam had received his transfer the week before. He had pulled in a favor, against protocol, with Harrison Currituck, whose life Liam and Mick's father had saved. Chief Alexander Liam Mrkonic had operated the harpoon when Harrison Currituck lost control and drifted dangerously far from the ship. "Thanks, Master Chief. I owe you, anytime, anywhere," he had promised. Captain Currituck, Commanding Officer, NAS *Pocono* granted the favor Liam's dad had never requested.

"He has his good days and bad days. I try talking to him, it's hard to do that with Neon around," Liam confessed.

"She's intrusive, isn't she?"

"The only reason I'm letting her stay at the house is for Asher. Once we head to the *Pocono*, she's gone."

"Where is she going?" asked Mick.

"She mentioned going to New Jersey, New York, New Hampshire, New Mexico, who knows," said Liam. "Now, you're still planning to stay at the house when I report early, right? Keep an eye on Asher? Make sure that he gets to the airport?"

"Relax, big brother. I got it covered."

"Thanks, Mick. It's just..."

"I know," Mick said in a rare, serious tone. "We're brothers and brothers stick together."

"I better get back to the house before Neon talks Asher into going to Jersey with her."

"You need to pay," said Mick.

"Pay? You said this was a gift for Asher." Chief was confused.

"I said the identity package is a gift to my nephew, not the cigars." Mick had on his all business look.

Chief sighed and pulled out his pay card again.

"These babies weren't cheap," said Mick as he slid the pay card across his computer.

Liam laughed. "I'll come by tomorrow before I head out."

"I'll be here."

Liam paused. Something nagged at him. He couldn't figure out what. It felt like everything had fallen into place too easily...as if someone had arranged it ahead of time. He shook away the feeling and shot his brother a smile. He threw Rufus one more treat and left.

Tuck came out of the trailer he lived in with his dad. The sun had broken the horizon. Normally, on mornings like this, Tuck would hop into his car and drive around peacefully to start his day. Not this last week, Ursula sat at the impound lot, stripped and alone.

"Tuck?"

He stopped and turned around. Xiao stood behind him. She brushed her hair over her ear, revealing her eyes gazing at the ground.

"What did you do, have a sex change?" Tuck asked in an agitated tone.

"Sex change? No, why?"

"You have a big set of balls coming around here." Tuck started to walk away.

"I'm sorry, Tuck," said Xiao.

"Sorry doesn't get Olivia out of the internment village or Ursula out of impound."

"You weren't answering my calls." Xiao lifted her head avoiding eye contact.

Tuck turned back around. "Why should I?"

"I was scared, angry."

"Because of you I lost my acceptance and scholarship to Clearview Prep. I got ambushed a couple of times being called a hybrid sympathizer."

"They called you a hysym?" asked Xiao. She combed her hair over her ear with her hand.

"They did and that's not the only thing, I'm on probation and my dad even lost his job because of your actions."

"You are a hybrid sympathizer."

"If trying to save a girl I liked from the hybrid police makes me a hysym, then so be it." He walked fast down the dirt road. Xiao had to take larger steps and double her pace to keep up with him.

"I didn't ask you to save me. This is Olivia's fault."

Tuck stopped dead in his tracks. Xiao bumped into him, almost knocking herself down.

"You're right. This is Olivia's fault. How dare she, a hybrid, try to do things that only us normals are allowed to do."

"I said I was sorry. Can't we still be friends?"

"No, I see what you do to people who consider you a friend. Now, if you don't mind, I have to go meet my probation officer." He continued walking.

This time Xiao did not follow.

Later that evening Tuck stood over the small stove, brooding over Xiao's nerve for coming by and berating himself for ever liking her to begin with.

His dad, tall and with a swimmer's built, came in. "Something smells good." His walrus like mustache twitched as he took in the aromas.

"I'm heating up a can of chicken noodle soup, nothing special."

"Still smells good." Tuck's father sat down on the couch and groaned as he took off his shoes. "I'm beat."

"Any luck?" asked Tuck.

"I might have some leads, nothing solid." Tuck's dad had lost his job at the bottle company after Tuck was labeled a hysym. Tuck's father nodded to the boarded window. "When'd that happen?"

"This morning after you left."

"You okay?" Mr. Tuckerson asked.

"Yeah. I'll fix it tomorrow."

He gently placed his hand on Tuck's shoulder. "Listen to me, son. This isn't your fault."

"You lost your job, I lost my scholarship, I'm on probation, other kids attack me and throw rocks at our home. Plus, Ursula was impounded. I'll probably never see her again. Once she's stripped of all her powers, they'll auction her off to a lowlife who probably doesn't deserve a car like her. All because I wanted to impress a girl."

"Welcome to the club." Tuck's dad smiled.

"Huh? What club?"

"There isn't a single man on this planet, or any other planet, who hasn't done something stupid because they wanted to impress a girl. I'm proud of you, Tuck. You saw what you thought was injustice and stood up to the man. No car, no job, no home, no school can even come close to getting through this crazy world of ours. That heart you have, well, that, my son, will put you above all others. Stay true to your heart."

"You lost your job. How are we going to pay the bills?"

"We've been through this before. You probably don't remember it. When we were trying to get your sister implants, I was fired from my job, and people vandalized our home, our cars. It got to the point that your mother couldn't handle it anymore. When she went out on her own to start her new life, you and I moved here to start ours—that part of the story you do know. If you're willing, we can move and start over, or we can stay here and stand our ground. There is nothing wrong with either choice."

A holopad started beeping. "Incoming call," said a cartoon-sounding voice.

"Maybe this is one of the interviews calling back with good news," said Tuck's dad. "Answer call," he said to the holopad.

A shimmery bust appeared of a middle-aged man. "Hello, is this the Tuckerson residence?"

"Yes, I'm Ely Tuckerson. How can I help you?"

"Good evening, Mr. Tuckerson. I'm Kevin Bannister, Dean of Academics at Black Rock Academy here in Buffalo, New York. I was wondering if Knute was available."

"I'm Knute." He stepped in front of the camera.

"Hello, Knute, I understand you lost your acceptance to Clearview Preparatory School."

"Yes, sir."

"May I ask why?"

Tuck didn't know how the dean knew he lost his acceptance.

"Sir, I um..."

Mr. Tuckerson put his hand on Tuck's shoulder. "It's okay."

"I lost my acceptance because I willingly and knowingly helped a hybrid escape from the hybrid police."

"I see," said Dean Bannister. "I take it you're on probation now?"

"Yes, sir, until my eighteenth birthday when I become an adult."

"Would you do this again?"

Tuck looked up at his dad for assurance. With a nod, Tuck looked back at the holoimage. "Yes, sir, I would. I don't agree with the govern-ment's stance on hybrids."

Dean Bannister grinned. "Dean Wu was right about you."

"Who's Dean Wu?" asked Mr. Tuckerson.

"She's the Dean of Academics for EFA's Junior Academy ship, NAS *Pocono*."

Tuck knitted his eyebrows. "I don't know her. How does she know about me? What was she right about?"

"Dean Wu has connections all around North America—the world, really, if not beyond. That's what happens when you teach at an academy for over fifty years. Her former students become connections for her, myself being one of them. She caught wind that you lost your acceptance to Clearview. She contacted me and put in a good word. If you knew her, you would understand how big of a deal this truly is."

"What are you saying?" asked Mr. Tuckerson.

"Knute, Black Rock Academy isn't as prestigious, big, or elite as Clearview Prep. We're small. We have an excellent two-year program, and our graduates have a fairly high acceptance rate to big-league universities. I was wondering if you and your family would like to come up here and take a tour of our campus. If you like what you see, then I have an open seat for you."

Tuck's eyes bulged out of their sockets. "Really?" he said in disbelief. "Why me?"

"I'll be honest. We don't make a habit of accepting students who are currently on probation. However, Dean Wu firmly believes in second chances to those she sees potential in. Like her, I see your potential because of your honesty about your probation and the willingness to stand up for your beliefs is enough to tell me you're the kind of student I want. If more people stood up for what they believe in, we would be living in a better world. When you come up for the tour, and if you like, we can get you registered while you're here."

"Yes, yes, yes," said Tuck. He quickly looked at his dad for approval. "We'll be there, sir. Thank you very much."

"I'll send you all the information. I look forward to meeting you in person, Knute."

"Thank you, sir!"

They said their goodbyes, and the hologram disappeared.

"I can't believe it. I got into a prep school." His heart pumped hard with excitement.

"I don't know who you are, Dean Wu, but I love you!" Mr. Tuckerson yelled. "It looks like we're starting over."

"Are you okay with that?" asked Tuck.

"I couldn't be happier."

Xiao stood at the top of the stairs, eavesdropping on her parents and the female hybrid police detective. Not long after she got home from seeing Tuck, the detective arrived.

"Because of your daughter's honesty and integrity, we managed to find three other hybrids that were related to Olivia."

"What happened to Olivia and her family?" asked Xiao's mother.

"Her parents were both arrested and sentenced to life in prison for harboring four hybrids. The three other hybrids were foster children they were taking care of. None of those foster children survived the cleansing."

"And Olivia?" asked Xiao's father.

"She survived. Tomorrow she will be taken to an internment village in Ellicott City, Maryland, not far from her house."

"What side effects does she have now?" Xiao's mother asked.

"She's deaf and blind."

Xiao couldn't bear hearing any more. She went to her bedroom and buried her head under the pillows. She couldn't stand it—couldn't stay here any longer. When she went out in public, she'd get mixed reactions from people—some commended her, while others threatened her.

Tuck wouldn't speak to her. She didn't know why she found that even more devastating. Considering she'd had no interest in boys until she met him, confusion swept her mind over why she felt this way when she barely knew him. She wanted to make it up to him, even if it took a lifetime. If only she could get him into another prep school as a peace offering. For now, she knew she needed to get away. She would tell her parents at dinner.

"I changed my mind, I want to go to EFA's Junior Academy," Xiao said in Chinese. She spoke in her parents' native tongue at home. Xiao played with the food on her plate, not looking up. She brushed her hair over her ear.

"Honey, I know it's been rough the last few weeks. You need to give this more thought." Xiao's mother placed her chopsticks down, laid her hand upon Xiao's, and gave it a gentle squeeze.

"I want to go. I can't stay here." Xiao pulled her hand away.

"Xiao, you did the right thing," her father assured her. He pressed his lips together. Xiao's father had never approved of her attending EFA from the start. Although he wouldn't admit it, Xiao knew he didn't want to lose his nǚ yīng.

"I know I did the right thing. I will do it again if I have to. This doesn't mean I have to like it. I want to contact Dean Wu to see if I can get my spot back."

"I tell you what," said Xiao's father. "If your mother agrees, let's sit on this decision for a couple of weeks. If you still want to go, we will contact Dean Wu. We are not sure the Academy is the best option for you anymore."

"I don't want them to give away my seat."

"If it's meant for you to go, a seat will be available for you in two weeks. We're waiting," her father ordered.

"Fine." She pushed herself away from the table and stormed to her bedroom. She went over to her holotable and pressed a speed dial button. Light shimmered over it.

"Answer, please." She bit her lower lip in anticipation.

Dean Wu said as her bust shimmied above. She looked disgruntled that Xiao had contacted her.

"Dean Wu, I'm sorry to bother you." She brushed her hair away from her eyes. "Is it still possible to attend the academy after all?"

Dean Wu gave her a cold, long stare. "From what I understand, you've already made your choice. You have to learn to live with the choices you make."

"Please, Dean, I'm begging here. I won't change my mind again. I promise." Xiao's eyes filled with tears. "I can't stay here."

"Ms. Li, if you are trying to run away from something, the *Pocono* is not your answer. However, though I initially gave your spot away, another opened up today. If you are willing to learn to live with the choices you make from here on out, I will grant it to you."

Xiao couldn't believe her luck. "Yes, ma'am," she said, overly zealous. "I can learn. Yes, I promise."

"I must go. Good day, Ms. Li." Dean Wu's bust disappeared.

Xiao fell back onto her bed in relief. Now, to convince her parents.

The door to Asher's bedroom flew open. He jumped.

"Hey! You're making a *huge* mistake going to that ship today." Neon plopped herself on Asher's bed.

Asher turned off his hBook. He wanted to yell at her again for not respecting his privacy, even though at this point he knew it would be like talking to an armadillo—they had the worst hearing of any animal on the planet.

Neon looked around Asher's room and whistled. "How is it that at Willow Wood, you had the cleanest room out of everybody, here it looks like..."

"Your room?" Asher chirped.

She smiled. "Yeah, my room." She laughed. "At least my room smells nice with cinnamon. Yours smells funky, like the time Timothy hid that dead squirrel under his bed."

"It does not."

"I hate to break it to you. It smells like boy in here."

"As if girls have nothing but pleasant smells," said Asher.

"Your uncle called. He can't take you to the airport. He has to take Rufus to the veterinarian."

Asher sat up. "Rufus is his dog. Is he going to be okay?"

"He didn't say. I told him I would make sure you get on the shuttle."

"That was a lie, wasn't it?" asked Asher.

She smiled. "I am going to talk you out of your biggest mistake ever."

"I will consider not going if you answer me one question."

"Anything if it keeps you here on Earth."

"The night we went to Park 84, what did you see behind the Coca-Cola truck?"

"I told you already, just an old lady. There, I answered your question. Now you have to stay here."

Asher wouldn't let her get out of this that easy. "You saw something that frightened you."

"I did not. I don't get scared. You know that."

"Say what you want, I don't believe you."

"Look, it was an old lady, okay? It's no big deal. Since you're not going, we have to figure out where we are going."

"I didn't say I wasn't going, I said I would consider it," said Asher. "We have to be at the airport in two hours."

"Good, then I have two more hours to talk you out of going. Honestly, I know you don't want to go anyway, right?"

Asher shrugged.

"See, that's what I mean. Stay here with me. You'll be happier."

Asher shrugged again.

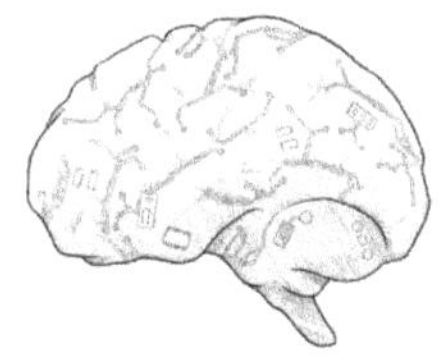

There were drop-off points all over North America. Against Neon's will, Asher and Neon arrived at the drop-off station at the air terminal in Pittsburgh. Asher had on his civilian clothes. All of his uniforms, reading material and equipment would be issued to him on the ship.

"What if his plan doesn't work? What if he's not the one on the medical scanner when you get scanned?" asked Neon. She refused to give up.

"He'll be on the scanner."

"You don't know that for sure. If they find out you're a hybrid up there, grab a space suit and abandon ship," said Neon.

Asher rolled his eyes.

With the help from one of Mick's sources, they managed to enter the airport undetected. There was a line formed at the Earth Force Alliance Junior Academy check-in station.

Asher could feel the hair on the back of his neck standup. Sweat formed on his forehead. He started biting his nails.

"Ha! I see it in your eyes. Reality hit ya, didn't it?" said Neon. "You don't want to go. You're scared to death. Let's get out of here and start our new life together."

"Where would we go?"

"Wherever you want." Neon smiled.

"Willow Wood?"

"We can't go back there—you know that. How about New Jersey?"

"Jersey? The pimple on the armpit of the country? Well, if that's where you want to go, why not?"

Asher turned and headed out of the terminal with Neon right next to him. He stopped, looked back for a second, then continued out the door.

"The cool thing is that Chief already got you an identity package. You can hide out in Chief's house while I see if Mick can get me one. I'll tell him that you're on your way to the *Pocono*."

"Okay."

"Things are going to be all right. You made the best decision of your life."

Asher stopped dead in his tracks. The blood that had returned to his face drained again.

"What is it?"

Asher didn't say anything. His eyes were on a Hispanic man and woman standing in the crowd—Cortez and Navarro, the hunters.

"You know them?"

"The woman," he uttered. "She killed Mom."

"Are you sure...of course you are, you have a perfect memory. Come on, we have to get out of here—like now."

Asher made the mistake of letting his eyes lock onto Navarro's. She tilted her head in disbelief; a sly smile appeared on her weather-worn face.

"Run!" yelled Asher. Neon and Asher turned and ran through the crowd. Navarro and Cortez chased after them.

*Oh shit, oh shit, oh shit*, Asher thought as he pushed himself through the crowd, hoping he would lose them among the other passengers.

Their path of escape ended in a T. Asher went right, while Neon went left. Asher didn't want to get separated from her. There was no going back now. Navarro followed him through every twist and turn.

Asher found himself back at the EFA check-in terminal. Cadets stood in front of the counter, waiting to be checked in. Asher scrambled over and pushed himself into the middle. He stooped down a little to blend in with the crowd.

"Hey, there's no cutting," said a boy wearing civilian clothes.

"Sorry," whispered Asher, watching Navarro as she stopped and looked around. He saw Navarro talk into her wristwatch. Moments later, a group of her goons arrived. She pointed, and they went off in different directions while she held her ground.

"Next."

"NEXT!"

Asher looked behind him. He didn't realize the line had kept moving. He couldn't risk running. He cautiously walked to the counter. Two cadets in their dress uniforms sat there checking in the arrivals.

"Name, please," said the young man sitting at a desk.

"I'm Asher. Asher Levi Smizik." It felt strange saying his whole name. He'd never had to do that at Willow Wood. He kept looking behind him, ensuring no one found him.

"Hello, Cadet Smizik. I'm Cadet Slater McGreggor." Slater typed Asher's name on the holopad. "Here you are. You're assigned to the NAS *Pocono*. That's the ship I'm on. It's a pretty cool ship. As soon as everyone is checked in, we'll head to the *Pocono*. Our shuttle is located at Terminal 11."

"Thank you," said Asher.

Asher tried to casually pass by. Navarro spotted him. He ran toward Terminal 11 with Navarro right behind him.

He dodged in and out of passengers as they disembarked from shuttles into the terminal. Glancing back, he saw Navarro falling behind in the crowd.

Once he rounded the corner and ducked off into a crowded gate, he stopped to catch his breath. *I lost her. I hope*, Asher thought. He had a dilemma, though. He couldn't go back unless he opened a fire exit, that would draw too much attention. He had no choice. He had to board the shuttle. Maybe he could sneak back to find Neon. He figured if anyone could outrun a hybrid hunter, it would be Neon.

He made his way to the shuttle gate and joined the ranks as they climbed on board. There were about twenty eleventh-level cadets still wearing their civilian clothes. The twelfth-level cadets had reported a few days earlier to help with in-processing.

Asher slid into a seat in the back row against the window. He slouched down with his knees pressing hard against the seat in front of him. He kept his eyes focused out the window, hoping he wouldn't see Navarro.

With Asher's attention fixed on the concourse, he didn't see the shuttle filling up.

"Is anybody sitting there?" said a kind voice.

Asher turned to see if the question was directed at him. There stood a girl with honey-brown hair and hazel eyes. She had a cute little nose that sat above a warm smile that reached toward two dimples. He had seen her before, at the souvenir store at the baseball game. Asher calculated the chances of this happening—too high to even admit to himself.

"Uh...umm...no." Asher's voice cracked. His heart sank.

She sat down in the end seat, leaving an empty seat separating them. There were no other seats available. He wondered if she would still have sat in his row if there were other seats open. He tried not to stare, he couldn't help himself. He would glance momentarily, only to whip his head back as casually as possible.

Asher wasn't one to start a causal conversation. He wanted to start one with her, he didn't know how.

Slater came on board with the other cadet. They secured the hatch, and the second cadet went into the cockpit.

"Settle down, fellow cadets. Take your seats and buckle up. We will be leaving shortly," said Slater. Asher tried to settle in as Slater strolled the aisle. He arrived at the last row where Asher sat.

"You, Cadet, strap in." He pointed to Asher.

Asher strapped himself in. Anxiety began to take over his mind. He had never been on a transport shuttle before. He had never left the ground.

"Move your butt over, nitwit," Slater said. "I get the aisle seat."

With a disgusted sigh, the young girl slid over. Asher couldn't believe how rudely Slater spoke to her. Neon would've given Slater a bruising if he'd said that to her.

"I told you not to call me that here, rock for brains!"

"Shut up, Nittany."

Nittany scrunched up her face and stuck her tongue out at him.

She turned and looked at Asher. "Do you have any brothers?"

Asher's heart felt like a pile of wet, decaying autumn leaves hugging the ground. "Yeah." Asher looked away, hoping no tears would escape his eyes.

"They are annoying, aren't they?" asked Nittany.

"Hey, I'm Slater. We met at the registration table. This is my sister, Nittany. Ignore her. Asher, right?"

Asher nodded.

"Which ship are you assigned too?" asked Nittany.

"NAS *Pocono,*" replied Asher.

"Me too. Have you've been on the *Pocono* before?"

"No." He wondered if she recognized him or not. If she did, she didn't show any signs of it.

"I have for family day. I normally wouldn't have checked in at this station, knowing Slater was working here, my family decided to venture to Pittsburgh. Besides, my uncle lives near here. It was fun seeing my cousins."

Asher couldn't find any words. Then he felt a weight lifting. The shuttle took off, and Navarro didn't find him. He looked out the window to double-check. As the shuttle rose, the ground turned into a city, a mass of land, then water, and finally into a giant, blue sphere.

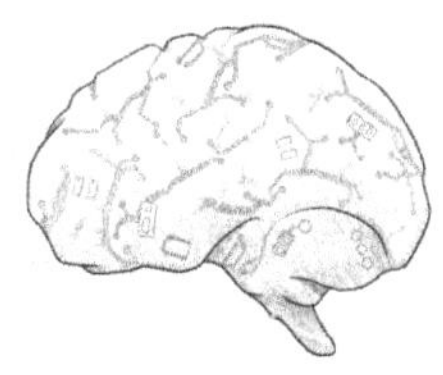

"Hello fellow cadets, this is your co-pilot, Senior Cadet Christian Myszkowski." The voice came over the loudspeaker.

"He's one of Slater's friends. Everyone calls him Ski," informed Nittany.

"We're going to make a pass of the *Pocono* before landing. You can see it out the port side window," echoed Ski's voice throughout the passenger cabin.

Asher looked out. He'd never seen anything as magnificent as the *Pocono*. It had to be the largest manmade structure he had ever seen. The main body reminded Asher of a 9mm gun from the twentieth century, minus the hand grip and trigger. The front revealed a glowing blue strip running from top to bottom. He marveled at the massive weapon that had helped to destroy the asteroid that once threatened Earth. The cold, gray skin of the ship was trimmed in bronze, and in the back were the propulsion engines. A giant ring circled the tail end, which contained the interstellar drives. The I-drives were what allowed the ship to speed through space. A transparent dome sat on top. On the belly of the ship, a glass tunnel outlined the edges. Asher could barely make out that people were walking about in them.

"Timothy, you would love this," Asher whispered to himself. The shuttle made a U-turn, headed towards the landing hangar.

Asher felt a hand placed on his shoulder. His body softened at her touch, and he turned to see Nittany's face close to his. She looked toward him and smiled. Any closer and their lips would be touching. This caused an unexpected arousal.

"Sorry," she said. "I wanted to see too." Her voice was sweet and innocent.

When Nittany sat back down in her seat, Asher tried to adjust himself downstairs without her noticing. He looked at her and saw a faint smile. His face felt warm. Did she notice?

The shuttle entered the *Pocono* and landed with a slight jolt. Yellow and red lights lit the hangar bay. Asher couldn't see well behind him, however it looked like other shuttles were landing too.

"Cadets, you may unbuckle your seat straps, but please remain seated," said Ski on the loudspeaker. "Once more shuttles land, they will pressurize the hangar."

Nittany looked at Asher. "You were that boy that kept looking at me in the stadium store, aren't you?"

Asher had words that wouldn't come out. He flashed her an awkward smile.

"I thought you looked familiar." Her eyes drew Asher in.

"Attention, cadets," bellowed Ski. "We are opening the hatch for departure. Please remain on board until your escort returns. The shuttle will be leaving shortly to take the remaining cadets to their academy ships."

"Do you know what squad you're in?" asked Nittany.

"No. I guess I applied too late. My welcome aboard package told me I would find out during in-processing. Do you know your squad?"

"Slater is being a butt and not telling me," Nittany replied.

"How many squads are there?" asked Asher.

"Each level has twenty-five squads. Each squad has six cadets."

Asher peeked over the seats. To his amazement, there were other new cadets that looked as scared and anxious as he felt. They were fidgeting, chewing their fingernails, biting their lower lips, and one girl stood with her eyes closed, breathing slowly in and out.

"*Pocono* cadets, stand up," roared a senior cadet who came up the ramp.

Asher jumped, hit his head, and fell back into his seat.

"You okay?" asked Nittany, her dimple showing playfully.

"No talking!" yelled the senior cadet.

Asher began chewing his fingernails again.

"When you exit the shuttle, the boys will muster on the starboard side of the hangar. The girls on the port side," said the senior cadet. "From there you will be taken to in-processing. There will be no talking. Let's move out."

With reluctance, hesitance, and a good amount of fear, Asher departed the shuttle.

Tuck got into his car. He still couldn't believe the hybrid police had let him get Ursula out of the impound. Ursula's electric shock treatment device had been removed, as well as the antigravity thrusters. Tuck didn't care, he got her back. He would reinstall them once he got the parts. He couldn't get caught, though, it went against his probation.

Tuck thought a guardian angel must have been looking out for him. How else could he explain everything that had unfolded over the past weeks? Black Rock Academy offered him a seat. The small academy held many opportunities that a normal high school couldn't afford. Plus, his dad received a job offer at Moog, Inc., a company that dealt with parts for interstellar and intergalactic space travel. Mr. Tuckerson would be making more money than he did at the bottle company.

If Tuck had to give his guardian angel a name, it would have to be Hai ying Wu, Dean of Academics onboard the NAS *Pocono*. He didn't know why she'd taken such interest in him. He'd never met her or even known anything about her until he lost his seat at Clearview. He had talked to her briefly on the holocomm after many attempts. She told him that she had two favors to ask. He didn't mind too much—both favors required him to drive Ursula. First, she requested he take two EFA junior academy cadets from Buffalo to Pittsburgh. The second was to pick a group of people up at a boat launch in the middle of December. He found the requests odd but it didn't matter. He'd do anything for Dean Wu after everything she had done for him and his dad.

What made the trip to Pittsburgh almost unbearable were the twins of his dad's boss. They were seniors on board the EFA Junior Academy ship, NAS *Arcadia*. All of their friends were meeting in Pittsburgh to fly to the *Arcadia* together. The boy twin had a wicked tongue, and he found new ways to use every curse word in the urban dictionary. Nothing pleased the self-absorbed twin sister.

Tuck didn't understand why the pair couldn't take a shuttle from Buffalo to Pittsburgh. As he bid them farewell, his stomach reminded him to check out the place that made Rueben sandwiches where the French fries and coleslaw were placed on the sandwich itself. He saw an ad on the way to the airport.

He jumped when his passenger car door opened. A girl with blue-and-green hair jumped in. She spoke boldly between broken breaths: "I'm a hybrid and I have the power to electrocute people. You can drive, or I can zap you and commandeer your car. Which is it?"

"I'm breaking my probation," Tuck said as he gunned it.

The girl looked back until they were out of the airport and onto the highway. Then she lay back, and her breathing slowed.

"I don't want no trouble," said Tuck. "Helping you makes me in complete violation of my probation."

"Probation? What did you do, litter on private property?"

"Aiding and abetting a hybrid."

"For real?" The girl sat up and looked at him.

"Yeah. My dad and I are shooting for a clean start. I don't want to ruin it."

"Relax," said the girl. "We're not going to get caught. Where you headed anyway?"

"Buffalo," Tuck replied.

"Buffalo? I guess that's as good of a place as any."

"You want to go with me to Buffalo?"

"Those hybrid hunters know I'm in Pittsburgh. It's not safe to stay here. I have to let things simmer down before coming back."

"You have family in Pittsburgh?" asked Tuck.

"No. I mean, there is this boy... he's probably dead by now." The girl became awfully quiet. She stared out the window.

"I'm sorry. Was he your boyfriend?"

"Asher? My boyfriend? Puh-lease." The girl crossed her arms and shifted her body to look in the review mirror.

"By the way, I'm Tuck."

"Neon. Now can we stop being chatty cats?" The girl spoke with a lump in her throat.

"Sure." Tuck looked over and saw her face in the window reflection. He couldn't tell for sure, it looked like she had tears rolling down her cheeks.

Navarro stormed into the back of her mobile ops van. JD, who lay peacefully on the floor, stood to greet his master.

"That's three times now that skinny hybrid got away from us. That's three times too many." Navarro slammed her mini-crossbow on the counter.

Cortez remained calm. "Sabastian has a hookup in the airport's security. He's checking out the security videos to see which shuttle the boy got on and to get the license plate of the car that took the girl. We should be hearing from him soon."

As if on cue, Cortez's watch buzzed. He tapped it, and a hologram of a man with a mustache appeared.

"What did you find out?" asked Cortez. Navarro came up to Cortez to get a better look at the hologram.

"I'm afraid not much. Every video that had those hybrids in it was scrambled. The imagery was unrecoverable," said the mustached man.

"Scrambled?" asked Navarro.

"Yes, however, we did manage to find this." An image of an old lady appeared.

"Alita Blackwood? What was she doing at the air terminal?"

"I don't know," the man replied.

"When I tracked that kid down at the cybercafé, Alita Blackwood showed up," said Cortez.

"Alita Blackwood and that boy are connected. I suspect the girl whose head looks like an Easter egg, is involved too. I can feel it in my bones," said Navarro.

"See if you can find anything else and report back," Cortez said.

"Yes, sir." The hologram disappeared.

"What do you make of the scrambled video, Cortez?" Navarro sat down in her chair. JD came up to her, and she brought her hand to his head.

"It sounds like it was specifically targeted. I know of only one hybrid that has the brain implant power to control such a large venue."

"The Phantom Prophet," said Navarro. "He's been dead for decades."

"They never found a body. Maybe he was in hiding," Cortez suggested.

"Let's say the Phantom Prophet is alive and he was the one who scrambled those videos. Why would he come out of hiding now?" Navarro looked up.

"Alita Blackwood and the Phantom Prophet worked together for a while to get civil rights for hybrids. That is, until they didn't agree on how to fight for their rights anymore. You think they're back together?"

"I don't know. Definitely the boy, and probably the girl, are key pieces to this puzzle. We find them, we get Alita Blackwood. The Phantom Prophet too, if he is indeed still alive. Have your crew start surfing the internet. Maybe a witness captured today's events and post them online. We could get answers that way."

"Yes, Navarro." Cortez excused himself.

"JD, what started off as a routine intercept has now become the closest we've ever been to capturing Alita Blackwood." Navarro closed her eyes and continued to work the puzzle in her head. Getting Alita Blackwood would mean putting a stop to the violence she spread across North America.

Cortez sat in his Jeep alone. He tapped his watch, and an older man in his fifties appeared, his face narrow and pale.

"What do you got?" asked the man.

"Dr. Monroe, I have reason to believe the Phantom Prophet is still alive."

"Really? How good is the source, or is this another fairy tale?" asked the doctor.

"Nothing solid yet. I have my crew working corners that Navarro doesn't know about."

"Good. We can't let her get ahold of him, if he is still alive. She would sell his implants to the highest bidder. I want them," he said. Cortez could see the doctor's greed. "What about Alita Blackwood? Did the tip pan out at the airport?"

"We didn't see her. We did see the boy from the Willow Wood raid there. He was with a girl. Both of them got away."

"Find them and bring them to me alive. I did the autopsy on that kid we found in the river. His implants are the most advanced I have ever seen. Problem is, we found the kid too late. It appears that the garrison chip only functions in a living body."

"Did you transplant it?"

"I did. Ten times, and not once did the chip turn on. The chip was fried. My best guess is if the host dies the chip does too. I've never seen before. I am working with the boy's DNA to see if that will turn it on or not. I placed the remains of the kid in a chamber. Now, if those two kids you saw have the same garrison chip..." The doctor paused. "Do you know where those kids ran off to?"

"The girl escaped with a boy named Knute Tuckerson. He's on probation for aiding and abetting a hybrid last month. We believe they're headed to Buffalo."

"And the boy?"

"He jumped on a shuttle to the NAS *Pocono*," replied Cortez.

"The hybrid police will be sure to capture him when he goes for his medical scan. At least the girl is still on the table. Does Navarro know about this Tuckerson boy?"

"No."

"Good. Keep it that way. She'll kill them first before we can get our answers."

"I'll take care of Navarro." Cortez looked up and saw her hopping out of the van. "I have to go. I'll keep you posted." He turned off his watch and got out of his Jeep.

"Navarro," he called.

"News?" she asked.

"We have leads on both the boy and the girl. Your idea worked. The boy hopped on board a shuttle that took him to Seattle."

"Anything on the girl?"

"Yes, she hopped into a car owned by a Carlos Rodriguez from Miami."

"Let's send a crew to each place to check things out. Seattle is too wet and Miami is too hot. We'll stay here until we get reports back."

Cortez didn't like this answer. "Navarro, I want to take my crew to Miami. I have resources down there that could prove valuable."

"Fine," she said.

Cortez hid his smile. He broke out a cigar and lit it. "I'll keep you posted."

The next day Cortez surveyed his crew. There were seven of them, including himself. Navarro had a huge operation, but these six members were the only ones he trusted. Even then, he wouldn't put it past a single one to betray him for their own benefit.

"Hey, when we get to Miami, maybe we can hit the beaches for a few days. Those beach girls are such easy lays," said one of the men. The others cheered in agreement.

"I'll show you an easy lay," said Dylan, the only female member of the group.

"Shut up, all of you," said Cortez. "We're not going to Miami. We're headed to Buffalo."

"Buffalo?" asked one of the crew members.

"If Navarro gets word of this change, I will kill all of you."

"Don't worry boss, we have your back," said Dylan. Cortez trusted nobody fully and she was the closest thing to full trust he had for a person.

"This is what is going to happen." Cortez laid out his plans to his crew.

# CHAPTER 22

Asher couldn't stand still while waiting to be told what to do next. He looked nervously around the hangar for ways to escape and places to hide in case he had to run. His stomach had the collywobbles at the idea of Navarro finding him.

He looked around for Chief even though he knew he'd likely be at the medical in-processing center.

There were about thirty boys in all, and every ten to fifteen minutes, a senior cadet would take ten boys with him and leave the rest to wait in the hangar.

"Man, I hope we get going soon," said a boy with black dreadlocks about twelve inches long. "I have to take a piss." He wore a personable smile.

Asher only shrugged. The boy looked strangely familiar. This bothered Asher. He never forgot anything. Yet he couldn't figure out where he might've seen the boy before. Maybe the umber skin threw him off. Not sure why, though—they had kids with umber skin at Willow Wood.

"I'm Crayon Flint. I go by Cray. I don't mind being teased about my name, what bothers me is how people act like their jokes are original. I've heard them all."

Asher still puzzled over Cray's familiarity—he didn't hear a word Cray said. Back at Willow Wood he could recite a conversation he'd had with his mother word for word at the age of four. He could describe an object in fine detail he'd seen fourteen years ago. Since he'd left Willow Wood, he had now experienced two encounters that left him wondering. This bothered Asher. Why couldn't he remember? He'd never experienced this feeling before.

Asher's thoughts were interrupted as Cray tapped him on his shoulder. "Huh?"

"Man, you were in a trance. What's your name?"

"I'm Asher Smizik," he replied shyly.

"Where are you from?" asked Cray.

Asher wanted to tell the truth—upstate New York—he followed the script of his new identity. "Pittsburgh, Pennsylvania." *At least for the time being*, he thought.

"I'm from Savannah, Georgia." Cray looked up at Asher.

"Cadet! There is no talking," ordered an EFA officer. He had a tattoo on his right arm—the North American flag in the background and a battlefield grave in the front. *Walter Mabus, Sept. 2146 – 23 Nov. 2167* was underneath the battle grave.

"Sorry, sir," said Cray. He shot off a quirky smile.

The officer walked away.

"Man, I hope not all of the officers are that anal," said Cray.

"Welcome aboard the NAS *Pocono*," said a senior cadet. He kept his hair of wheat and straw short on the sides and thick and wavy on top. "I'm Cadet John Barfly. Follow me."

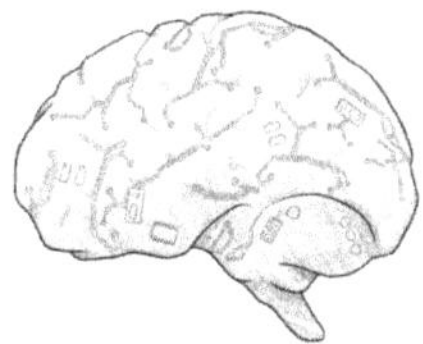

Cadet Barfly stopped in front of a hatch after a maze of passage-ways and shipyard ladders. "Okay, guys, this is the boy's locker room," said Barfly. "Once inside, you will basically shit, shower, and shave. Plus, you'll be given your preliminary uniform. Good luck, and see you around." The senior cadet motioned for the group of boys to head in.

Asher entered the locker room. His nose instantly picked up a rank scent, and the steam from the showers made it ten times worse.

Black and yellow-gold lockers lined the walls, and the back two corners each held a pile of boxes.

"I hate black and gold," said Cray. "I know it's our school colors, but really?"

"Cadets, there is no talking in here," said a bulky chief. "You will grab a box from over here." He pointed to the more orderly stack. "Inside you will find a pair of shower shoes and a ditty bag that contains your toiletries. In the shower kit, you will find shampoo, a soap dish with soap, deodorant, toothbrush, toothpaste, shaving cream and razor blades. You will take off your clothes and place them in a box. You will label and seal the box. Do not, I repeat, do not seal up your shower shoes and shower kit. You will then place your box in this pile." He pointed to the other pile of haphazard boxes. "Your box will be returned to you when you make your first trip back to Earth."

Asher wondered when his first trip back to Earth would be. He noticed a small tunnel on the opposite side of the locker room. It had shower spigots on both sides. There were cadets already in there taking showers.

"You will enter the shower tunnel," continued the chief. "You *will* use your shampoo and soap and wash thoroughly."

Cray raised his hand.

"Yes, cadet?"

"I already took a shower today."

The chief smiled. "Good. When you finish taking this shower, you will be extra clean." He gave Cray a sarcastic look. "As I was saying, on the other side, you will be given a uniform. Don't dawdle."

The cadets each got a box. They prattled among each other.

"This task does not require talking," said the chief.

Regret started to join Asher's doubt. The only people who saw him naked was his mom and Dr. Emily when she had him drop his pants and underwear and turn his head to cough at his annual physical. Of course, Neon too, thanks to her X-ray vision.

"No standing around, cadets! Take your clothes off, into the shower tunnel. Keep moving!" burst the chief petty officer.

Asher slowly undressed, feeling the most vulnerable since he'd escaped from Willow Wood.

"Cadet," the chief bellowed to Cray, "put on your shower shoes, unless you want to get foot fungus."

Asher walked to the shower tunnel. He grabbed his soap and hung his shower kit on a nearby hook. He stepped in the hot, steamy showers. Asher heard a snap, and the boy showering next to him jumped.

"Stop it! That hurts!" said the boy.

Another snap, this time Asher felt a sharp sting on his bum. He jumped and slipped, grabbing the shower nozzles to keep from falling completely.

The boy who'd towel-whipped him laughed.

"Stop grab-assing around!" The chief shot the boy with the towel a look that meant business.

"Chill out!" said the towel-whipping boy, giving the chief the middle finger. He had a tattoo of a snake and skull on his back and what appeared to be a naked lady on his right forearm.

After showering, Asher grabbed a towel by the exit, dried himself, and wrapped it around his waist.

On the other side of the tunnel, a senior chief barked more orders.

"Cadets, you will brush your teeth, use your deodorant, and shave.

I don't care if you only have one strand of peach fuzz on your face. You will shave. If you don't know how, I will show you."

Asher went to a sink and took out his shaving kit.

The boy with the tattoo stood at the sink next to him. The boy showed off his artistic skills by drawing part of a male's anatomy on the mirror. He gave Asher a coprophagous grin. "Now for the finishing touch." He sprayed shaving cream in his hand and dabbed his finger in it. He wiped the steam away with it, leaving a trail of white cream behind.

"Michelangelo! Wipe it off now, cadet!" ordered the senior chief.

"This is a masterpiece," the boy joked.

"Cadet, last time. Wipe it off."

"Fine!" The boy took his towel and erased his drawing. "He's obviously not a fan of the arts."

"Nice tattoo," another cadet said to the towel-whipping artist.

"If you like this one, you should've seen Pinocchio before I had it removed."

"Shaving does not require talking," the senior chief said.

Asher finished up and received a pair of black coveralls, one pair of briefs, a black T-shirt, socks, and a pair of military boots.

A senior cadet came into the locker room. "Who's ready?" He moved his eyes to the raised hands, counting. Asher's hand was one of them.

"Okay, you seven with me."

Asher, Cray, and five others joined the senior cadet. Once out in the narrow passageway, the cadet pulled out a pad.

"I'm Senior Cadet Blake Swisher. When we're not around instructors, officers and active duty crew members, you can call me Swish," said the teenager. "Give me your names, one at a time."

"Crayon Flint," Cray blurted.

The senior cadet scanned his hPad. "Echo 88. That is your squad. Remember that."

Asher knew there were twenty-five squads. The cadets would keep their squad number, which represented their graduation year, for the duration of their time at the academy.

The other boys gave their names. Whiskey 88, Tango 88, Yankee 88, Lima 88, and Mike 88 each had a cadet in the group.

"Name?" Swish asked Asher.

"Asher Smizik."

The senior cadet scanned the pad. "You're in Echo 88 too."

"Cool," said Cray.

"Follow me, and I'll drop you off at your berthing." Swish led them down a passageway and up three decks with the same drab white bulkheads, a variety of pipes snaking through the overhead.

"Echo 88, this is your stop," said Swish.

Cray opened the hatch partway.

"Come on in. Names, please," said a lieutenant junior grade officer. Her shiny black hair was done up in a tight bun. She had toned muscles on her arms. Her natural golden-brown tan added a sense of beauty to her.

"Cadet Asher Levi Smizik."

"Cadet Crayon Flint."

"Yes, here you are. I'm Lieutenant Junior Grade Sequoya Meoquanee, your assistant squad leader. Lieutenant Mabus is your squad leader," said LTjg Meoquanee. "He's helping with in-processing. He will be joining us later. Now, through that door is your berthing. On the side of each rack is a panel with directions on how to register the rack to yourself. If you have questions, come and get me and I will show you. Once you're done, come back out here and let me know what rack number you have."

"Yes, ma'am," said both boys.

Asher and Cray went into berthing and shut the door. The small compartment had two sets of racks, three bunks high, one set on each side of the space. The small aisle between them made it tight quarters. The foot of the racks landed right up against the bulkhead they'd stepped through. At the head of the racks, lined up against the wall, were three stand-up lockers about six feet high. On the back bulkhead, a door opened into the head.

Asher looked at the other racks. None of them had names on them yet. He and Cray were the first ones here.

"I call tops." Cray climbed up the rack ladder on the right and pretended to be asleep.

Asher didn't say a word. He decided to follow suit and take the top rack on the left side. He followed the instructions on the panel. The top of his rack opened up, revealing a coffin locker where cadets kept their uniforms and personal items. After Asher finished, he went into the head. He needed time alone. The small compartment had two changing stalls, each with their own shower, two toilet stalls, and four stainless steel sinks, each with a mirror.

Asher stood in front of the mirror. He replayed in his mind the past weeks that had brought him here. He thought of his mom, Timothy, Neon, and Willow Wood. Then he thought of Navarro, Cortez, and the fact that he had to conceal his true identity.

"I have to take a load off my mind," said Cray as he entered the head. "Three squad members are here. All girls. Pretty cute, too, if you're into that sort of thing." Cray disappeared into one of the stalls.

"Girls?"

"Yeah, this is a coed berthing and head," said Cray.

Asher cracked open the door. He first saw a girl typing her name on the middle rack under Cray's. She had black hair tied up into a bun. Another girl with shoulder-length strawberry-blond hair knelt down and worked on the bottom rack. He opened the door wider and saw the girl typing her name on the middle rack, under his. He shut the door.

*It's her!* he thought. Of all girls to be in the same squad and take the rack directly under his, it had to be her.

He put his hand in front of his mouth and checked his breath, then lifted his arm to smell his pits.

"Asher, right?"

He froze and saw Nittany behind him in the reflection of the mirror. She had her hair tied up in a tight bun. Unlike the other girl with a bun, Nittany had hers braided. He lowered his arms and flashed her his awkward smile and nervous laugh.

"Hi."

"I thought you were in my squad. I saw your name on your rack. I picked the rack below you."

Asher stood there silently, still flashing a crooked smile, showing off his dimples.

The silence soon became awkward.

"You don't talk much, do you?"

"I do," Cray said from the stall, followed by a flush.

"Berthing and the head is cramped, isn't it?" asked Nittany.

Asher shook his head. He didn't know why he couldn't find any words to speak. When looking at her, his body felt strange. Looking at Neon had never made him feel this way.

Cray came out of the stall and washed his hands. "Sorry for the smell." He laughed.

"Cadets! Muster in the common room," bellowed LTjg Meoquanee.

"We better go." Nittany turned and left.

"I think she likes you." Cray gave a lighthearted punch to Asher's arm.

"She what?" Asher mumbled as he followed Cray.

When Asher entered the berthing, Xiao-Niao Li's name was on the rack below Cray's, with Tabitha Dorney's under hers. Squatting at the bottom rack on the same side as Asher's, a boy put his toiletries in his coffin locker. He did not appear to be happy and slammed his rack shut as he stood up. Asher recognized him—the towel-whipping artist.

"What are you looking at, weathervane?" He flicked one of Asher's protruding ears, laughing as he headed to the common room.

"Why did he call me a weathervane?" Asher wondered aloud. He looked at the boy's locker and saw the name Brett Lundy.

# CHAPTER 23

Asher, Cray, and Brett stood in line behind their three berthing mates. They were waiting for their medical scans. "What do you think the girls are talking about that's making them giggle like that?" asked Cray. The girls were talking in hushed voices.

"They're probably debating who has the biggest dick and nicest ass," replied Brett.

"If that's the case," Cray said, "I'm sure there is no debate." He tapped his chest with his index and middle fingers, smiled and nodded his head.

"Don't flatter yourself," said Xiao, turning to face the boys.

The conversation made Asher nervous. What if Nittany had seen him adjust himself on the shuttle? He looked at her giggling, and his heart pounded. If Neon had joined the academy, she would've tried to talk him out of his feelings for Nittany. Neon did not like or trust normals.

"Make a hole, coming through," shouted one of the *Pocono's* master-at-arms.

Asher stepped aside as two mater-at-arms escorting a cadet in handcuffs walked by. Asher recognized him as one of the boys Brett had whipped in the showers.

"I bet he's a hybrid," whispered Cray. "I heard last year they caught over twenty!"

"Where are they taking him?" Asher's thoughts managed to sneak out of his mouth.

"They're taking him to a holding cell with the others," Nittany replied. "When everyone has been scanned, they'll take the hybrids to Earth to be cleansed."

Asher watched as they disappeared down the passageway. He feared he would be next—and what would Nittany think? Would she hate him or turn him in if she ever found out? If only he knew for certain that Chief had a foolproof plan. They were next in line.

"You okay, Asher?" asked Nittany. "You look petrified."

"Umm, uhhh, I'm afraid of needles." Asher told the truth, just not the full truth.

"If you're caught up on your vacs, you won't need any."

Asher started to calm down a tad bit. Her sweet melodic voice soothed him. They moved forward.

"Name," asked the second-class hospital corpsman sitting at a table.

Asher could hardly find his voice. "Cadet Asher Levi Smizik, ma'am."

The corpsman plugged in his name and read the results. "Don't call me ma'am, I work for a living. Go stand in that line over there. You need vaccinations."

"I already had mine," said Asher. Chief had ensured Asher received all of his vaccines before coming to the *Pocono*.

"According to our records, you need vacs. Next!"

Asher started chewing on his fingernails. He felt his heart beat hard and fast as if he drank a six pack of energy drinks. His stomach felt queasy. Hesitantly he joined the vaccine line. He watched Nittany go to the girls' line to be scanned and examined.

His anxiety rose higher. Could this be the wrong line? How would he avoid the scanner? And now he needed to get vacs. His mind raged on, and he scanned the room for Chief.

"Next!" called a familiar voice. Chief stood there wearing gray camouflage pants and a hospital scrub top with the *Pocono*'s logo over the left breast.

"Hi, Asher. I see you made it up here. You're doing okay?"

"Hello, Chief," said Asher softly. He saw Chief fiddling with a cigar box. "Aren't you doing my scan?"

"The chief medical officer wanted to do it. He out ranks me, so I couldn't argue."

Asher gave him a peculiar look. The look of "how am I going to pass the scan?"

"Relax, Asher. Thanks to Mick, I have a backup plan. He says it's flawless, although I can never take my brother at his word."

"That's supposed to make me feel better?"

Chief put Asher's chart up on the computer screen. "Let's see here. You need tetanus and a dose of multivitamin 2-part."

"Three shots?" Asher's stomach turned. "I had my shots already, remember?"

"Actually, only two," Chief corrected. "The multivitamin 2-part is one shot and one pill." Chief mouthed words to Asher so no one could hear him. "This is the backup plan."

Asher's eyes grew to the size of quarters. "Really? I have a hard time swallowing pills. I cough and gag, and then if I get it down, I throw up."

"You'll be fine, Asher."

"Since it's only a vitamin…oww! That hurt." Chief gave Asher the first shot.

"Sorry, just a little sting. It will be okay. How's Neon doing?" Chief asked, changing the subject.

"Okay. She didn't want me to come."

"I know. I'm glad you did. I take it you didn't have any issues coming here," Chief said.

Asher didn't know if he should tell Chief about Navarro or not. He decided to hold onto this secret a little while longer. He couldn't tell the full story with lots of people around. They would have to find a time to talk in private later.

"No, everything went okay," he lied.

"Swallow this." Chief handed Asher the pill, the size of a large lima bean.

"I can't take this."

"Asher, you have to trust me. Okay?"

Asher took a deep breath. He knew he was acting childish, to him his fears were real. He reluctantly put the pill in his mouth, gagging before it even rested upon his tongue. The gagging was replaced with a dry heaving sound. Asher spit the pill back out.

"I can't do it."

"Okay, let's try something different." Instead of getting a new pill, Chief Mrkonic took the old one from Asher. With one hand he held the pill and in the other a bottle of water. "Okay, you will place the pill on your tongue as far back as possible and then put the mouth of the water bottle in your mouth, forming a tight seal with your lips. Lean back and drink as much water as you can before breaking the seal."

Chief's tone caused him to relax. He couldn't figure out why.

"You ready?"

Asher nodded, although his thoughts felt otherwise. He would never be ready for a pill that size.

Chief placed the pill as far back as he could without risking Asher choking on it. "Form the seal with your lips and drink!" Chief quickly pulled his hand away. With much gagging, Asher placed the bottle between his lips and formed a seal. He proceeded to drink down the entire bottle of water, along with the pill.

"See that wasn't bad now, was it?"

"If you say so," replied Asher as his tongue combed the inside of his mouth.

"Now, I can give you one last shot."

Asher sighed. He'd forgotten about the shot portion of the 2-part vitamin.

"What is that?" Asher didn't like the size of the needle. He'd never seen one that big. "You're not sticking that in my arm."

"You're right. I'm not."

"Oh good." Asher began to relax.

"Pull down your coveralls and expose your doopa."

"My what?" exclaimed Asher.

"Doopa is what my grandmother used to call my backside. Bend over."

"Doopa? You sound like I'm a baby."

"I know you're not," said Chief. "Some words have a habit of sticking with you. Now show me a cheek."

"Is this part of the backup plan," mouthed Asher.

Chief nodded.

Asher sighed in defeat. He dropped his coveralls.

"Asher, where do you get your stubbornness from? Your mom isn't like this. At least she didn't used to be."

"She told me all the time I get it from my father."

Chief couldn't help but smile.

Asher yelped as he felt the cold, sharp sting of the needle enter his butt cheek.

"Aren't you done yet?"

"Sorry, I can't shoot this with one quick blow, I have to gently inject it into you." Chief wiggled the needle a bit, and finally the entire vitamin shot had entered the cushingness of Asher's rear end.

"Okay, you can get dressed and head over to the scanning line." Chief lowered his tone. "You have nothing to fear. I have your back."

Asher's nerves took over as he prepared for the scan. He didn't know how the shot and pill played into the backup plan. Chief had not been clear.

Once again, Asher waited in a line.

Asher went into the changing room, followed the directions posted on the bulkhead. He put on a paper hospital gown, and a draft ran up his legs to his barc bottom, giving him the chills. The red light above the door that led to the scanner room turned green. Asher knew he would be caught and escorted down to the holding cell. He felt sick. Very sick. His muscles wouldn't move. Fear took over his entire body.

A knock came from the other side of the door. It opened, revealing a petty officer first class corpsman.

"Come on, cadet. The doc is waiting for you."

"I don't feel well," Asher said softly. The corpsman walked away as if he didn't hear him.

Dr. Mitsuru Morimoto sat at the control panel of the scanner. The scanner itself stood tall in the center of the room. It had a clear cylinder with one opening and a large control box connected to it where Dr. Morimoto sat.

Beads of sweat formed on Asher's brow, and he started to hyperventilate. A mater-at-arms stood in a nearby corner of the room.

Asher stepped into the scanner. An inner cylinder began to rotate. It scanned his body. As it ended, his stomach piqued. Unable to prevent it, Asher opened his mouth and regurgitated all over the clean, sterilized deck. In the remains of his breakfast, Asher spotted the pill. As the disgruntled corpsman rushed over to assist him, Asher fell to his knees as though he would vomit again. He grabbed the pill and hid the spew-covered bolus in the palm of his hand. The corpsman helped Asher up, gave him a puke pot, and took him back to the changing room. A corpsman met them there.

"I don't believe this," said Dr. Morimoto in a disgusted tone. "Petty Officer Verbeck, grab his uniform and take him to an examination room. He passed the scan. It's probably transitional sickness from Earth gravity to artificial gravity."

Throwing up helped Asher feel better, especially when the doctor said he passed the scan.

"Asher? What happened?" asked Nittany as she spotted him.

"You smell!" said Brett. "Yuck, is that puke on your face?"

Asher covered his mouth with his hand and, without saying a word, followed the corpsman to the exam room. He could feel the warm, drizzly vomit on his chin.

"You might want to close the back of your gown, cunnerman!" shouted Brett in a raucous tone.

Asher looked and saw the back of his open gown bared his doopa to everyone. *Great, first Nittany saw me adjust my boner on the shuttle, and now she saw my bare ass,* Asher thought.

Petty Officer Verbeck led Asher into the examining room. "Here you go. There's a sink if you want to clean yourself up. You can lay down on the exam table. I'll be right back. You going to be okay?"

Asher nodded. He knew the corpsman would be getting the ship's master-at-arms. He knew it.

Autumn Fletcher sat at the piano, her fingers dancing over the keys like ballerinas. She hit the wrong key and stopped. She massaged her right hand with her left. The one thing that truly made her happy, that took her away from all her problems and strife, had joined the list of disappointments. She had acquired arthritis in both hands and could no longer play the piano as well as she used to. What had once brought her joy now brought pain.

She looked around the dark hotel bar. Though people bustled in and out of the hotel's lobby, the bar remained empty. When she'd checked in earlier, she stumbled upon the piano. Autumn had a hard time passing up a chance to play. She hasn't had time to play much lately. Always on the go. Keeping an eye out for Alita Blackwood.

Autumn had never liked Alita Blackwood. She met her way back in the day when she attended an academy. Blackwood transferred at the start of their senior year. Or was it in the middle of their junior year? She couldn't remember anymore. Her memories seemed to blend in with each other the older she got. Back then, Alita Blackwood instigated hate and discontent. Being a hybrid, she did her best to cause an uprising against the normals with the few hybrids on board who managed to get past the scanning.

The last uprising she'd instigated at school caused a riot. That memory didn't blur itself into nonexistence. Autumn wished it would, though. Losing one of her closest friends had killed a part of her heart. If she'd known back then what she knew now... Nothing had changed. Alita Blackwood still terrorized normals. Autumn wished she had what it took to kill Alita Blackwood, to stop the killing. She'd known a long time ago that her heart didn't come equipped to perform the job. All she could do now was keep an eye on her and hope she didn't hurt any more people. The older she got, though, the harder it became.

Gully Jumper watched Kane sniff each tree, leaving his mark. Buffalo had a certain chill to it, different from his log cabin near the river. He didn't mind though.

Gully had never imagined that in his old age he would be tracking down Alita Blackwood. It made perfect sense that she would come to Buffalo, since Neon came here. He knew Alita Blackwood had great interest in Asher and Neon, especially Asher. He shuddered at the thought of Alita Blackwood grabbing Asher and brainwashing him into joining her cause. He understood the cause she fought for; he didn't approve of her methods. Gully knew she intended to use Asher for her own gains—taking great strides for hybrids' liberation, with great destruction for many.

A few months ago, Alita Blackwood had discovered the true power of Asher's implants. Having been one of two men who'd built Asher's hybrid chips, Gully knew the stakes. Asher himself was none the wiser.

Kane came up to his master and wagged his tail.

"Ready to go in?" They walked around to the front of the hotel. An ambulance had parked out front, medics racing into the lobby.

"What's going on?" he asked a spectator next to him.

"I heard an old lady died in the bar while playing the piano," she replied.

Gully tapped his watch. "Call Autumn." There was no answer.

Asher watched as the corpsman left. He didn't lock the door behind him. That might be a good sign. Asher went to the sink and splashed cool water onto his face. He cupped his hand and rinsed out his mouth. He cleaned up and put his uniform on.

Asher took a deep breath and sighed. He reached into his pocket and pulled out the pill and rinsed it off in the sink. He looked at it closely. Most of the outer coating had dissolved, exposing what look liked a microchip.

The pill must've given the scanner a false readout.

Asher jerked and slipped the pill back into his pocket as the door opened and Chief walked in. Asher relaxed.

"How are you feeling?" Chief asked. "I heard you got sick."

"Better, I guess."

"You passed the scan. Your 2-part vitamin worked."

Asher pulled the pill from his pocket. "I swiped this from my vomit."

Chief grabbed a latex glove and had Asher put the pill in it. He wrapped it up and held it in his hand. "I'll dispose of this."

"What if I need it again?" asked Asher.

"I have another one."

"Oh."

The corpsman came back into the room. "Sorry, Chief. I didn't know you were in here."

"It's okay. I was checking on my son. Asher, this is Petty Officer Verbeck."

"This is the son you were talking about. I should've guessed by the looks," said Petty Officer Verbeck.

"He has his mother's eyes though," said Chief. "It's a small case of transition sickness. I gave him a shot."

Asher looked at Chief. He didn't get any transition sickness shot. He didn't correct him either.

"You feeling any better?" asked hospital corpsman second class (HM2) Verbeck.

"My stomach feels much better. Now I'm getting a headache."

"I'm glad your stomach is feeling better, Cadet Smizik. You're not alone—the fifth case today. I can get you a couple of pills for your headache."

"No, thank you. I'll be fine," replied Asher.

There was a knock on the door. Chief opened it. "LTjg Meoquanee."

"Chief, I heard one of my cadets got transition sickness." She looked at Asher. "You feeling okay now? Usually after a big throw-up like that, the transition sickness goes away."

"I'm feeling better. Chief gave me a shot for it," he lied.

Verbeck squinted and gave Chief a peculiar look. "He should be okay to join the rest of his squad."

"Good. The rest of Echo 88 is ready. We are going to the mess decks for noon chow. Are you up to it? You can rest in berthing if not."

"I'm okay," Asher assured her. "I have a light headache, I'll be all right."

She smiled once more, and they headed out of medical.

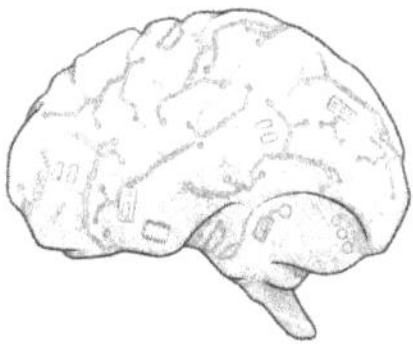

Asher looked forward to touring the ship, which LTjg Meoquanee announced during lunch. He felt more relaxed with the weight of the scan now off his shoulders. Plus, he enjoyed lunch with Nittany. She joined him on the mess deck, and their light conversation could cure anything. They entered the bridge together as another squad left. There were officers and enlisted manning various stations. Asher felt his headache returning.

"Hello, Cadets, I am Lieutenant Commander Xavier Crumb, the officer of the deck. Welcome to the bridge of the NAS *Pocono*. If engineering is the heart of the *Pocono*, the bridge is the brain." LCDR Crumb's eyes scanned Echo 88. Asher noticed that the officer paused for a quick second on him.

He had a strange sensation, as though someone had reached into his brain.

LCDR Crumb gave Echo 88 permission to explore the bridge and ask the enlisted and officers on watch about their stations.

Asher looked around. Unlike the movies and holoshows he watched, this bridge didn't have a giant viewscreen up front. It looked like a submarine bridge, only bigger.

The oval-shaped room had numerous computer stations with blinking lights around the bulkhead. He walked around and looked at the helmsman station, weapons station, environmental station, and the rest.

A large holotable sat in the center of the bridge. On each side sat a chair. The large chair that looked more comfortable than the others was where the commanding officer sat. The navigator and officer of the deck would occupy two of the remaining chairs. The last chair, for cadet training, looked the most uncomfortable.

Asher felt a stabbing pain that seemed to be emitted from the area of his brain where the chips were implanted. He winced, and it left as quickly as it came.

As Asher exited the bridge, he had an odd sensation. He turned to see LCDR Crumb staring at him, not blinking. Asher took a deep breath and exited the bridge.

Neon watched the sunrise through the window. At Willow Wood, her bedroom faced west, letting her view the sunset each night. Even if her room had been on the east side like Asher's, she wouldn't have seen the sunrise anyway. She made it a point to never get up that early.

Today she had a perfect view of the sun rising. Tuck had sneaked her into the cottage he and his dad were renting. The house had two bedrooms, the first on the ground floor and Tuck's on the second. Each bedroom had its own bathroom, which made it easy for Neon to stay hidden. Neon figured she would stay here for two or three days and then head back down to Pittsburgh to try to track down Alita Blackwood. She wanted to avoid going to the Buffalo safe house. She didn't want other people peeking into her business. She liked her freedom.

She scanned the house with her vision and stopped briefly when she found Tuck in the shower. She let out a little smile and continued to scan. His dad must already be at work. She didn't see anyone else in the house.

Tuck came out of the bathroom. He had a towel wrapped around his waist. "You're awake."

"Yeah, a loud noise from the bathroom woke me up."

Tuck laughed. "You heard that?"

"How could I not? I bet Asher heard that on the *Pocono*."

"I find great enjoyment in shower farts." He laughed. "You hungry?"

"Starved." She crawled out of the bed and stretched as Tuck fumbled to put on his boxers while still wearing his towel. "Are all you guys the same? You're as bad as Asher. I have X-ray vision, you know."

"What are you saying? You already took a peek?" Tuck smiled.

"What if I did?"

"Impressed?"

"Hardly," she replied. She disappeared into the bathroom and shut the door.

Neon came downstairs. A wonderful aroma flooded her nose as she joined Tuck in the kitchen. He stood over the stove, spatula in hand.

"How do you want your eggs?" he asked.

"You cook?" She sat down at the bar that divided the kitchen from the living room.

"Dad says everyone should know how to cook." He looked over and smiled. "Nice outfit."

Neon had changed clothes and put on a Weed Whackers T-shirt and a pair of gym shorts.

"You have the worst wardrobe ever," she said. "You do know there are livelier colors than black, brown, and gray, right?"

"Hey, I have maroon, navy blue, and khaki in my closet."

"Whatever, dude." She grabbed a piece of toast off a plate and took a bite.

"Scrambled work for you?" he asked.

"That's the way I like them," she replied, taking another bite of toast.

"I know your plan is to head back to Pittsburgh in the next day or two, you're welcome to stay longer."

"You got a crush on me?"

"We just met. Maybe in a week or two, I will."

"Yeah, okay, I wouldn't hope for anything if I were you. You're not my kind."

"What is your kind?" He dished a spatula full eggs onto a plate.

"You're a normal. I'm a hybrid. No way would it work, even if I did like you."

"I kind of resent that. I saved your life from those hybrid hunters."

"Relax, my savior," she said in a sarcastic tone.

"Why do you hate normals?" He put two plates of eggs on the counter and poured them both a glass of orange juice.

"Gee, let me think." She wrinkled her nose back and forth. "Normals want to cleanse my ass, where I will probably die."

"Not all normals think that way." He shoveled egg onto a piece of toast and took a bite. "I don't, anyway."

"Good for you. What do you want, a blow job?"

"You don't have to be such a bitch," he returned.

"Look, I appreciate your help, and these eggs are delicious. Maybe if things were different, I would give you a chance." She had gathered her composure.

They spent the rest of breakfast in awkward silence.

Cortez sat in his Jeep, smoking his panatela. He watched the parked purple-and-black car in front of a small house. Dylan opened the passenger door and hopped in.

"It's them, all right," she reported.

"How many?" Cortez asked, not taking his eyes off the house.

"Only the girl and the boy that picked her up at the airport. Are we going to take them tonight?"

"No. If she's on the move, she might not be here tonight. We go in now. Remind the crew that we need her alive."

"And the boy?"

"I'm sure he can fill organ orders we have."

"I'll let them know." She hopped back out.

"I don't know who you are, but soon I will and you'll be mine." His eyes stayed fixed on the house.

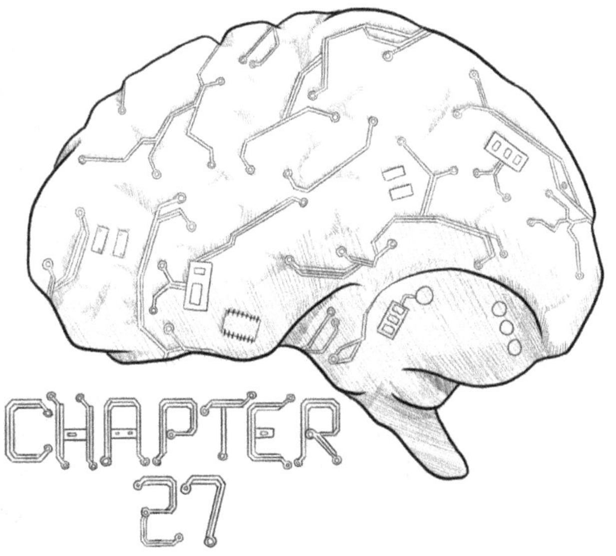


Asher woke up earlier than anticipated, an hour before reveille. He grabbed his shower kit and towel and walked into the head. Nittany stood in front of the sinks. She leaned into the mirror and squeezed a pimple on her forehead. She jumped and turned.

"Uh, Asher. Good morning." She brushed her bangs down over her forehead as her entire face grew red.

Asher immediately put his towel and shower kit in front of him.

"Um, hi," he said. He hadn't expected to see her up.

"You're an early riser too?" asked Nittany.

"Not usually," he replied.

"My body is used to getting up early to do farm chores. I figured I would grab a shower before anyone else."

"Yeah, me too," said Asher.

Each of them stepped into their own shower stall. Asher felt odd taking a shower when the girl he liked took a shower in the stall next to his. He felt a little guilty wishing he had Neon's x-ray vision. He hurried to finish before she did and decided to go explore the ship.

Asher wandered several decks and passageways until he found a small space that had a porthole. He peered out and watched as Earth became smaller and smaller—the NAS *Pocono* left Earth's orbit to begin workups, a time for both the cadets and crew to prepare for longer excursions.

As Asher watched Earth, he had an overwhelming sense to say a final goodbye to his mom and Timothy. His heart hurt. He secretly hoped the ghosts of his family, which haunted him in his dreams, would be left behind.

The bells and whistles sounded at reveille. Asher needed to get back to berthing. He took one more look as the *Pocono* initiated the interstellar drives. As the I-drives powered up, he wished he could stick around to see what see what it would look like to travel at such speeds. Asher's commitment and excitement for his classes overpowered his desire to stay and watch. Besides, he was curious to see what classes were like out in the world. He's only been homeschooled up to now.

Asher placed his hand on the glass of the porthole. "I love you, Mom. You too, Timothy." He headed back to berthing.

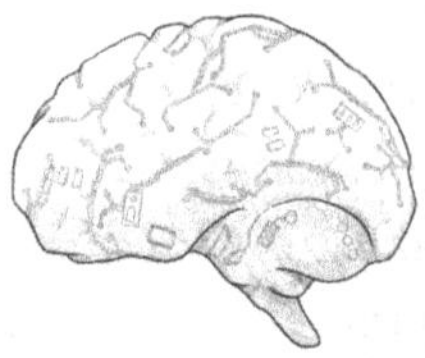

Asher had no problem staying focused in math. He loved math and found it easy—he always wondered how much impact his brain implants had on his ability to learn.

Three squads were combined for each academic class—Echo 88, Oscar 88, and Lima 88 took math class together.

"To start things off this semester, Oscar 88, each of you step up to the equation wall. You all will have the same equation to work on. Let's see who gets theirs done correctly first and how much you retained from your 10th level classes down on Earth," said Professor Chip Middleswarth. The short and stocky man who spoke firmly and loudly stood with a wooden pointer in hand. The lights in the classroom glared off his sweat-covered bald head.

The six cadets from Oscar 88 took a writing tool and turned to the equation as it appeared in front of them on the bulkhead. They immediately began work.

A short, stout boy finished first. He circled his answer and tapped the complete icon. A big red X appeared over his work. He let out a disgusted growl and hit the reset button. His area of the wall cleared, leaving the original problem behind.

A girl finished next. She tapped the complete icon, and a green star appeared over her work. She had the correct answer.

Each member of Oscar 88 eventually finished the problem. Three of them had to go back and redo it, until they figured out the correct answer.

"Echo 88, please take the wall," said Professor Middleswarth.

Echo 88 stood ready. The bulkhead revealed a new equation. All the cadets began at the same time. As his classmates worked through the math, Asher wrote one line and tapped the complete icon. A green star appeared. Gasps echoed through the classroom.

"Very good, Cadet Smizik. Where is your work? You're missing your work."

"Pardon, sir?"

"You must show your work on how you had arrived at the answer. Next time, let's see your work."

"Yes, sir."

Asher sat down as he watched the rest of his team work out the problem. Xiao finished second. Cray and Nittany had to redo theirs. Everyone finished, except for Brett. His nostrils flared, the veins in his neck bulged, and his taps on the reset button turned into full-on punches.

"Cadet Smizik. Please help your fellow cadet. Remember, show your work." Professor Middleswarth shook his head as he watched Brett struggle.

Of all the cadets to help out, it had to be Brett. Keeping his calm, Asher explained how to solve the equation. Brett didn't seem to pay any attention. He worked through the problem on his own, again coming up with the wrong answer.

"Cadet Lundy, are you even listening to Cadet Smizik?" grunted Professor Middleswarth.

"I can do this on my own," Brett insisted.

"Enough. Both of you sit down." Professor Middleswarth's stern look made Asher feel like he'd done something wrong. He slumped to his desk.

Asher watched the others write out their work. He didn't know why he had to do that if he knew how to solve the problem without it. Eventually Echo 88 took another turn at the bulkhead. The equation appeared, and Asher knew the answer in an instant. This time, instead of writing the answer, he wrote out all the work before tapping the complete icon. A green star appeared. Brett struggled again.

The boatswain mate's whistle sounded over the intercom system, signaling the cadets to move on to their next class.

"I assigned homework for tonight. You can access it on the computer in your academy account under assignments."

The cadets shuffled out of the room.

Neon stepped outside. After breakfast, she felt tempted to head back to Pittsburgh today. Ahead of her on the street were two men coming toward her. She did a quick scan and saw weapons hidden under their jackets.

"Oh shit!" She scrambled into the house and shut the door. She found Tuck in the kitchen, cleaning up. She grabbed his wrist. "We have to go, like, now."

"Why?"

"Hybrid hunters tracked us here." The two of them fled out the back door. "Which way?"

"This way." Tuck headed toward the back of the small yard. They climbed over a short chain-link fence.

"Where are we going?" asked Neon.

While running, Tuck tapped his watch. "Report to the corner of Chandler and Bridgeman. My car will meet us. This way."

They turned down a side street and, out of breath, jumped into Tuck's car. He peeled out. "Did we lose them?"

Neon scanned the area. "I think we did. They're not within my range."

"Where to?"

"Any place where those drones can't follow us." Neon bit her lower lip as she watched five drones buzz their way.

"Ursula might not have her lightning anymore, but she still has her thunder. Hang on." Tuck stepped on the gas and made a hard right. Neon thought for sure he had Ursula up on two wheels.

"If the drones don't kill me, your driving will," said Neon.

"Relax, I haven't had an accident yet." Tuck pushed hard on the pedal and shifted Ursula into her highest gear.

"Yet being the key word there?" Neon closed her eyes. If she believed in any kind of god, now would be the time she would pray to it. At least ten more drones joined the chase.

"The drones spotted them and now are in pursuit," said Dylan. She watched the pad that showed the pair's location. "Good thing you had us put a drone tracker on the car before reporting back to you."

"This isn't my first rodeo," said Cortez. He took a long inhale of his panatela and blew it out slowly.

Gully sat next to Autumn's bed. She rustled, and he sat forward. "You're awake."

"Where am I?" she asked in a weak voice.

"We're at the hospital. You had a minor heart attack. Doctor said you're going to be okay, though."

"Alita Blackwood? Neon?"

"I don't know. The only thing I care about right now is you."

"The others?"

"They all know. Thane thinks you're putting on an act to get more attention."

She let out a weak smile.

"You rest. I'm going to get something to eat."

She closed her eyes.

On his way to the cafeteria, Gully got turned around and ended up in the emergency room. Gully watched as paramedics brought in a boy on a stretcher.

"What happened?" a doctor asked as he hustled to the stretcher.

"Car accident."

"Do you have a name? Stay with me, son." The doctor looked into the boy's eyes.

"Was anyone with him?" asked a nurse.

The medic replied, "Witnesses said they saw a girl with blue-and-green hair climb out and run off. That's it."

"OR, stat," said the doctor.

After evening chow, Echo 88 headed to their common area to study. Asher whizzed through his homework. He didn't want to make it too obvious that he'd finished ahead of the others, so he took the opportunity and started reading a new book from the ship's online library.

Brett let out growls of frustration.

"Brett, why don't you let Asher help you?" asked Nittany.

"How many times do I have to tell you cunnermans that I don't need anyone's help?"

"It's really easy. I can help you," said Asher. He didn't really want to help Brett, he did want to impress Nittany, since she'd offered his help. If any of the other cadets had suggested it, he probably wouldn't have volunteered. He would've made up a lame excuse not to help Brett.

"No," said Brett.

"Everyone has their weak points," Cray said. "Mine is grammar mechanics. Math is yours. Maybe Asher can make it easy for you."

Brett clenched his teeth. His nostrils were flaring, and the veins in his neck bulged. He picked up his gear, stomped off into berthing, and slammed the door.

"What a moron!" said Cray.

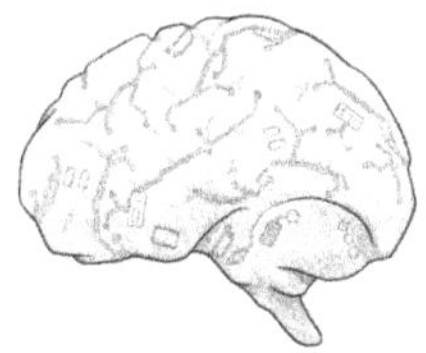

Asher had been with his squad all day long and needed time alone. He sought solitude in the head. A warm shower would give him time to think and reflect on the day's events—and a moment to remember his mom, Timothy, and Neon. Fortunately, his surroundings had no connections...no memories of them. This made it easier to forget them, to forget the pain, to forget the mistakes he'd made the night of the Willow Wood raid.

He stepped under the warm spray and let the water wash over him. Since he'd been on the *Pocono*, there had been no signs of Navarro or Cortez. Did this mean he could stop running? It almost felt too safe to be true. Maybe the *Pocono* would replace Willow Wood as his safe haven.

As he headed into berthing, a sudden pain slammed through his head. He flew up against the lockers and found it hard to breathe or swallow. He opened his eyes and saw Brett pushing him up against the lockers with his lean forearm on Asher's throat.

"Consider this your only warning, cunnerman! You don't mess with me. You don't offer me help. You don't talk to me. You do nothing. You make me look stupid in front of the others again, I will kill you. Do you understand?"

Asher used his own stubbornness to will back any tears. He refused to let Brett, or anyone else for that matter, see him cry. He nodded.

"Good, we have an understanding." Brett threw Asher onto the floor.

"Hey, what's happening?" Cray asked as he entered berthing.

"Nothing. I was giving Weathervane advice on his homework." Brett pushed his way past Cray.

"Asher, you okay?"

"Leave me alone." Asher wanted to appear strong. He pulled himself up and made his way to his rack to be alone.

"Did you want me to get Meoquanee?"

"I said I'm okay. Now leave me alone," Asher snapped.

"If you say so." Cray turned and left Asher to himself.

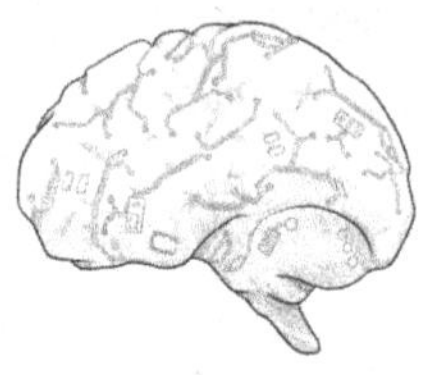

Asher stood in front of the door to medical. During his sad times, he could always depend on his mom, Neon, and Timothy to cheer him up. They weren't here. Maybe Chief could help.

Asher stepped inside sickbay. He didn't know where Chief hung out after working hours.

"Can I help you? Sick call is over with, unless it's an emergency."

Asher recognized HM2 Verbeck, the corpsman who'd examined him the day of in-processing. Asher rubbed his head. He felt a small headache coming on. Tension, he thought.

"I'm looking for Chief Mrkonic. I want to ask him a question."

"I remember you. He's in his office. Go down the corridor and into the infirmary. His office is on the right. You can't miss it, listen for the uncontrollable shouting." He paused. "Actually, follow me, I'll show you. I need to talk to him anyway."

"Thank you." Asher wondered what the corpsman meant about the shouting. They entered the infirmary.

"Way to go, Brockhouse, my grandmother could pitch better than that and she's dead." An orotund voice came from the office, obviously not happy. Asher remembered that same voice when the Pirates had given up nine runs in the first two innings of the game he'd seen with Chief.

Petty Officer Verbeck tapped on the door.

"It's open," bellowed Chief.

Verbeck opened the door. Chief was watching a holoimage on his desk that appeared to be the Pirates game.

"Chief, Cadet Smizik wanted to see you."

"Asher, come in."

"Chief, I'll see you tomorrow. I'm headed out."

"See you tomorrow, Verbeck."

Asher stood there, not sure what to say or do. If they were back in Pittsburgh, Asher may feel more comfortable. He didn't know how to act around Chief onboard the *Pocono*.

"Have a seat. You okay?"

Asher sheepishly sat down. "Chief. I, uh...uh..." His voice was wobbly; his tongue couldn't form any words.

"NO!" Chief screamed as the Pirates gave up a second homerun in the bottom of the first inning.

"What's wrong, Chief?"

"Brockhouse. Why would they use this bum when they're neck-and-neck in a pennant race?"

"Who is Brockhouse? He didn't play when we saw them."

"An awful trade. He was on the team for one day and ended up on the disabled list. Then he spent a couple of weeks in the minors on rehab. This is his first game back, and they should send him back to the showers. The Pirates are in a race to win their division. It's tight. We still have a month left in the season. A lot can happen during that time."

"Why did the Pirates trade for him if he's bad?"

"That's what I've been asking myself since the day they traded for him. What's up?"

Asher shrugged. He had trouble putting his thoughts into words.

"Let me guess. You needed a break from your homework, and coming here to watch the Pirates game with me was your perfect excuse."

Asher let out a muffled laugh. "Yeah," he agreed. It sounded like as good an excuse as any.

It didn't take long for Chief Mrkonic's passion to spread to Asher, and before long, Asher found himself getting into the game with Chief.

Chief asked, "How you feeling now?"

"Better. I guess I was a little homesick. Stupid, huh?"

"Not at all, Asher. When I first joined EFA after high school, I was homesick every day. I really missed your mom."

"Does the missing her feeling ever stop?"

"It hasn't for me."

This surprised Asher. Chief still missed his mom.

"Look what time it is. It's after Taps. I'll take you to your berthing. We don't want you to get dinged on bed call."

"Chief, can I come up here again and watch more baseball games with you?"

Chief smiled. "I would enjoy that. When baseball season is over, we can watch the Steelers, Penguins, and Anvils too if you'd like."

Asher smiled. "I think I would like that."

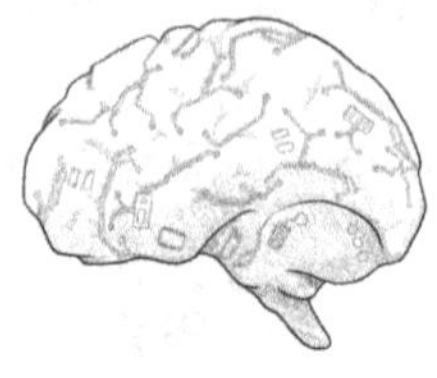

Asher entered Echo 88's common area to find Nittany sitting on the couch, reading.

"Asher." She stood and went right to him. "You okay?"

"I think I'm a little homesick is all."

"Cray said something happened between you and Brett."

"I'm okay. Like I said, I'm a little homesick."

Nittany wrapped her arms around Asher and gave him a hug. He'd known her less than forty-eight hours and she gave him a hug—Asher couldn't wrap his head around it. He didn't mind Nittany being the touchy-feely type. He had a feeling course through his body as her embrace held him for a couple of seconds. He never felt anything like this before. Then she let go.

"Maybe that will help you with homesickness," she said.

"Thanks." Asher felt weak in the legs. Not sure what else to do or say, he went into the head to get ready for bed. Cray stood in front of the sinks, brushing his teeth.

"You know she likes you, right?"

"Huh?" he replied.

"Nittany. She likes you. One of the hottest girls on the ship likes you."

Asher looked at Cray, confused. "Have you..."

"Have I what?"

"Have you liked someone before? I mean really liked them?" asked Asher.

"You got a whiff of Venus's common myrtle, didn't you? Haven't you ever had a girlfriend before?" asked Cray.

"No. Do you have a girlfriend?"

"Nah, my boyfriend and I broke up a few months ago. I'm taking a break from dating." Cray showed his big toothy grin. "Man, you got it bad. I can tell. You better buckle up and fasten your seatbelt. You're in for a ride."

# CHAPTER 29

After ten days on board, Asher became more comfortable with the situations presented to him. He tried reaching out to Pandora a couple of times to let her know his status. She never answered his video calls anymore. He wondered if she'd gotten mad at him for not meeting up with her and her father.

The *Pocono* took a long and roundabout way to the Tekulve-Lockley wormhole. They could've been there in a day. Chief had told Asher that due to ship operations and getting cadets and crew qualified to enter the wormhole, they would zigzag, practicing and preparing for the trip through.

Echo 88 had science class in the dome instead of the classroom for a change of scenery. The dome had gym equipment and a pool. Cadets met there three times a week before breakfast for physical training.

"Come on in," said Mr. Irwin LaTrobe. He stood with bare feet on the observation deck. Dean Wu kept her civilian instructors under tight restrictions. She believed that teachers were to look professional while in class. Mr. LaTrobe, in his mid-twenties, managed to keep off of Dean Wu's minimum dress code radar.

He wore a pair of board shorts with bright colors swirling into a surf scene. A florescent-yellow muscle shirt complemented the shorts. His dirty-blonde ponytail hung to the middle of his shoulder blades. His arms and legs had surf-themed tattoos. Around his tanned neck, he wore a men's shell necklace with a shark tooth pendent that matched the anklet on his right ankle. Each ear had a black huggie hoop earring attached to it. A thick, trimmed goatee, light stubble on the jawline, and a mustache decorated his face.

"Today the *Pocono* gets to surf through the Tekulve-Lockley wormhole. It is named after the two scientists who discovered it, Dr. Phillip Tekulve and Dr. Janet Lockley." Mr. LaTrobe stomped his bare foot a couple of times. His Nebraskan accent did not match his looks.

"Why does he keep stomping his foot?" asked Brett.

"If you would've paid attention on the first day of class, he strongly hinted that's his way of telling us the information is going to be on a test," replied Xiao.

"That's lame," Brett scoffed.

Mr. LaTrobe typed a code into a keypad on the bulkhead. The room vibrated as the metal ceiling and bulkheads divided, unveiling a glass dome. Beyond it, stars painted a dreamscape.

"If you look toward your twelve o'clock position, you will see the wormhole entrance."

"Hey, look, I can see the other academy ships," Cray claimed.

Asher kept silent. The stars pulled him in. Timothy would have loved seeing the stars this way, completely among them. Neon would want to go wormhole surfing. He could see his mom standing here, amazed. He pushed his memories away and focused on the wormhole.

"Who can tell me what a wormhole is?"

Xiao shot up her hand. Before being called on, she spoke. "A wormhole is a tunnel in the geometry of space-time postulated to connect different parts of the universe."

"One cool bean to Cadet Li. It is a passageway to other solar systems that takes years off of travel time." He stomped his foot. "Lucky for us, the Tekulve-Lockley wormhole is stable. There are unstable wormholes out there, like the Festerine wormhole in the Odessa sector that is only available for travel every thirteen years. It stays open for less than a week. There are also whipping wormholes, where the mouth and/or tail of the wormhole whips around, causing you to have no idea where it will appear or let you out … if it lets you out."

"Is that what happened to the Lost Fleet?" asked a cadet from Oscar 88.

"We don't know why the Crusader Fleet, commonly referred to as the Lost Fleet, disappeared sixty years ago. There are theories that it entered a whipping wormhole or a wormhole that only opens once every so many years."

"Can wormholes take you into the future?" asked the same boy.

"In theory, a wormhole can cause time travel, it's only in theory though. A time travel wormhole has not been discovered to date."

The *Pocono* vibrated as it gained speed and moved toward the mouth of the wormhole. Everyone looked up through the glass observation dome with anticipation. Mr. LaTrobe continued his lesson about wormholes as they traveled through the brilliant blue and green streams. When they exited the wormhole, Mr. LaTrobe dismissed the class.

Asher's watch vibrated. He'd received a text from Dean Wu.

*Cadet Smizik, come to my office before heading to your next class.*

Asher gulped and headed down the hall, wondering what he'd done to earn a trip to the dean's office. He tried not to entertain the thoughts buzzing in his head.

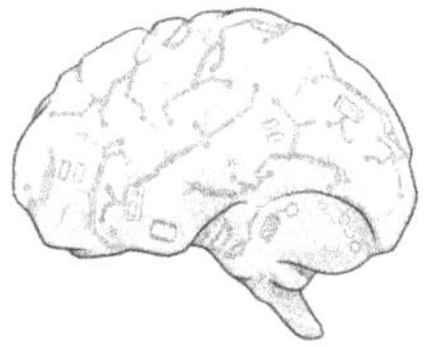

Asher stood in front of Dean Wu's desk. His stomach tight with knots, he tried not to look at her. He'd only dealt with her twice, for his interview and again on his third day on the ship for indoctrination. Both times she came across as an intimidating, no-nonsense person.

"Cadet Smizik, do you know why I summoned you?" She placed her hands on her desk, with the right hand on top.

"No, ma'am." Asher noticed the scar on her hand again. Why would she choose not to keep it?

"It has been brought to my attention that you have special abilities. Do you know what those abilities are?"

"No, ma'am." Asher stumbled over his words. Had the dean realized his secret?

"I checked all your grades. You have a perfect grade point average. All of your tests and assignments were errorless."

Asher started to tremble. His schoolwork came easy to him, thanks to his implants.

"Cadet, I am going to ask you this once, and I expect the truth. Are you cheating?"

The question caught him off guard. "No, ma'am." He spoke the truth.

"In the fifty years I've been teaching, I've never told a student what I am about to tell you. You need to tone it down."

"Pardon, ma'am?"

"The last time I saw a cadet do this well, they ended up being a hybrid with brain implants. We know what happens to hybrids."

Asher's heart grew tight in his chest. Could this be the end of his academy days?

"Your medical scans came back normal, that rules out any chance of you having these same implants. I don't have to have you cleansed and sent to an internment village. However, if you continue to receive perfect grades on all of your exams and assignments, which will raise suspicion, many will accuse you of cheating. Cheating is a serious matter. I have zero tolerance for it."

"Yes, ma'am," said Asher.

"To prevent any more attention to the matter, I suggest you get an answer or two wrong in math or misspell a word on your paper. Understand."

"You want me to make mistakes on purpose?" This baffled him.

Dean Wu stood, walked around her desk, and looked the boy in his eyes. "Asher, by observation, you are a quiet, shy individual who doesn't like attention. Correct?"

"Yes, ma'am." He looked down at the floor.

"What I am trying to say is if you continue to do this well in all of your classes, you will draw unwanted attention to yourself. Understand?"

"I think so."

"Please understand it's nothing against you. I'm looking out for your best interest."

"Yes, ma'am,"

"Any questions for me?"

"No, ma'am."

"You're dismissed."

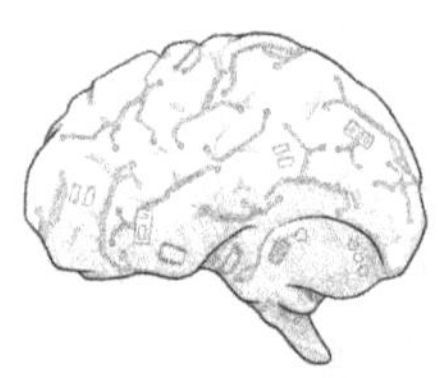

Asher sat in his math class thinking about what Dean Wu had told him earlier. Did she suspect he was a hybrid? If so, why didn't she send him to medical to be rescanned? If she thought he was a hybrid and didn't tell anyone, did that mean she was an ally?

"Cadet Smizik!" boomed Professor Middleswarth.

Asher shook his head to bring his attention back to class. "Yes, sir."

"Please join Cadet Li up at the equation bulkhead. We will see who gets the correct answer first." Xiao stood up front, waiting. When they did these races, Xiao always came in second, with Asher being first. They were the two best students in their class. Professor Middleswarth called the two top scoring cadets from the other two squads. They joined Xiao and Asher.

"I chose the two cadets from each squad who scored the highest on yesterday's exam. You will race to get the problem done. The first squad to get the correct answer gets a free night of no math homework."

"We got this," said Cray confidently.

"Today it's the top two from each squad, next time it might be the third and sixth best or the top and bottom two. I will change it up."

Asher thought about his conversation with Dean Wu. He wanted to win the free night of no math homework for his squad. He didn't want unwanted attention either. He started to work on his problem, taking an unusual amount of time.

"Why is Asher taking this long?" asked Cray. "He never takes this long."

Xiao did her work and pushed the complete icon. A green star appeared. "Yes, I finally beat Asher. I can't believe it." Xiao's normally expressionless face showed a slight smile of satisfaction.

"No way!" said Cray.

"Come on, Asher!" cheered Nittany.

A boy from Oscar 88 finished with the correct answer, then a girl from Lima 88. The other cadet from Lima 88 tapped on the button and red X appeared and she had to start over. It became a tight race. Asher, the cadet from Lima 88, and a cadet from Oscar 88 were neck-and-neck. All three quickly pushed the complete icon. Asher saw the red X appear over his work for the first time.

"NO WAY!" Cray gasped.

Embarrassed, Asher turned and saw the shock on his classmates' faces. Even Professor Middleswarth had a look of surprise painted on his face. Lima 88 started cheering as a green star appeared over their teammate's work. The Oscar cadet earned his green star right after.

"It appears Lima 88 has no homework tonight."

Asher returned to his desk. He felt bad. He knew he could have finished first. He kept hearing Xiao making snobbish comments about beating him.

"Loser! You're such a cunnerman," Brett said to Asher.

Asher tried to ignore him. He didn't know what he hated more, willingly getting a question wrong or letting his squad down.

After class, the cadets went into the hall.

"Yo, Asher, what happened? You always finish first and never get any wrong," said Cray.

"I don't know. That problem was hard, I guess."

"You guess?"

"It goes to show that Asher isn't as smart as he appears," said Xiao.

Asher held back as the rest of his squad continued to their next class. He didn't think it would be this hard acting like a normal in the real world?

"It's okay, Asher. You'll do it next time." Nittany stood on her tiptoes and gave Asher a quick kiss on the cheek. "That's to make you feel batter."

# Chapter 30

Cortez watched Navarro from a distance. JD rooted through the dirt as Navarro watched. Every time Cortez looked at the pig, he saw it with an apple in its mouth, steaming over a hot smoker. He hated that pig. He hated Navarro even more. He stuck with her for her resources, which he didn't have access to. Thanks to Dr. Monroe, Cortez didn't have to rely on Navarro's resources much longer. He had started to get his own now.

"Any word?" asked Navarro, returning from the play area.

"The crew in Bangor found three hybrids, which led them to five more in Stroudsburg. They are deconstructing them as we speak."

"What about the girl?"

"Nothing since we lost her after the raid on Rodriguez's house." Cortez refrained from telling Navarro the whole truth.

"If they didn't have that vehicle accident, you could've tracked them down again." Navarro's eyes gazed toward the sky. "Too bad the boy didn't live. She might have come back to him, and then you could've nailed her."

"We'll find her," said Cortez.

"You'd better. Until the boy steps foot on ground, he is useless. We need to find that girl. I am almost certain she will bring out Alita Blackwood."

"I'll keep you posted." Cortez lit up a panatela. He watched Navarro disappear into the mobile ops center.

"Does she suspect anything?" asked Dylan as she came up to Cortez.

"No. Any word from them?"

"They staked out the hospital in the beginning. Now that he's been released, we have all our bases covered both at his house and school," she replied.

"We have to be patient. She'll return to him to make sure he's okay."

"How can you be sure?"

"He rescued her twice. She'll come."

"We have the area bugged, if she makes contact, we'll know about it."

"Good." Cortez exhaled more smoke.

Neon had experience living on the streets. She'd received her hybrid implants at the age of five. About a year later, hybrid police arrested her parents and took her brother to be cleansed. She never found out why the hybrid police left her behind. The question bothered her every day. She remembered the surgeries that turned her into a hybrid. She saw fine beforehand, even better afterward. Her vision became much more powerful.

She remembered her brother walking around, playing with her. Then he went away for a couple of months. When he returned, he could run super-fast and jump much higher than before. Her mom told her that he went and saw the hybrid fairy. Neon had looked forward to the time she would get to see the hybrid fairy.

Later, she figured out that she and her brother were the kind of hybrids that normals hated. They had no ailments. No disabilities. They were given hybrid implants to be better than most. Her parents must've had money. She didn't know who performed the surgery or where her parents got the implants from. She wished she knew more about her family and how everything had come to be.

The last few days blurred together, causing her to lose track of what day it was. She couldn't remember how long ago the accident had happened. She forced her weary eyes open. Her stomach growled, reminding her that she hadn't eaten much the last few days. Her shoulder ached. She had dislocated her arm in the car accident. She managed to get it reset by a doctor before running off. She saw him talking to a nurse, who immediately got on a holocomm.

*Living at Willow Wood for five years made me weak*, she told herself. Her head pounded, causing her to lose her sense of direction. She had to get to Pittsburgh to find the old lady who spied on her. Things went black.

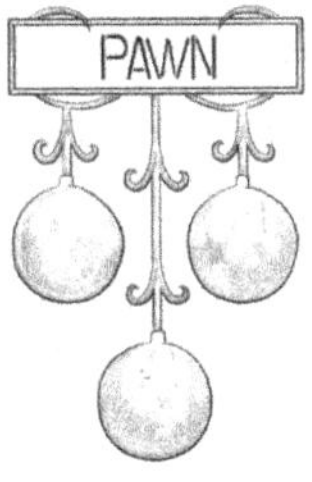

The door chimed, followed by a bark. Mick came out from the back room of his pawnshop. An elderly woman with red hair from a bottle stood holding the door open as an umber man with a white goatee and white rim around his head carried a girl in his arms.

"Is that...?"

"She needs medical help," said the woman.

"You go back to the car and rest. You don't need to have another heart attack on me," said the man.

"I'm fine," she said.

Mick looked at the girl. "Neon," he said. "I have a couch in the back office."

Mick tapped his watch.

"What are you doing?" asked the old woman.

"I'm no doctor, and your friend in there says she needs medical help."

"You can't call for help. She's...special."

"I know that," said Mick. "That's why I'm calling one of my sources who handles special patients."

"She's burning up," said the man as the woman entered the back room.

After the call, Mick locked up his shop and flicked on the "closed" sign.

"What happened to her?" asked Mick.

"She was in a car accident a couple of weeks ago and never got medical attention," said the old man. "At least, that's what she told us before passing out."

"Help is on the way. How did you know to bring her here?"

"One of your sources told us to come here," said the old man.

"I see. Speaking of sources, you two better go. The person coming here to help doesn't like an audience, if you know what I mean."

"Understood. We'll be on our way," said the old woman.

Mick unlocked the door and let them out. He watched the old couple get into a car and drive off.

Walking across the street was the detective he'd met at the Pirates game with Liam, Asher, and Neon. "Shit," said Mick. "How did they find out this soon?" The detective walked toward the pawnshop. "You got this, Mick. Play it cool."

"Mr. Mrkonic." Mac waved to him.

Mick wished he had drawn the curtain. He unlocked the door and opened it. "Mac, right?"

"Yes, do you have a few minutes?"

"Not really." Mick shifted his weight and crossed his arms.

"I'll be quick." Mac entered the shop, not waiting for an invitation. "Is all this stuff in here legal?" Mac waited a second and added, "Never mind, I don't want to know."

"Detective, if this is about the stuff I sell, I have legitimate records to account for everything."

"I'm not here for that. I tried contacting your brother. I found out he's on the *Pocono* and was out of range."

"Is something wrong?" asked Mick.

*Thump...crash* came from the back office.

"Who's back there?"

"No one, sir."

"That sounded like a bad crash," said Mac. He walked to the counter.

"Detective, what did you want to see me about?"

Rufus came walking out of the back room.

"Must've been your dog making all the racket."

Mick let out a small sigh of relief when the detective turned and faced him again. "We are done with Vicki Smizik's body. We had her cremated. Since she doesn't have any living relatives, I thought maybe he would want them. If not, we will send them where we send all the other unclaimed remains."

"I'm sure he would. Since he won't be back for a few days, can I get them?"

"No, it has to be your brother. Can you let him know for me?"

"Yes, I will, thank you." Mick escorted the detective out. He locked the door and pulled the curtain down. He sighed in relief and dashed to the back room.

"You okay..." He stopped and looked around the empty room. The back door was ajar letting a cool autumn breeze inside the shop. "Damn, where did she go?"

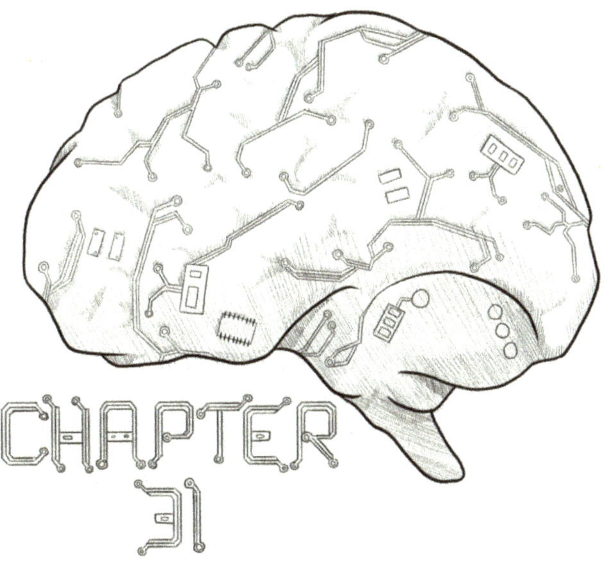

# CHAPTER 31

Asher looked out of his secret porthole. Earth and all the space stations orbiting looked no different than when they'd left over a month ago. He didn't know what to think about returning to Earth. The last month on board the *Pocono*, he'd felt healed from the death of his mom and Timothy. Asher didn't like grieving. He had never experienced it at this level before. Keeping busy with schoolwork and getting to know Nittany better kept his mind off his past.

Asher leaned up against the window to get a better look at the North American Cosmic Hub. The massive, upside-down, teardrop-shaped space station orbited Earth. The bottom quarter of the hub housed all the engines and systems that kept the station running. The second quarter consisted of the operations center. This was where the air traffic controller worked, as well as other operations personnel. The remaining portion housed restaurants, hotel rooms, a movie theater, lounges, a casino, and other entertainment that kept waiting passengers occupied, while spending their money.

It looked like a giant donut cut into thirds and placed it around the business section of the teardrop. Glass tunnels connected the donut pieces to the teardrop. The donut pieces were called the military wing, the civilian wing, and the recreational wing.

EFA ships and shuttles temporarily moored in the military wing, waiting to get underway. Shuttles ran between the hub and various EFA staging points in North America. Within the next few hours, the *Pocono* would be moored there. Civilian ships and shuttles frequently came in and out of the civilian wing. Civilian shuttles ran between the hub and various cities in North America.

The sports arcade wing had eight transparent domes. The domes housed football, soccer, softball, and baseball fields, plus a track-and-field complex and an empty field for miscellaneous events.

Inside the arcade, there were basketball courts, pools, ice skating rinks, laser tag arenas, mazes, and video games, among other things. Both EFA Junior Academy and Senior Academy utilized the facilities for intramural sports and team training.

LT Mabus had informed them that eleventh-level cadets only participated in escape rooms for the first semester. They were popular on Earth. Asher had never done an escape room before. He didn't know what to expect from it. If it was like anything trying to escape hybrid hunters, these rooms were going to be very difficult.

"What're you doing?" asked Nittany, walking up behind him.

"Nothing," he replied. Asher smiled and perked up when he saw Nittany. He wondered how she'd found him. He didn't tell anyone about this spot.

"Do you have any plans tomorrow?" she asked, rather shyly.

"Chief is taking me out for dinner, nothing besides that." Asher's chest tightened. Did she want to spend time with him?

"Since it's a holiday and there are no classes tomorrow, would you like to explore the hub together?"

"Uh, sure," he stumbled. He hoped that spending time with

Nittany on his birthday would help him forget that this would be his first birthday without his mom and Timothy.

Nittany smiled and stood up on the balls of her feet for a quick second.

"Is this us going out as friends or a date?" Why was it Asher's tongue never stopped the words that shouldn't come out of his mouth?

Now Nittany looked nervous. She grabbed onto her cross necklace and massaged it with her thumb. She bit down on her lower lip. "Which one do you want it to be?"

*Great*, Asher thought. She'd thrown the question that shouldn't have come out of his mouth in the first place right back at him. What would happen if he said date and she only wanted friends, or he picked friends and she hoped for a date? This girl stuff confused him. If only he could read her mind.

"Nittany, I think there's something you should know about me. You can't tell anyone."

There he went again. Speaking words he shouldn't have. Now what was he going to do?

"I won't tell anybody," replied Nittany.

*Think, Asher, think. You can't tell her you're a hybrid.* "Um, I've never been on a date before." *Nice save*, he thought. Then he had second thoughts.

"I would be honored to be your first date," she replied. She shot him a smile that made her even more beautiful.

"Really?" Asher sat up straight in shock.

"I like you...a lot." She looked toward the deck and turned red.

"Me too."

She scooted next to him and gently snuggled her shoulder into his side. He had no place to put his arm except wrapping it around her.

"Can I tell you something personal?" she whispered.

"Okay," he replied.

"There are five kinds of love languages. Mine is touch. That's why I tend to grab your arm in the passageways, touch you, hug you and all."

"I've read about the love languages."

"Which one do you have?" asked Nittany.

"Quality time," he replied.

"Like what we're having now." She snuggled in a little closer.

"Yeah." Asher hadn't felt this happy since before the raid. He gave her a little squeeze. Then a new thought popped into his head. *Did we just tell each other I love you?*

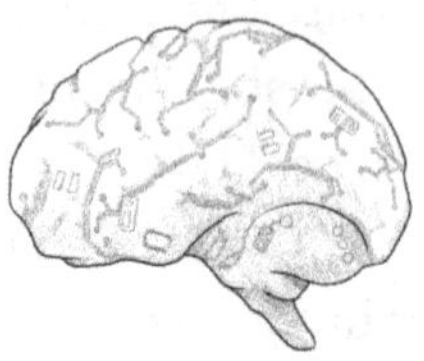

Asher lay in his rack. Unlike normal weekdays, berthing stood still, dark, and quiet. The 1MC speaker system kept silent, not releasing any bells or whistles that would echo throughout the ship. Asher enjoyed sleeping in, especially since he'd stayed up until 2:03 a.m. texting Nittany. Like their conversations, her texts were long, and his were of few words.

October 13th, a Wednesday, marked North America Unification Day. The last country in North America, Cuba, had signed the Unification Constitution declaring them a state in the country of North America ninety-seven years ago. The United States of America and Canada were the first two countries to sign. Then came Mexico, and once they signed, most other North American countries soon followed. Except for Cuba. It took bartering and negotiations, eventually they signed.

North America became the first continent to turn into one single country, not counting Australia, who had been their own country for centuries. Within the next fifty years, other countries united in similar fashion. Resources, economy, famine, and wars motivated the merges. Earth had ten countries in all: North America, South America, Australia, Eastern Europe, Western Europe, Eastern Asia, Western Asia, North Africa, South Africa, and Antarctica.

Asher shared his birthday with Unification Day. This would be his first birthday without his mom, the first one without Timothy in eleven years, and his first with his dad. He imagined what his mom and Timothy would do if they were here and heard about Asher's first date. He could see his mom getting all excited, taking pictures and shedding a mother's tear without anyone noticing. He laughed to himself when he pictured Timothy coming out of nowhere and shooting him and Nittany with his super soaker. This time he would probably have tomato juice in it. Nittany, of course, would be invited to his birthday dinner to celebrate him turning seventeen. He could see her getting along with everyone at Willow Wood...well, almost everyone. Neon wouldn't like Nittany because she wasn't a hybrid.

Every morning on his birthday, he would wake up on his own, which meant he would have breakfast for lunch. Every year he would have root beer pancakes and home-fried potatoes. For dinner his mom made him stir-fried veggies in root beer sauce, homemade perogies sautéed in garlic butter, and root beer float birthday cupcakes. At least he got to spend his last birthday with his mom. Seventeen was not a milestone birthday like thirteen and sixteen were. Even with that thought, he still hurt inside.

"Good morning, Asher! Are you awake?" Nittany tapped on Asher's privacy panel.

He pulled it open and poked out his head. A warm smiled greeted him.

"I thought I would go get breakfast at Galaxy Joe's on the station. You want to join me?"

"Sure." Asher had mixed feelings—he was excited to be with Nittany that conflicted with the heaviness of his heart for the loss of his mom and Timothy.

He crawled out of his rack. When the day lights were turned off, berthing was illuminated by red light. It kept berthing dark enough to sleep in, yet if a cadet had to get up in the middle of the night, they could still see.

Asher noticed that Cray's, Tabitha's, and Xiao's racks were empty. He'd never heard them get up and leave. Asher could hear faint snoring coming from behind Brett's privacy panels. Asher wondered what

Brett would be doing today. He seemed to have no friends other than the girls he claimed to sleep with.

Asher grabbed his towel and shower shoes and disappeared into the bathroom. Nittany followed.

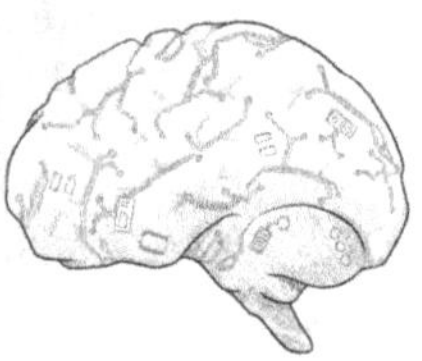

Asher started to relax after being tense and nervous throughout breakfast. He didn't know what created more paranoia: Nittany finding out he was a hybrid, or the worry of Navarro and Cortez finding him there.

"Chief wants me to have dinner with him tonight." Asher didn't want to tell her why. He didn't want to make a big deal of it being his birthday. Besides, he figured Nittany would ask more questions about his family. He'd kept his answers brief and vague thus far. How could he talk about his family honestly with Nittany without revealing his secret? He didn't want to take the risk. His thoughts were interrupted when his hand bumped Nittany's. This had happened three times already, with less time between each bump. He didn't know what to make of it or how to deal with it.

"That's cool. I can see if the others are doing anything. Hey, look, they have a merry-go-round here," said Nittany, pointing.

"I've never ridden one."

"You've never been on a merry-go-round?" Nittany's jaw dropped with disbelief. "Come on, you have to ride with me." Nittany led him over to the ride.

Asher climbed onto a horse. With ease, Nittany climbed onto the horse next him. She held onto the pole and shot him a smile. In return, Asher gave her his awkward, crooked smile.

A bell sounded, and the merry-go-round started to move. Asher relaxed with the silly music that serenaded the ride until eventually he laughed along with Nittany. He felt free and safe. He turned and smiled at her. She smiled back and reached out to him. He grabbed her hand. They held onto each other until the ride ended.

When the ride stopped, Asher and Nittany climbed off their horses, standing together in the cramped space, face to face. Without much thought, Asher leaned in.

"Please exit the merry-go-round," bellowed the attendant. The spell broke, leaving Asher wondering if he would've kissed her if the attendant hadn't interrupted them. He felt a little overwhelmed, yet in a way, relieved that the attendant had. He knew Nittany had experience in kissing with her past boyfriends. He, on the other hand, had only kissed a girl twice.

Asher stepped off the merry-go-round first. He offered his hand to Nittany to help her off, and she took it. Their hands remained intertwined as they explored more of the hub.

"Tell me something about you that I don't know yet," said Nittany.

"Like what?"

"What's your favorite color?"

Asher shrugged. "Blue, I guess. Yours?"

"Green. Now ask me something."

"I don't know." Asher asked the first question that popped into his head. "What's your favorite food?"

"That's easy. A true Philadelphia cheese steak. None of these knock-offs that places outside of Philly sell. What's yours?"

"Root beer."

"That's a drink. What food do you like?"

"Root beer isn't just for drinking. Mom used to make root beer flavored stir-fry for my birthday." Asher's tongue betrayed him. As soon as the word *birthday* fell from his lips, he immediately knew the next question, a question he didn't want to answer.

"That sounds good. When is your birthday?"

"Um, uh, today," Asher mumbled as he looked down to the deck.

Nittany stopped walking and swung in front of Asher, still holding his hand. "Today is your birthday and you didn't tell me?"

Asher shrugged.

"Happy birthday," said Nittany.

Asher watched her kiss the tip of her index finger. Chills swept through his body, causing a stirring below as she placed her finger on his lips. Asher pictured Timothy's lifeless face wedged between the rocks. "Not now, not now, not now," Asher said to him. He managed to avoid another embarrassing moment.

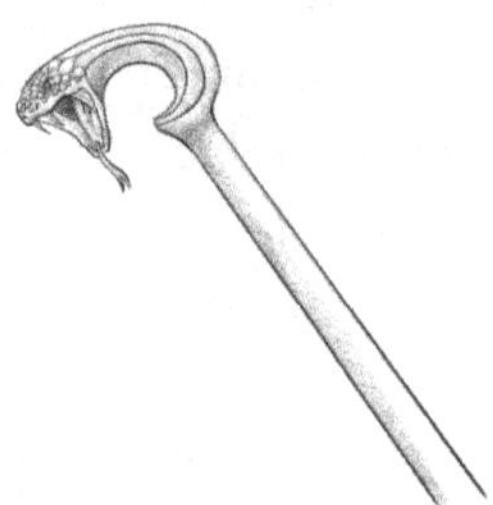

"I thought I would find you here," Dean Wu said to a man in a gray hood. She shuffled with her cane and stopped to look at the couple riding the merry-go-round.

The man in the gray hood didn't respond. His eyes were focused on Asher and Nittany. He watched Nittany place her finger upon her lips and then bring it to Asher's.

"Hai ying, when did you get here?" asked the man in the gray hood.

"About five minutes ago," she replied.

"You saw it then?"

"I did."

"You know what has to be done."

"It will crush them," she replied. "Rules are rules."

"Don't you think I know that?" The words came out a little curt. "If the wrong person sees them together like they are..."

"I know what is at risk here. I will take care of it."

The man in the gray hood let out a small sigh. "Sorry, Hai ying."

"I know, old man, I know," said Dean Wu.

# CHAPTER 32

Asher sat at a table at Brother Bruno's, a pizzeria in the space station. His unfinished slice of pizza sat in a puddle of orange grease that dripped from the slice. Even though he had been with Chief most of the evening, his thoughts were with Nittany. His morning with her had proved to be a good distraction after all.

"Happy birthday, Asher." Chief picked up a wrapped box and handed it to him.

"Thanks." He carefully ripped the wrapping paper. In a glass case on a wooden base sat a baseball and baseball card. Both of them were signed by Gehrig West.

"Gehrig West hit his five hundredth homerun ball, and my grandfather caught it. West contacted him, and he gave my grandfather an autographed bat and jersey plus tickets to all the playoff games, including the World Series, in exchange for the baseball. Many years later, my grandfather received this. Gehrig West had died and left the ball and a baseball card to my grandfather. He passed it down to my father, and my father eventually gave it to me. I thought I would continue the tradition and pass it down to you."

Asher marveled at the gift. "This won't fit in my coffin locker."

"I tell you what, I can hang on to it until we go home. Then we can put it in your bedroom."

Asher knew where he would have put it in his bedroom at Willow Wood. He still didn't consider the room he slept in at Chief's house as his bedroom on a permanent basis.

"What's her name?" asked Chief.

"Huh?" Asher didn't understand the question that came out of nowhere.

"You have what your grandmother used to call the žiara lásky šteniatka." Chief smiled.

"What does that mean?" asked Asher.

"It's Slovak for puppy love glow." Chief gave Asher a sly smile and a wink.

Asher looked away, trying to hide his smile. His face warmed up again.

"Nittany," he said softly.

"Cadet McGreggor?" Chief's smile turned into a look of concern.

Asher bit his bottom lip. "Yeah."

"Does she know you like her?"

"We held hands today when we walked around the hub." Asher's heart hammered at the thought.

Chief leaned back into his chair. "Asher, I don't have to tell you that fraternization with a fellow squad member is unauthorized."

"I know."

"I don't think you do. You have to walk away."

"Why?"

"Because I said so."

"No, I won't do it." Asher's wonderful day turned into miserable one.

Chief let out a long sigh. "You need to walk away."

"Fine, I will." He stood and headed off.

"I meant from her, not me."

Asher knew what he meant, he didn't care. He would not walk away from Nittany. He never would.

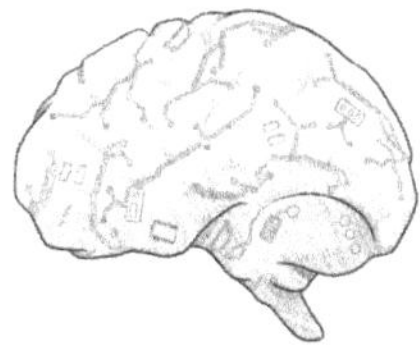

Asher had calmed down by the time he reached Echo 88's common area. He didn't know if he and Nittany would become a couple or not. He wanted her to be his girlfriend, and he hoped Nittany wanted him for a boyfriend. Regardless of what Chief said, he still wanted to work toward a special relationship with Nittany.

"Asher? I didn't expect you back this soon." Nittany came into the common area from the ship's passageway, her hand looped through the handle of a plastic bag. "What's wrong? You don't look happy."

"I'm better now. Chief and I had a disagreement at dinner."

"What did you two disagree about?" Nittany sat next to Asher.

"Nothing really." Asher didn't want to tell her about the conversation, afraid she would shy away from him. Plus, he didn't want to reveal his feelings yet. "What did you do tonight?" Asher changed the subject.

"I know you didn't want me to make a fuss over your birthday, but I couldn't help myself." She pulled out a TastyKake tandy kake from the bag along with a candle and lighter. "I would've attempted to make you a cake if I had the time and facilities, since I don't, this will have to do."

"Thank you, it's not necessary." His mood changed for the better at Nittany's gesture.

"Sure, it is." Nittany opened the package containing three thin cupcakes. She inserted a candle into the center one and lit it. "Would you like me to sing you 'Happy Birthday'?"

Asher couldn't help but chuckle inside. "You don't have to."

"You sure? I don't mind."

"Okay." Asher gave in. He smiled and felt a little embarrassed as Nittany sang to him with her soft, sweet voice. Asher blew out the candle once Nittany had finished.

"I didn't know what to get you." Nittany reached into the bag and pulled out a six-pack of root beer in glass bottles. "I got you this."

"Thank you," said Asher. He gave her one of his crooked smiles.

Like on the merry-go-round, his eyes were drawn to hers. Their faces drew closer and closer. Nittany closed her eyes and lifted her head toward Asher's. His stomach grew tight. He leaned in.

"Cadet Smizik! Cadet McGreggor!"

Asher and Nittany pulled apart before their lips connected. Asher looked toward the doorway. There stood Dean Wu with a hard, firm glare. She had a box in her hand. Asher couldn't see it completely.

"What?" Nittany jumped.

Dean Wu's lips were pressed together. "He never told me this," she mumbled. "Cadet Smizik, Cadet McGreggor, I want to see you two in my office before you go to breakfast."

"Yes, ma'am," Asher and Nittany replied in unison.

"What's wrong?" asked Nittany.

"Nothing that we can't fix." The dean turned to exit.

"Was there something you needed?" Nittany looked at Dean Wu's hand with the box in it.

"No, no, cadet. I like to make my rounds every now and then to ensure that no one is misbehaving. Good day, Cadet McGreggor. Cadet Smizik."

"How much trouble do you think we're in?" asked Asher.

"I don't know. It's not like we...we did anything wrong."

If Dean Wu had caught them two seconds later, their lips would've been connected and he would be having his first kiss with the girl he liked. Asher couldn't believe his luck. First the merry-go-around guy, and now Dean Wu interrupted and ruined the mood. They took away any magic that might have been happening. Asher hoped he would get another chance before the day ended.

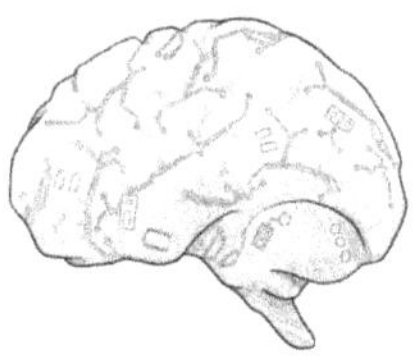

Asher took a sip of his root beer float. Next to him, Nittany had a half-devoured hot-fudge sundae with coffee ice cream in front of her. After their run-in with Dean Wu, they decided to go to Big Star, an ice cream joint on the space station.

"You doing anything special during autumn break at the end of the month?" asked Nittany.

Asher shrugged and took another sip of his float.

"For Halloween weekend, I'll be at my uncle's house, the one who lives near Pittsburgh. He throws a big Halloween party in his barn every year. Maybe we could go together if you like." Nittany shied away from Asher.

Asher loved the idea, even though he had mixed emotions. He didn't know how one could be excited as well as being scared at the same time. "Yeah, I'd like that. I would have to ask Chief first."

Nittany smiled. "Most everyone wears costumes to the party. Would you like to dress up as a couple?"

"A couple?"

"A couple, like "you could dress up as a Baker Bros. Waffle and I could be Vermont maple syrup. Or you could be salt and I could be pepper. A cool one would be for you to dress as a lifeguard, and I could be a swimmer in distress."

"A lifeguard? I can't swim."

Timothy's face with the doll-like eyes flashed before him. In his mind, he could feel the river water hitting his back again. All his joy was suddenly replaced with guilt, fear, and sadness.

"We're not going swimming. It's only a costume," said Nittany.

"I know, I don't want to be a lifeguard." Asher looked down at his float thinking about Timothy drowning.

"That's okay, we can be something else." Nittany filled her spoon with ice cream. Fudge dripped off her spoon and onto her chin. "Can you hand me a napkin, please?"

Asher reached across the table. As he brought his hand back, he knocked over his float. A flood of dull brown liquid flowed across the table and onto Nittany's chest and lap. She yelped as she bolted out of her chair.

"I'm sorry." Asher jumped out of his chair and started dabbing Nittany's chest to clean off her shirt. He looked up and into her eyes. She had a peculiar smile about her face. He stopped dabbing.

"Uh, Asher?" said Nittany. "Your hand is on my boob." She turned red and gave a shy smile.

Asher's eyes almost popped out of their sockets when he realized what he had done. He removed his hand and hid it behind his back. He looked down at the floor. "I'm sorry, I didn't mean..."

Nittany lifted Asher's chin with her finger. He looked into her eyes.

"It's okay, Asher. I know you didn't mean to cop a feel." Her eyes were honest and true.

Asher felt that invisible force again, pulling him toward her. Her head tilted upward, and her eyes closed. He closed his eyes, and their lips touched. A feeling he'd never experienced before whipped through his body. The sensation that swept through him hadn't happened the time he'd kissed Neon to see what the big fuss was about when they were twelve years old. Their lips parted, and Asher opened his eyes.

Nittany seemed to be in a daze. "Although my experience in kissing boys is very limited, I've never had one like that. It was...electrical."

"I liked it too," Asher admitted. They closed their eyes a second time and kissed again.

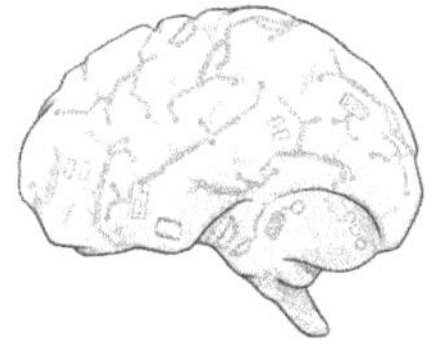

Asher came out of the head after his nightly brushing. This had to be the best birthday ever, despite the argument with Chief. With Nittany still in the shower washing the root beer float's stickiness off, Asher climbed in his rack to read before going to sleep. He felt a hard object under his back. He pulled out a wrapped box. He opened an unsigned card that read "Happy Birthday."

He neatly unwrapped the present, revealing a box of root beer candies—root beer barrels, root beer licorice, root beer jelly beans, root beer gummies, root beer lollipops, and root beer fizzy nuggets.

Asher looked all over the box and card. He found no evidence of who'd placed it on his rack. His squad knew Asher liked root beer, no one, other than Nittany and Chief, knew today was his birthday. Chief had already given him a present. *Who else knows?*

Asher rolled on his side, facing the bulkhead, and heard a tap on his privacy panel. He turned to look behind him as it slid open a crack.

"Asher?"

Asher rolled over and saw Nittany peeking in. "Yeah."

"I had fun with you today."

"Me too."

Nittany stepped on the tiny ladder to bring her face even with Asher's. She leaned in and kissed him. He kissed back.

"Take it to the fan room," said Brett as he entered berthing and disappeared into the head.

Nittany pulled away. The fan room was known as a hideout for cadets who wanted to make out and have sex.

Nittany gave Asher a bashful smile. "Good night." She slid the panel shut.

Chief sat down at his desk. The evening had started off good, then went south real fast. He figured he would talk to Asher in the morning, giving him a chance to cool down a bit. He tapped on his desk and pulled up a student file.

*Cadet: Nittany Lynn McGreggor*

*Father: Bram "Mac" McGreggor*

*Father's Occupation: Detective, Hybrid Police*

Chief pulled up the point of contact information the hybrid detective had given him when he first came to ask him about Vicki. They were one and the same.

Asher and Nittany came out of Dean Wu's office, both glum.

"Who do you think told her that we kissed?" asked Nittany.

Asher shrugged. Two times now he'd been to Dean Wu's office, and he didn't like either one.

"I can't believe she threatened to put us in different squads if we continue our relationship." Nittany shook her head. Her nostrils were flaring.

"It is the rule. We both knew that," said Asher.

"I know, but we're almost adults. They act like we don't know how to keep our relationship separate from school. It's stupid," said Nittany.

"Actually, she didn't say if we *continue* our relationship, she said if we continue to *show* our relationship," said Asher, remembering the conversation word for word.

Nittany stopped and looked at him. "What are you saying?" She had an inquisitive look on her face.

Asher shrugged. "Maybe we need to whisper through cracks is all."

"Okay, now you lost me."

"Pyramus and Thisbe were tragic lovers in Ovid's *Metamorphoses*. Their parents were rivals. They whispered their love to each other through a crack in the wall that divided their two houses."

"That sounds kind of romantic, Asher. I bet they end up getting married and causing a truce between the families."

"Actually, Pyramus thought a lioness had killed Thisbe, so he fell on his sword and killed himself. Thisbe finds him dead, so she kills herself."

"That's horrible," said Nittany. "It sounds like that holomovie that came out a few years ago, *Dash and the Alien*, where a human and an alien fall in love, their races were at war with each other. Both of them end up dying at the end. I cried."

"Actually, the director, Arthur Clydesdale, took that trope from Ovid. He wasn't the first to do that, though. Shakespeare's *Romeo & Juliet*, Laurents, Bernstein, and Sondheim's *West Side Story*, Galisper's *Anna's Tale...*"

Nittany interrupted. "I get the picture." She smiled. "You know, you're cute when you discuss your knowledge of books."

Asher's face warmed.

"All of those stories you named, they had a forbidden love because they were in different houses, so to speak. We are in the same squad. Now, if you were a hybrid and I was a normal, that would fit the trope, especially if we committed suicide in the end."

"You would knowingly date a hybrid?" It happened again. He'd opened his mouth, and words that shouldn't have come out, did.

"Me hook up with a hybrid?" She laughed. "Not on your life. Come on, we have to meet the others. It's our first escape room challenge today. It should be fun."

Asher watched as Nittany headed down the passageway. His heart deflated. He wondered if he would kill himself if he thought she'd died.

He didn't believe he would; however, he knew he would give his life for hers.

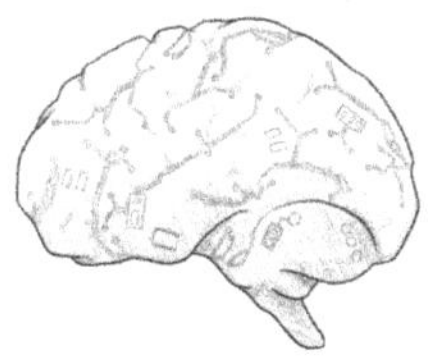

Echo 88 and Whiskey 88 stood in one of hundreds of challenge rooms on board the hub. They were used for both the junior and senior EFA Academies. The room appeared as if they were in the woods. The trees created a nice shade from the artificial sunlight. There were two sets of obstacle courses.

"Echo 88, Whiskey 88. I am Game Master Thane Blass. You will address me as Game Master or Game Master Blass." He stood tall and proud despite his large belly and the gray hair only on the sides of his head. His white goatee and piercing eyes made him every bit intimidating.

"This will be one of your easiest challenge rooms. Squad leaders, hand out the puzzle pieces."

LT Mabus handed one puzzle piece to each of his cadets. Whiskey 88's squad leader did the same for them.

The Game Master explained what each obstacle consisted of. "Squad leaders, you have sixty seconds to prep your cadets."

"Echo 88, I know you guys have this," said LT Mabus. "Work as a team. Remember, it doesn't matter how many puzzle pieces you carry. As long as we finish, you guys get an award."

"I don't want no ice cream social," said Brett. "We're going to win the 'get out of one exam' pass."

"Squads, take your positions," bellowed the Game Master.

A hologram of a red ten hovered in front of each team. It began counting down. When it reached five, the numbers changed to yellow.

"Here it goes," said Cray.

All the cadets watched as the yellow number one turned into a green "GO."

"We have to get to the next obstacle without any part of our bodies touching the ground by using these two 2x4s and those ropes."

"You don't have to tell us what to do. We know already," said Brett. He grabbed a board from Nittany and put it on the ground with it stretching into the "no feet" zone. He balanced himself on the board and started walking to the other end. "Now give me the next board," he demanded.

"It's not going to work," said Xiao. "We can't touch the boards with our hands.

"Yeah, it will," Brett replied.

"What are they doing with their boards?" Tabitha asked, referring to Whiskey 88.

"They're tying rope to them," replied Cray.

"That's stupid. What are they going to do? Drag themselves across?" Brett asked as he came back to the squad.

Asher knew what needed to be done. He kept his mouth shut, though, heeding the dean's words.

Xiao, Cray, and Brett stood arguing with each other over how to get to the next obstacle.

"Guys! Look!" yelled Nittany. She pointed to Whiskey 88. They had put the two studs parallel to each other. The cadets stood in a line behind each other with one foot on each board. They had tied one end of each rope onto the board, with the other end clutched tightly in the cadets' hands.

"Right foot!" yelled Kyle Knoebel at the head of Whiskey 88. The entire squad lifted up their right feet and hands, which caused the board to move up. They moved it forward and stepped down awkwardly, almost losing their balance.

Echo 88 grabbed the ropes and started attaching them to the boards. They pushed and shoved each other trying to tie the ropes to the board. In the chaos and miscommunication, they tied both ends of the rope to one board and had to start over. Whiskey 88 made it to the second obstacle before Echo 88 got everyone ready to cross the first.

After four tries, they made it to the next station. A web of red laser beams hung before them with the lowest hole no lower than their waists.

"We need to make our plans before we do this," said Xiao.

"Let's do it already," said Brett.

"We can only use a hole once. We need to look at this strategically," said Xiao.

"Xiao, you're the shortest and lightest. You should go last," Tabitha said.

"I'll go through this one," Brett said, pointing to the lowest hole.

"We should save the lower ones," said Xiao.

"Cray, Weathervane, slide me through this hole," Brett ordered.

"Xiao has a point," said Cray.

"Do it."

"Give him what he wants," said Xiao, shaking her head.

Brett made it to the other side. Nittany went next.

"Maybe we should put Asher through that one!" Nittany pointed. "It's one of the smaller ones. We can use Asher's skinniness to our advantage."

Brett, Xiao, and Cray argued about who went next, ignoring what Nittany had suggested.

"Stop arguing!" she yelled. "Whiskey is way ahead of us." Nittany suggested her idea about Asher again.

Asher fell into the arms of Cray, Xiao, and Tabitha.

"Lift!" said Cray.

The threesome lifted Asher about head level and carefully slid his pointed feet through the hole. Brett and Nittany were on the other side, taking his feet. Asher watched the top of the trees sway as he slowly passed through the web. He tried being as stiff as a corpse in rigor mortis. He sucked in his stomach to prepare himself to be passed through the beams.

"He's halfway through," said Cray as the beams surrounded Asher's waist.

"Good thing he doesn't have a boner, he wouldn't fit," mocked Brett.

"That's gross," said Nittany.

Asher made it to the other side. Amongst the arguing, each cadet made it through.

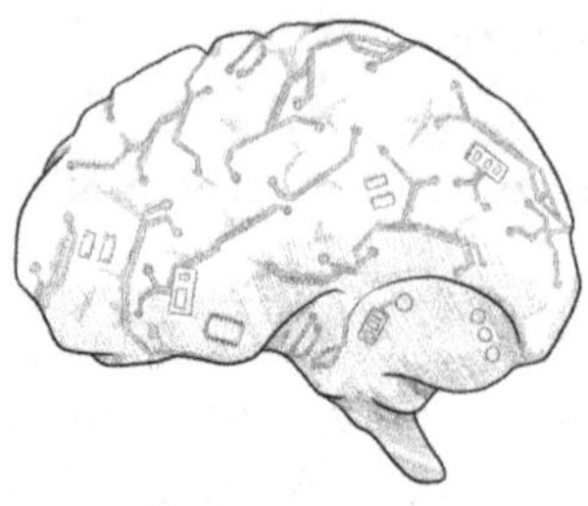

Whiskey 88 completed the course forty-five minutes before Echo 88 made it to the last obstacle. Their lack of teamwork was a bigger obstacle than the course itself. By now, everyone had had enough of Brett, and Brett had had enough of everyone.

A block of wood one foot high, one foot wide, and one foot deep stood fastened to the deck before them. Once five team members were balanced on the block with no body parts touching the ground, the sixth member could work on solving the puzzle. If any of the five touched the ground, the puzzle solver had to stop working and step away until everyone was back on the block.

After much debate, Tabitha became the puzzle solver. Cray, Brett, Asher, Xiao, and Nittany began working themselves onto the block. Asher kept his mouth shut yet again by not suggesting he could be the puzzle solver. His implants would make it easy for him.

Brett and Cray got on at the same time, bumping heads.

"You cunnerman!" yelled Brett. He clenched his fists. Cray kept his mouth closed as he rubbed his forehead.

At least one foot of the five were on the block. Getting their second foot off the ground became the challenge. They were a tangled mess.

"Hey! Watch where you're grabbing," said Xiao.

"It was an accident," replied Brett.

"You try to cop a feel again and I'll show you an accident." With the back of her hand, she wacked Brett in the stomach, causing him to fall off, bringing everyone else with him.

After several attempts, they all made it on the block. Tabitha began to work on the puzzle.

"Damn, who shit their pants?" asked Cray, winkling his nose.

"That would be me," Brett said with a devious grin.

The cadets started gagging and slipped off. Tabitha stepped away from the puzzle until they got back on.

Brett yelped. "Ouch! Who kneed me in my sack?"

"It's was an accident," Cray said in a mocking tone.

"Accident my ass." Brett pushed Cray off the block. Everyone else tumbled after.

Cray shot up and gave Brett a giant shove. Brett delivered a right fist to Cray's eye.

Game Master Blass held a hand up, stopping LT Mabus and LTjg Meoquanee from ending the fight. "Wait. They need to get this out of their system."

The three adults watched as Asher and the girls broke up the fight. The brawl ended.

# CHAPTER 34

"I knew we were going to get our butts chewed tonight, just I didn't expect LT Mabus to chew us out while we did push-ups the entire time," said Cray, rubbing his arms.

"I hated taking laps around the Hull Tunnel while it was Meoquanee's turn to ream us out," replied Tabitha.

Brett uncharacteristically kept silent as his sweat-covered body crawled into his rack, sweat and all, and shut his privacy panel.

"Aren't you going to take a shower first? You're all sweaty and nasty," said Xiao.

"He hasn't changed his sheets since day one," Cray informed her.

The privacy panel slid open partially. Out came a fist with the middle finger up.

"Xiao asked if you were going to take a shower, she didn't ask for your IQ." Cray smirked.

"At least it's higher than the number of targets you shot in the escape room," Brett said as he opened the privacy panel all the way and slid out of his rack.

"Give me a gun now, and I will show you I can hit the target."

"Enough, you two," shouted Xiao. "I don't want to have to go through any more torture."

Brett grunted. He opened his coffin locker, grabbed his toiletry bag and towel, and disappeared into the head.

"We're never going to be a team as long as he's in our squad," said Cray. He grabbed his bathroom gear and headed toward the door that led to the common room.

"Where are you going?" asked Tabitha.

"I'm going to get my shower in the locker room. The farther I stay away from him, the better."

"Good idea." Xiao followed suit, with Tabitha right behind.

"Are you going to the locker room?" asked Nittany.

Asher shrugged. He grabbed his toiletry bag and towel and disappeared into the head.

Asher walked past the first shower stall. He heard Brett in there with the water running. Asher listened closely. Brett was talking to himself—an explosion of anger emerged from the stall. The metal side of the shower hollered in pain as something slammed against it a few times.

"Take that, LT Mabus, you fricken asshole!" Another punch. "Fricken Cray, you motherfricker. I should rip you a new asshole, you gay bastard." More punches. "I wouldn't even have to fricken be here if the fricken senator wasn't such a motherfricker. I'm wanna fricken kill of all of them."

Asher thought about asking Brett if he was okay, decided to keep his mouth shut. He entered the second shower stall.

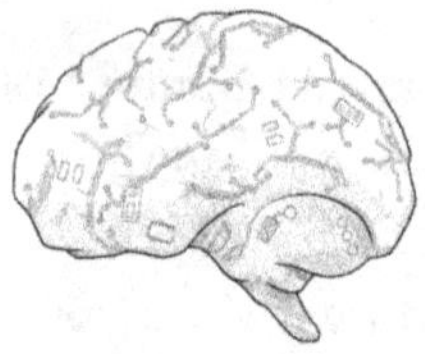

After his shower, Asher walked into berthing. The empty room showed no evidence that the others had returned from the locker room yet. He looked at Brett's empty rack and wondered where he'd gone.

The door opened and in came Brett from the common room. His eyes were puffy and bloodshot. His right hand lay bloody and swollen in his left hand.

"I think I broke my fist," he said in a defeated tone.

Asher grabbed a clean uniform and slipped it on.

"Where are you going?" asked Brett.

"You need to go to medical. I'll go with you."

"Why would you go with me?"

"I don't know. It seems like the right thing to do."

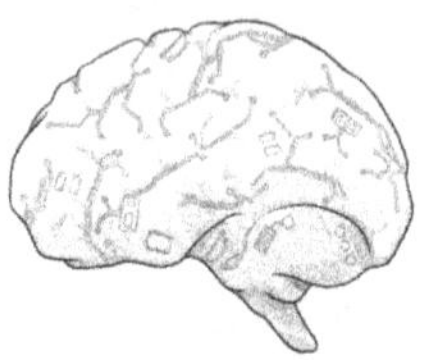

Asher sat in the waiting area of medical. Dr. Morimoto, HM2 Verbeck, and a couple people Asher didn't know took Brett into the operating room. Asher stayed behind waiting with his 'don't leave anyone behind,' mentality. He rubbed his temples; he had that strange feeling in his head again.

"Cadet Smizik," said LT Mabus as he entered medical.

Asher stood up immediately. "Sir."

"What happened?"

"I think Brett broke his hand," he replied.

"How?"

Asher thought for a second. He knew exactly how. "I don't know."

"Good job bringing him here and staying. That's a trait of a good cadet. I got it now. You go hit your rack."

The doors to the operating room opened. Dr. Morimoto walked out. "He'll be fine."

"Good. Can I talk to you privately, Dr. Morimoto?" asked LT Mabus.

"Come to my office, Lieutenant."

LT Mabus followed the doctor, and they disappeared into his office.

"Cadet Smizik, you're still here?" asked Petty Officer Verbeck as he came out of the treatment room.

Asher's head started to throb. "I waited to see how Brett is."

"He's fine. We gave him the treatments needed. He'll be as good as new in the morning. Are you okay?"

"I have a headache. Just tired is all."

Chief and Brett came out of the surgery room.

"You're still here?" asked Brett.

"Yeah," replied Asher.

Brett didn't say anything.

"Hey, Asher, you doing okay?" Chief asked.

Asher shrugged.

"You boys go hit your rack," said Chief.

"Yes, Chief," Asher said.

The two boys headed to berthing. As they made their way back, Asher's head started to feel a little better. Once he got into his rack, it took no time at all to fall asleep.

# CHAPTER 35

Echo 88 gathered in the common room. The cadets were preparing for their next escape room. LT Mabus, LTjg Meoquanee, and HM2 Verbeck were with them.

"Echo 88, it's been a privilege to be your squad leader the last month and a half," LT Mabus said. "Unfortunately, I received emergency orders to report to the NAS *Saipan*, where I will be the chief engineer. LTjg Meoquanee will be your squad leader, and Petty Officer Verbeck graciously volunteered to be the assistant squad leader for the remainder of the semester. Good luck at today's match. Maybe our paths will cross again."

Everyone wished LT Mabus good luck. They had mixed feelings about his leaving.

"Okay, Echo 88, let's head out," shouted Meoquanee. "It's game time."

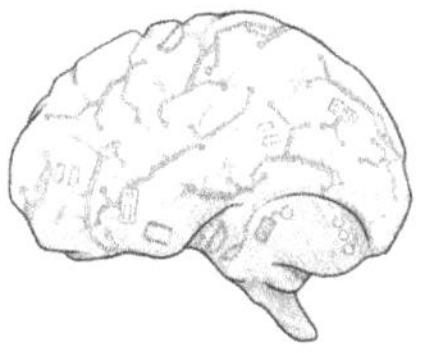

"Echo 88, this is our last escape room before we go on autumn break," said LTjg Meoquanee. "I have a good feeling about this one."

"We are oh and five," said Cray. "We suck. Romeo 88 is going to beat us like everyone else has."

"With that attitude, you've already lost. As we discussed before, you all work as individuals and not as a team," said LTjg Meoquanee.

"We worked as a team in the Victorian room," said Xiao. "Well, most of us did." She glared at Brett.

"You all go in as individuals and work by yourself until it eventually brings you all together. If you start off as a team, I think you will see a real improvement."

"LT Meoquanee is right," said Cray. "Let's do this." Unlike the others, Cray showed his excitement.

They entered the starting room.

Asher entered last. He had another headache. They had been coming on more frequently of late.

The game started, and Echo 88 found themselves in a brig aboard a nineteenth-century pirate ship. To complete this escape room, everyone had to get topside. An actor pretended to be a villainous pirate. He rattled the chains that confined his wrists to the wall, causing an eerie clanking noise.

The actor called himself Captain Iron Fist. He kept trying to talk the kids into freeing him. No one did. He continued to rattle his chains.

Everyone neglected to search for clues as a team, with the exception of Asher and Nittany, who stayed together. Cray tried to get everyone to work together, no one seemed interested.

A large explosion outside the room caused it to shake violently. The cadets stopped what they were doing. The emergency alarm sounded.

"There is an emergency," said a computerized voice. "Please exit topside in the mustering bay."

The door opened. Smoke crept in as a flickering orange glow from the right side of the door lit the passageway. Another explosion shook the room again. Tabitha and Nittany screamed as they left the room, trying to get to the mustering bay.

"Wait," said Captain Iron Fist. "The chains are malfunctioning. They're supposed to automatically open when the emergency alarm sounds."

Brett and Asher looked at each other. "We need to help him," said Asher.

A third explosion boomed.

"Screw this, I'm out of here," Brett said, and he ran out.

"Hey, cadet, this isn't funny. Help me out."

There were minor rumblings, and Asher thought back to the night of the raid. The chaos, the deaths, the unknowns. The memories made his head pound—his body frozen and unable to move.

"Cadet! You okay?"

Asher got a whiff of smoke, which knocked him back to reality.

"I'm trapped. Get me out of here." Panic washed over the actor.

Asher ran to the cell door and shook it. "It's locked."

"Damn safety measures never work when you need them to." Another explosion occurred nearby shaking the escape room. "You'll have to solve the clues to find the key."

"Don't you know where the key is?" asked Asher.

"The Game Master didn't tell me. The bastard locked me up."

Asher closed his eyes. He brought up all the clues he had before the explosions started. He opened his eyes and smiled. He worked at an alarming rate, finding one clue after another. He found the key to the cell as well as to the shackles.

"Thank you, cadet. I've been doing this for many years. This was the fastest I've ever seen one person find the keys." The actor rubbed his wrists. "Let's go!"

The room shook. Asher, the actor, and the props in the room that weren't fastened down began to float.

"What's happening?" Asher's eyes went wide, and fear coursed through his body.

"The gravity generator must've gone out. We get to swim in air to the exit. Be careful of the fireballs. Fire burns differently in zero gravity."

Iron Fist let Asher lead the way. Asher had experienced zero gravity once before in Mr. LaTrobe's science class.

They exited the room and saw a ball of flame a few feet down the right-hand passageway. They turned left like the others and floated as fast as they could. Rounding the corner, they saw Romeo 88 and their actor floating toward the door to the mustering bay. Asher saw all seven of them go in.

"Wait!" Asher yelled. The hatch slammed shut with the clashing of metal hitting metal. Asher unhinged the door, and he and Iron Fist floated through the hatch and into the mustering bay.

"Time!" said the Game Master. "Romeo wins." He stood in the mustering bay, wearing gravity boots.

Asher furrowed his eyebrows. Bewildered, Asher wondered if this was part of the game.

"Everyone brace for gravity," said the Game Master. The cadets went to the bulkheads, placed their feet on a rung, and grabbed onto another rung with their hands. The Game Master ordered the gravity to be turned on.

Asher's stomach felt heavy as the gravity pulled him toward the deck.

"This was part of the room. The goal wasn't to escape the room, it was to escape with all of your team and the pirate," bellowed the Game Master. "I want to be perfectly clear. This is the only time the alarms will sound during a game. If you hear those alarms again, it's the real thing."

Everyone in Echo 88 looked disappointed.

"LTjg Meoquanee told us to stay together as a team," Xiao said, "and we didn't listen."

"How were we supposed to know that saving the actor was part of the game? This was messed up and unfair," Brett whined.

"Asher was close to winning the game for us," Nittany remarked.

"If we would've worked together," said Tabitha, "we would have had this game easily."

Cray clenched his jaw, mad at himself for not sticking around to help Asher. "Now we're oh and six. This was no treat. It was a trick."

"How's your hand?" Nittany asked Xiao.

"It hurts!" She cradled her injured hand.

"What happened?" asked Asher.

"The asshole over there pushed me out of his way. My hand brushed up against a leaking steam pipe."

Asher looked over at Brett. If he was sorry for what he did, he didn't show any sign of it.

"This is going to leave a scar too. I am allergic to scar tissue meds."

"Something needs to be done about him," said Cray.

LTjg Meoquanee and Petty Officer Verbeck came up to the group. Echo 88 conducted their debrief, and, with that, autumn break had begun.

# CHAPTER 36

Asher tapped on the door to Chief's office.

"It's open," Chief bellowed from behind the door.

Asher peeked inside. "Uh, Chief, can I ask you a question?"

"Sure, come in. What is it?"

Asher bit his fingernails. "Uh, I was wondering. Since autumn break starts after lunch today and you have to stay here for duty weekend, can I go to your house today by myself?"

"You want to get off the ship as much I do, don't you?"

"Yes."

"You're not still seeing Nittany, are you?"

"She will be with her parents."

"You didn't answer my question," said Chief.

"I stepped back," Asher said, taking a nervous step backward and biting another fingernail.

"Do you have any idea where Neon disappeared to?" asked Chief.

"No, I already told you that."

"I don't have to warn you about opening the door to strangers, do I?"

"I'm not a kid, Chief," Asher insisted.

"When you get home, check in with Mick."

"I will. Thank you, Chief!" Asher's heart filled with excitement. He turned to exit.

"One thing, Asher," said Chief.

"Yeah?"

"What do you plan on doing this weekend alone?"

Asher shrugged. "Read and enjoy the quiet."

Chief smiled. "You have enough money on your cash card for a shuttle ticket?"

"I do, I could always use more for food."

"I'll get online and transfer you more cash."

"Thank you, Chief." Asher rushed out of the medical spaces to where Nittany paced back and forth in the passageway.

"Well?" she asked.

"I'm allowed."

Nittany squealed and gave him a hug and a kiss. He hugged and kissed back. They pulled apart before they were caught.

"That's great. Mom said I can stay at my uncle's house for the weekend. She already bought me my shuttle ticket. We're going to have a blast. My uncle makes the best corn mazes, plus the Halloween party in the barn is always fun."

"I don't have a costume for the party," said Asher. "We don't have time to order one, do we?"

"Do you trust me?" She gave him a keen smile.

"Yeah."

"Good, I'll take care of the costumes then, okay?"

Asher shrugged. His thoughts drifted back to Willow Wood. Each year at Halloween, everyone would dress up and have a party. Timothy would be The Flash. Asher always dressed up as a villain to Timothy's

Flash. He was Heat Wave one year, Captain Cold another, Reverse-Flash, and his personal favorite, the Thinker. He always let Timothy pick the villain du jour. Asher showed a slight smile, liking the idea of Nittany choosing their costumes.

"As long as it's not a superhero or a supervillain, okay?"

"Deal," she said.

That belonged to him and Timothy.

Cortez, with his smoking panatela sticking out of his mouth, stormed into Navarro's private quarters. He found her on her knees giving JD a bath. "I thought pigs liked to be dirty," he said with a Cuban accent that made it hard to understand.

"Pigs don't have sweat glands. They use mud to cool themselves off. What do you have for me, or do you like barging in while I am having me and JD time?"

"Krankshaft spotted that blond kid that got away from us last summer during that New York raid. He spotted him at the hub."

Navarro sat up with interest. "Please say Krankshaft is following him." She grabbed a towel and dried her hands.

"That's the bad news. He got on a shuttle to Pittsburgh. Krankshaft couldn't get on the shuttle," said Cortez.

Navarro's face tightened. "Tell me one of my crews started tailing him in Pittsburgh."

"Sabastian's crew is on it. They're already at the terminal waiting for the shuttle."

Navarro smiled. She dried JD off and got him out of the steel tub. "Tell Sabastian to follow. Do not engage. I'm on my way. My gut feeling is he's the piece we need to bring Alita Blackwood down once and for all."

"I would rather shoot first and scan later. They can't be trusted." Cortez gave her the comment she'd expected to hear. In reality, he had to capture the kid alive for Dr. Stroud Monroe. He would earn big dollars if he sold him to the doctor.

"Patience was never one of your strong points. Come on, let's go have ourselves a happy Halloween." Navarro smiled.

Xiao walked down the streets of the Baltimore internment village, escorted by an armed guard. Not many people visited the confines of the interment village. Goosebumps ran up and down Xiao's arms. This could be a setting for that writer from the 1900s that Asher had told her about. What was his name? Kane. Stephen Kane. No, that wasn't it. King, yes, Stephen King.

The houses that the former hybrids lived in looked like they should've been condemned years ago. The smell of death was potent. The streets were trashed with debris.

They stopped in front of a house at 17 Clipper Lane. This was where Olivia had been living since her cleansing. The house looked haunted. Actually, all the houses in the neighborhood looked like they should be torn down and rebuilt.

Xiao carefully placed her foot on the step that led to the porch. Her heart stopped as the guard's hand came down upon her shoulder, forcibly holding her in place.

"Didn't mean to scare you. Normals aren't allowed into dwelling units," he said.

"How am I supposed to see Olivia, then?"

"You yell her name. Then she'll come out," said the guard.

"She's deaf and blind."

"I'm sorry, miss, I can't let you in there."

"Fine, we can go back then," said Xiao.

The guard relaxed his grip. She ripped her shoulder from him, ran up the steps and pushed open the door. The smell pushed back at her. Flies buzzed around a lifeless figure that lay on the floor at the bottom of the stairs.

Xiao knew at once it was Olivia. She must've fallen down the stairs and died. The living conditions were not even suitable for the dead.

Olivia's head started to turn toward Xiao. Her eyes were black holes. The mouth opened, and out slithered a snake. Xiao screamed as the guard fired his laser pistol. The snake and Olivia's head splattered with some remnants landing on Xiao's uniform.

"I hate snakes. Nasty creatures. Now we have to go."

Xiao shook her head. She walked outside and vomited. If only the images and memories she'd acquired would all go away. She was afraid they were there to stay.

Xiao lay in her bed with her red, swollen eyes hidden in her pillow. She tried calling Tuck. She found out he'd been in an accident and couldn't take her call. She had to talk to someone other than her parents. Olivia had always been that someone. Xiao couldn't call any of her squad members. Cray and Tabitha tended to have diarrhea of the mouth. She'd heard that Asher and Nittany were planning a big weekend together. That left one person. There was no way she was calling him. No way in Hell.

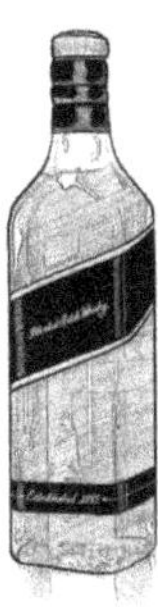

Brett and Jinx lay in bed, both out of breath.

"I missed that," said Jinx.

"This is much better than going with my dad to DC for campaign speeches."

"I'm glad you stayed. I like it when you explode in me." She kissed him on the lips.

"That was pretty good. You should try it in zero gravity though."

Jinx sat up. The sheet dropped, exposing her nipple-pierced breasts and tattoos that clothing normally covered. "How would you know?"

"There's a room on the *Pocono* where you can control the gravity generator."

"You had sex with other girls up there?"

"Yeah, what's the big the deal?"

Jinx spun around on her bare butt and pushed Brett off the bed with her feet.

"No big deal? Get out of here!" she yelled.

"What the hell? We always had sex with other people."

Jinx stood and threw on her panties and a shirt. She poked at his chest. "You always had sex with other people. Not no more. You have a choice. Sex with only me, or you won't see me ever again."

"If that's what you want." Brett got up and started dressing.

"You asshole, get the hell out of here!" Jinx threw an object from her dresser, hitting Brett in the head.

"You're such a bitch," Brett responded. Before he knew it, flying objects were soaring past him. He managed to get his pants on, he grabbed his remaining clothes and ran out.

"If I ever see you again, Brett Lundy, I will make sure you can't have sex again in any gravity."

Brett's holowatch buzzed. He knew Jinx wouldn't keep him away too long. He answered it. "I knew you would miss me too much not to call," he said.

"Miss you? Don't flatter yourself," said Xiao.

"Why are you calling me?" Brett asked. "No one to bitch at where you're at?"

"I needed someone to talk to," she replied.

"And you picked me?"

"Believe me, you weren't my first choice."

"I'm nobody's sloppy seconds," said Brett.

"You're not my second either. More like my sixth." She started to cry.

"Hey cunnerman, I don't deal with crying girls."

"For once, Brett, can you keep your damn mouth shut? I need to talk, and you listen."

Brett bit his bottom lip. What could she want to talk to him about? Why was she crying?

"Where are you at?" he asked.

"I'm home near Baltimore."

"That's near Washington, DC, right?" asked Brett.

"Yes."

"If I'm not too late, I can be there in a couple of hours."

"I want to talk. You don't need to come here."

"It's best if I come down there." He looked at Jinx's house. "There are hostilities up here."

"Okay. I guess."

"I got to run if I'm going to catch my dad's flight." He hung up before Xiao could start her next sentence. He dashed to the house, hoping it wasn't too late. He wondered if he was going down to see Xiao or to stay away from Jinx. It had to be because of Jinx. Why would he want to see Xiao? Her legs were locked at the knees. At least it would help him kill time until Jinx cooled down. Who knew, maybe he would get lucky anyway.

Asher walked into his bedroom at Chief's house, and a wealth of emotion rushed over him. Back on Earth, memories of his mom and Timothy and Willow Wood flashed before him. The *Pocono* became his safety harness that allowed him to separate from his harsh past on Earth.

Asher took off his uniform jacket and hung it up in the closet. He threw the rest of his uniform pieces into a pile in the corner. He would wash and iron them later this week. He felt grimy. He smelled like...the ship. He didn't realize the *Pocono* had a distinct, lingering smell until he left it. He wondered if Nittany smelled the same way. Whenever they were together, her hair smelled tropical, like mango and coconut. He loved the smell of her hair.

"I might as well get a shower," he mumbled to himself. He slipped off his briefs and headed to the bathroom down the hall.

"Nice package."

Asher screamed. He whisked around to find Neon. His hands automatically, instinctively, covered up his crotch.

"Dammit, Neon. You scared the shit out of me. What are you doing here?"

"We haven't talked in almost two months and this is how you greet me?" She walked over to Asher, as if nothing fazed her. "Wow, what do they got you doing up there? Is this the start of a six pack?" She tapped his abdomen. "You don't seem happy to see me, Asher. He sure does." Her eyes glanced down to his groin.

"Don't you ever fricken listen, Neon. Stop doing that." Asher stormed into the bathroom and grabbed a towel to wrap around his waist.

"You act like that's the first time I've seen your boner," she said.

"You know I don't like when you do that stuff. Yet you continue," Asher said in disgust.

"Aren't we cranky tonight."

"I'm tired, and I don't like it when people sneak in the house while I'm here alone."

"I didn't sneak into the house while you were here. I've been staying here the last few days," said Neon.

"Uncle Mick said you were sick. Then you disappeared from his shop."

"That is true," she said. "The person I was looking for actually found me."

"Who were you looking for?" asked Asher.

Neon poked her head in and gave him a devilish grin.

"You didn't. Say you didn't," said Asher, afraid she wouldn't say she didn't. He shut the door on her in disgust.

"She's not what you make her out to be," said Neon.

"Alita Blackwood is a terrorist."

"She is fighting for our freedom, for our rights," Neon insisted.

"I'm too tired to argue with you. If you want to associate with a terrorist, you go right ahead. I'm not going to stop you." He turned on the shower.

Nittany and Asher had made plans for the two of them could be alone together all weekend. Chief wasn't coming home until Monday morning, and Nittany came up with a story where her cousin's friend would be covering for her. Asher wanted one-on-one quality time with her. They couldn't get much one on one time on the *Pocono*. They'd agreed to sleep in separate bedrooms. Nittany didn't want to give up her virginity until she was married. He respected that.

"You locked the bathroom door doesn't mean I can't still see you," Neon said from behind the door.

Asher flipped her the finger.

"Is that what they're teaching you up there?"

"Neon, just go away. Go to Alita Blackwood, go to Dr. Emily, I don't care where you go, disappear like you do at times."

"Geez, Asher, tell me how you really feel. If I'd known you would change this much by going up there, I would've tied you up and not let you even go to the terminal let along the *Pocono*. You know, I thought you were dead until Alita Blackwood told me you weren't."

"Neon, if you go away for the weekend, then I will spend all next week with you, okay?"

"You want me gone for the weekend?" She cocked her head. "You have something planned. It must be good if you're not telling me what it is. What is it?"

"I want to be alone for the weekend. Chief isn't here, and I want to charge up my batteries is all. I don't get alone time on the *Pocono* like I did at Willow Wood." Asher didn't lie, the last thing he needed was for Neon to know about Nittany.

"I'm sorry you feel that way. I told Alita Blackwood I would keep an eye on you. She seems to think there's something worse out there than the hybrid hunters and police that could take you from us. She wouldn't elaborate though."

What could be worse than hunters and police Asher wondered. All he knew was that he didn't need or want Neon here to watch out for him. He didn't want anyone to look out for him anymore. He could do it himself. He'd had a taste of freedom and a normal life, and he wanted more.

B rett got out of the car. He could feel Oscar's watchful eyes following him. Brett hadn't wanted Oscar to come. The senator gave him no choice.

He looked up at Xiao's house, a duplex. The neighborhood didn't look like the slums or anything. He could tell Xiao lived in a working-class community by the make and models of the vehicles parked in the driveways and along the curb. He walked up to the door and rang the bell.

The door swung open, revealing a small man with silver-and-black hair.

"May I help you?" asked Mr. Li.

"Uh, yeah, I'm here to see Xiao."

The man's eyes scanned him from head to toe like a hybrid scanned by the police. "Do I know you?" asked Mr. Li.

"I don't think so."

"You look awfully familiar. What's your name?"

"Look, I'm not here to play Twenty Questions. Xiao asked me to come over."

"My daughter would never ask a boy to come here, especially not before asking her father. Besides, it's after nine o'clock. Off with you." The door slammed in Brett's face.

"What a dick," Brett mumbled. No wonder Xiao was the way she was. He didn't come all this way to have a door slammed in his face, though. He rang the doorbell again and again and again, until it finally opened, this time with Xiao on the other side.

"What did you say to Fugin?" asked Xiao.

"Nothing."

Mr. Li spoke in gibberish, Brett guessed Chinese or Japanese. If only he had his interpretive earplugs in, he would be able to understand what they were saying. Finally, Xiao grabbed him by the shirt and yanked him away from the house.

"What were you two talking about?" asked Brett.

"He is very protective of me and doesn't like a boy calling this late at night. Especially if it's a boy he's never met before."

"I can see why you never had a boyfriend then," said Brett.

She stopped and looked at him. "How do you know that? Oh, Tabitha."

"You know she and Cray can't keep secrets." Brett opened the back of the car and climbed in first.

"Such a gentleman." Xiao climbed in.

"Why do you keep staring at me like that?" Xiao sat across the table at Flood's, a local ice cream establishment. She put a spoonful of pistachio ice cream in her mouth.

"I'm not used to seeing you with your hair down, wearing normal clothes," Brett replied. Xiao wore a long navy-blue skirt with a white blouse. "You know, you are kind of hot."

"Don't throw your lines at me. It's not going to work. The store hasn't had her grand opening yet, and it isn't happening anytime soon."

Brett leaned back and smiled.

"What?" asked Xiao.

"You know what your problem is?"

"I already told you about Olivia." The first part of their night they'd spent talking about Olivia. Brett would chime in every now and then with one of his lame jokes. He actually listened to her—or pretended to listen—as she got her feelings off her chest.

"I'm not referring to that. Your problem is that you're too stiff. You don't have fun."

"I have fun," Xiao said.

"Tell me the last time you let loose and had fun," Brett insisted.

Xiao didn't say a word.

"That's what I thought. What are you doing tomorrow night? Wait, why am I asking? Of course you have nothing planned for tomorrow night. Come out with me."

"What makes you think I don't have plans tomorrow night?"

"Because you're Xiao."

She didn't want to admit that of all people, Brett knew her better than she knew herself. "I'm not like you, Brett, whose father can afford to send you to the Academy. I have to go on scholarship. If I don't keep up, I risk losing the opportunity."

"Really? You have the second-highest GPA in the eleventh level. Like if you skip one night of studying, you're going to slip down to my rank?"

Curious, Xiao asked, "What do you have in mind?"

"I don't know yet," replied Brett.

"I'm not saying I'm going. If we do meet up tomorrow night, it is not a date, and I will not be one of your cheap slorches."

"Relax, even though you're kinda hot with your hair down like that, I won't let the womb raider explore your tomb." He gave her a mischievous grin.

"You really think I'm hot?" asked Xiao, pushing her hair back behind her ear. She obviously hadn't heard Brett's womb raider comment.

"I said kinda hot. If you didn't have mosquito bites for tits, then you would be hot."

"Mosquito bites?" asked Xiao. "If we're going to talk about something small, then we should discuss your member."

"I knew you had some fun in you."

"What does that have to do with your member being small?" she asked.

"You took notice." Brett smiled.

Xiao rolled her eyes. "It wasn't hard to do. Every time I logged into my computer, someone posted a picture or video of you and Pinocchio. You know how many memes are out there with your version of Pinocchio?"

"You saw that?" asked Brett.

"I don't think there is anyone on this ship that hasn't."

"Cool," replied Brett. "Let's get going. Oscar will take you home."

"No, I think I'll walk." She gave him a forced smile and left.

Brett stood up from the table as Xiao walked away. "I'll pick you up tomorrow at six," he yelled.

Nittany rang Chief's doorbell. She'd deviated from the plan. Instead of meeting him at the corn maze, she came to his house to surprise him. Besides, she didn't want to bring her weekend getaway bag with her to the corn maze.

Her eyes grew wide and her jaw dropped when the door opened to reveal a girl with green-and-blue hair where there should have been Asher.

"What do you want?" the girl asked.

"Uh, hi. Is Asher here?" asked Nittany.

The girl's eyes grew. "How could I not see it? You're the reason Asher wanted me out of the house. Asher has a girlfriend." She opened the door wide, giving Nittany room to come step inside. "I'm Neon."

"I'm Nittany. Asher has talked about you before."

"Funny, he never talked about you." Neon crossed her arms and put the majority of her weight on her left leg.

"Neon, we're not supposed to answer the—" Asher stopped halfway down the stairs wearing a pair of jeans and a T-shirt. "Nittany?" His face lit up and he rushed to greet her. Their lips connected.

Neon cleared her throat. "Why don't you two go upstairs to Asher's room? Don't make any loud noises. I have sensitive ears."

Nittany and Asher pulled apart. Asher shot Neon a nasty look, then turned his attention back to Nittany.

"What are you doing here? I thought we were meeting at the corn maze."

"Corn maze?" asked Neon. "No one mentioned nothing about a corn maze. Sounds like fun. When are we leaving?"

Asher gave her another glare.

"I didn't want to bring my overnight bag to the corn maze."

"Overnight bag? Oh, this is getting better by the minute," said Neon.

"Neon, don't you have something to do, like clip your toenails, clean the toilet, or watch the leaky faucet in the kitchen drip?" asked Asher.

"I see I'm not wanted. That's fine," said Neon. Asher thought she left a little too easily.

"That's Neon?"

"Yeah, I didn't know she was going to be here," said Asher.

"That's okay," said Nittany. "As long as I'm with you, I'm happy."

They gave each other another hug and kiss.

"Come on, I'll show you where you'll be sleeping." Asher led her upstairs.

Neon stood in the kitchen. Through the walls, she watched the two little lovebirds kiss and walk upstairs. They headed to Chief's bedroom. Now she knew what Alita Blackwood meant when she said something worse than the hybrid police or a hunter was coming their way. Not only was it a girl, she was a normal.

"Don't worry. I can handle this." Neon spoke as if Alita Blackwood stood next to her. "Oh boy, can I handle this." A mischievous grin appeared on her face.

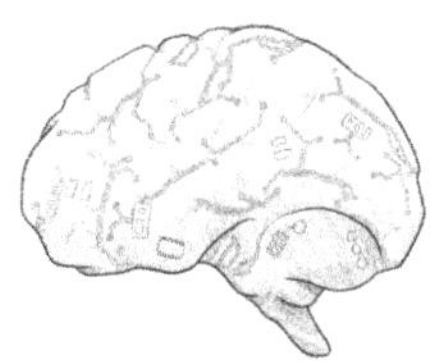

Nittany, Neon, and Asher walked around Cooper's Farm. They had a corn maze and a hay maze, plus booths selling hot apple cider, kettle corn, candied apples, and other autumn treats.

"I'll be right back." Nittany stood on her tiptoes and gave Asher a kiss on the lips, then disappeared into the women's restroom.

"She wants to make me gag," said Neon.

"It's obvious you don't like her, couldn't you at least be nice, since you invited yourself along?"

"She's a normal. If you think I'm going to sit by and watch you ruin your life by falling in love with a normal, you have another thing coming."

"She's not ruining my life. She is making it better," Asher said.

"When are you going to tell her your little secret, then?" asked Neon.

"I don't know." Asher wanted to tell her. He wondered what would happen if he did?

"That's what I thought," said Neon.

Asher saw Nittany come out of the restroom. "Can you do me at least one favor and let Nittany and me do the hay maze together?"

"Fine." Neon rolled her eyes.

"What's next?" asked Nittany.

"You want to do the hay maze?" Asher asked.

"Sure," Nittany replied.

"Asher you take your pooky in the hay maze. I'll sit this one out. I have hay fever you know." Neon sneezed unconvincingly. "I'm going to get kettle corn. My nose likes that smell better," said Neon. Knowing that she could still spy on them gave her comfort.

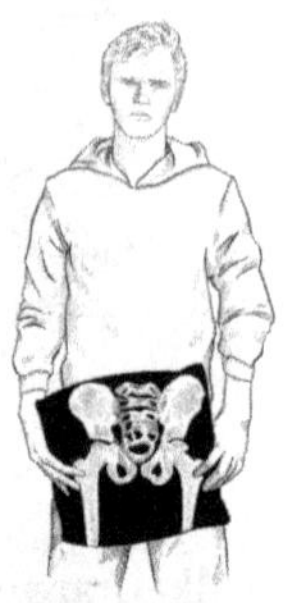

Neon stood by, watching and snacking on her popcorn as Nittany and Asher entered the maze. Three men entered after them, and Neon scanned them for fun. Bored watching Asher and Nittany, she did a quick scan of the maze and found four men of similar stature standing by the exit. "Son of a bitch," she said. "Hybrid hunters."

etective Bram "Mac" McGreggor sat at his desk at the East Coast Region Hybrid Police Department. Most detectives who worked in his department looked for hybrids and hybrid smuggling rings. They captured the hybrids and took them to be cleansed. Not Mac. He tracked down hybrid hunters and put the vigilantes behind bars.

Hybrid hunters took the law into their own hands. They didn't give the hybrids a chance to live through the cleansing process. They killed them on the spot. The reason was different for each hunter. Some did it to sell their implants on the black market, some did it because they loathed hybrids, for revenge, and for sport.

One of the problems with hybrid hunters was that the innocent tended to become collateral damage. They didn't care who got injured or killed as long as they got their target.

Mac was good at his job. Ten years ago, during his second year with the division, he and his partner had set a record high of hunters apprehended. The last four years, after his partner resigned, Mac had been going solo—he preferred to work alone. He always worked on three or four cases at a time. When one case's lead became hot, another one got cold. The trail leading to Cortez and Navarro sizzled. They were the worst hybrid hunters of all, and with Mac's determination, he would find them. After five years tracking them down, his instinct told him he was right behind them.

Mac sat at his desk looking at the various holoimages floating above of evidence and information collected over the last five months pertaining to the Willow Wood case. Normally, he wouldn't investigate this hunter raid, since it had happened out of his area of operation. The hoofprints of a pig and remains of exploding darts were signs that Navarro led the raid. There was a little stub of a cigar that matched Cortez's brand of choice. He'd gone to the scene, hoping to find clues that led him to Navarro and Cortez. Tired of being the hybrid police's lead on Navarro and Cortez's case, he wanted to close this once and for all.

"Hey, Mac, pull up file BUF6573," said Mac's supervisor, Captain Briggs.

"Buffalo?" Mac's fingers maneuvered over his desk, and all the holograms were replaced with a police report.

"This might be nothing, a couple of weeks ago, a kid on probation for helping a hybrid escape a raid, crashed his car during after being chased by unmarked drones."

"What does this have to do with me, Captain?" Mac asked as he pulled up the file and paged through.

"Witnesses saw a girl run from the scene. The guys up in Buffalo believe they were being chased by hunters."

"Captain, I don't have time to take another case. I'm already giving up my weekend with my family to be here. Slater and Nittany are back on Earth from school. I hope to see them before they head back."

"Turn to page three in the report. The kid had a camera in his car, and it started recording when he summoned the car to meet him."

Mac found page three, a picture of low quality on it. "I'll be damned." He tapped his desk, and a picture popped up next to the one already there.

"Looks like the same person, doesn't it?" asked Captain Briggs.

"It sure does." Mac got up and grabbed his jacket. "I'm headed to Buffalo to talk to this kid." Mac took a gander at the report. "Knute Tuckerson." He tapped his desk, and the two images of a girl with blue-and-green hair disappeared.

Mac woke up from his short nap during the ride from the airport. His rental car had parked itself in front of the Tuckersons' house. He stretched and let out a yawn that could've summoned any moose in the area. He could feel the difference in temperature compared to Philadelphia.

He paused to surveil the area. The neighborhood consisted mainly of small two-story houses with a ranch style thrown in the mix here and there. Cars lined both sides of the street, making a narrow passage that would allow one car to pass at a time. One car in particular caught Mac's attention. A high-class all-terrain vehicle sat amongst the middle-class cars used to commute to work, school, or run errands. He saw a figure sitting in the driver's seat. He couldn't make out any details. He climbed from his car and made sure his eyes didn't stop when he scanned the parked car ahead of him. He didn't want to let on that he knew they were there. Then again, it could be a neighbor sitting in the car waiting for their spouse to come out. Mac had learned over the years to never rule anything out too early.

He walked to the door and rang the doorbell. Mr. Tuckerson answered.

"Hello, Mr. Tuckerson, I'm Detective McGreggor; we talked on the phone." Mac flashed his badge.

"Yes, please come in," said Mr. Tuckerson. "Detective, I know my son is on probation and there is evidence that he broke it. He is a good kid, truly he is."

"Relax, Mr. Tuckerson, I'm not here to arrest your son. I'm not from the Hybrid Advocate division, nor am I from Search and Seizure."

"Then what division are you from?" Mr. Tuckerson asked with a perplexed expression.

"I'm from the Cabal division. I track down hybrid hunters." Mac scanned the area. "I have reason to believe your son was with a girl who might be connected to a case I'm working on."

"He was with no girl," Mr. Tuckerson assured him.

"Evidence says otherwise. Like I said, I have no interest in arresting or even detaining your son. I want to ask him a couple of questions."

"Okay, he's up in his room." Mr. Tuckerson led Mac up the stairs and down the hall. He tapped on the door and walked in. "Knute, there's a detective here to speak with you." Knute fidgeted nervously in his bed.

"Detective, I wasn't doing anything wrong. I lost control of my car. I had got it from the impound, and she wasn't road worthy after being stripped of everything."

Tuck's room faced the street. Mac walked over to the window and peeked out, trying not to be conspicuous to the driver.

"Mr. Tuckerson, do any of your neighbors have a forest-green road massacre?"

"If you're referring to the one parked down the street, no."

"How long has it been out there?" asked Mac.

"A few days, I guess," replied Mr. Tuckerson.

"Did anyone report it?"

"Not that I know of," Mr. Tuckerson replied. "Should I contact the police?"

"No, I'll take care of it." Mac turned his attention to Tuck. "Knute, I'm Detective McGreggor."

"I told you—"

"Relax, I'm not here to arrest you or anything like that. I want to ask you a couple of questions. I believe you might be a witness in a case I'm working on."

"What case?" asked Tuck.

"Navarro and Cortez are the worst hybrid hunters out there. I'm trying to capture them for justice can be served the proper way, not their way." Mac noticed Tuck grow a little pale at the mention of Cortez. His gut and experience told him the kid knew something.

"I've heard of them," said Mr. Tuckerson. "They're in the hybrid police's top ten most wanted. I believe they hold the number two and three spots, with Alita Blackwood holding number one."

Mac ignored Mr. Tuckerson. "Tuck, who is this girl?" Mac pulled up a holographic image of Neon from his watch.

"I don't know." Tuck's eyes looked toward the left as he answered.

"I don't care if the girl is a hybrid or not. You could tell me that you have a hundred hybrids in your basement and I wouldn't care unless one of them was her. She is a witness to my case. I need to know why she was up here."

Tuck looked at his dad, then at Mac, and back at his dad. Mac turned his attention to Mr. Tuckerson. "Sir, may I have a moment alone with your son?"

"Do I need to get a lawyer?" asked Mr. Tuckerson.

Mac smiled. "I can't tell you either way. What I can tell you is that I am not here to arrest your son. Once he gives me the information I need, then I'm gone, and you shouldn't be bothered by the department again. May I have a few moments with Tuck?" Mac could tell that Tuck was a little scared from the way he kept glancing at his father.

"Tuck, I'll be out in the hall if you need me." Mr. Tuckerson left, closing the door behind him.

Mac sat on the edge of the bed to pull up the pictures of Neon. He accidentally pulled one up of Nittany with two other girls.

"Xiao?" Tuck said in a low breath.

"Oh, you know her? She's in my daughter's squad onboard the NAS *Pocono*. I keep asking for a picture of her entire squad. For unknown reasons she won't send me any photos of the boys in her squad. I think she has a crush on one and is afraid I'll come up there and arrest him." Mac let out a stifled laugh.

"Her." Tuck pointed to Xiao. "She's the one who turned me in for helping a hybrid this summer."

"The one not smiling." Mac changed topics as he changed photos. "You know this girl, don't you?"

Tuck looked down toward his lap.

"You have nothing to be afraid of. Who is she?"

"I only know her first name. Neon."

"Where did you meet her?"

"I was at the Pittsburgh airport. I dropped off two academy cadets, and she jumped in my car and told me to go."

"Was she being chased?"

"I believe it was Cortez or Navarro. I'm not sure which."

"I see. Tell me about the accident."

"I'm not going to get in trouble? Dad already lost my sister and mom. If he loses me too…"

"He won't lose you. Tell me about the accident."

"Hybrid hunters showed up at the house here. Neon and I escaped out the back. I had my car come and get us. We were being followed by drones. I tried using my lightning strike on them. I had installed it. It fried the drones and my car. That's the last thing I remember before waking up in the hospital."

"What did this Neon tell you?"

"Nothing really. She wanted to get back to Pittsburgh."

"Do you know this boy?" Mac asked as he pulled up a picture of Asher.

"No, never seen him before."

"Can you tell me anything about the hybrid hunters that were after you?"

"I didn't really see them. It was Neon who spotted them."

"I appreciate your cooperation." Mac tapped his watch. "I transferred you my contact information. Call me if you think of anything else or if Neon contacts you again."

"Okay, sir."

Mac stood and walked to the window. The forest-green road massacre had gone.

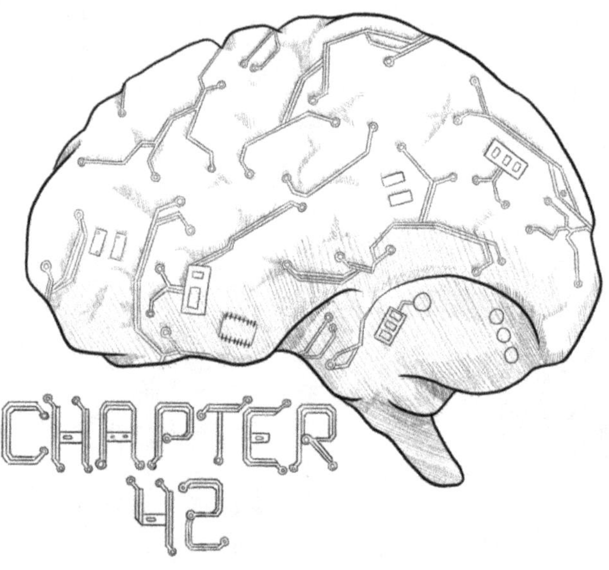

# CHAPTER 42

"Timothy would've loved these mazes." Asher held Nittany's hand, a spark of energy going from her hand to his. He found himself laughing as they made a wrong turn into a straw-laden dead end.

"If my brother Flem were here, he would be climbing over the hay and through it instead of trying to find the way out," Nittany claimed.

Asher smiled. "Timothy would've done the same thing." His smile turned solemn when the vision of Timothy climbing over the hay walls turned into the dreadful image of him climbing over the stonewall the night of the raid, the night he died.

"You okay?" asked Nittany.

Asher shrugged and continued down the path.

"How come you don't talk much about Timothy?"

Asher stopped as if his feet were trapped in Gorilla Glue. He tried to pull his hand away. Nittany tightened her grip. She stopped and faced Asher. He looked up at the sky, avoiding her eyes to avoid crying. Not now.

"It's being back on Earth," he managed to say.

"Asher, you can talk to me. If I can help…"

"There's nothing you can do." Asher stepped around her and headed down the passage. "Come on, I think the exit is this way." His grip tightened on Nittany. He wanted to tell her everything. His heart ached knowing he couldn't. How could he explain his loss without revealing his true identity? He stumbled ahead, pulling her along, willing himself not to cry, when he heard a bunch of scrambling up ahead, followed by screams.

They stopped. There were more screams, and the wall collapsed onto the path. Asher yanked Nittany away from harm's way, only to see Neon on an antique John Deere tractor.

"Neon?" Asher asked as he coughed and sneezed from the floating hay that swirled around them.

"What happened?" Nittany coughed and gagged as she wiped off the stray straw on her clothes.

"I thought you guys were lost. I made an exit for you."

A crowd of people started to congregate around the tractor.

"We weren't lost," Asher said between clenched teeth.

"Get down from there now," said a large man in bib overalls. "Leave the premises or I will call the police on you."

"I'll leave. Geesh. Come on, Asher," said Neon.

Asher started to climb over the fallen hay bales.

"Wait! We don't have to leave. This is my cousin's property," said Nittany.

Asher shrugged and continued climbing. He met up with Neon. "Why did you ruin this?"

"You have uninvited company," Neon said.

"Yeah, and her name is Neon." Asher's voice rose in frustration.

"Not me, them." Neon flashed her eyes to a couple of men.

Asher recognized one of them from the airport. "Hybrid hunters," he mumbled.

"They had both entrances blocked. We better get out of here."

Asher looked at Nittany. She had furrowed her brow and opened her mouth a tad. Bewilderment and disappointment flooded her eyes. "I'm sorry, Nittany. I'll make it up to you." Asher reached his hand out to her. She walked past it.

"That worked better than I thought it would," Neon mumbled.

"What?" asked Asher.

"Oh, nothing. Come on, let's get out of here."

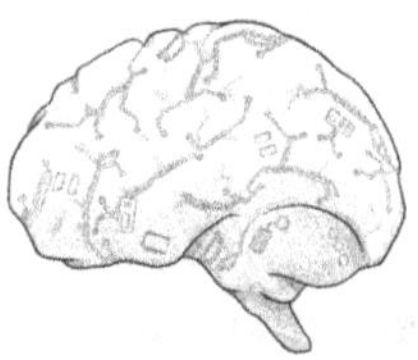

Asher, Nittany, and Neon arrived back at Chief's house. Neon bounced inside.

"Asher," said Nittany.

"Yeah?"

"Why did you go with her today instead of staying with me?"

Asher shrugged. "I don't know." He lied.

"Maybe I should get my stuff and go back to my uncle's."

Asher's heart broke. "No, please don't go. I want you here. I do. Don't worry about Neon."

"Asher, I feel like you're keeping secrets from me. The last guys I dated kept secrets from me."

Asher closed his eyes. Maybe he should tell her the truth.

"I am keeping a secret," said Asher.

"What is it?" Nittany asked.

"Please don't tell anyone. Okay?"

"I won't. What is it?"

"This past summer..." Asher bit his lower lip and looked toward the sky. "My brother, Timothy, drowned."

"Oh, Asher, I'm sorry. Why keep that a secret?"

"Because I killed him."

Nittany took a step back. "What do you mean?"

"We got into a canoe, and I told him we would be safe. We capsized in rapids and he drowned."

"Asher, that was an accident. You didn't kill him. I don't see one ounce of killer instinct in you." She gave Asher a hug.

Asher hugged her back and looked into her eyes. "Please stay."

Nittany gave Asher a huge hug. "I'm not going anywhere."

"I told you to keep a distance," Navarro said through her teeth.

"Sorry. We thought we were at a safe distance," said Sabastian.

"That girl spotted you. Otherwise, why would she drive a tractor into a hay maze?"

Cortez whipped out a switchblade and rested the tip upon Sabastian's Adam's apple. "You know why she's pissed?"

"The hybrids knew we were tailing them?" Sabastian gulped.

"Give the man a head-of-the-line privilege. He got the correct answer," Cortez said.

"Cortez, find me a new crew to replace Sabastian's. They will be doing a special assignment for me."

"Yes, boss."

Navarro smiled wickedly, showing her perfect teeth. "We need to fill organ orders. I think you and your crew are perfect for the task."

Cortez escorted Sabastian to the butcher room at one of their operation centers.

"Cortez, we did what you told us to do, including lying to the boss lady. We almost had the boy if it wasn't for that girl crashing into the hay wall. You're not going to make us organ donors, are you?"

Cortez smiled, his panatela sticking out. "I can't risk the chance of the witch finding out our little secret." Staring directly into Sabastian's eyes without blinking, his hand thrust upward, a switchblade piercing the skin under Sabastian's jaw. Blood streamed down his gloves. Sabastian's half-open jaw revealed a bloody metallic reflection running vertically. He gripped Cortez's wrist, trying to move it. Cortez removed the knife, and Sabastian's body fell to the floor.

A man with a thick salt-and-pepper beard came out of the back room. His gloves and apron were bloody. "Cortez?" He had a raspy voice.

"Sabastian here won head-of-the-line privileges. He is being kind enough to help fill outstanding organ orders. I'll have a few more donors for you shortly."

The man smiled, revealing missing teeth. "Excellent."

"I've had enough of this shit," Cortez said to himself. "I'll get the kid myself." He left the butcher room, focused on his new mission.

B rett walked up to Xiao's duplex. He gave a *rap-a-tap-tap* on the door. Within a minute, the door opened, revealing Mr. Li.

"You again," he said. "Come on in, she's upstairs. She'll be down in a minute." Mr. Li turned around.

Brett mocked Mr. Li behind his back, mouthing, "You again," as they went to the living room.

"Xiao says that your father is Senator Lundy, the one running for president."

*Great*, Brett thought. The last thing he wanted to do was to talk about his father. "Yeah."

"I'm not voting for him," said Mr. Li.

"That's something we have in common," Brett replied.

Mr. Li let out a small *hmm*. "What are your plans with my daughter tonight?"

"We're going to find trouble."

"If you get my little girl in trouble, I will see to your cremation personally."

Brett laughed mockingly.

"What time will you have her back?"

"Probably by seven," replied Brett.

Mr. Li looked at his watch. "It's 6:03 now. That's less than an hour." Mr. Li showed no emotion and kept his eyes locked on Brett.

"I'm not bringing her back in an hour. I meant seven a.m. I'll have her back by 0700."

Mr. Li returned the artificial laugh.

"Let's go," said Xiao as she came down from the stairs with Mrs. Li.

Brett stood and patted Mr. Li's shoulder. "It was nice talking to you, Pops."

"Mr. Lundy," said Mr. Li. Brett turned his attention back to Mr. Li. "No Pinocchio business."

Xiao grabbed onto Brett's arm and dragged him outside.

"Wow, you didn't say bye to your parents," Brett said once they were in the driveway.

"If I did, I would have been interrogated again about what we're doing tonight. What are we going to do tonight? Is Pinocchio going to make a guest appearance?" asked Xiao.

"He can if you want," said Brett with a devilish grin. He walked around the car and climbed behind the wheel. Xiao opened her door herself and got in. She gave him the stink eye.

"What?"

"You've could've opened the door for me."

"Why? You made it clear that this wasn't a date. Now let's find ourselves some trouble."

"Where's Oscar?" asked Xiao.

"I gave him the night off."

"You gave him the slip, didn't you?" she asked.

"Yep! Now let's get this night started." Brett tapped a button on the dashboard, and the car began to move. He stretched over the front seat and pulled out a bottle from a cardboard box. He opened it and took a swig. The liquid sent a burning sensation down his throat and across his chest. "Good stuff," he said, passing the bottle to Xiao.

"Talismon Barnes? What kind of whisky is that?" asked Xiao.

"Rare, expensive and the best damn whisky on this planet. Go ahead, take a swig."

"I don't drink. Now, what are we going to do tonight?"

"Come on, you said you wanted to loosen up. Take a swig."

"Fine." Xiao brought the bottle to her lips. In under a second, she coughed and gagged, and whisky came out of her mouth and nose. "That stuff is horrible. How can you drink that?"

"Simple, like this." Brett grabbed the bottle and took another drink. "Here, try again."

"Getting drunk is not my idea of having a good time," said Xiao.

"Come on, you won't get drunk off one swig."

Xiao took another gulp. She managed to keep it down this time.

"All right!" Brett cheered.

"Where are we going?" asked Xiao.

"354 Wigwam Drive."

"What's there?"

"You'll see." Brett smiled and took another swig.

"You brought me to an abandoned house from a horror movie that looks demon-infested?" Xiao and Brett stood in front of an old, deteriorating house. It reminded her too much of the houses in the internment village. The windows that weren't boarded up were broken. The house's once-white paint was now gray and peeling. Shingles were missing from the roof. Brett set the box from the backseat down on the ground.

Xiao already felt the effects of the whisky.

"Here, take this and throw it." Brett handed her a roll of toilet paper.

Xiao took the roll and threw it down the sidewalk. "This is supposed to be fun?"

"Really? You're such a cunnerman. This is how you do it." Brett unwrapped a roll and tossed it into the tree in front of the house. They got caught on the limbs leaving a streak behind as it fell back down.

Xiao took another swig. She handed it to Brett, and he did the same. "I can do that." Her speech began to slur.

After they used up all the toilet paper, they moved on to eggs.

"It's not my fault," Xiao slurred. She flopped down on the ground next to the last carton of eggs and took another swig from the bottle.

"What?" asked Brett.

"Olivia's death. If she would have left the party without me, she could still be alive. And I could be with Tuck."

"Who's Tuck?" asked Brett.

"A boy I danced with." She began to laugh. "I had to turn her in. You know? Hybrids are bad people. Do you like hybrids?"

"Personally, I don't give a shit either way," said Brett.

"You should give a shit." Xiao rested her head on the ground. "I tell you why. You can study your ass off, and who gets the scholarship or the promotion? The hybrids—that's who. All because they could afford to purchase a garrison chip. It's not right."

Brett took another swig and passed the bottle to Xiao.

"It's not my fault." Xiao stumbled as she tried to stand up. She managed to pick up the carton of eggs. "Tuck blames me." She threw an egg at Brett. It barely missed him. "Olivia's parents blame me." She threw another egg at Brett. This time he blocked it with his arms. "Olivia blames me, Mugin blames me, Fugin blames me, you blame me." With each name, Xiao threw an egg at Brett.

He laughed at each hit, trying to block the incoming egg bombs.

"Why are you laughing?"

"I never thought I would see the day that Xiao-Niao Li was wasted."

"You have egg on your hoodie." Xiao plopped down next to him. "You better take that off. You can get salmonella." She reached over and grabbed both sides of Brett's hoodie, pulling it off. "Oops. I took your shirt off too."

"You are drunk." Brett smiled.

"You know, your chest makes up for what your flat ass lacks." She ran her hand down his body and pushed him onto his back, then fell on top of him. "It's not my fault." She leaned in and gave Brett a deep, hard kiss. Brett returned it.

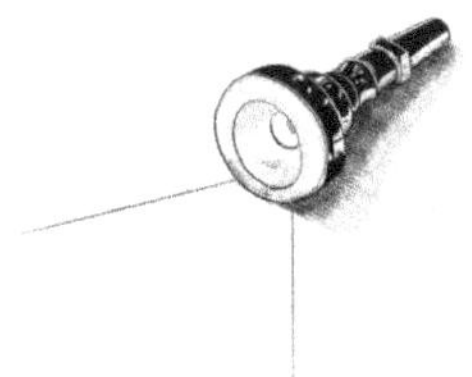

"It's almost sunrise and we managed to not get called for any mischief night crimes," said Officer Purnell, sitting in the passenger seat of a police car.

"You spoke too soon; look there," replied Officer Hanson. He pulled the police car up to an abandoned house. Toilet paper hung from the trees, eggs shells spattered across the front porch.

Officer Purnell got out and turned on his flashlight. He walked over to a car that looked abandoned.

"Hey, Hanson, we have two naked kids in the back seat here. By the look of things, they've been drinking the good stuff."

Officer Hanson walked over to the car. "Looks like drinking wasn't the only thing they were doing. There on the floor is Little Peter's raincoat." He pointed the light to a used condom.

"At least they used protection," said Purnell. "Let's wake these two darlings up and haul them down to headquarters."

"There goes our paperless night." Hanson tapped on the window with his flashlight. "Rise and shine."

Cortez sat in his Jeep, smoking his cigar. He watched as people wasted their money to get scared inside a man-made haunted house. If they only knew the real terror waited outside. He had to admit, the outside looked intriguing, but nothing to get the adrenaline flowing through the veins. A man with an antique chainless chainsaw hid behind a tree. When unsuspecting idiots walked past the tree, he would let the chainsaw make its deafening scream and jump out at them. Nothing but child's play.

The chainsaw's constant roar and the screams of pitiful people started to irritate him. This was why he preferred to kill his prey quickly and silently. If he wanted to torture them, the first thing to go would be their voice box.

His holocomm vibrated. He tapped it, Dylan's image shimmied over his arm.

"This better be good," said Cortez.

"You were right. A detective from HQ showed up at the Buffalo boy's house," said Dylan.

"That's all you have for me? We knew that was bound to happen." Cortez didn't know what got on his nerves more, this worthless news or the guy with the chainless chainsaw.

"It gets better, Cortez. The detective was McGreggor."

"Bram McGreggor, Navarro's old partner from the force." He took a deep inhale of his cigar and let the smoke flow through the hologram. "He's good at his job. We need to keep an eye on him." Cortez looked at the man with the chainsaw, his patience getting thinner with each buzz of the saw.

"That's not all. You're going to like this," said the man.

"What?"

"We intercepted a call to the *Pocono*. That boy who got away at Willow Wood, guess who he's dating."

"I don't care who the kid screws. I want that kid."

"Oh, I think you'll care. It's Nittany McGreggor."

"The detective's daughter?" asked Cortez.

"One and the same."

The saw coursed through his ears one more time with high-pitched screams. A group of kids running and laughing, not paying attention, ran into the Jeep. "That's it, I've had enough." Cortez slapped the holowatch off and opened the door. As he exited the Jeep, he pulled out his knife. He marched across the road and up the grassy hill toward the chainsaw man.

The man popped out from the tree. The chainsaw sounded its battle cry as Cortez stopped. His left hand immediately gripped the man's neck and pinned him to the tree. The man had no strength. Cortez wasn't surprised. That was why the guy needed a chainsaw.

With his right hand, he pressed the tip of the blade up under his jaw, slightly piercing it. "Drop the chainsaw," Cortez said through gritted teeth. The man complied. "Chainless chainsaws are not scary. A knife pressing against your throat, now that is scary." Cortez looked down and saw a wet spot growing on the man's groin. "How many kids did you make piss their pants? I bet zero. You're not going to have any more chances either." Cortez thrusted his hand upward. He kept his eyes fixed on the chainsaw man's eyes and watched the life drain out of them. He pulled his knife out, let the body drop to the ground, then smashed the chainsaw against the tree. Three kids exited the haunted house. He smiled and went back to his Jeep to follow his target.

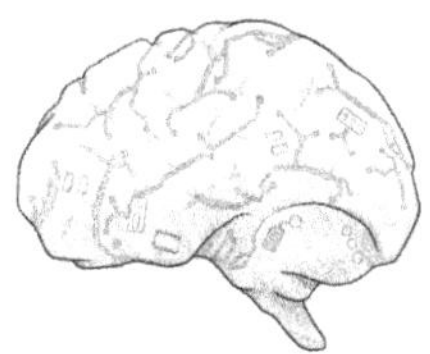

Asher, Nittany, and Neon arrived back at Chief's house and climbed out of the car. Neon seemed to be having the time of her life, whereas Nittany seemed gloomy and perplexed. Neon skipped into the house, leaving Asher and Nittany alone outside. Asher stopped and glanced around. He had this strange feeling they were followed from the haunted house. Paranoia, Asher told himself. It's only paranoia.

"Asher?" said Nittany.

"Huh?" he replied, only half paying attention.

"Were you and Neon ever more than friends?"

"You mean like us?" asked Asher.

Nittany nodded.

"We kissed two times, to see what the big deal was. That happened four years, six months, two hundred ninety-four days, one hour, and twenty-seven minutes ago. It meant nothing," replied Asher, still not paying full attention to Nittany or what he was saying.

"It meant nothing, yet you remember how long it's been, down to the minute, since you kissed her?"

Asher shrugged. "Yeah," was all he could get out.

Nittany bit her bottom lip. She grabbed the cross on her necklace and massaged it. She kept silent and went into the house. He waited a few more minutes and then headed inside himself.

Asher went down into the man cave. Neon was sitting on a couch watching a holoshow. "Is Nittany down here?"

Neon looked up into the ceiling. "She's in your dad's room."

"Thanks," he said as he trotted back up the stairs. When he arrived at Chief's bedroom, he found the door shut. He tapped lightly. "Nittany, you in there?" The door opened. "You going to bed?"

"I guess. Are you?" she said quietly.

"I'm going to grab a quick shower, then I'll go to bed. I had fun with you tonight."

"Me too." Nittany gave him a weak, forced smile.

"Good night." He leaned in and gave her a kiss. Her kiss in return was weak and not full of energy like all of her previous ones.

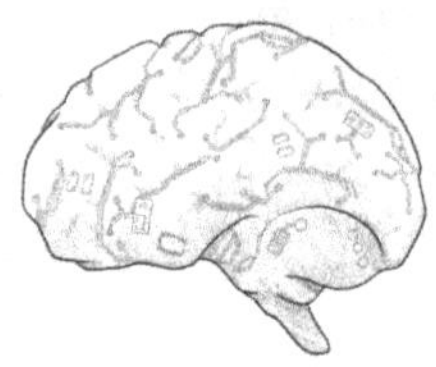

Asher entered his bedroom after his shower. He dropped the towel around his waist and pulled out a clean pair of underwear.

"Nice tush."

Asher jumped! "Neon! I told you..." He turned around. Nittany lay under his covers. She had the bedspread pulled up above her bosom, her shoulders bare. He realized he had no clothes on and quickly held his underwear in front of him. He could only hope that she didn't see anything. Which was very unlikely.

"Nittany, what are you doing in here?" Asher bent down carefully to not expose himself to her. He grabbed his towel and wrapped it around his waist again.

"I would like one-on-one time with you is all. We haven't gotten any of that today."

"I know, I'm sorry."

"Can we have alone time together before we go to sleep?" asked Nittany.

"Most definitively." Asher looked at her in his bed. Her beauty put a smile on his face and caused things to stir under his towel. He was finally going to get alone time with Nittany without Neon wedging herself between them.

He pulled his underwear up under the towel. He kept the towel wrapped around him, hiding the uncontrollable bulge in his underwear.

Asher sat down on the edge of his bed. It felt strange having her in it. He crawled into his sheets and stayed as close to the edge as he could.

"Let's cuddle," Nittany suggested.

Asher knew touch was her love language. He didn't know what Nittany would do if she found out he had a boner. He wanted to respect her wish to wait but didn't know if he could overpower the temptation that lay next to him.

Asher and Nittany moved closer together. She rested her head on his chest and her free hand on his abdomen. Asher wrapped his arm around her. He began to relax. As awkward as this felt, it also felt natural and peaceful.

Without warning, Nittany pushed herself up and started kissing Asher hard and deep. He wrapped his arms around her and felt her bare skin. Then he realized Nittany's naked breasts were pressing against his chest.

"Nittany?" He pulled away. "I thought you wanted to wait until you get married."

"I lost two boyfriends because I wouldn't sleep with them. I didn't mind really. I never had feelings for them like I do you. I know you want to do it. I don't want..." She trailed off and looked toward the sheets.

Asher pulled himself up a little. Nittany covered her breasts with the sheets. "Nittany, I respect you and your wishes and dreams."

"You do?" asked Nittany.

"I do. You think I'm going to leave you because you don't want to have sex until you're married?" he asked.

"I got scared with Neon being here. I thought maybe you would do it with her because I won't."

Asher looked her in the eyes. "Nittany, I would never do that to you. Neon means nothing to me; at least not like you do. She's a friend, a sister at best. You, you're my friend, you're my girlfriend. I want to spend all my time with you, not Neon. I've tried to get rid of her several times. It's not easy trying to get Neon to do something she doesn't want to do."

"Really?"

Asher nodded.

She leaned in and gave him a simple kiss. "Thank you. Now close your eyes so I can get my nightie back on."

"You saw me, don't I get a peek?" Asher smiled.

"Not this time."

Asher complied, and Nittany reached down on the floor, grabbed her nightie, and put it back on.

"You can open your eyes now."

Asher stared at her. "You're beautiful."

"I'm going to bed now." She leaned over and gave him another simple yet loving kiss.

Once Nittany had left, he let out a deep sigh and slid back into bed. He had no idea how he'd managed to deny her like that. No, he did know. The love he had for her knew that if he had proceeded, it would've hurt both of them. He went to sleep knowing he did the right thing.

Nittany tossed and turned in bed. Anger filled her heart for what she'd done to Asher. She'd embarrassed herself in front of him. Fear that she would lose him to Neon overpowered her. She knew without a doubt that if she had done what she did with Asher to her first two boyfriends, she would have gone all the way. Or at least to a point where she got too scared and pushed out of it halfway through.

Then there was Asher. She knew he wanted more by the way his kisses became deeper and deeper, his hands exploring more parts of her body, where she had to replace them a couple of times. Then there was his member. It seemed to always be ready to take the plunge. She felt it pressing against her leg and moved when she kissed him. The thing she liked about Asher was that he would catch himself starting to cross the line, and before she could say anything, he would step back of his own accord. The way all her friends talked, not many guys would do that. She felt her heart grow for Asher, knowing he was willing to sacrifice his needs, wants, and desires for hers.

Her bladder reminded her that she'd had too much hot apple cider while waiting in line for the haunted house. After she finished going to the bathroom, she stopped by Asher's door, which stood ajar. She heard him mumbling and stirring in his sleep. Asher did this on a regular basis on board the *Pocono*. After their talk in the hay maze, she knew why he had nightmares. He blamed himself for his brother's death.

"Mom!" Asher sat straight up. He trembled as sweat covered his entire body. His breaths were short and sporadic, as if he were trying not to cry.

"It's okay," said Nittany, immediately going over to Asher and crawling into bed with him. She held him tight, giving him comfort.

"They're dead." Asher managed to say between breaths.

"Shhhh," whispered Nittany. "I'm here. You had a nightmare is all." Nittany knew that wasn't true. To her it was a nightmare, to Asher, it was reliving the darkest night of his life.

She eased his shaking body back down. He rolled onto his side, facing away from her. She wondered if he usually slept facing outward. She couldn't help to think that maybe he didn't want to show her the fear on his face. Or maybe the tears that leaked from his eyes.

She pulled the covers up over both of them. She spooned up against him and wrapped her arms around him. She sent soft, comforting words to him, and the trembling slowed down until he fully relaxed in her hold and went back to sleep. She leaned over and gave him a kiss on the cheek. "I love you, Asher," she said. She snuggled back down, not letting go of him, and finally sleep overcame her.

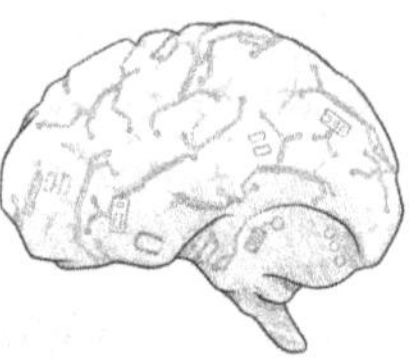

The autumn sun dawned through Asher's bedroom window. He woke up and felt something pressed tightly behind him. He rolled onto his back and found Nittany snuggled up close to him. Not knowing what to do with his arm, he wrapped it around her. She snuggled in to his embrace. This comforted him. He felt completely content with Nittany asleep next to him in his bed. He watched her sleep. She looked at peace. He tilted his head down and kissed her on the forehead. "I love you, Nittany." The peaceful feeling consumed him, and he fell back to sleep.

Cortez stifled a yawn. The sun started to come up over the horizon. He sat and watched the house that Asher, Neon, and the McGreggor girl had gone into when they came back from the haunted house. He could have easily sneaked in while they were all sleeping and given them an injection that would ensure they wouldn't wake up until he needed them to. His instinct told him not to. He'd learned to listen to his instinct long ago when he lived in Santiago De Cuba during his childhood. If he hadn't, he would have never seen his teenage years.

If Alita Blackwood could be involved with these kids, he wanted to see for himself. What a bounty she would bring if he managed to capture her before Navarro did.

An autotaxi pulled up along the curb in front of the house. A man got out with a duffle bag. Cortez punched a few buttons on his dashboard, and a holographic image appeared. Under the hologram, it read, *Chief Hospital Corpsman Liam Asher Mrkonic.*

Xiao pulled the pillow over her head. The bright morning light coming through her window made her head hurt all the more. She licked her lips, trying to wet her mouth. She had thrown up too many times to remember, and it felt like a Muay Thai tournament going on in her head. She didn't know if she wanted to die because she felt like a shuttlecraft had run her over or because of the fallout that would come with her parents—maybe a little of both.

Mrs. Li entered Xiao's room carrying a tray holding a small teapot and cup. Using her native tongue, she spoke. "I brought you green tea. It will help."

Xiao forced herself to sit up in bed. Her head throbbed. Speaking in Chinese, she said, "How mad is Fugin?"

"If I were you, I would stay away from him for a while," replied Mrs. Li.

Xiao took a sip of the hot tea. Warmth spread across her chest. "How much trouble am I in?" She took another sip.

"No charges are being pressed for vandalism or anything. Your father's biggest concern is if that boy you were with pushed himself on you. Did he get you drunk to take advantage of you?"

"Actually, I pushed myself on him. He didn't resist, though." Regret flooded her body. Why did she let herself get out of control like that? She'd become one of Brett's notches, and that alone made her sick to her stomach without the help from the hangover.

"Did you use protection?" asked Mrs. Li.

"The first time we did," Xiao said with complete confidence. "The second time, I believe so. I'm not sure about the third time."

"How many times did you do it?" Mrs. Li had a worried look on her face.

"I think three," said Xiao.

"Since you're not sure if you had protection for...for all the times you had sex, later today we will go get you the shot."

Xiao placed her hand over her stomach. The idea of getting a shot didn't feel right. After seeing what had happened to Olivia, feeling responsible for her death, she didn't want to be a part of that again. Even if it was a day-old zygote.

"Mugin, I made a huge mistake. I don't want to get the shot." She took another sip of her tea.

"Xiao-Niao, it only takes one sperm to get you pregnant."

"I know. I just..." She paused and closed her eyes.

"You what?"

Xiao let out a long sigh. "Friday, before coming home, I stopped at the internment village that Olivia was living in."

"Really? Why didn't you tell us?" Mrs. Li sat on the bed and placed her comforting hand on Xiao's leg.

Tears swelled in Xiao's brown eyes. She tried blinking them away and they still streamed down her cheeks. "It was horrible, Mugin. I found Olivia dead."

Mrs. Li gasped and placed her hand over her heart. "Xiao, I'm sorry. You can't blame yourself. You were in the right."

"I know I was. I didn't do anything wrong, does that make it right?"

"That's for you to figure out," said Mrs. Li.

"I was afraid you were going to say that."

"Xiao, you are very smart. You are very brave. Your father and I love you very much, and we are proud of your accomplishments. You are at the age when you start thinking with both your mind and your heart. At times they supply you with different answers. Only you can decide which one you follow."

Xiao let out a long sigh. She took another sip of her tea and placed the cup on her nightstand.

"I believe that right now, your brain is telling you to get the shot later today and your heart doesn't agree. Your father and I prefer you get it. Chances are you're probably not pregnant. Do you want to risk that chance? I trust you, Xiao. I'll let you make the decision and I will support you."

"What about Fugin?"

"I'll handle him. Now get some rest. We'll talk more about this later."

"Thanks, Mugin." Xiao slid down into her bed. The tea did make her feel a little better, the thought of going back to the *Pocono* and facing Brett made her feel sick. She wanted to blame him. After all, he brought the alcohol, made her take a sip, took her to the abandoned house. He brought the raw eggs. He could've stopped her. For every excuse she made putting Brett at fault, she came up with five reasons she could blame herself.

Mac walked up the hill toward the haunted house. He wore the same clothes he'd had on the day before. Metal stakes with round glass tops strategically stuck out of the ground about four feet high. Holographic police tape connected to all the stakes, made of a hologram. He flashed his badge to a young police officer who was making sure no one crossed the tape who shouldn't. Mac walked up to the tree.

"May I help you?" asked a well-toned woman.

"Yes, I'm Detective Bram McGreggor from Hybrid Police Headquarters."

"I'm Detective Melissa Grady, homicide. We didn't call for your assistance. We have no idea if hybrids were involved or not."

"I heard on the radio that the victim was stabbed up under the chin, going into the roof of his mouth."

"Yes."

"Do you have any leads or suspects?" asked Mac.

"No, people thought he was acting the part of being dead for the haunted house. When he didn't come home last night, his mother contacted the person who runs this haunted house. She came over to see if he was sleeping here. The actors often do that. This is when she found the body," said Detective Grady.

"What's his name? How old?" asked Mac.

"Dennis Rivertree. He was eighteen. A senior in high school."

"Damn. Just a kid."

"Detective, what's your interest in this case?"

"The stab wound. Rarely will a killer stab their victim in the jaw like that. Did you find anything else? Anything out of the ordinary?"

"We found a cigar next to the body. We're running a DNA check. It could be anybody's."

"Cortez," Mac said, more to himself than to Detective Grady.

"Detective, we have something," said a young officer coming out of the haunted house. "You're going to want to see this."

"Care to join us, Mac?" asked Detective Grady. Mac nodded.

Detective Grady led Mac inside the haunted house to the control room. Sitting at a holotable were two men.

"What do you have?" asked Detective Grady.

"We were looking at the holofootage," said a man with a mustache.

"They recorded pretty much the entire property, including inside the house here."

Mac saw the frozen frame of the holoimage. A familiar figure stood next to the victim. "Cortez."

"Shit, it is Cortez," said Detective Grady. "Play it through."

The man without a mustache played the holovideo. They watched as Cortez came up to the victim and stabbed him.

"Stop it there," said Mac. "He's looking at something."

"Maybe to see if anyone saw him?" suggested the man with the mustache.

"No, it looks like something caught his attention," said Mac. "Can you move the hologram so we can follow his line of sight?"

"Yeah," said the other man.

"Stop!" yelled Mac. "Blow those three up." The man enlarged three teenagers walking together. One was a very tall boy, another a girl with blue-and-green hair, and the third... "Son of bitch!"

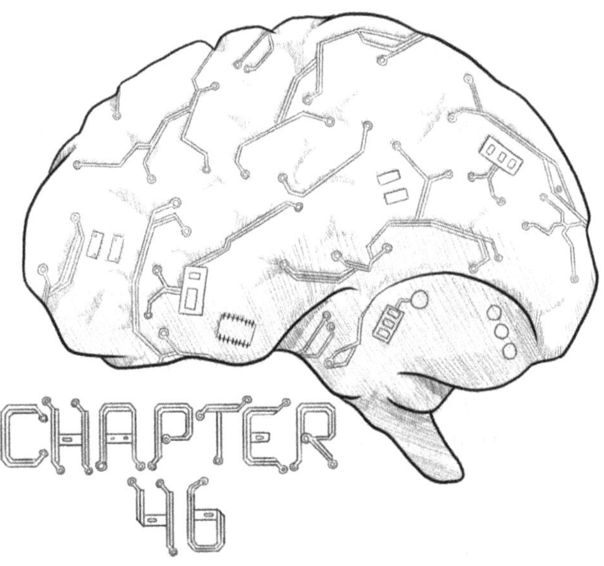

# CHAPTER 46

"What is this?"

The sound woke Asher up instantly. He immediately recognized the voice. The voice that should've still been on the *Pocono*.

"Chief, what are you doing here?" Asher sat up about the same time as a petrified Nittany.

"I live here." Chief's nostrils flared over his reddening face. "That's more than I can say about Cadet McGreggor."

"I can explain," said Asher. *The one time I break the rules, I get caught.*

"You two get dressed. I'll meet you downstairs in two minutes." Chief left before Asher could reply.

"I'm sorry, Asher." Nittany's eyes were tearing up.

"It's okay." Asher had known he would be in trouble if he got caught, and he got caught. Oddly, a part of him didn't care.

Asher and Nittany went downstairs and sat on the couch in the living room. Chief stood in front of them, pacing. He opened his mouth to speak when the doorbell rang.

"Don't go anywhere." Chief walked over to the door and peeked through. "Nittany, it's your father."

"How did he know to find me here?" whispered Nittany.

"Maybe Chief called him?" Asher whispered.

"Detective, I believe I have something of yours here." Chief opened the door and invited Mac in.

"Nittany is here?"

"Yes, she's in the living room," replied Chief.

Mac walked in and saw Nittany. He shook his head in disgust. "Your mother said you were staying at your uncle's this weekend."

"I'm sorry."

"Get your stuff and go to the car." Mac gave Asher the evil eye. Then he turned his attention to Chief. "May I speak to you privately?"

"Yes, come in the kitchen."

Asher tried to listen, their voices were too low for him to hear. He wished he had hybrid ears. Nittany came downstairs with her overnight bag, evidence of tears on her face.

"I'm sorry, Asher," she said.

"It's okay." He gave her a hug and held her.

"Not acceptable," said Mac. "Get to the car, Nittany."

Nittany gave Asher one last tight squeeze and left. Mac gave Asher another evil eye and followed his daughter out.

"Do you mind telling me what the hell you were thinking?" asked Chief.

Asher sat back down on the couch and shrugged.

"Answer me this, Asher. Did you have this planned when you asked me if you could stay here by yourself? I want the truth."

Asher nodded.

"You lied to me." It was more of a statement than a question.

Asher nodded.

"When Neon called me last night and said you and Nittany were having sex in the house, I didn't believe her. Until she sent me an image from her eyesight."

"Wait a minute," Asher finally spoke. "Neon called you?"

"Yes, she did. I can't believe you went behind my back to have sex with your girlfriend under my roof. The girl I specifically told you to stay away from. You know what her father does for a living? I'll tell you. He tracks down hybrids and has them cleansed. Do you understand that?"

"We didn't have sex. That wasn't the plan for her visit."

"I don't care what the plan was. You lied to me like your mother, keeping the truth from me about you."

Asher stood. "Don't you dare bring my mom into this."

"Why shouldn't I?" Chief roared.

"Because I said so," said Asher.

"Oh, I'm supposed to listen to you like you listened to me? I am so angry right now, Asher. There will be consequences."

"Oh, what? You're going ground me?"

"That's a start," said Chief.

"I spent the first sixteen years of my life grounded. This isn't new to me."

"Don't get smart with me. If your grandfather caught me bringing in a girl to sleep with while he was away, he'd lock me in the attic and throw the key away."

"I told you, Nittany and I didn't have sex, and we weren't going to. That wasn't the plan," said Asher, his voice now rising.

"I was a seventeen-year-old boy like you once. I know what goes through your mind."

"No, you don't," said Asher. "Have you ever had to hide your entire life because if you're caught, you're dead? Did you watch your mother murdered in front of your eyes? Were you ever responsible for your brother's death? Were you ever chased knowing that if you were caught you would be dead? Don't stand there and tell me what I'm thinking. You don't have a damn clue."

"Maybe not. Thanks to Nittany's dad, what I do know a boy was murdered at the haunted house that you all went to last night."

"He thinks I killed a boy?"

"No, he knows it was Cortez, a hybrid hunter. For all I know, that hunter could be waiting outside for the perfect time to kill you."

"From what I've read and experienced from Cortez, if he was going to kill me, I would be dead by now." Asher's thoughts shifted. "Does Nittany's dad know I'm a hybrid?"

"I think he knows; he's not admitting it yet. Which is lucky for you. Get your bags, we are going back to the *Pocono*. If a hybrid hunter is stalking you, you'll be safe there."

"I'm not going. I'm going to a Halloween barn dance with Nittany tonight."

"You really think I'm going to let you go to the dance? For someone who has to hide the fact he gets straight As, you sure are dumb."

"I'm going to the dance, and you can't stop me."

"Try again. You are not going to the dance and I am stopping you. Now go pack," Chief insisted.

"No, I'm not going. I'll quit school if I have to," said Asher.

"You're like your mother. Quitting when things start to sting. She quit on our relationship. She didn't even give me a chance to help her."

"I told you to leave my mother out of this."

"Like it or not, Asher, she was a selfish bitch."

"Frick you!" Asher headed toward the front door.

"Get back here!" yelled Chief.

"NO!"

"I'm warning you!"

"Go to hell!" Asher opened the front door, stormed outside and slammed it shut.

*Damn it*, Asher thought. He had many emotions piercing through his body. Anger held him in a tight grasp.

"Asher, wait up," said Neon as she ran down the sidewalk toward him.

"Leave me alone," he said.

"I want to talk," Neon said, finally catching up.

"I don't want to talk to you. Of all the times I covered for your ass, the one time I needed you covering me, you betrayed me. I don't get it, Neon."

"I had my reasons."

"Like you had your reasons for not warning my mom about that guy with the night vision goggles the night of the raid? She and Timothy could still be alive if you'd turned yourself in."

"Don't you go blaming me for their deaths. That wasn't my fault."

"Of course, nothing is your fault, you selfish bitch."

Neon took a step back. "What did you call me?"

"You heard me," he replied.

"You are my best friend. If it's selfish of me to get you to join the right side of our cause, then yes, I am selfish."

"My best friend? That's a joke," said Asher.

"We are best friends," Neon replied.

"No, we are not. If you were my friend, you wouldn't have ratted me out. We're done, Neon. I want you the hell out of my life."

"You want me out of your life? Fine. When Nittany's father comes to take your ass to cleansing, don't try to come find me for pity, that shuttle left orbit and it's not coming back."

"Good." Asher stormed away from her. Neon turned and stormed in the other direction.

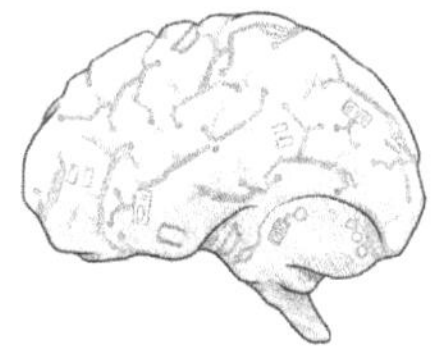

Asher sat on a park bench. The autumn sky had started to cloud over. Asher had so much anger and rage in him, that he didn't notice he hadn't brought his coat. He didn't know what to do. It was easy to blame Neon for his mom's and Timothy's deaths. Like it was easy for Chief to blame his mom for not telling Chief about him.

"Is this seat taken?" asked a tall man with a gray hood.

Asher shook his head.

The man sat down and offered Asher a root beer barrel.

"Is that honey to catch the fly?" Part of Asher hoped the old man would say yes.

"If I were Cortez, I would not be catching you with honey. Hell, for Cortez, using vinegar is still too sweet." The old man laughed. "Oh no. I'm no hybrid hunter."

"Then who are you?" asked Asher, not looking at him.

"I am an old man who cares."

"Great, are you going to talk bad about my mom and squeal on me?" asked Asher.

The old man laughed. "No, I'm not. I know what it's like to have a friend betray you and a father angry at a mother."

"How do you know this?" asked Asher.

"I've been around. That's why I have to tell you that there are three people you need to forgive, sooner rather than later."

"I'm not forgiving Neon or Chief. And you're wrong, there is no one else I'm mad at."

"That is where you're wrong," said the old man. "You have to forgive yourself."

Asher finally looked over at him. His hood cast a dark shadow on his face.

"That's not happening." Asher stood.

"The sooner you forgive yourself, the sooner your heart will start healing," he said.

"I don't have to take this from you." He turned to walk away.

"Asher," said the old man.

Asher stopped dead in his tracks. How did the man know his name? It was as if he knew everything about him. "What?"

The old man sighed. "Watch yourself. You haven't hit rock bottom yet."

"Okay, whatever." Asher shook his head. *Crazy nut bag*, he thought as he headed down a side street.

"Does he know?"

The old man turned and saw an old lady standing next to him. "Alita Blackwood, aren't you taking a risk coming here?"

"No more than you," she replied.

"I'm not on the top of the most wanted list anymore."

"You gave up. You quit."

"I shifted strategies is all."

"Call it what you want," said Alita Blackwood. She stretched her neck in the direction Asher had headed.

"Neon brings you here, doesn't she?"

"Yes, she's pissed. I'm taking her back where she belongs. It's where Asher belongs too."

"We've been through this already. 579 times, to be exact," said the old man.

Alita Blackwood shook her head in disgust. "You never change. Bullheaded as always. I still think we can bring him to our side."

"Your side, not ours. Let's be very clear on that."

"I'm not giving up, and you know that."

"It's never going to happen. And you know that," said the old man.

"Because you're the Phantom Prophet doesn't mean you know everything."

"No, it doesn't. I always hated that name for that very reason."

Alita Blackwood shifted her attention to the houses in the direction Asher had gone.

"You see him approaching, don't you?"

"We can save Asher from that son of a bitch."

"In order for Asher to persevere, he needs to hit rock bottom first."

"You're going to hand Asher over to Cortez like an appetizer at a cocktail party?"

"Asher is stronger than he thinks he is. He'll be okay. I suggest we leave before Cortez spots us as well. That would change the game as we know it."

"You never answered my question."

The old man stopped and looked at her. "No, he doesn't know."

Cortez drove toward the boy, constantly looking for signs of Alita Blackwood. The need to wait disappeared the moment he found the boy walking alone. If Alita Blackwood had been in the area, he missed the opportunity.

Cortez pulled his car up to Asher. "Excuse me, can you help me?"

Asher stopped and looked. A swift *psst* came from the Jeep. Asher slapped the side of his neck as if swatting a mosquito. His body swayed, and he fell to the ground. Cortez placed his tranquilizer gun on the dashboard and got out. He opened the back door and put Asher inside. He looked around to ensure that no one saw him. Once satisfied, he got into the Jeep and drove off.

$M$ ac leaned back in his chair, studying the holophotos above his desk. Eerie shadows formed on Mac's face, especially around the eyes. He swirled a glass of Hendrick's gin and tonic, the ice making a soothing, clicking sound.

"You were awfully quiet at dinner tonight," said Heather as she took her long hair, balled it up on top of her head, and put a pencil through it.

Mac looked up at the doorway, seeing his wife's silhouette.

"A lot going on."

Heather walked behind her husband and rubbed his tensed shoulders. Her hands and arms were toned. She looked at the holophotos.

"Are you still mad about what Nittany did? We did worse at her age."

"It's not that." He took a sip of his drink. "Well, part of it is."

"Nittany thinks she got Asher in a lot of trouble. She can't get ahold of him by holowatch or online," said Heather. "He probably got grounded from them."

Mac sat up and turned his attention to his wife. A strange twisting feeling filled his stomach. "What was that?"

"Nittany hasn't talked to him since she left his house. He isn't returning any of her calls or messages."

"Shut the door," said Mac. Heather did. "Phone Liam Mrkonic."

A hologram popped up over his desk. It read "Calling…"

"Hello," said Chief as his bust appeared over Mac's desk.

"Hey, Chief, I'm sorry to bother you, with Sunday's fiasco, I forgot to tell you why I was in town to begin with."

"Detective, this isn't a good time." Chief had multiple days' worth of growth on his face, and his clothes were matted as though he had been sleeping in them.

"I'll make it quick. I have Vicki Smizik's ashes, and I thought you might want them."

"Uh, yeah, sure."

"Is everything okay, Chief? You look a little worried there, a little preoccupied."

"I kind of am, Detective," said Chief.

"I'll be coming to Pittsburgh soon to see my brother. I'll bring them then, if that's okay."

"That's fine, Detective. Now I really have to go."

"Actually, before you go, Nittany would like to talk to Asher. Is he around?" asked Mac. Heather gave him a puzzled look.

"Sorry, he's already asleep. He's been sick all day."

"Sorry to hear that. Could you see if he is awake? Nittany really wants to talk to him."

"I'm sorry, Detective, I have to go." The holoimage of Chief disappeared.

"What was that all about?" asked Heather, placing her hand on Mac's shoulder. "Why would you want to wake a sick boy?"

"Asher's not at the house," said Mac.

"He said he was sick in bed." She crossed her arms and gave him the wife's look. "What aren't you telling me?"

"Heather, you know I can't discuss work with you."

"Bram." Her look got stronger.

"I have reason to believe Asher is a hybrid."

"What do you mean a hybrid?" asked Heather.

"I suspected it when I met him at Park 84 this past summer. The kid seemed out of his element, plus his father said he had no other relatives other than his brother. Now this kid shows up claiming to be his son shortly after the Willow Wood raid where the ex-girlfriend was murdered. Then I heard he went to the Academy, never thinking he would be put into the same squad as Nittany. I saw the list of hybrids caught, and he wasn't on it. Even though my gut said one thing, I believed another."

"Wouldn't he have been caught during the medical scan?" asked Heather.

"You would think. His father works in medical. I should've thought of that sooner."

"Bram, if you're thinking of going back to Pittsburgh to scan him—"

"It's my job. Besides..." His thoughts drifted.

"Besides what?" asked Heather.

"He's probably dead," said Mac.

"What parts are you leaving out?"

"I have reason to believe that Cortez, and probably Navarro, were targeting Asher."

"You think Chief lied about Asher being in bed? You think Cortez got him?"

"I do."

"I sure hope you're wrong about this, Bram."

"If Asher is still there, then I'll have to scan him."

"Bram. You can't scan him."

"I sure the hell can. If he is bringing danger to my family, I have to stop it."

"Bram, listen to me. You can't scan Asher."

"Why not?"

"Let's say he is a hybrid. You scan him and you'll be required to have him cleansed. You know how that's going to affect Nittany? She's never going to talk to you again."

"She would get over it as soon as the next crush came along." Mac took another sip of his drink. "I know you don't like my job…"

"Me liking your job or not has nothing to do with this. You have to trust me here, Bram. You cannot scan Asher. This will break Nittany's heart, and she will blame you for it. Can you live with that?"

"If it means keeping her safe, yes. For all I know, when I picked up Nittany on Sunday, Cortez could've been hiding in the house and no one knew it. Besides, if Asher is a hybrid, which I'm pretty sure he is, and I don't turn him in and the word gets out that I knew, I could lose my job, like what happened to Navarro."

"That's not necessarily a bad thing," said Heather.

Mac gulped the last of his drink down and placed his glass on his desk. "My job is a necessary evil. Don't you get that?"

"Evil, yes. Necessary, that's debatable. I try to keep my opinions to myself about your job. I know you work hard, and you are good at it. Your job is about to cause another family rift like it did eleven years ago. We barely survived the first one."

"Scanning Asher has nothing to do with Remington."

"He was our son! Flem's twin brother. If it wasn't for your job, we could've gotten him hybrid implants instead of a coffin."

"I don't hear you complaining about my job when I bring home the Christmas bonus each year."

"How can you sit there and defend the agency when it kept us from saving our son? Nittany was too young to understand the death of her baby brother. She is not too young to see her boyfriend outed by her own father," said Heather.

"Okay, say he is a hybrid and I don't scan him, Navarro or Cortez track him down and kill him to sell his implants on the black market— if they haven't already. The same thing could happen to Nittany that happened to Asher's mom, Vicki Smizik. I would not be able to live with myself knowing I could've prevented it, and I know you would feel the same way."

"Fine, do what you feel you must, don't come to me crying to help pick up the pieces." Heather shook her head in disgust. "Your job caused us to lose one child. Don't let it make you lose a second." Heather left the room.

Mac let out a long sigh. He pulled up the haunted house video and watched Cortez kill the boy. He turned it off before the part where Nittany appeared.

"Let's see if I can talk my way out of having to sleep on the couch tonight," Mac mumbled to himself. He got up, turned off the pictures, and walked to the door. He looked over his shoulder to a cabinet that contained his scanning wand. He shook his head and left.

# Chapter 48

Cortez stood over a body completely stripped of its clothes and slumped in a chair. The hands and feet were strapped to the chair with wires hooked up to his head. Slobber drooled from his mouth. Dried blood was caked under his nose and at the corner of his mouth. His black-and-blue eyes had swollen shut. His body had bruises, cuts, and other wounds from head to toe.

"Did you kill him?" asked Cortez.

Dr. Stroud Monroe stood looking at a hologram of a brain with three hybrid implants and the garrison chip. The light from the hologram reflected off the top of Dr. Monroe's bald head surrounded by strands of white hair.

"My suspicion was correct. This boy's garrison chip is of the same make as that kid we pulled out of the river this past summer. However, this one isn't fried. I need him alive to get a better feel for how his implants work."

"I don't remember other hybrids passing out like this."

"They don't. My patients claim that it feels like someone is trying to reach into their memories. In my twenty-five-plus years, not one hybrid claimed to get a headache when I hack into their garrison chip. This boy, on the other hand, he screamed in such pain and terror that he passed out. Odd, very odd." His eyes stayed focused on the hologram.

"Why all the bruising and cuts?"

"You have your way of extracting information and I have mine."

"Couldn't you penetrate his firewall? You're Akron Industries' leading specialist in hybrid technology." Cortez grumbled with impatience.

"Have you ever heard of the Dalin?" asked Dr. Monroe.

"They're a galaxy myth."

"What if I told you his garrison chip can prove the Dalin exist?"

This sparked Cortez's interest. "Go on."

"Roughly sixty years ago, a crashed shuttle was found that had advanced technology. This could be that same technology."

"Where is this shuttle now? I didn't know it existed."

"It doesn't anymore. From the stories, about a week after it was discovered, the shuttle, all reports of it, and anything related to it up and disappeared. Supposedly the Dalin returned and reclaimed what was theirs. I can't wait to crack open this lad's head and examine the garrison chip closer—while he is still alive, of course."

"If what you say is true, I guess this is why Alita Blackwood risked getting caught to get this hybrid," said Cortez.

"If that's the case, why now?" asked Dr. Monroe.

"What?" Cortez asked in confusion.

"From my examination, the garrison chip has been in this kid for fifteen or sixteen years. Why is she chasing him down now?"

"Maybe she recently found out or was leaving him alone until we chased him out," Cortez suggested.

"Could be, I think there is more to it." Dr. Monroe walked around the table with the holographic brain, not taking his eyes off the image. "A lot more."

After learning the new information about the boy's chip, Cortez wondered if maybe Navarro had the same thoughts, trying to use the boy as bait. Cortez kept silent. He would keep the doctor alive for now. If he got in the way of capturing Alita Blackwood, the doctor would have the same demise as Sabastian and the chainsaw kid. Navarro wanted to kill Alita Blackwood for personal reasons. Cortez wanted to kill her. She was the biggest trophy out there.

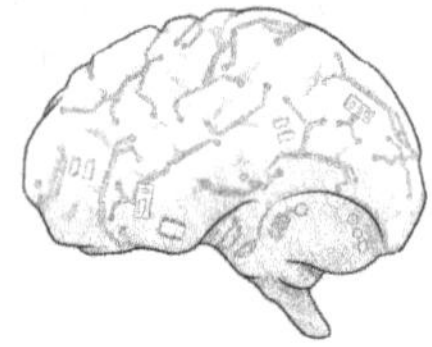

Asher drifted in and out of consciousness. He felt his body vibrating as if he were in a vehicle. His head still hurt. His whole body wracked with pain. His stomach wrenched, and his muscles were limp. Fading in and out, he eventually realized he lay trapped in the trunk of a moving vehicle.

Asher had no idea how long he'd been unconscious. Whatever they did to him seemed to screw up his internal clock, and he had no focus. The vehicle stopped, and Asher startled as the door opened. The large Cuban with a panatela in his mouth peered down at him.

"Here's your stop, kid," said Cortez as he threw Asher onto the sidewalk in front of Chief's house. "The only reason you're still alive is because I'm not through with you yet."

Cortez kicked Asher in the stomach. Asher grunted and coughed up blood as he lay on the cold concrete. "We'll see how lucky you are the next time I see you." Cortez got into his vehicle and sped off right before Chief and Mick came running out of the house.

C hapter 49

Chief came downstairs from Asher's room. Mick stood up from the couch. "How is he?" asked Mick.

"They really tortured him. Physically and mentally," said Chief.

"Did he say what happened?"

"All he said was that he was walking the streets angry and a Jeep pulled up to him. A Cuban guy shot him with a tranquilizer."

"This doesn't make sense. Why did they let him go? Did you check for a tracker? They might be trying to use him to lead them to other hybrids," said Mick.

"I did. He's clean."

"And Neon?"

Chief shook his head. "He has no idea what happened to her."

Chief plopped down on his recliner and closed his eyes. "What do I do now, Mick?"

"What do you mean?"

Chief sat up. "He's not safe here. The day Asher disappeared, Detective McGreggor pulled me to the side and said Cortez was spotted at the haunted house where Asher, Nittany, and Neon were. Although he didn't admit it, I could tell Detective McGreggor suspects Asher is a hybrid. McGreggor had to know Cortez was onto Asher."

"Wait, if he knows Cortez is onto Asher, then he must know—"

"—that Asher is a hybrid." Chief finished Mick's sentence.

"If he knew, how come he didn't come back to apprehend him?"

"I'm guessing that has something to do with Nittany." Chief leaned back and closed his eyes again.

"You have two options here. The first one is you and Asher go back to the *Pocono* and go on with your lives. Or I can talk to one of my sources, get both of you new identities, and you and Asher move to Argentina."

"Argentina? The armpit of South America?" asked Chief. The doorbell rang. "Who can that possibility be this early in the morning?" Chief pushed himself up, went to the door and looked through the peephole. "It's the detective."

Chief opened the door. The morning light flooded in as a silhouette of Mac stood before him. "Detective? When you called last night, you didn't mention anything about visiting us today."

"I apologize for the intrusion. I find it more comfortable sleeping in my car on the way here than the couch we have back home." Mac had bed-head and markings across his face, no doubt from the seams in the seat of his car. "May I come in?"

"Please." Chief opened the door wider, and Mick stood up to join them.

"What can I do for you?" Chief eyed the box.

"As promised, I brought Vicki's ashes," replied Mac as he handed Chief the box. "I apologize that they're not in an urn."

Chief looked at the box. He had wished many times over to have had one more chance to hold Vicki in his arms. A blanket of sadness covered him. This wasn't what he'd had in mind. He could feel his heart aching. It finally happened. Vicki's death started to become real.

"Liam?" said Mick. "You okay?"

Chief shook the memories from his head. "Yeah, I'll be fine." He turned his attention back to Mac. "Thank you, Detective. I appreciate this."

"I wish it was under better circumstances," said Mac. "Before I go, can I see Asher? My little girl wanted me to check up on him since he was feeling under the weather."

"He's asleep, I don't want to disturb him," said Chief.

"I understand. Can I pop my head in on him though?" Mac started walking slowly toward the stairs. Chief stepped in front of him and blocked his path.

"Detective, he is sleeping. Once he wakes up, I will inform him that Nittany was checking up on him."

"I'll only be a minute, and I'll be as quiet as a hybrid being smuggled through a checkpoint." Mac stepped to the left. Like a mirror image, Chief followed him.

"Detective, unless you have further business here..."

"Chief? Mr. McGreggor?"

The three men looked up the stairs. Asher stood there, confused. Chief saw the look of shock and surprise on Mac's face.

"Good morning, Asher. How are you feeling?" asked Chief, hoping Asher would play along.

"I still don't feel good," replied Asher.

"Asher, is that a black eye?" asked Mac.

Asher placed his hand over his swollen and bruised eye. He answered before Chief could. "Yes. I have purpura pneumonia. Am I still contagious, Chief? I'm hungry."

"Uh, yeah." This caught Chief off guard. Brilliant answer, though. If the detective looked it up, he would see that one of the symptoms was bruising. "The fact that you're hungry and walking around means you're well on your way to recovery. I would hold off another day or two to be sure you're no longer contagious."

"I'll make you one of my famous omelets," said Mick.

"Okay, thank you. Uh, Mr. McGreggor. Tell Nittany I said hi and

I'm sorry I haven't answered any of her messages. My apologies for Nittany and I going behind your backs the other day."

"As the missus pointed out to me, I've done worse at your age. Don't tell Nittany I said that."

Asher smiled. "I won't. Tell Nittany I said hi and that I miss her."

"I will, and I'm sure she will understand. I could see her trying to come here to be your nurse."

"Really?" Asher seemed to perk up.

"Sorry, no visitors until we know you're no longer contagious," said Chief. He could see disappointment flood Asher's body.

"I better get going, Chief. I took up enough of your time."

"Thank you, Detective."

Mac said his goodbyes and left.

"Whew!" said Mick. "Good thing Asher was here. I think he knew Asher was missing."

"You're not kidding," said Chief.

Asher came downstairs. "What's in the box?"

"Detective McGreggor brought your mom's ashes."

Asher stood there with tears beginning to glisten in his eyes.

"May I have them?" he said softly.

Chief nodded and handed over the box. "If you want, we can pick out an urn for her or sprinkle her ashes at Point State Park in Pittsburgh. She used to love going there."

"That's okay." Asher held the box close to his chest and went back to his room.

Xiao walked into berthing, which showed no signs of anyone's return. She threw her stuff on her rack and went into the head. A stench slapped her nose hard. A toilet flushed, and Brett came out of the stall still buckling up his uniform.

"Hey—" Brett started to say.

"Stop right there, Brett Lundy. It was a mistake. It will *not* happen again. If I find out that anyone on this ship knows about it, then I will cut your balls off and shove them so far up your flat ass the doctor will think you grew a new pair of tonsils. Do I make myself clear?"

"Can you tickle them with your tongue like you..." He lost his breath as Xiao gave him a hard backhand in the stomach.

"I mean it, don't mess with me," Xiao said with a firm face, fire in her eyes.

"Okay, fine. I won't tell anyone what happened."

"I'm glad we have an understanding." Xiao, disgusted, went into a stall.

"Such a bitch," Brett said to himself.

"I heard that!"

"If I didn't have to go see Dean Wu, I would let you hear something else."

"Go away!" Sounds of urine flowed into the toilet followed by a flush emitted from the stall.

When Xiao came out, Brett had left berthing.

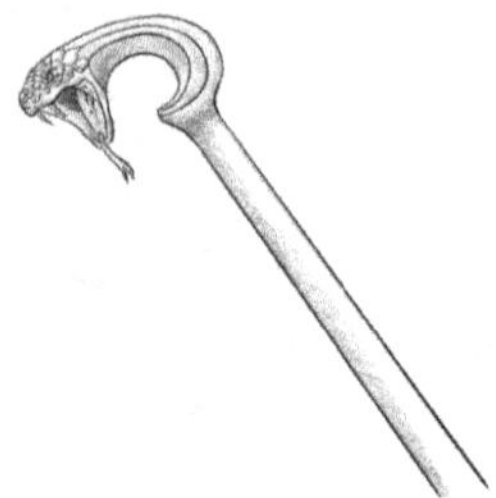

Dean Wu hated to deal with parents of the cadets. She dreaded it every time she had to. She swore they were as thickheaded, if not more, as their own children. She had one on her holocomm now.

"Senator Lundy, thank you for joining me," said Dean Wu. "I would like to talk to you before Brett arrives..."

"What's so urgent that my assistant, Oscar, couldn't handle it? I don't have time for this. I have a campaign luncheon I need to get to," interrupted Senator Lundy. A holoimage of Senator Lundy sitting in a chair shimmered in front of her desk. His arms were crossed, and every few seconds his attention went elsewhere. This gave Dean Wu a sense that the senator had as much interest in Brett's grades and success as a cat had interest in jumping into roaring rapids. Her lips tightened. No one dared interrupt Dean Wu, and if they did, she would let them know.

"Senator, Brett is failing..."

"Of course he's failing," grunted the senator. "That's why I tried to keep him from going to the Academy to begin with. He doesn't have what it takes to succeed up there, or in life for that matter. He is nothing but loud, rude, and disrespectful."

"I can assure you, Senator, we didn't teach him those qualities. He learned that elsewhere." She gave him a stern look.

"I only sent him up there to keep him away from the press. I had no doubt in my mind that Brett was going to fail and eventually drop out or get kicked out, whatever came first."

Dean Wu thought otherwise. "Potential."

"What?" asked the senator.

"Brett has much untapped potential."

"If he has any potential, I sure as hell don't see it."

Dean Wu kept the first words that landed on the tip of her tongue to herself. "It's going to take everyone to reach him, and I mean everyone." She gave the senator another firm stare.

"I don't have the time for this. You need to do your job, and if you continue to harass me about Brett, I'll make sure you no longer work for the Academy."

Dean Wu stood up. "First of all, Senator, you have no control over my job whether you're elected president or not. Secondly, I am seventy-eight years old. In the unlikely event you do find a way to fire me, then you will be doing me a favor—"

Senator Lundy opened his mouth to say speak.

Dean Wu put up her index finger to quiet the senator before he got a word in edgewise. "Finally, I will not have you come into my office on my ship and tell me that I am not doing my job. I can stand here and tell you with better evidence that you are not doing your job as a father."

"Don't go there, lady." Senator Lundy sat up tall in his chair, jutting out his chest.

"I am the Dean of Academics on board the NAS *Pocono*. You will refer to me as such. What I would like to say to you right now would make me anything but a lady."

"I don't mean to get your granny panties in a wad. Look, the boy's mother died when he was seven. Good thing, it would've hurt her severely seeing her son growing up to be such a loser and menace to society. The kid lacks smarts. He doesn't care about anything or anybody other than himself. He is a true embarrassment with no brains."

"I'll show you true embarrassment," said Brett, standing in the doorway.

Senator Lundy turned toward Brett.

"Brett, step into the camera's view." The senator spoke strongly and firmly.

Brett locked his jaw and clenched his fists. His nostrils flared, and veins bulged on his reddening neck. He stood next to Dean Wu.

"Brett, you know what I mean."

"No I don't. I wish you were half as concerned about me as you are about becoming president or that trophy bitch of yours, asshole. You think I care only about myself? Frick you! If I didn't care about myself, no one would, all you care about is yourself. It's all about your image. You don't fricken care about me. Go to hell!" Brett ran out. Senator Lundy stood in a fury, knocking over his chair.

"He can't act like that to me. Bring his ass back now!"

"Senator, Brett said the words that I chose not to, although he barely got the shovel into the ground. This conference call is over." Dean Wu turned off the transmission as the senator opened his mouth to speak.

Dean Wu stood looking at the space that had once occupied the senator's image. "If you weren't so damn important to our world's future, I would take you down this instant," she said aloud. Dean Wu grabbed her cane and exited her office to find Game Master Blass standing in the passageway.

"Mr. Blass, why am I not surprised to see you here."

"The senator is such a prick." The Game Master shook his head in disgust.

"For once, I can't disagree with you," said Dean Wu.

"You're going to go talk to him?"

"You know I am. I must."

"Take it easy on the kid. He's fragile." Gamemaster Blass smiled.

Dean Wu gave him a backhand slap in his oversized stomach.

"Fragile my ass. Some things never change," murmured Dean Wu as she headed down the passageway.

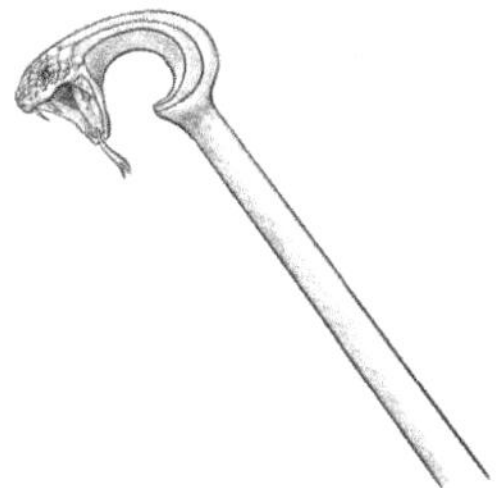

Dean Wu found Brett in his room, alone. He managed to tear the door off the hinges that led into the head.

"Cadet Lundy."

"Get the frick out of here."

"I have two things to tell you. First, you will not use such language when addressing me. Second, I believe in you," Dean Wu said earnestly.

"The senator said..."

"Your father is a typical politician. His mouth is bigger than his brain. Look at me, Brett."

Brett looked toward her.

"I can't make you learn. Your dad can't make you learn. I can, however, give you the tools necessary to learn. You have to want it."

"I don't belong here. Everyone knows it. I only came here to get away from the senator. Besides..."

"Besides what?" asked Dean Wu.

"The only reason I got into this school is because a former student of yours talked you into it."

"You must be referring to Oscar Drake. Well, Cadet Lundy, let me set things straight. No one talks me into doing anything I don't want to do."

"Then why did you accept me? You have to know I've been kicked out of schools, failed most of my classes, and spent a night or two in jail, detention centers."

"I know more about you than you think I do."

"Then why?" Brett repeated his question.

"I have a very dear friend with whom I went to school. He had the same kind of issues as you. With help from his teachers, and eventually me as a friend, he worked really hard and proved to his father—and more importantly to himself—that he did indeed belong here. Do you want to prove the senator wrong? Do you want to prove to yourself that you do belong?"

Brett nodded. "I'll do anything to prove that bastard wrong."

"It's going to take a lot of work on both of our parts, especially yours. Are you ready to work hard? Give all it takes?"

"Why bother? I'm a disappointment no matter what I do."

"I don't see it that way. What I see is a boy who desperately wants attention from his father. The only way he knows how to do it is to be a paper cut on his tongue. I think it's safe to say that strategy isn't working. Let's try the other route. Work hard and show the senator what you are truly made of. Even if he still ignores you, though you deserve his attention regardless, so be it. His loss. Don't let the actions of your father keep you from becoming the person I know you can be."

Brett shook his head again.

"It will mean making sacrifices, like giving up free time in the evenings. Are you willing to do that?"

"Why can't I have free time? That's when I please all the girls."

"You will come to my office and we will work on your studies together during free time."

"Tutoring over pleasing girls?"

"I know you, Cadet Lundy. You have sex on the brain twenty-five hours a day."

"There are only twenty-four hours in a day, Dean."

"Exactly. You need to tame your appetite for drugs, sex, and alcohol and turn it to your studies. It's the only way."

"What do I tell people when they don't see me at free time?"

"You'll have to tell them the truth. It takes a man to say the truth. Tell them you are doing extra studying. If they make fun of you for that, then screw them. You can't worry about what other people think of you. You need to know that you will do whatever it takes to improve your studies." Her lips were firm, and her eyes focused on his with intensity.

"Okay, I'll try it for a week."

"A week? This is a full-time, rest of the year commitment."

"I want to see how it goes first."

"Fair enough." Dean Wu started to leave the room.

"Hey, Dean, do you remember the first time you had sex?"

Dean Wu stopped and turned her head to look at him. "That is of no concern to you." She exited the room, only to find Game Master Blass waiting for her.

"Well?"

"I will be tutoring him," said Dean Wu.

"Not that," said Game Master Blass. "Do you remember the first time you had sex?" He winked at her.

"Unless you want to see a throat specialist, I suggest you go back to your games." Dean Wu headed down the passageway with the tiniest of smiles on her face.

# CHAPTER 51

A crowd of people bustled down the corridor in Terminal H on board the hub. Asher's head weaved between passengers, looking for Nittany.

"Asher!" Nittany yelled. She waved and shot him a huge smile.

Asher smiled back, excited to see her again.

She ran up to him and gave him a massive hug. He returned it.

"I missed you," said Nittany, kissing him.

"Me too."

Asher picked up her bags off the deck. He wanted to hold her hand. He knew he couldn't, fortunately, carrying her bags kept his hands occupied.

"Are you feeling any better?" asked Nittany.

"Yeah, the bruising and swelling is pretty much gone."

"I wish I could've been there to take care of you," said Nittany.

"Me too."

"I'm surprised Chief let you off the *Pocono* to greet me."

"He lifted my grounding this time only," replied Asher before changing the subject. "Where's Slater? Wasn't he on the same shuttle as you?"

"He was. He's stuck in the way back with Ski, Barfly, and Swish. I wasn't waiting for them. I wanted to see you."

"Should we wait for them?"

"Nah! They can find their way. Is anyone else back yet?"

"I think Brett is back. I don't know about the others, unless they returned while I was out here waiting for you."

"How long were you waiting for me?"

"All morning."

Nittany opened the door to berthing for Asher. "Nittany!" called Tabitha as they entered.

"Hey!" said Nittany. "How was your week?"

"It was spectacular. My boyfriend surprised me with tickets to see Mitch Kalon."

"You saw Mitch Kalon! No way!" said Nittany.

"Our seats weren't the best though. Not close enough to be picked for the Kalon's Kiss at the end of the concert."

"Still you got to see him in concert."

Asher threw Nittany's gear on top of her rack and disappeared into the head.

"How was your break?" Tabitha asked with a sly smile and a wink.

"It was great until Asher's dad caught us sleeping together," said Nittany.

Tabitha's mouth gaped open. "You and Asher got busy? I thought you wanted to wait."

"No, we didn't have sex. We spent one night in the same bed. Chief came home a day early and found us."

"Boy, would I have loved to see your faces when Chief found you." Tabitha laughed.

"Hello, ladies!" Cray strolled in.

"Cray, you'll never guess who slept with each other on autumn break."

"You promised."

"Am I supposed to be surprised?" replied Cray.

The girls looked at him.

"What? We all know you two are dating. You don't hide it very well. It was only time until he plucked you."

"He didn't pluck me," said Nittany. "See, Tabitha, this is why I didn't want anyone to know."

"Relax, Nittany," said Tabitha. "Cray, they only snoozed together, no fun time...so she says." Tabitha gave her friend another wink.

"Yeah, okay," said Cray.

"How was your week, Cray?" asked Nittany.

"It was great. I earned my junior life saving certificate. Now I can assist the lifeguards at the beach this summer."

"That's cool."

"I even got to practice mouth-to-mouth with a boy whose family moved in to help with financial issues on both ends."

"Does this person you mouth-to-mouthed with have a name?" asked Tabitha.

Cray gave a shitty grin. "Wouldn't you like to know his name," replied Cray.

Asher came back out of the head.

"There he is. The big dog himself, my man Asher! What's up?" Cray gave Asher a high five that awkwardly turned into a handshake.

"Uh, hi, Cray. Nothing," said Asher.

"I heard you had a great week, you hound dog, you."

"It started off good. Then I got sick," Asher lied.

"I'm starving. You all want to head to the student lounge? The snack shack should be open," Nittany said, coming to Asher's aid.

"Yes, I'm in. I'm hungry," said Tabitha.

"Okay," Asher replied.

Cray and Tabitha walked out of berthing.

"Umm, Asher?"

"Yes?"

"I really missed you."

"Me too." The two gave each other a deep kiss.

"Hey, you guys coming?" Cray poked his head back in berthing.

Both of them snapped out of the trance. "Yes, we're coming."

"Why was Cray acting all weird?" asked Asher.

"I don't know. I think it has to do with him getting his lifeguard certificate."

# CHAPTER 52

Asher sat at Chief's desk in his office on board NAS *Pocono*. The end of November had approached. Asher had his hands on the side of the box that contained his mother's remains. When he put it down on the desk, he couldn't part with it. Chief stored the box in his office after Asher scored penalizing points for having it in his locker during a health and comfort inspection.

"I thought I saw you come in here," said Chief. "The Pittsburgh Anvils are playing against the Boston Celtics. You want to watch it with me?"

Asher shrugged.

"You've been pretty distant since autumn break. Are you okay?"

Asher shrugged again.

"I can't imagine the horror you've gone through the last few months, with your mom, Timothy, and the incident during autumn break. I am here to listen. No judgment, no lecture, no yelling, only to listen.”

“I'm okay,” said Asher.

“It's not good to internalize your feelings.”

“I said I was okay,” Asher snapped.

“As a son myself, I know it's hard to say things to your parents. I get it. Maybe Mick has a source who could help you with your emotions. Besides, I feel a lot of this recent anguish you had to deal with was my fault. If we didn't fight over Nittany staying at the house, you would've never been caught.”

“I miss my mom and Timothy, okay? You happy now that I admitted my feelings? It has nothing to do with our fight.” That wasn't entirely true. He felt agitated, and hostility flowed through his veins.

“I know it's tough on you missing your mom and Timothy and not knowing if Neon is okay,” said Chief.

“Neon is okay. She's not dead,” said Asher.

“How do you know that?”

“I talked to Pandora the night before we came back here. She is a friend of mine I talk with on the computer. She assured me that Neon was alive.”

“Pandora? I haven't heard you mention her name before,” said Chief.

“I only talk to her a little bit. I don't think Nittany likes it when I talk to other girls,” said Asher.

“You really care for Nittany, don't you?”

“Yeah.”

“I don't want to get into another fight about the same topic, it's too dangerous for you to date her.”

“I don't care. I love her, Chief.”

“I'm sure you do. Don't let cupid's arrow fool you, it's more of a puppy love than a deep relationship love.”

“It's not puppy love. I know you don't believe me.”

“Maybe I don't. You two only met three months ago,” said Chief.

“I know. I knew it when I first saw her,” said Asher.

“Asher, I hear what you're saying...”

"You loved my mom, right?"

"Yes," replied Chief.

"How old were when you realized you loved her?" Asher asked.

"It was our first date. I was fifteen."

"That's two years younger than I am now. It can happen."

"Asher, I'd known your mom since elementary school. It's different."

"It's not different."

"Okay, how about we agree to disagree?" Chief suggested.

Asher shrugged, followed by an awkward silence.

"Did you mean what you said?" asked Asher.

"About agreeing to disagree, yes."

"No, not that. I heard you tell Uncle Mick during autumn break that your life would've been a lot easier if I never showed up on your doorstep."

Chief sat down in the chair across from Asher. "I meant every word of it," he replied.

Asher scrunched his eyebrows in disbelief. Did Chief actually admit he didn't want him?

Chief continued. "My life would have been easier, but not better."

Asher looked at Chief. "Huh?"

"The last few months watching games with you, you sharing about your day during school, me getting called into Dean Wu's because she thought you were cheating. Even our disagreements and fights. It all filled a gap that was created in my life the night your mom and I called off the engagement." Chief closed his eyes. Then he started talking again. "I tried to fill that gap with too many things to mention over the years. When I finally realized the only thing that could fit inside that gap was your mom, I stopped trying. Then a quirky teenage hybrid showed up on my doorstep saying I was his father."

Asher reluctantly let out a hint of a smile.

"I didn't realize it until the day you ended up missing," said Chief, "You actually had what it took to start filling in that gap. Other than your mother, you are the only one who could've done that."

Asher stayed quiet, his mind worked overtime taking it all in. He wondered if Chief could fill the same gap that had formed when his mom and Timothy died. In order to do that, he would first have to let Chief fully inside, showing his vulnerabilities, and he didn't know if he wanted to, or if he even should.

"You know what tomorrow is?" asked Asher.

"I do. December 1st," replied Chief.

"I mean…"

"It's Vicki's birthday. I haven't forgotten. Have you decided what you want to do with her ashes yet?"

Asher shrugged. "I don't know. I thought maybe take them back to Willow Wood."

"I wish we could. It wouldn't wise to take you there. I'm sure hybrids are staking out the place to see if anyone comes back, if not, then the hybrid police are staking it out to see if any hunters or hybrids show up."

"It wouldn't take long," said Asher.

"Let's give this some thought, and then next time we go to Earth, we can discuss it, okay? There is no reason to be in a hurry over this," said Chief.

"I guess."

"How about we go get ice cream before Taps and you can tell me how you're going to ask Nittany to the winter semi-formal dance before Christmas break—since I know you're going to do it with or without my consent."

"I wasn't planning on going," said Asher.

"Does Nittany know this?"

"No, I haven't told her yet."

"Let's go get ice cream and we can discuss this on the way."

Asher got up and placed his mother's remains back on the shelf. "I'll pass on the ice cream," said Asher. He left Chief standing alone in his office.

*Clank, clank, clank!* "Everyone out of their racks now. On the double," yelled LTjg Meoquanee. "Move it, move it, move it!"

"What the hell time is it?" asked Brett.

"It's time for your next escape room," replied LTjg Meoquanee.

"It's two thirty in the morning," said Cray. He slid out of his rack, almost hitting Xiao's head.

Nittany rolled out of bed and started to open her rack.

"Cadet McGreggor, do not go in your rack," said LTjg Meoquanee.

"Don't we have to get dressed in our uniform for the escape room?" Nittany asked with a yawn.

"Whatever you're wearing is the only thing you are taking with you. Out in the common area."

Cray, wearing his boxers and a T-shirt, exited berthing first, followed by Xiao in a lavender pajama suit with feet. Nittany, wearing her white nightie, waited as Asher climbed out of his rack in his briefs. They were followed by Tabitha, wearing an oversize T-shirt she'd gotten when she went to the Mitch Kalon concert.

"Cadet Lundy, you're the last one up. Out of your rack," ordered LTjg Meoquanee.

Brett pulled himself out of his rack and gave LTjg Meoquanee a wink.

"This is going to prove more interesting than I thought," said LTjg Meoquanee as she watched Brett's bare bum leave the berthing area. She shook her head in disbelief and entered the common room.

"I figured you would show up for this match," said Game Master Blass, perched high on his chair overlooking the two holotables. The first table showed the room Echo 88 would be assigned. Yankee 88 had the second. The rooms were identical.

"Hello, Thane," said Dean Wu as she walked up to the holotable that showed Echo 88's room. Dean Wu nodded to LTjg Meoquanee and Petty Officer Verbeck, who were sitting at their control station for the table.

"Is anyone else coming?" asked Game Master Blass.

"If you are referring to Gully and Autumn, no, they won't be coming. If they're in their right mind, they're still sleeping. Besides, they have to get ready for the storm that's almost upon us."

"What about—"

"You know he won't come," Dean Wu answered before Game Master could finish his question.

"He got us into all this, yet he doesn't come around. I don't get it," said the Game Master.

"For as smart as he is, his heart is a hundred times as big. Seeing these events taking place brings out memories of his own that he doesn't like facing."

"He will have to face them one day."

"He knows that, until then, all we can do is be patient."

The Game Master grunted and turned his attention to the squad leaders. "Squad leaders, prepare for countdown."

Echo 88 stood in the starting room, ready for their next escape match.

"I have a good feeling about this one," said Cray.

"We're going up against the only other squad who hasn't won a match yet," said Xiao.

"I'm ready for our first win," said Tabitha. She had given Brett her night shirt to cover himself up. Fortunately, she went to bed with her panties and sleeping bra that night.

"I don't understand why they have it in the middle of the night," said Nittany.

The timer counted down. The starting buzzer sounded. The first clue appeared on the door.

"Oh good, a water bottle," said Cray. He picked up the bottle and swallowed half the contents. He noticed everyone looking at him. "What? The ham we had for dinner made me thirsty."

"The first clue," said Tabitha. "Floating is the key."

The door hissed opened. Everyone entered and stopped. The room did not bear any appearance of previous rooms they'd played. Two pipes were attached to the floor vertically, about one foot in length, each standing in the middle of the escape room about half the size of a basketball court. Pipes, valves, discharge valves, and all sorts of plumbing plagued one bulkhead. The valves all had a lock with a tag attached to it.

Tabitha looked up to the ceiling, which hung approximately three stories high. It looked like it had a sprinkler system attached to it.

"How are we supposed to get to those locks?" asked Nittany.

"I can climb that," said Cray.

On the left side of the room were two levers on the bulkhead; both were locked in the up position.

"There are locks on everything. What are we supposed to do?" asked Xiao.

"You see anything in there?" Asher asked Nittany.

She looked into the two pipes poking out of the deck. "It's too dark. If there is something in there, I can't see it."

If only he had Neon's vision.

"What's that writing on the side of the pipe?" asked Asher.

Nittany read it. "Pour it out here." She looked up. "Pour what out?"

"Cray? Where's that water bottle?" asked Asher.

"Right here."

"Let me see it." Asher took the half-empty bottle and poured it into the pipe. A ping-pong ball came to the top, fell out, and rolled across the floor.

Nittany picked it up. "Look, it's a bunch of symbols."

&@*%%#

"Hey, one of the lever locks has a symbol combination," said Xiao. Nittany took the ball to her. They dialed the combo, and it unlocked.

"Pull it down," said Cray.

Xiao pulled the lever down. A hiss came from the ceiling. They looked up, and the door to escape opened.

"There's our exit," said Cray.

"How do we get up that high?" Xiao asked. "It's too far to jump if we climb the pipes."

"Let's see what happens once we pour the water in the second pipe," said Tabitha.

"There's no water left," said Asher.

"Great job," Brett said to Cray. "Such a cunnerman."

"Don't start on me!" said Cray.

"Calm down, everyone," said Nittany. "Maybe there's another water bottle hidden."

"There isn't; I already checked," Cray assured her.

"There's the second clue," Brett said with a grin.

Everyone saw Brett taking a piss in the pipe.

"That's gross!" said Nittany.

"Stop it!" Tabitha said.

"Hey, it worked!" Brett said.

"I'm not touching that ball," said Cray.

Brett pulled the T-shirt back down and specks of wetness appeared towards the bottom.

"Remind me to burn that," said Tabitha.

"Ha ha," said Brett. He read the numbers off the ping-pong ball. "Five, nine, zero, two, six."

Cray went to the combo lock and put in the numbers. The combo unlocked.

Cray pulled down the lever. With a strange hiss from above, it began raining on them.

"You set off the overhead sprinklers, cunnerman," said Brett.

A steady rain beat down upon the cadets.

Cray tried pushing the lever back up without success. The sprinklers could not be turned off. Water immediately formed puddles that grew quickly.

Asher scanned his surroundings. "Does anyone see a drain?" he asked, trying to stay calm.

"What?" asked Brett.

"I see no drains," said Asher.

"So?" Brett replied.

"If there are no drains, then this room is going to flood." Asher started to worry.

"That's it," Cray said. "That explains all the pipes. I bet we're supposed to flood the room and float to the door." He stepped on the pipe to the lowest lock and tag.

"The most common double play in baseball," said Cray. "The lock is a three-digit combination."

"Six, four, three," said Asher. Keeping score with Chief helped him with that. A specific number represented each position.

"Asher's right," said Nittany. "In baseball, it's when the third baseman throws the ball to the second baseman, who throws it to the first baseman for a double play."

Cray dialed in the numbers. "It worked."

"Please let this open the drains." Asher pushed back against the wall holding the pipes as the water lapped over the top of his feet.

Cray took the lock off and twisted the valve. Water came out of a discharge valve about ten feet above.

"Tabitha, what does your tag say?" asked Cray.

"It's a six-letter combo, and the clue is a demon-like animal found in Madagascar."

Nittany smiled at Asher. "Aye-aye."

Tabitha dialed it in. The lock opened, and she twisted the valve. The discharge valve by Brett's head opened and shot water, knocking him onto the deck.

Asher took in a deep breath as the water crawled up his ankles.

"I think you're right, guys," said Xiao. "I think we're supposed to open those locks and cause the room to flood, so we rise to the door. Floating is the key."

Everyone started toward the lowest locks, trying to flood the room faster, except for Asher. He stood frozen to the pipes, watching the water rise with all of his focus.

Nittany saw Asher clinging to a pipe like a pale, frozen snow sculpture.

"Asher? You okay?" She waded up to him.

"I have a severe case of aquaphobia and the room is flooding. What do you think?" he said.

Nittany placed her hands on his pale cheeks and turned his head so he could see her. "Asher, I am here. I am not going to let anything happen to you. You will be okay."

"The room is flooding." Asher's body trembled.

"We can use you two cunnermans' help," yelled Brett. Nittany ignored him; Brett looked closer at the scene. "What's his problem?"

"He'll be fine. He has an acute case of aquaphobia. We'll get through this."

"I knew he was a cunnerman, but a wuss too?" Brett tried to open the locks to make the room flood faster.

Cray stopped. Once he heard Asher had aquaphobia, the game room enthusiast inside him stepped aside and let the lifeguard in him come out.

"Asher? Can you swim?"

"He almost drowned last summer in a boating accident," Nittany shared. "His brother did."

"Not good. Okay, bud, you have Nittany and me here with you," Cray said. "Remember, I got certified to be a lifeguard during autumn break. I'm a good swimmer. I'm not going to let you drown."

"Leave the cunnerman be," said Brett. "You want to win this game or not?"

"Shut up, Brett!" yelled Cray.

"Asher, focus on my face. Do you see my face?" asked Nittany.

Asher nodded. The water wrapped around his waist.

"Cray and I are here with you. We are not going to leave you. We will climb the pipes as the water lifts us up, okay?"

Asher didn't say a thing. Filled with horror and panic, his body trembled harder with fear. Timothy's dead eyes kept flashing in front of him.

Cray nodded to Nittany to keep encouraging Asher. The water lapped against Nittany's throat while it lapped upon Asher's chest. He started to flail his arms and breathe heavily when he saw that Nittany had to tread water.

"Asher, look at me, I am okay. I know how to swim and so does Cray."

Asher could feel the water creep over his shoulders. A little wave slapped him in the face. His chest and throat tightened up. His stomach churned, making him nauseous. He shivered uncontrollably as sweat dripped down his forehead. His arms flailed wildly.

"Asher, it's okay. Reach for the next pipe and pull yourself up."

"Yeah, bud," said Cray. "I'll hold your waist and help you up. Try not to drink the water. Brett took a piss earlier, remember?"

Asher flashed a faint smile.

"That's it, we don't want to drink Brett's pee," said Nittany. "On the count of three, you reach for the next pipe and Cray will give you a boost. Okay?"

Asher nodded. Cray prepared himself.

"One, two, three."

Asher grabbed the pipe.

"Good job, Asher, look at me," Nittany said.

Asher grabbed the next pipe, his hand slipped, and he went under. Cray and Nittany grabbed him. Asher panicked. He gasped for breath and choked on the water he swallowed.

Asher let out a scream. He didn't see Nittany. He didn't hear Cray. He could only see Timothy stuck in the rock, blaming Asher for his death.

"I got you, bud," said Cray.

Asher clung to the pipes, his knuckles turning white.

"Asher, you're okay. Cray and I are still here," said Nittany. "Asher, focus on my voice. Do you hear my voice?"

Timothy's face and voice faded away, replaced by...an angel.

"Asher, we're almost to the top. You're doing a great job," Nittany continued. "We have you. You are not alone. We are with you."

"Xiao, I have a math question on this one," said Tabitha. "The ages of a father and son add up to sixty-six. The father's age is the son's age reversed. How old could they be?"

"How many numbers?" asked Brett.

"Four," replied Tabitha.

"I don't know guys," said Xiao. She squinted, trying to come up with the answer.

"Nittany, it's math," said Cray.

"Asher, listen to me. The ages of a father and son add up to sixty-six. The father's age is the son's age reversed. How old are they?" asked Nittany.

"How old are they?" asked Asher.

"How old are they?"

"Fifty-one and fifteen," Asher said in a worried tone.

"Try five-one-one-five," said Nittany.

"It doesn't work," Brett said. "It figures the cunnerman would get the wrong answer when it's most important."

"Forty-two, twenty-four," said Asher.

"Try forty-two, twenty-four," yelled Cray.

"Nope, didn't work," replied Brett.

"Did you tried reversing them?" Cray asked. "Twenty-four, forty-two."

"Yes, I tried reversing them," mocked Brett.

"Sixty, zero six," said Asher.

"Brett, try six-zero-zero-six," yelled Nittany.

Brett dialed in the numbers. It didn't open. He reversed them to zero-six-sixty. The lock opened.

Asher, Nittany, and Cray reached for another pipe. Slowly they climbed, Asher on the cusp of shock and insanity. Nittany's voice and Cray's presence kept him from falling over that edge.

"Guys, we made it!" said Xiao.

Nittany saw Brett climb out first. The sprinklers shut off, and the water stopped entering the room.

"Look, Asher, the water stopped. We're at the top," said Nittany.

"Can you swim at all?" asked Cray.

"No."

"That's fine. Nittany, I want you to swim alongside Asher and keep talking to him. Can you do that?"

"Yes."

"Hurry up, cunnermans, we're the first ones out!" yelled Brett. "We can win this!"

"Asher, do you trust me?" Cray asked.

Asher nodded.

"Good." Cray maneuvered himself to face Asher's profile. "I want you to lean back on me."

"I can't do it. Oh God, Timothy. No."

"Who's Timothy?" Cray mouthed to Nittany.

"His brother," she replied.

"Asher, I am not going to let you drown. You have my word. Okay? You have to trust me. I'm going to reach around you and grab onto your chest. Then we will fall backward slowly and float. All you have to do is float. I'll do the work."

Asher felt Cray's arm wrap around him. Visions of Timothy flashed before his eyes. He felt himself being pulled. "I got you, bud," Gully Jumper said in Asher's mind.

"Do you need our help?" yelled Tabitha.

"When we get there, I'll need you to help pull him out," said Cray.

"Okay, we are standing by," said Xiao.

"On the count of three, Asher, let go and fall back toward me. Nittany, as soon as he lets go, start talking to him constantly, giving him reassurance."

"Okay."

"Here we go. One, two, three." Cray gently pulled Asher, he wouldn't let go of the pipe.

"Asher, you have to let go, bud; we're going to get you out of here, you have to let go. Let's try this again. One, two, three."

Asher continued to grip the pipes.

"You have to let go," Timothy's words echoed in his mind. "Let go."

"I can't do it," said Asher.

"Okay, Asher. I love you, stop acting like a fricking baby and let go of the damn pipe," Nittany said with force.

"Damn, you go girl," said Cray when Asher released his grip.

"Asher, I am proud of you," said Nittany. "You are doing great. We're almost there. This room is almost done. You are brave, Asher, for not giving up. You have friends who won't give up on you. You are doing this."

They reached the entrance of the door.

"Hurry, the water is receding," said Brett. "The other team is coming out. Let's go." Brett helped Tabitha and Xiao pull Asher out. Exhausted, Asher fell against the far wall.

Cray gave Nittany a push up to exit as the water drained out of the room.

Nittany got out and went over to Asher. She sat next to him and held him in a comforting hug.

"Get my hand," said Brett. He reached down to Cray. The water receded past his reach.

"I can't reach," said Cray.

"Damn it." Brett fumbled getting the wet nightshirt off. Once he managed to pull it off, he flung it over the side, and it slapped against the wall.

"Here, grab this," Brett yelled to Cray. Then to the others, "Pull!"

He, Tabitha, and Xiao pulled Cray up. Cray grabbed onto the deck and lifted himself out. When Cray got out of the water, the other team pressed the finish button. They were excited to win their first match.

Brett scowled.

# CHAPTER 54

"I can't believe we almost won," said Cray as Echo 88 entered their debriefing room.

"We could've won if it wasn't for Asher," Brett said. "Like the instructors would let us drown."

"Brett, it wasn't Asher's fault." Nittany stuck up for Asher, who felt bad enough already.

"It was too his fault. If he wasn't such a poltroon, all six of us could've opened more valves and pipes, and the water would've come in faster. Then we would have made it to the top faster."

"He doesn't know how to swim," said Nittany, still sticking up for the silent Asher.

"You would stick up for your boyfriend." Brett gave Asher a little shove in the chest.

Asher failed at holding his tears and his thoughts back. "I have a fear of water, okay?"

"No, it's not okay. It's a dumb fear. Especially here! The officers won't let us drown."

"I'm sick and tired of you, Brett, trying to tell me what to do or how I should act. You don't know the first fricking thing about being me." He looked at Nittany. "Six months ago, I saw my mom murdered. The last thing she told me was to get my younger brother to safety. He was eleven years old. He was entrusted to me. I failed my mom's dying wishes. I failed him. He died when we tried to escape in a canoe."

"Escape? From what?" asked a bewildered Tabitha.

"I'll tell you from what. Hybrid hunters. The only way to escape was the river. It was dark, I didn't know what I was doing or where the river was taking us. I didn't have a paddle and we ended up in rapids. The canoe flipped, and Timothy died because of me. There isn't a night that I don't go to bed seeing his face, my mom's voice constantly echoing in my head to get him to safety." Asher's face contorted. His lips quivered and his body trembled as he shook with sobs. It felt like he had a lump in his throat that he couldn't swallow.

"Did the hybrid hunter kill your mom? Why were they chasing you?" Brett asked sarcastically, as if he didn't believe a word Asher said. "Was the boogeyman there too?"

"Navarro killed my mom while we were trying to escape. She was protecting me and the other hybrids."

"Other hybrids?" asked Nittany.

"You mean you're a..." Cray started to ask.

"Hybrid." Asher stopped. He couldn't believe he'd announced it to his team.

Everyone froze, including Nittany. Asher felt a weight fall from his shoulders, and he breathed clearly.

"I'm a hybrid and so was Timothy. Just because a person is a hybrid doesn't mean we don't have a fear of dying. We have it more so. We all have heartbeats. We have joys and sadness. We cry and laugh. We are like you in every way, except part of our anatomy is technology. I don't think that makes me any less human than you. That's why I am the way I am. I had to spend all semester long with people who could not relate to what I was going through...the fear of being captured during medical scans. I am tired of hiding who I am. I didn't ask to become a hybrid. If it wasn't for my hybrid implants, I would have died years ago." He looked at his squad, who were silent.

Nittany shook her head, looking petrified. Tears ran down her cheeks. Asher realized he lost the only friend he had. He lost the girl he treasured in his heart.

"Oh, screw you all!" he said and ran out of the debriefing room, leaving his squad in silence, including Brett.

Nittany came out of the head with a set of dry clothes on. She put her wet hair up in a bun. Xiao, Tabitha, and Cray were already dressed.

"Has he come back?" asked Nittany.

"No. He hasn't. Brett left after getting changed."

"Should we tell Lieutenant Meoquanee about him?" asked Xiao.

"If we do, he will be cleansed," said Tabitha.

"Nittany?" Cray asked.

"I don't know, if my father found out..." Nittany's brain and heart were at war with each other, trying to process what had happened.

"I can't imagine carrying a burden like that for such a long time," said Cray.

"Asher is a forbidden shadow," said Tabitha.

"Huh?" Cray asked.

"My grandfather was a hybrid. He used to tell me that hybrids were forbidden shadows. They had to hide within shadows to survive."

"All he wanted was to fit in," said Nittany. "He wanted to be like us, and we made it difficult for him. I didn't realize all the pain he had to hide from us."

"What do we do?" asked Tabitha.

Nittany said, "I told Asher that I loved him."

"Not once all year did Asher do anything against us," said Cray.

"He took in all our trash talk in the beginning, especially what Brett divvied out." Nittany wiped tears from her cheeks. "He tried to fit in, he didn't know how. I told him I was his girlfriend."

"Nittany, this isn't your fault," said Tabitha.

"For as long as I can remember, Dad always went out and got the bad guy. He tracks the bad guy down and destroys them. I was always excited to hear when he caught them, it made me feel safe. The bad guys he caught and destroyed were only considered bad guys because they had technological implants. It didn't bother me. They didn't have a face. Now what we call the bad guys, they have a face. That face is Asher, and Asher isn't a bad guy."

"No, he's not a bad guy," Cray agreed.

"You're right, Tabitha, it's not my fault. It's not your fault, or even Brett's. It's the fault of society. We're scared of people being smarter or stronger than us and taking over the world that we let the worst in us come out. I told Asher I was more than his friend. Friends don't give up because society says it's wrong." Nittany started to leave.

"Where are you going?" asked Tabitha.

"I am going to find him." Nittany darted out of berthing.

"I'm coming too," said Cray.

"I'm right behind ya." Tabitha looked behind her and saw Xiao standing there. She kept pushing her hair over her ear. "Are you coming, Xiao?"

"I turned in a hybrid once and told people I would do it again if I had to."

"Oh, Xiao, you wouldn't?" asked Tabitha.

"What those people don't know is since then I took a silent vow that I wouldn't do it again." She gave Tabitha a smile of honesty. "Let's go find him."

"What about Brett?" asked Tabitha.

"What about him?" replied Cray.

"Do you think he'll tell?"

"Not if he knows what's good for him," Cray replied, holding up his fist.

"Let's worry about Brett later. Let's fine Asher first," said Nittany. She headed out of common room, and the others followed.

"You feel good right now, don't you, boy?"

Brett looked up from the table he was sitting at in a café on board the hub. "Screw off!" he said to the Game Master.

"You finally dealt enough bull to break down the one person who truly didn't deserve it."

"I don't know what you're talking about, and it's none of your fricken business."

"You're nothing but a cunnerman," said the Game Master.

"You don't know what you're talking about. You know nothing about me."

"Oh no? I know you're scared that you'll never meet your father's expectations. That's why you do the things you do. If you purposely fail, then you can't blame yourself."

"Shut up. No one asked you to butt in."

"You're a cunnerman. It's easier for someone not to like you when you act the way you do, than if someone doesn't like you for who you truly are. Like the other boy, he kept to himself to hide who he truly is because he was afraid to show his true self. You hide your true self by being loud, rude, and obnoxious. You guys are similar in a lot of ways."

"I said shut up!"

"What are you going to do? Hit me?"

"Yes!"

The Game Master stood, revealing his heavy weight and height.

"You don't scare me," Brett insisted.

"Go on. Hit me."

"Why bother?"

"I knew you didn't have the balls." The Game Master sat back down.

"Leave me alone. Like I said, you know nothing."

"I know that you're hurting with your own personal pains. I know you feel you have no friends. Whenever a person wants to be your friend, it's because they have a hidden agenda, since your dad is the president. That's why you haven't tried to befriend anyone."

"The senator is not the president."

"Not yet. If you stopped being a cunnerman to Echo 88 long enough, you would find out that you have the most trustworthy group of friends right there with you. All you have to do is be a friend back."

Uncharacteristically, a tear strayed from Brett's eye.

"You want to be a leader. You think it makes you cool and stuff. If you're part of a team of friends, leader or not, that's the coolest you could ever be."

"How do you know all this?"

"I used to be in the same shoes you're in now." The Game Master pointed to the boots on Brett's feet. "I know exactly how you feel."

"You don't know how I feel. Now get lost!"

"You listen to me!" The Game Master got stern with him. "This boy tried to help you with your schoolwork, and you threatened him and pushed him around. When you needed someone to escort you to medical because you injured your hand punching the bulkhead in the shower, he was there. Once you got to medical, he sat there waiting for you. Hell, he could've not taken you to medical at all, yet he did. How many times did you mock him, yell at him, threaten him, tease him, turn your back on him, and make fun of his ears?"

Brett lowered his head. The tentacles of guilt, shame, and regret were starting to grasp tightly around Brett's heart, as small as it was.

"All that boy ever wanted was to be a part of the group, to fit in. To have a team that would consider him an equal and a friend. You did everything in your power to keep that from happening. The sad thing is, that boy would still give up his life to save your sorry ass if the need arose. All that time and energy you waste on being a bully—try using it to be a friend and a team player instead. I know firsthand that if you do, it will make your life a helluva lot easier. And more enjoyable."

"What do you want me to do?"

"An apology would be a step in the right direction."

"Okay, I'm sorry. Now leave."

"Not me, you cunnerman," said the Game Master. "Asher."

"Apologize to weathervane? Yeah, right."

"Then, after you apologize, try being his friend. Get to know him. You'll find out that you have more in common than you think."

"Like what?"

"You both watched your mother die."

Brett kept quiet.

"You never thought of that," said the Game Master.

"Even if I do want to apologize and become his friend, I don't know where he is. He ran away." Brett gave the only excuse he could think of.

"If one is going to run away, the transport terminal would be a good place to start. Maybe you should help your team and show that you can be a friend to them. Look, here they come now."

Brett saw Nittany, Cray, Tabitha, and Xiao come into the snack shop.

"Brett, did you see Asher?" asked Nittany.

"No, he isn't in here." The four kids started to walk away. "Hey!"

They stopped and looked at Brett. He turned to look at the old man, he had left without Brett noticing. He turned to the other kids. "Did you check the transport terminal?"

"Not yet," said Nittany. "We'll go there next."

"Can I come?"

"Look, dude," said Cray. "We're trying to find Asher to be his friend, not to turn him in."

"I'm cool with that."

"No funny business?" asked Tabitha.

"I want to help..." Brett tried swallowing a lump in his throat. "I was wrong."

Cray smiled. "Right. Why should we believe you?"

"I guess I gave you no reason to believe me." Brett hung his head low.

"I believe you," said Xiao.

Brett perked up. "You do?"

"Yes, I do." She gave him a backhand slap into his stomach.

"What was that for?" asked Brett.

"To remind you that if you're ever an asshole to any of us again, I will slice it off and feed it to the cockroaches that infest your coffin locker."

"I love it when you talk dirty to me," Brett said with a wink and a pucker.

"A little rough on him?" Dean Wu asked as she went up to the Game Master, who had stepped away from Brett.

"He can handle it. Besides, I had to be. He's a little thickheaded, you know." The Game Master smirked.

"Oh, I know, trust me, I know." She smiled back.

"Seeing them all year sure makes you wonder if they will actually become a team."

"Oh, I know. If we managed to do it, they will too."

The Game Master and the dean watched as the young group left the snack shop.

"He's not here," said Nittany, disappointed.

"Hang on a second." Xiao went up to the ticket counter. "Excuse me, ma'am, I'm looking for a friend. His name is Asher Smizik. He's tall and has blond hair. Did he come by here?"

"Here's a picture of him." Nittany held up her holowatch and projected a selfie of herself and Asher eating candy apples at the hay maze.

"Yes, I saw him."

"Where did he go?"

"He left on a transport to New York a few minutes ago."

"New York?" said Cray. "Why New York?"

They all were trying to figure out why Asher had headed to New York. Then it dawned on Nittany.

"He's going home."

"I thought he was from Pittsburgh," said Tabitha.

"That's what he told us. If Asher is…" She looked around for possible threats. "…you know what, he would give false information, right?"

"Okay," Xiao said, "let's say he is from New York—we have no idea where in New York."

"New York is a pretty big city," said Brett. "I got lost there once when my dad was on business."

"Asher doesn't come across as a city boy," said Xiao.

Nittany's eyes opened wide. "I know where he's going. He's not from New York City. He's from a small town in upstate New York, a place called Detrick Falls."

"How do you know?" asked Cray.

Nittany ushered the group away from the ticket counter where they wouldn't be heard. "Listen, he thought he was running from hybrid hunters, it is worse. My dad mentioned that these rogue hunters, Navarro and Cortez, raided a hybrid community filled mainly with kids. They botched the operation, and everyone got away except a woman. That must be his mother. C'mon." They moved back up to the ticket counter.

"Excuse me, ma'am, can we get tickets for the next transport to New York?" asked Xiao.

"I'm sorry, that was the last transport to New York until tomorrow."

"What's the closest can you get us to New York?"

The ticket assistant looked on her computer. "Bridgeport, Connecticut, that leaves in six hours."

"What terminal is closest to Detrick Falls?" asked Nittany.

The ticket assistant's fingers ran across the computer. "There's a shuttle leaving for Erie, Pennsylvania, in forty-five minutes—oh, wait. It's fully booked. I can get you on a flight to Toronto. It leaves in four hours."

"Can we be put on a waiting list?" asked Xiao.

"I can. The likelihood of you getting on is slim. All but two people are checked in."

"That's okay, we'll take our chances," said Nittany.

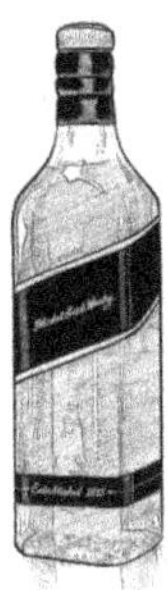

"I'm all for helping Asher, I have a slight problem though," said Cray.

"What?" asked Nittany.

"I don't have enough money on my pay card. I can't ask my mom for more either. I'm on a scholarship for a reason."

"I didn't think of that," said Nittany. "I won't have enough either."

Xiao and Tabitha looked dismal as well.

"What are we going to do now?" asked Nittany.

"Guys, I got it covered," Brett assured them. "I have enough money on my pay card for all of us to go to the Tekulve-Lockley wormhole and back. We need to get on the flight."

"Is it wrong of me to want people to get sick so they have to take another flight?" asked Nittany.

"That's it," said Brett. "That's how we can get on."

"Get people sick?" asked Cray.

"Find a group of passengers going on the flight to Erie. Hang out by them and keep scratching. When I come back, follow my lead." Brett dashed away from them and headed to the station store.

"I don't know what Brett has in mind, I hope he gets back soon. They're about to load the shuttle," said Nittany.

"Hey, guys. Sorry, the line was long at the station store. I got the shampoo." Brett talked louder than usual. He held up a maroon-and-white bottle with a penguin on it. In big letters it read "Artic Pubic Lice Shampoo."

"I wish we had time to take a shower before our flight to Erie leaves. The itching is really getting to me," said Brett, a little too loud. He purposely scratched in areas without any modesty.

Echo 88 kept the routine up. One by one, people around them shifted away.

"Hey, it's almost time to board. Let's go get in line for the shuttle to ERIE," Cray said rather loudly.

The five cadets went and stood in line, all five scratching in areas they shouldn't in public. Brett made a point to drop the shampoo bottle a couple of times.

"Hey, look." Brett nodded toward the ticket desk.

"Excuse me, miss," said a man who looked to be in his fifties. "My wife and I decided to change our tickets from Erie to Philadelphia, if that's okay. Our daughter lives in Philly, we want to stop in and say hi to her. Can we exchange our tickets please?" He kept looking at the cadets.

"Here comes a family of four," said Tabitha.

When the family finished at the ticket desk, the attendant called for boarding.

"Why aren't they calling us?" asked Nittany, a little worried.

"They better call us. I didn't scratch in embarrassing places for nothing," said Xiao.

People avoided the cadets as they entered the tunnel that led to the shuttle.

The attendant finished checking in the passengers. She went over to the desk and got on the intercom system. "Will passengers Brett Lundy, Crayon Flint, Nittany McGreggor, Xiao-Niao Li, and Tabitha Dorney please come to the ticket desk."

"I think we did it," said Nittany.

"Who would've thought?" said Cray.

"Let's go bring Asher home," Nittany said.

Brett followed the others on board the shuttle. He spotted the last seat open between two heavyset women in their sixties. Brett smiled. "This is going to be fun." He squeezed into his seat, not before scratching his crotch first.

"Excuse me, can you hold my shampoo while I get my seat belt fastened? I almost missed the flight running to pick this up!" He gave the lady on his right the shampoo. Brett started cracking up when both ladies' efforts to push away failed due to their sizes.

"Thank you," Brett said as he took the shampoo back and gave her a wink. He looked at his watch as a text came. Jinx had replied to his text. He'd asked if her brother still lived in Erie. Three words appeared. *Yes, frick off!*

"Chief Mrkonic," said LTjg Meoquanee as she hustled into medical.

"You need me?" asked Chief.

"Have you seen Asher?"

"He was here a little bit ago. I was busy with a patient and couldn't talk to him."

"Chief, I got word that everyone from Echo 88, except for Asher, got on a shuttle headed to Erie, Pennsylvania."

"Why would they go there? I'll find Asher to see why they all went."

"That's the thing. Asher hopped on a shuttle to New York before the others. I think something happened that caused Asher to run away, and the rest of the kids went after him to bring him back."

"New York? Son of a bitch." Chief ran to his office and looked on the shelf. The box with Vicki's ashes was gone.

"You want me to call authorities?" asked LTjg Meoquanee.

"No, if Asher went to New York, I know exactly where he's going. I'll go get him and the others," said Chief.

"Are you sure?"

"If he's going to New York, I'm positive."

"I can fly you there if you want. That way you don't have to wait for the next flight out."

"I don't want you doing anything that will get you in trouble. I can handle this."

"Chief, I outrank you. They're my squad. I'm going with you."

Asher stood looking over the coffee-brown stain that had wicked its way into the grains of the oak flooring at Willow Wood. A winter storm brewed outside. The bitter winds swept leaves and other debris around Asher's feet through the large hole in the wall that Navarro and Cortez had created the night of the raid. Asher could see his breath as a chill swept through his body. He wished he would've grabbed a heavier coat and not his gray hoodie.

With the box that contained his mom's ashes clutched to his side, Asher knelt down and gently touched the bloodstain. A chill ran down his spine. Asher placed the box next to the stain.

"I failed you, Mom," he said, fighting back tears. "I killed Timothy. I didn't get him to safety like you told me to." Droplets of guilt, grief, anger, and sorrow flowed down his haggard cheeks.

"You didn't deserve to die. It should've been me. I'm the hybrid, not you. Nittany says you're in heaven. Nittany is...was my girlfriend. I went to school with her. Chief says I haven't known her long enough to love her, but I do." Asher talked to his mom as though she were sitting there, intrigued with every detail, like she would when he shared the excitement of the last book he read.

He talked about Nittany, Brett, and the rest of Echo 88. He shared memories of his first baseball game, his nightmare with Dr. Monroe, Neon and Alita Blackwood, and he shared his feelings about Chief, his dad.

"I have this friend, Pandora. Do you remember her? She's the one that Dr. Emily caught me talking to on the laptop," said Asher. "She's a hybrid too. She lives in an entire village with hybrids. Her father is coming to get me. I wanted to say goodbye to you and Timothy before I left. I won't be coming back." Asher kissed the tip of his finger and pressed gently on the stain. "I love you, Mom. I miss you." He let out a sigh. He didn't have much time left. He stood up with the box in hand and proceeded to climb the debris that led to the second floor.

He walked into his old bedroom. His bed was cut to shreds, his belongings tossed about. The condition of his room was no different than the rest of the house.

Asher found his old pillow ripped, half the stuffing missing. He picked it up and brought it to his face. He took a deep inhale, trying to bring his fond memories of Willow Wood back with the aroma. It didn't work.

Asher continued through the house, room by room, looking for memories that he could salvage before going to Pandora's community. He stood outside the door to one of two rooms he hadn't searched yet. This would be the toughest room to search thus far. He wasn't sure he could go into Timothy's room. Trying to hold himself together the best he could, he took a deep breath and opened the door and stepped in.

Timothy's room reflected the other rooms in the house. It looked like a shuttlecraft had zoomed through. He walked over to Timothy's bed and placed his hand on it. He spotted a black fury object barely sticking out between the bed and wall. He crawled onto the bed and pulled out Berman, the stuffed gorilla that had belonged to Asher before he gave it to Timothy years ago. He curled up on Timothy's bed, clutching Berman to his chest.

People envied Asher how he could recall his memories perfectly. He could bring back any memory he wanted to. That was what they were. Memories. You couldn't talk to a memory. You couldn't hug a memory. You couldn't interact with a memory. He felt a memory's purpose was to take his heart on an emotional shuttle ride through an asteroid field.

Asher yawned. He had to get up; otherwise he would fall asleep on Timothy's bed.

He stretched as he got out of the bed. He headed down the hall toward his mom's room, taking Berman with him. Her bed was turned upside down on the floor, her personal items strewn about. He went to the window seat. The seat had been removed, and any contents inside were gone. He reached in and wiggled a piece of floorboard. It came up, revealing a small safe. A sigh of relief escaped his lips. No one had found his mom's secret hiding place.

He closed his eyes and brought up a memory of his mom opening the safe six years, seven months, sixteen days, twenty-two hours, four minutes ago. He saw her dial in the combination. He hoped she hadn't changed it since then. He dialed in the numbers from his memory—0516. The safe opened. He realized the combination matched Chief's birthday, May 16.

He fumbled through the contents, not looking for anything in particular. He wanted to see what his mom thought was valuable that she had to hide it away. He found memory chips and placed them next to his watch. Within a few minutes, his watched beeped. Asher pulled up the content from the first chip.

They were photos of what appeared to be her childhood, from birth to high school graduation. He wondered why he didn't see any pictures of Chief. He transferred a second chip. This one contained documents, one being his true birth certificate. His mother's and Chief's names were listed as his parents.

He found a chip with a video recording. When he brought it up, he saw Uncle Mick's face. He played it.

"Vicki, I got what you wanted, and I haven't told Liam. You really need to tell him. I know you're scared, worried, and Liam can be an ass at times. Deep down he still loves you. I know that once he lays eyes on Asher, he will love him too and will support you with everything he has for Asher's surgery."

Asher gasped. He didn't know Uncle Mick had helped his mom get a garrison chip off the black market. Uncle Mick knew all this time and kept his word to Asher's mom, even after she died.

Asher continued to watch the video. "Oh, and I got this stuffed Pirate Parrot for my nephew. I hope to give it to him next time you're in town." Asher felt a tear. His uncle held onto that parrot for sixteen years. He'd made good on his promise and given it to him. Now he wished he would've brought the parrot with him.

Asher pulled out the last item, a small navy-blue plush fabric box. He opened it up and revealed a simple diamond ring. His mom's engagement ring that Chief proposed with. He pulled his dog tags out from under his shirt. He unsnapped the chain and slid the ring onto it, then snapped it back together.

Asher shoved the dozen chips into his pocket. He gave his mom's room one last look, then headed out to the grounds.

He stopped and looked up at tree house. Snowflakes were beginning to dance down from the overcast sky. He climbed up, shivering.

He stooped inside the tree house. It seemed smaller. Leaves left-over from the autumn madness were huddled in the corners. Ivy and vines found their way through the windows during the summer growing season.

He went to the far side and knelt in front of two handprints painted on the wall. The red one belonged to Timothy and the blue one to Asher. The handprints had their names etched into the wood above them. Underneath, etched into the wall, was *Brothers Forever!*

Asher placed his hand over the blue one. His hand had grown since he'd painted it on the wall. He placed his other hand over Timothy's. A sudden chill surged through his body. He took a deep breath and fist-bumped the wall between the two handprints, and their secret hiding place swung open. In it lay a metal box—Timothy's time capsule.

Inside were odd little trinkets. Asher pulled out one of Timothy's favorite action figures from The Flash universe. He tucked it into his pocket. He saw a thumb drive that had his favorite books stored on. He put it with the action figure. He removed Timothy's rusted pocketknife and placed it into his pocket.

Clutching onto Berman the Gorilla, he wept. "I'm sorry, Timothy. I think of you every day. I will never forgive myself for your death. I miss you terribly. Everyone described you as being the closest thing I had to a brother. I disagree. You *are* my brother." Asher stayed there, crying, releasing all the anger, grief, and guilt that he kept bottled up over the past six months. He let everything out. Asher finally began his journey down the path of healing.

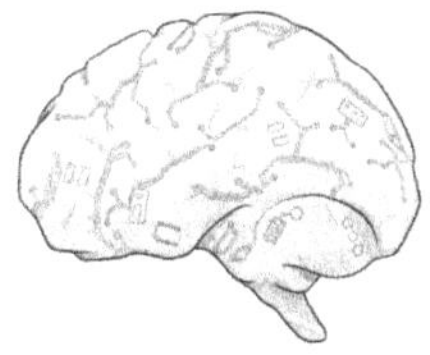

"Hey, weathervane!"

Asher looked up and saw Brett, Nittany, Xiao, Tabitha, and Cray. He stood up and wiped the tears off his face. "What are you guys doing here?"

Led by Brett, the members of Echo 88 crammed themselves into the tree fort.

Brett took a step closer to Asher. "For a hot minute you've been carrying a secret by yourself. I'm here to tell you that you no longer need to carry that secret alone. You have friends here to help. I lost my mom too. I know how it feels." Brett stuck out his right hand.

Asher looked at Nittany. She nodded.

"Don't leave me hanging, cunnerman."

Asher let out a small chuckle and shook Brett's hand. Brett pulled Asher toward him and gave him a hug. One by one, they all joined in until the whole squad was one.

"This was your home?" asked Nittany.

"Yeah."

"Who's that in the photo with you?" asked Cray.

"It's my brother, Timothy. If it wasn't for him, I would be dead. He saved my life." Asher wiped the tears from his face. Another group hug formed, and Asher sobbed, taking another step down the path of healing. Not one cadet let go until Asher was ready.

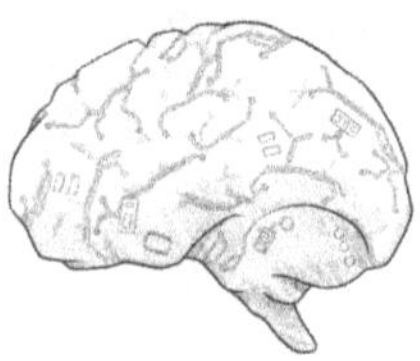

Asher and the others stood around the naked Japanese maple tree that Asher called his quiet spot. With his fingers tremoring, he opened the box. He pulled out a sealed plastic bag that contained black particles that were once his mom. He opened the bag and sprinkled her ashes onto a snowy blanket around the tree. After he finished, he turned to Nittany. She opened her arms and hugged Asher tight. He buried his head into her shoulder and cried.

"Let's give them some time," whispered Tabitha.

Cray, Xiao, and Tabitha headed back to the house. Brett placed his hand on Asher's shoulder. He gave it a little squeeze and followed the others.

After a few minutes, Asher lifted his head. "I got your shoulder wet." He looked into her eyes. They were different than normal, and he realized why. "You don't like me anymore, do you?" Asher could feel more tears, he fought them back.

"It's not that I don't like you. I mean, I'm still your friend. If my dad found out you're a hybrid..."

"It's not your fault. You didn't know, and I didn't know he was in the hybrid police."

"You really put me in the middle," said Nittany.

"I'm sorry. I didn't mean to. I tried to keep to myself."

"I know you did." Nittany's eyes were glossy. "I still want to be your friend. If word got out and my dad found out I knew, I don't even want to think about it."

"I'm okay if you want to turn me in. If that would keep you out of trouble, I'll do it."

Nittany's tears flooded over her eyelids. "You'd do anything for anybody, wouldn't you?"

"Anything for you, Nittany."

"This makes what I am about to say all that much harder."

"Then don't say it. I understand. I'm not going back to the *Pocono* anyway. I can't put all your lives in danger, especially yours. When you didn't know, you were safe, now that you know, I don't want you to go to prison for aiding and abetting. I contacted a friend, Pandora, and her father is coming to get me and take me to their secret community."

He knew Nittany wanted to change his mind. He figured she was too scared and too confused. He knew her heart battled with her brain, and her heart was losing. Asher had the same battle going on with his heart and brain.

"I'm sorry, Asher." Nittany ran away, crying.

Asher stood there, knowing he'd ruined everything. There was no other time in his life that he hated being a hybrid more than this moment. His implants caused him to lose the girl who carved her initials into his heart.

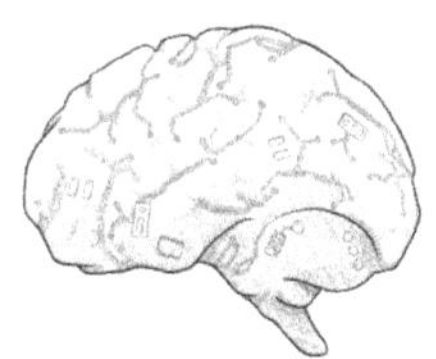

"Asher, let's go. We don't have much time." Neon emerged out of the tree line.

"What are you doing?" asked Asher. "How did you get here?"

"Alita Blackwood is waiting for us."

"I told you, Neon. I'm not going with Alita Blackwood. Besides, I'm waiting for someone."

"I know. You're waiting for Pandora."

"How?"

"Yeah, about that." Neon showed a side of herself that Asher had never seen before. Nervousness. "You know how you had to put up a façade and not tell those normals who you truly are?"

"Yeah," said Asher.

"I wear a mask too."

"What are you trying to say?" Asher thought he knew what she was going to say. He hoped he was wrong.

"I wanted to talk to kids our age about stuff. Topics that 'Neon' would never discuss. One night, I saw through the wall that you were exploring chat rooms. That's when I created Pandora. I could express things about myself without you getting all weird on me."

"You lied to me?"

"It wasn't supposed to get out of hand. You're my best friend, Asher, nothing more, nothing less. I didn't do this to hurt you."

"Nothing less? Best friends are supposed to be able to share their darkest secrets without worrying that the other will judge them."

"I know, and I'm sorry."

"Wait! If you were Pandora, how did you answer my call at the cybercafé? You couldn't answer my call. You were in Jamestown by then with no access to the internet."

"I'll explain everything. We need to leave. Cortez is on his way."

"Are you sure?" Asher started to worry.

"Yes, let's go."

"I can't go. I have to warn my...friends."

"Asher, if you go trying saving those normals, you're going to get yourself killed."

"I don't care." Asher took off toward the house.

"Look! There's one," yelled a hybrid hunter. The weapon he fired sounded mighty strong. At the same time, lightning and thunder clashed in the snow bearing sky.

"Oh crap!" The weapon fire missed. Asher doubled back. He needed to lose the hunters first before he could go back and see if his friends were safe. "I need to hide. Think, Asher, think."

Up ahead, he saw the well and ran to it. He looked over his shoulder to make sure the hunters didn't see where he went. "Damn it," he said when he saw his tracks in the fresh fallen snow.

Laser fire hit the ground in front of him, and more followed. He dodged out of the way and scurried down a moss-ridden ladder. "You cunnerman," Asher said to himself. "You trapped yourself."

He climbed down until his feet were on the last rung before it became a sheet of ice. Asher tested the frozen well water before putting all of his weight on it.

"Now what?" he asked himself. The ladder rungs made a grinding sound as they disappeared in the wall. "Huh?"

*Click.* Asher heard latches detach from its surface. The sound of rock scraping across rock echoed in the well. At the ice line, a secret hatch appeared. He opened it wider. Without hesitating, he scurried into the tight crawl space. If anything, he would be out of sight from the hunters when they peered down.

He slithered his way into the hole and closed the door with his feet. His shoulders scraped the sides. Again, he wished he had Neon's eyes. He twitched his nose from the foul and stale air. He army-crawled forward, into total darkness, bumping his head along the way. The loose dirt falling down on the back of his neck made him itch.

Asher pulled himself out of the cramped crawl space and into a cavern. He stood and stretched his aching muscles. Loose dirt fell from his clothes. The air felt much warmer inside the cavern than on the outside. It felt refreshing to his chilled bones.

"Is that...?" Asher squinted. In the darkness of the underground cavern stood dimly lit running lights of a shuttlecraft. It showed extreme wear and tear.

Asher placed his hand on the name of the Dalin-class shuttlecraft: Hank Morgan NAS *Pocono* RT-25. Ashcr jolted as the hatch opened with a wisp. He crept up the ramp and poked his head inside.

"Come inside, I won't bite you," said a familiar voice from the pilot's seat.

Asher walked up to the cockpit. The pilot's seat spun around, revealing a familiar gray-hooded figure.

"It's you," said Asher.

The man lowered his hood, revealing an aged and worn face. He pointed toward Asher with a nail-bitten finger. "It's me...well, at least a younger me." The man laughed at his own joke. "Please sit, we have much to discuss with little time. I know you have many questions."

Not taking his eyes off the old man, Asher moved a cigar box off the co-pilot's seat and sat down.

"I know the first question you have on your mind. Go ahead, ask it."

Asher stared at him. This was like a story from one of his books coming to life. "Who are you?"

"You already know the answer to that."

"Me?"

"Yes, a much older you. Much older."

"Were time machines invented in the future?" Asher's brain tried processing all of this.

"Hell if I know. It wasn't a time machine that brought me here...or should I say *you* here? It was that damn wormhole that caused the Lost Fleet to disappear."

"The theory of wormholes connecting time is true?"

"Yes, it is," replied the man.

"I go back in time and become you?" Asher started to make sense of everything.

"You do indeed."

"If that's the case, why didn't you stop the raid? Keep Mom and Timothy from being killed?"

The old man let out a long sigh. A look that combined guilt, regret, and grief covered his face. His glacier blue eyes became glossy with tears. "Time is a ruthless creature that cannot be tamed. Regardless of what you do to change time's habits and goals, it will continue to wreak havoc until it gets what it seeks. In this case, it was Mom's life."

"You didn't even try."

"I did try, several times, it's hard to fight the inevitable."

Anger and rage whipped through Asher's body. "I don't believe you. You're making this shit up."

"I wish I was. You know how you thought you knew Cray and Alita Blackwood when you knew you've never met them before?"

"Yeah." It dawned on him. "Neon is Alita Blackwood?"

"Yes, she is."

"That explains how Alita Blackwood found me at the cybercafé. She pretended to be Pandora."

"Yes, she did. Unfortunately, Navarro had bugged all public computers, hoping any escapees from Willow Wood would use them."

"That's how Cortez found me." Another notion popped into his head. "Dean Wu, Gully Jumper, Autumn Fletcher, and the Game Master."

"Yes, they are Xiao, Cray, Tabitha, and Brett all grown up like me."

There was one name missing from that list. He was afraid to ask it. He refused to believe it. "No, this is a dream or brainwashing. This can't be real."

The old man let out another sigh. He closed his eyes and placed his fingers by his temple.

Asher blinked and shook his head. Visions popped into his mind. He saw the dead glare of Timothy wedged between the rocks in the water; he felt the tingle when he had his first kiss with Nittany. His skin felt wet and clammy as a memory from the flooding escape room focused in. His thoughts and feelings that flashed before him were the exact thoughts and feelings he had. His memories seemed to be in syndication.

There were other visions that popped into his head. They weren't old memories or feelings. They felt like memories. He didn't remember any of them though. He felt pain in his right hand as a vision flashed where he cut his hand climbing down the stairwell debris. Goosebumps covered his arms as he saw a canoe on a riverbank in the snow. It felt like the night of the raid, this memory seemed different. A chill coursed his body as he saw Nittany fall into a canoe. She appeared...injured.

"What happened?" asked a confused Asher.

"I shared memories with you. Memories you already acquired and never shared with anyone, and ones you haven't experienced yet."

"How?"

"Our hybrid implants can transfer files to other computer systems, whether it be the computer system on the *Pocono* or to other hybrids. Even the computer in your father's man cave. You could say it's a hybrid's version of mental telepathy."

"You mean I can talk to computers with my mind?"

Asher heard the old man's voice in his head. His lips weren't moving. "Not now, you will eventually. That door on your implants hasn't been unlocked yet."

"When? How?"

The old man continued to talk through their garrison chips. "Soon enough. Mind reading other computers isn't new technology. There are other hybrids out there who can hack implants. Ours can't be hacked, though. There are other surprises will unveil themselves when the time is right."

The old man spoke with his voice again before Asher could ask his question. "Yes, our implants have a firewall."

He continued to answer Asher's questions before Asher spoke them. "I helped a little to create our implants. The real credit goes to Gully and Heath. They had advanced knowledge of the technology from our time. Heath is from my...your time. You know him as Kyle Knoebel."

"Kyle from Whisky 88?" Then another thought came to Asher. "How can you access my thoughts when Dr. Monroe couldn't?"

"Gully and Heath created a superb firewall that only I have the capability of getting through. No one can access your implants, although a few have tried and many more will follow. That's why you were having all those headaches. Gully, Heath, and I couldn't figure out a way to prevent the headaches."

Asher's mind flashed in all directions.

"Yes, that is why you've been getting headaches."

Asher closed his eyes, remembering each time he had a headache. The same face appeared in most of those memories.

"Petty Officer Verbeck."

The old man let out a small smile. "Yes, I will start speaking normally again," said the man. "Verbeck is a hybrid on the *Pocono*. Look, we don't have much time left. Echo 88 are being held captive by Cortez's mongrels in the wine cellar. You need to get them to safety."

"How do I do it?"

"I can't tell you. It would wind up that creature known as time. The creature is stirring from what I told you already. Remember this: because you know you grow old doesn't mean it will happen. You are still at risk of dying, especially if you step off the written timeline. Don't think you're immortal, you're not. And neither are our friends. Now we must go. You have to rescue them."

The old man stood up and headed to the exit of the shuttle.

"Wait!"

The old man stopped and turned. "Yes, I am the Phantom Prophet." He'd done it again. He'd read Asher's mind. "There's a head in the back of the shuttle. Cups by the sink. I know you remembered what your father taught you. Now hurry up. I'll show you an easy way to get out of here."

"One more question."

"Special sensors," replied the old man.

Now he knew how the Phantom Prophet had kept Neon from finding the secret passageways and the cavern with her hybrid eyes.

The old man disappeared from the shuttle.

Brett pounded on the wine cellar's wooden door. "You're going to regret this!" he yelled. Cortez's men caught Echo 88 and locked them in the cellar until Cortez knew for sure they weren't needed alive.

"They can't hear you," Xiao said. "Besides, they locked it from the outside."

"My holowatch is being blocked. I can't contact my dad," said Nittany.

"Maybe Asher will rescue us," Cray said.

"I hate to say it, he's probably dead," Tabitha chimed in.

"He's not dead," Nittany insisted.

"If he is still alive, he's probably long gone, and we came here for nothing," said Brett.

"Asher's not like that," said Nittany. "He'll come for us. I know he will."

"They'll kill him if he does," Tabitha said.

"That's proof that Cortez hasn't killed Asher yet. If he did, we would be dead too," said Nittany. "I heard enough Cortez stories from my dad that I know his MO." Nittany let out a high-pitched shrill. "Something bumped my leg." She looked down at the wall, and a hidden door popped open and brushed against her leg. Asher's head popped out.

"Asher?" asked Nittany. "God, you scared me."

Asher pulled himself out. "There are hybrid hunters outside the door. I had to use this secret passageway to get to you."

"Where've you been?" Nittany asked.

Asher wanted to tell her the truth even though the Phantom Profit had told him to keep his secret. Asher wished he didn't have to keep any more secrets. From what the Phantom Prophet had said, he would be holding secrets for the rest of his life.

"I was looking for you guys without getting caught. It wasn't an easy task."

"Where does that lead to?" asked Brett. "Is it a way out?"

"Of course it's a way out," said Cray. "How else would Asher get in here?"

"I'll get you all out of here. I promise." Asher might have failed his mom and Timothy, he wasn't going to fail his friends.

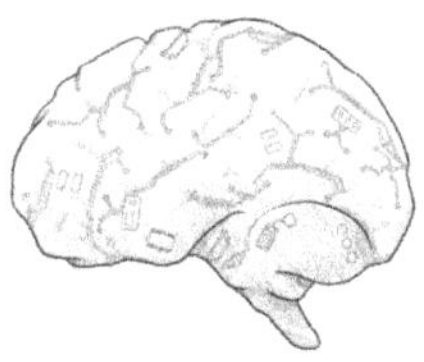

Asher took them through the passageway, through Neon's room, and eventually ended up in his bedroom.

"Are you taking us in circles?" asked Brett.

"No. I was able to sneak in through the back door and up to my room. I couldn't go through the basement. Cortez had guards standing by."

"This is your room, Asher?" asked Nittany.

"Umm, yeah." Asher felt almost ashamed of it. He didn't know why.

Asher cracked open the bedroom door. He looked to ensure no hybrid hunters were patrolling the second floor. "Come on, this way."

Echo 88 crept down the hall. A wind blew through, giving Asher the chills.

Asher looked over the side of the staircase debris. "It's clear. Be careful climbing down." Asher led the way. He lost his footing and grabbed onto a piece of wood, and a nail went through his hand. As he suppressed a scream, a memory of the Phantom Profit's now became his too.

He glanced up at Nittany. Would she get injured like he'd seen in the Phantom Prophet's memory? The future memory didn't reveal how or when. He didn't know if it would be a life-threatening injury or not. This scared him. He'd met all of Echo 88's older selves, except for Nittany. Why?

He pulled his hand off the nail, tore a piece of his shirt off and wrapped it around his hand, wincing in pain.

"You okay?" Nittany asked when she arrived at the bottom.

"Yeah, just a scrape." He looked at her oddly.

The future memory of her injured in the canoe flashed before him. The image terrified him.

Cray looked out the gaping hole where the front door had once stood. "I see hunters out there. We can't go that way."

"This way," said Asher. "Don't step there." He pointed to the dark stain on the floor.

"What's that?" asked Tabitha.

"My mom's blood." He stepped around the stain and headed toward the back of the house. Asher led them through the ransacked rooms to the back porch. He would've taken the egress tunnel inside the house if the entrance wasn't being guarded by one of Cortez's men.

"Oh no," he said.

"What's wrong?" asked Nittany.

"There was an outhouse over there before getting destroyed,"

"Cunnerman, now is not the time to worry about taking a shit," said Brett.

"That was our way out. It was an egress tunnel."

"Over here!" yelled a hybrid hunter.

"We gotta go now," said Cray.

The image of Nittany in the canoe flashed in Asher's mind again. He shook his head in disbelief. He knew, deep down, they had to go to the river.

# CHAPTER 58

"And where do you think you're all going?" Navarro asked as she stepped out from behind the tree that held Timothy's tree house. Echo 88 came to a skidding halt.

"Detective Navarro," said Nittany.

"Hello, Nittany. I'm not a detective anymore. Your father made sure of that."

"It's not my father's fault you got kicked off the force."

Navarro fired a dart and hit Nittany in the leg. She yelped and fell.

"You bitch," said Asher. He went to tackle Navarro, she raised her crossbow at his head. He stopped and retreated to his friends again. He knelt down to check on Nittany's leg. At least this dart didn't explode.

"You realize you and your friends won't see what tomorrow brings, right?" asked Navarro.

"Let them go," said Alita Blackwood. She emerged out of the woods, showing that her hands were empty. "It's me you want, not them."

"That's where you're wrong. Their young organs will sell at a fine price on the black market. You know I can't let them leave."

Alita Blackwood looked at Asher, then shifted her attention to Navarro again. "You know I'm going to kill you, right?"

"Let's see here. My men are surrounding you. I have a weapon. You don't. How do you figure on killing—" A weapons blast came from the tree house. Navarro dropped to the ground, dead. Asher saw green-and-blue hair duck down.

"Told you I would kill you," Alita Blackwood said in a boasting tone.

*Neon*, Asher thought.

Hybrids who belonged to Alita Blackwood's army emerged. Weapon fire and snow danced the swing, the jive, and the quickstep, causing disarray on the grounds. "Get to the river. It's your only way out," said Alita Blackwood.

Asher took a deep breath. He went over to Nittany. All of his friends were taking cover behind trees.

"Asher, you need to get out of here," said Nittany.

"I'm not leaving you! Can you move?" Asher asked.

"I think so." Nittany moaned.

Asher helped her up. He turned himself into a human crutch. "This way!" he yelled. The rest of Echo 88 followed Asher into the woods.

"Where are we going?" Nittany asked in pain.

"To the river. It's the only way out of here." The future memory that the Phantom Profit shared led him to the decision of escaping via the river. He prayed to Nittany's God that he wouldn't fail this time.

"Is there a boat?" asked Brett.

"No, a canoe."

"A canoe? Asher?" Nittany wiped the snow that melted on her brow out of her eyes as it pounded against her face.

"I know, I'm not going to let you die. No one dies. Not this time!"

"We're going to need more than one canoe," said Xiao.

Asher could hear multiple gunshots. With newfound strength and courage, Asher helped Nittany through the woods and the field. They made it to the wall, the same spot where Timothy had been shot.

"Are they following us?" asked Nittany.

"I don't see them," Tabitha replied between breaths.

Asher looked around and decided that they couldn't rest any longer. "Come on. Let me boost you up over the wall." Asher made a stirrup with his hands. Nittany put her good leg into the stirrup and winced with pain as she shot up to the ledge of the wall. She managed to grab onto it and pull herself up the rest of the way. Brett and Cray helped Xiao and Tabitha up.

"Hurry, Asher, I see hunters coming," yelled Nittany.

Asher helped Cray over the wall. "Here, Brett, you're next." As soon as Brett was up, he lay down and reached for Asher. Asher jumped and grabbed onto Brett's hand. Brett lost his balance and yanked Asher over the wall. Both of them landed on their backs next to the others.

"You guys okay?" asked Xiao.

"I'm going to feel that in the morning." Brett massaged his arm.

"Nittany, you okay?" He could see her face crinkled up in pain.

"I don't think I can go any farther. I need to rest. My leg feels tingly and numb. I think there was a numbing agent on the dart."

"We can't stop; we're almost to the river." Asher did the unthinkable. Taking what he'd learned in his first-aid class during a general quarters drill, Asher swooped in on Nittany, put her in a fireman's carry over his shoulders, and dashed toward the river.

"Asher! Careful!" Nittany grunted.

The wind picked up and snow came down harder. They made it to the riverbank and Asher gently put Nittany down on the sandy gravel. He gasped for air, his chest swelling and shrinking with each breath he desperately needed.

"There's three canoes here. How did they get here?" asked Cray.

"A group of people are looking out for us," Asher replied.

Before anyone could react to Asher's answer, Nittany mumbled, "I don't feel good. I feel dizzy." She fell onto the pebble beach.

"Nittany!"

Old haunted memories invaded his mind. He didn't know if he could go any farther. He didn't know if he could get into that canoe after what had happened last time. He didn't know if he could see the rocks again where Timothy's corpse had lain.

"They went this way! Follow their footprints." Voices were approaching them.

Asher's ears perked up as he heard the voices coming from the woods. Without hesitation, he picked up a weak Nittany and put her into the bow of the canoe. The Phantom Profit's memory had become his too.

Brett and Xiao got into the second canoe, Cray and Tabitha in the third. Asher pushed the canoe into the river and jumped in. He let out a sigh of relief when he saw a paddle in the canoe. Now if he only knew how to steer with it.

"Look! There they are," yelled one of Navarro's men from the shore. They fired a few rounds and missed. Asher sighed again as they made it around the bend. He heard the familiar sound of a scorpion approaching.

"Drones!" yelled Cray.

A chorus of hisses came from the other side of the river, and a ball of light sped through the air, exploding the drone on contact.

"Dig hard, everyone," said Brett. They headed toward the rapids.

From the other side of the river, two sets of eyes were hiding behind a bush as a third pair walked up.

"I see you got them on the first try this time." The Phantom Prophet smirked.

"I had it on shotgun setting with heat seeking ammo this time. Besides the last time wasn't my fault," said Gully.

Both men smiled.

Brett and Xiao were in the lead canoe. They hit the first rock, which had massive clearance on either side.

"I knew I should've been in the stern," Xiao snapped.

"Relax, sister, I got this," said Brett. The canoe weaved in a serpentine path. Pieces of ice floated along with them.

"Can you at least keep us going straight?"

"Shut up and paddle, here we go." A splash of cold water reached out and swiped Xiao's face. The canoe wobbled and almost tipped.

"Brett!" yelled Xiao. "This water is freezing. If you tip us..."

"Hey, this isn't as easy as driving a road vehicle."

"I've been with you when you drove a road vehicle. I knew I should've taken the stern."

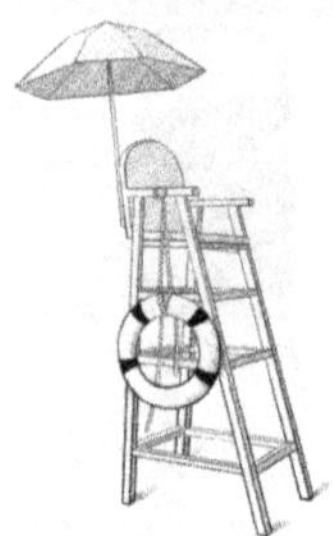

"Get up on your knees. Regardless of what happens, don't stop paddling, and yell when you see rocks," said Cray. He knelt.

The canoe jerked as it hit a rock.

"Rock!" yelled Tabitha.

"A little sooner next time would be great."

"Sorry. Rock five feet."

"Port or..." The canoe hit the rock. "Starboard?" Cray wished his cousin Jacoby manned the bow. Jacoby's dad, Uncle Izaak, would take them camping every summer. Canoeing and white-water rafting were the highlights of the trips.

"I'll do better, I promise...Rock four feet starboard."

Cray used his paddle as a rudder and managed to stay clear of it.

The canoe started to move faster. "Okay, Tabitha, here we go!" The canoe entered the white water.

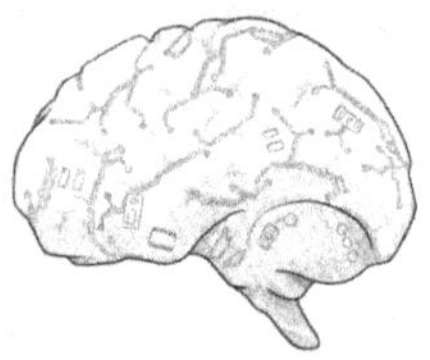

Asher whispered a prayer to a God that Nittany had shared with him on more than one occasion. The snowstorm camouflaged his tears of fright as they began to enter the rapids. He couldn't tell if his hands were shivering from the cold or if fear had set in. Asher closed his eyes to pull himself together. He could not be weak. Not this time.

"Asher," Nittany said as she held on to the side.

"Yeah?"

With the sincerest tone possible and nothing but truth from her heart, Nittany said, "I believe in you. You can do this."

Asher didn't say a thing. However, he sat up a little higher and stuck out his chest a little further.

"Okay, downward Vs," said Asher.

"What?"

"I have to aim for downward Vs. I read that in a book after last time."

The canoe entered the white water with haste. They banged against rocks peeping out of the water. Asher did his best to keep the canoe shooting down the rapids.

"Rock!" yelled Nittany. Too late. The canoe ran up and over the hidden rock, causing it to stop and pivot a bit. "What now?"

Timothy's dead eyes flickered in front of Asher. "You killed me," Timothy's voice echoed in his head. Asher remembered these rocks. He'd found Timothy's body here six months ago.

"Asher!" yelled Nittany.

Asher closed his eyes and saw Timothy's pale, dead face. He forced himself to replace the cold memory with Timothy on the lawn, giggling while Asher tickled him. Asher let out a little smile.

"Asher! You okay?" yelled Nittany.

"Yeah." Asher tried shifting his weight in jerking motions to wiggle the canoe free. It didn't work. He took the paddle and pushed it against nearby rocks. Still not enough.

"I can't get us off this rock! I'm going to have to get out and push us off."

"Asher, you can't do that. It's too dangerous. The water is too cold."

"I can't think of any other way. I can see the bottom."

Tears ran down Nittany's red cheeks. Asher took a deep breath and slowly and carefully stood, still holding on to the side of the canoe. His bottom pointed to the snow-filled sky.

Asher lifted his right leg and stuck it over the side of the canoe, placing it on a slick underwater rock. The coldness of the icy water cut through his foot like an icicle stabbed into his heart. He tried to push off, the canoe wouldn't budge. Hanging on to the canoe, he managed to get his other leg out. He slipped and recovered fairly easily. Both feet stung as the winter water coldness pierced the skin of his feet., and they were rapidly growing numb.

He pushed and shoved; the canoe wouldn't move. "I wish I had Timothy's strength right about now." With a grunt, he gave the canoe a huge shove, and it rocked. He jumped in and, with no grace, landed on his bottom as the canoe took off.

"You did it!"

Asher looked back. He could've sworn he saw a flash frame of Timothy...no, it couldn't be. Maybe his anxiety was causing him to see things.

Asher grabbed his paddle. Kneeling on the canoe floor for better balance, he managed to steer them through more of the rapids. When he thought he'd conquered the worst part, it showed up in front of him —a three-foot drop that stretched across the river. Asher stood to get a better look. The snow limited his vision. It looked like a rabid beast foaming at the mouth. Beyond the falls, one canoe had already capsized, and the second followed shortly after. With the chaos and danger, Asher had one thought. He wondered why such a thought would pop into his head at this very moment, regardless, he followed it through.

"Nittany."

"What?"

"You wouldn't want to go to the winter semi-formal dance with me, would you?"

"You ask me that now?"

"Yeah," Asher replied.

"Does this mean you're coming back to the *Pocono* with us?"

"I guess so." Asher hadn't realized that by asking Nittany to the dance, he'd committed himself to going back to the *Pocono*. Oddly enough, he didn't mind.

"I'm glad you're coming back. I wouldn't want to go to the dance with anyone else except with my boyfriend. What I said back there, well, I'm sorry. We will work this out. I want you with me up there on the *Pocono*. I can't lose you."

Brett pulled himself onto a rock, shivering. "Motherfricker that water is cold." Wrapping his arms around himself, he saw Cray on the shoreline trying to run up the river on the rocky banks. Xiao swam hard upriver. "What are you doing?" he yelled.

"Asher and Nittany. Nittany is injured, and Asher can't swim," Xiao replied through chattering teeth.

Brett looked up toward the final rapid. He could see the canoe go under. "Oh shit!" He dove back in, fighting the current.

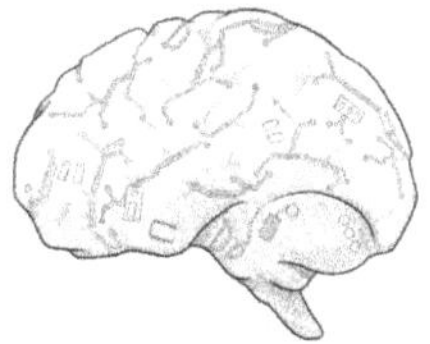

Nittany held on to each side of the canoe the best she could with numb hands. She looked back at Asher, who struggled with controlling the canoe. "Are we going to die?"

"Not today!" He paddled with all his might to get a good running start. Not knowing where it came from, a startling, out of tune, cracking battle cry trumpeted out of Asher's mouth as the canoe flew over the final hurdle. The canoe wobbled letting water in. They did it. They made it through the rapids. Both of them started laughing and celebrating. The cheers of the others rang out around them.

"You go, weathervane!" yelled Brett as he threw his fist up in the air.

"You did it, Asher! I knew you could do it," Nittany said with blue lips.

"Thanks for believing in me."

"Asher, I will always believe in you. I love you!" She looked back and shot him a smile.

"I love you too, Nittany."

"Yo, cunnermans! Over here!"

Asher saw Brett nearby, treading water. Asher steered the canoe over to him. Brett hoisted himself up, almost flipping them.

"Careful, Brett," said Asher. "Don't be a cunnerman." Asher gave Brett a crooked smile.

Brett pointed at Asher. "Don't be an Ash. Let's go get the others before they die of hypothermia."

Asher paddled up to Xiao as she treaded water. Her bun had fallen out, and her hair stuck to her face.

"Need a lift?" Brett said as he reached out to help pull her into the canoe.

"Pppp-lease," said Xiao.

Almost tipping the canoe, Xiao reached out and grabbed Brett's hand. She gave it a big yank, causing him to fall over the side. "I knew

I should've taken stern." She grabbed onto the side of the canoe, lifting herself in.

"You bitch!" Brett grabbed onto the canoe to pull himself up.

"I swear to God, if you flip us over..." Xiao started to say as Brett hoisted himself into the canoe, almost flipping them.

"Damn it, Brett!" yelled Xiao.

"Look!" Nittany yelled.

"I see them," Asher replied. Up on shore, at what looked to be a boat launch, stood Tabitha and Cray, waving.

Asher let the canoe run aground. Brett and Xiao jumped out. Asher climbed out and helped Nittany. Cray wore his toothy grin.

"My man, Asher," said Cray. "The only one who managed not to capsize."

Xiao gave a backhand slap to Brett's stomach.

"What was that for?"

"What do you think?" asked Xiao. "For tipping us."

Asher walked Nittany up to shore. With his free hand, he gave Cray a high five.

"Now what?" asked Xiao. All six of them were shivering and their lips were blue.

Asher shrugged. "Follow the dirt road?"

"Listen," said Cray. The sound of a vehicle came from the dirt road.

"Someone is coming," said Brett. "They must've known we'd end up here."

Echo 88 dispersed, trying to find a place to hide. Xiao stopped at the cry of a...pterodactyl?

"Xiao!" said Brett. "Move it!"

Xiao stood in the middle of the road. From around the corner, a purple-and-black car appeared with a pterodactyl hood ornament and the name Ursula on the license plate.

"Tuck?" Xiao said. "How?"

"Get in!" yelled Tuck.

Echo 88 all crammed into the car. Tuck put it into gear and headed back the way he came.

"Turn the heat all the way up," Tabitha said from the back.

Asher held onto Nittany. She sat on his lap, snuggling into him. She shivered, and her teeth clattered. "Stay with me, Nittany."

"Dude, this car is wicked!" said Brett.

"I got out it out of the shop. I haven't finished upgrading it though."

"What are you doing here?" asked Xiao, interrupting the boys' conversation.

"Dean Wu from the NAS *Pocono* got me a seat at a prep school in Buffalo. I asked what I had to do for such a gift, and she replied that one day she would need my services to pick up people who needed a ride. I didn't realize it was going to be you."

"How did Dean Wu know?" asked Xiao.

"I don't know," Tuck replied.

The road ahead forked. The left took them to the main road, and the right to a gravel road that followed the river.

"Shit!" Tuck swerved from the left fork to the right as a Jeep cut him off.

"We're being chased!" said Tabitha.

"Can you fly across the river?" asked Xiao.

"I haven't installed that upgrade yet. At least I have my backroad snow tires on," said Tuck. "Otherwise we would be in serious shit."

"Like we're not already?" Xiao said sarcastically.

Asher felt sick to his stomach. He tried to replace the nauseated feeling with another good memory.

The car jerked as Cortez rammed them in the rear.

"Dude, you can go faster than this," said Brett.

"If it wasn't snowing, yes. Even my backroad snow tires have their limits."

Cortez rammed them again. On the driver's side stood a cliff going straight up. On the passenger's side, a cliff went straight down into the river. Cortez pulled his Jeep between the cliff wall and Tuck. Both swerved toward each other. With a crash and bang, both vehicles flew off the cliff toward the water.

LTjg Meoquanee flew the shuttle up the river. Chief sat in the co-pilot's seat with Mac leaning over between them. Chief and LTjg Meoquanee arrived at Willow Wood the same time as the hybrid police, including Mac. The hybrid police were given an anonymous tip that a war broke out at Willow Wood between hybrids and hunters.

"Are you sure Neon said they got into canoes?" Mac asked with a nervous and doubting tone.

"I'm sure," replied Chief. "I wish we could see better through the snow."

"Look!" LTjg Meoquanee pointed. The three watched a muscle car and a Jeep drive off a cliff and into the waiting river below. "Hang on, we're going down." Meoquanee did a deep dive and pulled up to level out a foot above the water. Chief and Mac opened the side door.

"Do you see anyone?" asked Mac.

"Look! Over there." Chief pointed to someone treading water. LTjg Meoquanee eased the shuttlecraft over to them. Another head popped out of the water, and another.

Chief threw out a rope. "Grab on to it!" Mac and Chief pulled the rope in. They reached down and helped Xiao, Cray, and Tabitha out of the water.

"Was Nittany with you?" asked Mac.

Out of breath and teeth chattering, Cray replied, "Yeah, Brett and Asher too."

"And Tuck," said Xiao.

Mac took his shoes and coat off. "I'm going in."

Brett and Nittany gasped as they broke the surface. Tuck soon followed.

"There they are," shouted Xiao.

Chief threw the rope to them and pulled them in.

"Hi, Daddy." Nittany cast her father an awkward smile that turned into a frown when she saw her father's eyes.

"Are you okay?"

"I was shot in the leg and it hurts. I think I'll be okay." She looked at the others. "Hey, where's Asher?"

# CHAPTER 60

It all happened fast. Asher shivered in the car with water up to his nose. His teeth clattered. He found an air pocket where he could breathe, at least until the oxygen ran out. Could this be one of those moments the Phantom Prophet had told him about where he could still die? Asher closed his eyes, trying to calm himself down. He knew Nittany got out and was pretty sure the others did too.

"Okay, Asher. This is just another escape room. No one is going to let anything happen to you," he said. "All I have to do is pull myself out of the car and use my legs to kick off and go toward daylight. Yeah, that's it. I can do this." He upchucked in his mouth and swallowed it back down. It had an acidic, metallic taste to it.

Asher took one last deep breath and held it. He forced himself under the water, leaving the security of his air pocket. He reached out blindly and pulled his way toward the open door. He looked straight up and saw daylight. He cleared the car.

An image of Gully Jumper flashed in his mind. Gully showing him how to tread water. Asher pushed himself from the stony bottom and started to do the motions that Gully did. His cheeks were burning. Panic pounded inside him, and he struggled harder, forcing himself up higher and higher. The coldness of the water suffocated him.

He coughed and gagged as his head broke the surface, doing a poor version of the doggy paddle to stay afloat.

"There he is!" Nittany shouted.

"Asher! Grab the rope!" yelled Chief.

Asher turned and saw the shuttlecraft. Chief threw out a rope. It landed a couple of feet away from him. He stretched out his long arms and grabbed.

"Hang on!" yelled Chief.

The water splashed in his face, going up his nose. He held his breath. It was difficult to hang onto the rope with numb hands.

"Take my hand." Chief reached down.

Asher reached up. He felt something clamp onto his ankle. It pulled him back down. He looked as his head went underwater again. Cortez. Asher kicked and struggled; Cortez's grip wouldn't weaken. He heard a plunge, and a body swam past him. Cortez released his ankle. He felt the back of his shirt being yanked and pulled him up. He gasped as his head broke the surface again.

Chief treaded water next to him.

"You okay?" asked Chief.

Asher didn't say a thing.

"Let's get you on the shuttle. This water is freezing."

Brett and Cray helped Asher on board. Mac's head popped out. Chief reached out, and Mac grabbed his hand and pulled him in. Both men climbed aboard.

"Where's Cortez?" asked Asher.

"He drowned," was all Chief said.

Chief sat in the co-pilot seat as LTjg Meoquanee flew the shuttle-craft to the nearest hospital with the heat on full blast. She looked over her shoulder and saw Echo 88 grouped together, telling Mac everything that had happened. She smiled.

"Why are you smiling?" asked Chief.

"After three months of trying to kill each other, they are finally a team."

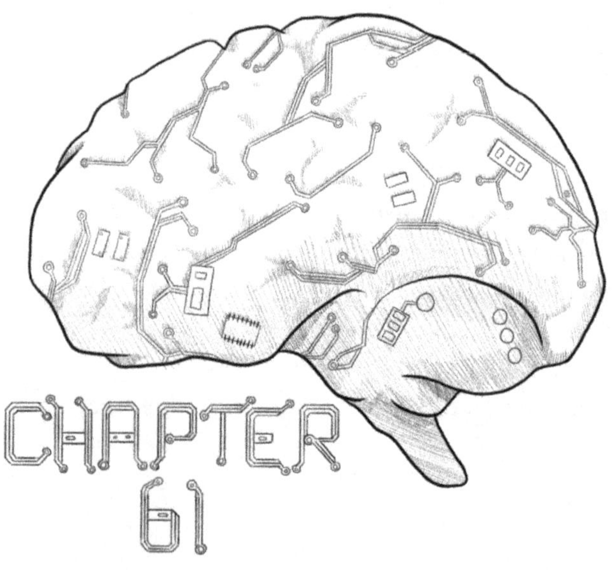

# CHAPTER 61

Asher sat in the hospital lobby. He felt sick to his stomach. Brett, Xiao, Tabitha, Cray, and Chief sat with him. All of them were wearing hospital scrubs. They stood up when Mac came out from the back.

"How is she?" Asher asked eagerly.

"She's going to be fine," he replied.

"Can I see her?" he asked.

Mac seemed troubled. "Asher, I have to take you in the back to be scanned."

"You can't do that," Chief jumped in.

"I'm sorry, Chief. With everything that has happened these past few months, it warrants a scan on him."

"I won't let you." Chief stepped between Asher and Mac.

"Dad, it's okay. Really," said Asher. For the first time, he called him Dad.

"Asher? I can't."

"All the scan is going to reveal is how healthy I am."

"How healthy you are?" Chief had a puzzled look on his face.

"I took my vitamin today." He gave Chief a wink. He never thought he would face many of his fears in the same day. He thanked the Phantom Prophet silently for the vitamins. He wondered if those vitamins always came in cigar boxes.

Xiao walked into the hospital room. It smelled of bleach, and the floor glistened. A soft whispering noise came from behind the pulled pale-yellow curtain along with a rhythmic beep. With her dislocated right arm in a sling, she cautiously pulled the curtain far enough to peek inside. Tuck slept on the hospital bed. His right leg hung in a brace. He had an IV drip, and wires hooked up to him that measured his heart rate and blood pressure. The monitor's green dot moved up and down in a slow and steady motion. She combed her hair over her ear with her fingers. She saw his chest moved slightly up and down. She winced as a lightning strike of pain jolted her shoulder.

"I know you're going to be okay," whispered Xiao. She paused, and with her good hand moved her hair behind her ear. "This is hard for me to say even with you sleeping, I'm sorry. I don't know how or when, one day I will pay you back for losing your seat at Clearview Prep and for getting your car...I mean, Ursula impounded." She placed her good hand on his wrist and leaned over. She gave him a simple kiss on the lips. "Thank you."

As she closed the curtain to leave, the beeping noise sped up. She flung the curtain open to see Tuck fiddling with the wire that monitored his heart. He looked up and smiled.

"You get my heart racing like an epinephrine drip." A mashup of a smile and a wince of pain appeared on his face.

"You scared me. Don't you ever stop?" She wanted to be mad at him, yet she wanted to reach out and hold his hand. She picked the latter. "Are you okay?" Xiao had a hard time looking him in his eyes. She kept her line of sight on her hand resting on top of his.

"I screwed my knee up again and I have a cracked rib. I'll be all right. Once Ursula is recovered, I'll be better."

"You love that car, don't you?" asked Xiao, still trying to avoid his eyes.

"I do. In a sense, she is my best friend. She and I have been through a lot."

"Tuck..." She finally looked at him. The words wouldn't come out.

"I know," he replied. "You said it once, you don't have to say it again." He gave her a reassuring smile.

"You were awake the whole time?"

"I think most of it." He rotated his hand, causing hers to fall into his light grasp.

Xiao felt weird. Normally she didn't care what other people thought of her. This felt different. She did care how Tuck viewed her. She felt tears building up. "Can we, like...I mean...maybe we can..." The words were coming to her, she couldn't figure out how to say them.

"Do you have a pencil?" asked Tuck.

"No, why?" she replied.

"Cause I want to erase your past and write our future." He smiled, followed by a wince of pain.

"You're willing to give our friendship a second chance?" This time she couldn't hold the tears back.

Tuck winced again. "I would like to start new if you want to."

"I'd like that," she said, looking down as her cheeks grew warm.

"I liked your kiss," he said softly.

Xiao's cheeks grew even warmer. "At the party you asked me to kiss you if you were wrong. I hate to break the news to you; dinosaurs no longer exist." Both of them laughed and winced in pain at the same time. Xiao brought her good hand up to her bad shoulder.

She leaned over and kissed him on the cheek.

"Oh!" He perked up. "The first president of North America was Obi-Wan Kenobi, right?"

"Don't press your luck," she replied, trying to hide her smile.

"Why the change of heart?" asked Tuck.

"Let's say I learned that because there are laws, doesn't make it right."

"I couldn't agree more."

"I better go. I wanted to make sure you were okay."

"I'm glad you stopped by." He paused. "I know how important your studies are to you, I was thinking maybe over winter break we can meet up."

"I'd like that," she replied.

"Really?"

"A friend told me I need to have more fun in my life. I would like that fun to be with you."

Brett ducked into the room next to Tuck's. He hoped Xiao didn't see him spying. He pressed himself up against the wall. A little girl with no hair lay in a bed, watching him. She was pale, and her cheeks were sunken in. Brett smiled at her, and she returned one along with a little wave of her hand. Brett put his finger up to his mouth to warn the little girl to be quiet.

He saw Xiao walk by. He waited a few seconds and then headed in her direction. "Hey, wait up," he said.

Xiao stopped and turned around. Brett jogged up to her. "How's the shoulder?"

"It hurts." She took her good hand and backhanded him in the stomach.

"What was that for?"

"For spying on me." She gave him a firm and hard look.

"I don't know what you're talking about," he replied.

"Yeah, I bet you don't." Xiao headed down the hallway with Brett at her side.

"Are you worried that we might get expelled?" asked Brett.

"Actually, I'm not. What happens, happens. I guess a little bit of you rubbed off on me."

Brett opened his mouth to speak, all that came out was an *oof*, as Xiao backhanded him in the stomach again.

"What was that for? I didn't say anything."

"That's for what you were going to say," said Xiao, not looking at him.

Brett stopped and placed his hand over his stomach. He watched her as she continued down the hall. "I love it when she plays rough."

LTjg Meoquanee sat down next to Chief in the waiting room. She handed him a cup of coffee. "Maybe this will help take the chill out of you."

"Thanks! Jumping in that river sure brought a whole new meaning to taking a cold shower." Both of them laughed. Chief took a sip and looked at her wide-eyed.

She smiled. "When you were in the back getting checked out, I contacted your brother like you asked me to. He told me to put Jack Daniels in a cup of coffee for you."

"You always listen to a strange man you haven't met yet?" He took another sip.

"It depends. I thought this was the right call."

Chief lifted his cup to hers. "Thanks, it *was* the right call." He took another sip. "What's in your coffee?"

"Actually, I have tea made with strawberry leaf, blackberry leaf, and juniper." She brought the cup up to her nose and breathed in the steam. "It's a recipe that's been handed down for generations. If you want, I have more out in the shuttle. I could mix you up some."

"No, thank you, this coffee is doing the trick." He took another sip. "I'm guessing you talked to Captain Currituck."

"I talked to him and Dean Wu on a three-way call."

"Expulsion for all six?" He held the warm cup with both hands, easing the chill.

"They will go to captain's mast, and he will award them their punishments. Both he and Dean Wu agreed they all deserve a second chance, even Cadet Lundy." Both laughed. "Of course, being the senior person involved, I have to write a report on this prior to captain's mast."

"What are you going to put in the report?" Chief looked directly at her.

"I'll tell you what the report will say," Mac said as he came up. "Cortez and Navarro knew Asher's mother ran Willow Wood. They figured he knew where other hybrid safe havens were. While he was transporting across the hub, one of their men spotted Asher and nabbed him and took him to Earth. Once they made it to Earth, Asher escaped and went to Willow Wood, not knowing where else to go. As for the other kids, including Nittany, they found out what happened, being teenagers, they thought they could handle the problem themselves. All of them ended up at Willow Wood. Navarro, Cortez, and their crews went there to get

Asher. Alita Blackwood found out the hybrid hunters were going to be there. She brought her army and attacked, thus killing Navarro. The kids escaped by canoe; a young man was out for a joyride and found the six kids on the shoreline wet and cold. He was going to take them to a place where they could get dry clothes and warm up, Cortez tried to head them off. We know what happened there." Mac looked at Chief first, then LTjg Meoquanee and back to Chief. "That's what is going in my report. Plus the fact that Asher's scan came out negative." He looked at Chief.

"Then that's what I will put in my report," LTjg Meoquanee replied.

"Thank you, Detective," said Chief.

"If our kids are going to be dating, I think we can finally call each other by our first names."

"Thank you...Mac."

"No problem, Liam. Now if you'll excuse me, I need to contact the missus. This is going to be fun."

"Chief, I want you to know something," said LTjg Meoquanee.

"What's that?" He took another sip of his coffee.

"Today those six cadets became a true team. They're helping each other carry the burdens they each bear. They stood by Asher, no matter the consequences, they are a team. I wanted you to know, as their squad leader, I consider myself part of the team as well."

Chief didn't say a word. He nodded in acknowledgment. He understood.

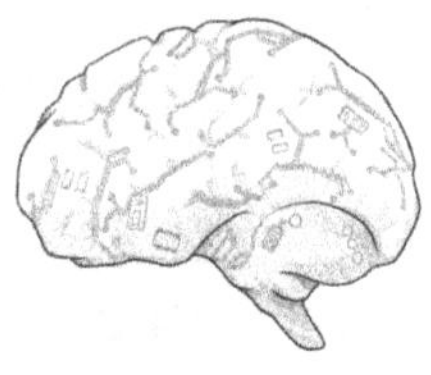

Asher poked his head through the door that led to Nittany's room.

A hospital gown was draped across her. She spun her legs over the edge, her back to Asher.

"You better be careful; those gowns have a way of illuminating the full moon."

Nittany turned her head. "Asher! You okay?"

Asher walked in. Nittany spun back with discomfort on her face, and with the help of the bed, she sat semi-upright.

"I'm fine. I have a black-and-blue mark on my ankle where Cortez grabbed it, other than that, I'm a little sore is all. I'm finally starting to warm up too."

Nittany scooted over to one side of the bed. "Can you sit here with me? We can warm up together." She smiled.

Asher didn't hesitate. He crawled into the bed with Nittany and gave her a sweet kiss. He wrapped his arm around her. She snuggled into him, and the two fell asleep.

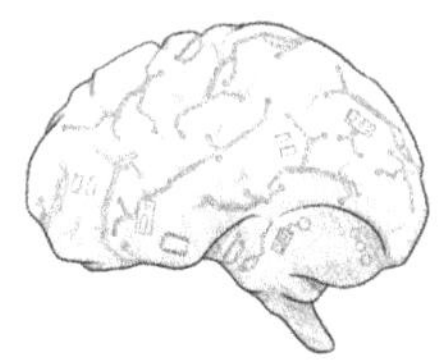

Asher woke with a jolt. He had a dream of Timothy, and this time they were laughing and playing at Willow Wood. His mom watched with a smile.

The dream didn't wake him up. Something else did. He looked at Nittany's sweet face, purring into his chest. Out of the corner of his eye, he spotted it. There, at the foot of the bed, Berman the stuffed gorilla sat looking at him. Asher had left it in the tree house when they fled. He carefully slid from Nittany and climbed out of bed. He grabbed Berman and raced out into the hallway. He looked around in the waiting room and saw a girl with blue-and-green hair exiting. He ran after her. The cold winter wind whipped through him as he ran outside.

"Neon!" he yelled.

She stopped and looked at him from a distance. Using only her index and middle finger, she pointed to her eyes and then pointed to him. After the second time she proceeded to get into a car. Asher saw Alita Blackwood sitting inside. He wrapped his arms around himself as they drove off.

"Everything okay?" asked Chief, walking up to Asher. "I saw you run out."

Asher brought Berman closer to him. "Yeah, everything's fine." He smiled.

"Good, let's get inside where it's not cold," Chief suggested.

Once inside, Chief stopped. "Oh, I have this for you." He pulled out Asher's dog tags and chain. "Mac said you left it in the scanning room." He handed it to Asher.

"Thanks, Dad." Asher held the diamond ring attached to the chain. "This was the ring you gave Mom. I think you should have it." He started to disconnect his chain.

"You keep it, Asher. You can give it to your true love in no less than twenty years." They both laughed.

"I'm sorry I've been such a butt," said Asher.

"Hey, like it or not, that comes with the territory of being a father. The things Uncle Mick and I used to put your grandparents through, I'm surprised they never disowned us." Both laughed again.

"Did you talk to Uncle Mick?" Asher wondered if he should tell his dad that Uncle Mick knew about him, and even helped get his implants.

"I did. I had a few choice words for him after seeing the communication chip that was in your pocket."

Asher looked down at the ground. "I'm sorry, I didn't know until I found the chip today."

"I'm not going to pretend I understand why Vicki kept you a secret from me all these years, despite the situation. What I do understand is that we can't change the past, however, we can help mold the future."

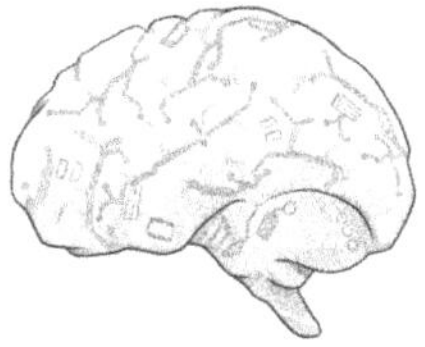

"There he is," said Cray as Asher entered Nittany's room.

"What happened to you?" asked Nittany, sitting up a bit perkier.

"A friend brought me Berman from Willow Wood." He held up the gorilla. "It's was mine as a kid before I gave it to Timothy. They thought I would want it."

"That's cool," said Tabitha.

"Did you hear we aren't going to be expelled?" asked Xiao. "Even Brett gets to stay."

"You make that sound like a bad thing," said Brett.

"The verdict is still out," said Xiao.

Echo 88 stayed in Nittany's room, laughing, talking, and sharing until each of their parents came to get their children, except for Brett. Oscar came for him.

"Was it this cold when we were that age?" asked Autumn as she, Game Master, Dean Wu, Gully, and the Phantom Prophet walked into the hospital cafeteria and sat down at a table.

"They survived the first semester," said Dean Wu.

"As we knew they would," said Gully.

"Winter break is going to be tougher for them," said Autumn Fletcher.

"They can handle it," said the Game Master.

"That friendship they developed this semester will get them through a lot in the coming years," said the Phantom Prophet. He looked at his lifelong friends gathered around him, gave a tiny shake of the head, and let out a soft grunt. Not only was it going to be tougher for the cadets who'd left the hospital, it was going to be even tougher for them now too.

Printed in the USA
CPSIA information can be obtained
at www.ICGtesting.com
LVHW040051071223
765524LV00036B/892/J